BEN RAINES HA

The secretary-general of ... ... Moon, said, "I believe you will find that everything is in order, General Raines. Once you have signed that document, the SUSA will be officially recognized as a sovereign nation, with all the guarantees and rights accorded such by the United Nations. In return, you will help us restore order in every country you're needed in."

"My people aren't peacekeepers, Mr. Secretary," Ben said.

NORTH AMERICA KNOWS IT . . .

The secretary-general smiled. "We don't expect you to be peacekeepers, General. Just restore some semblance of order around the world."

Ben nodded. "I want it known, up front—no matter what country my people go into, we aren't going to screw around with two-bit warlords and punks and thugs. If they oppose us, they're dead."

"You are in full command of the entire operations. All concerned understand that," the secretary-general said. "Where do you plan on making your initial landing in Europe?"

"France." Ben smiled. "Normandy."

NOW THE WORLD WILL FIND OUT!

D-DAY
IN THE
ASHES

WILLIAM W.
JOHNSTONE

PINNACLE BOOKS
Kensington Publishing Corp.
http://www.kensingtonbooks.com

PINNACLE BOOKS are published by

Kensington Publishing Corp.
119 West 40th Street
New York, NY 10018

All Kensington Titles, Imprints, and Distributed Lines are available at special quantity discounts for bulk purchases for sales promotions, premiums, fund-raising, and educational or institutional use. Special book excerpts or customized printings can also be created to fit specific needs. For details, write or phone the office of the Kensington special sales manager: Kensington Publishing Corp., 119 West 40th Street, New York, NY 10018, attn: Special Sales Department, Phone: 1-800-221-2647.

Pinnacle and the P logo Reg. U.S. Pat. & TM Off.

ISBN-13: 978-0-7860-2078-2
ISBN-10: 0-7860-2078-4

First Pinnacle Printing: March 2000

10 9 8 7 6 5 4 3

Printed in the United States of America

This nation will remain the land of the free only so long as it is the home of the brave.

—Elmer Davis

Laws that forbid the carrying of arms . . . disarm only those who are neither inclined nor determined to commit crimes . . . Such laws make things worse for the assaulted and better for the assailants; they serve rather to encourage than to prevent homicides, for an unarmed man may be attacked with greater confidence than an armed man.

—Thomas Jefferson

Prologue

Long before the United States of America collapsed under the sheer weight of liberal programs, as the touchy-touchy, kissy-kissy group took over Washington, there were millions of people who were looking for a way out of the morass caused by our elected ninnies and nannies in Congress. Political correctness was the order of the day. Fat people could no longer be called fat; now they were calorically adventurous persons—thanks to liberals. There was no such thing as true juvenile justice, so consequently many kids could and did thumb their noses at law and order, discipline, and respect—thanks to liberals. Minors could kill in cold blood and know that if caught, they wouldn't spend much time in the bucket—thanks to liberals. The public schools went to shit—thanks to liberals. It wasn't that teachers couldn't teach, for this country had the most qualified teachers of any country in the world. But when teachers are in fear for their lives, how the hell can they be expected to teach? Teachers could no longer spank due to restrictive legislation, the parents couldn't spank for fear of being hauled into court on child abuse charges, so discipline went right out the window—thanks to liberals. The minority-elected president and his nonelected czarina went on television—and to the surprise of those who knew the facts—declared that guns were the nation's number-one health hazard. Really? According to the latest statistics available for the year that piece of liberal Democratic hysteria-inducing bullshit was uttered, motor-vehicle accidents were number one with 40,300 deaths, falls were number two with 12,400 deaths, poisoning was number three with 5,200 deaths, drowning was number four with 4,300 deaths, fires and burns number five with 4,000 deaths, suffocation by ingested objects number six with 2,700 deaths, and firearms were number seven with 1,400 deaths. So much for the accuracy of mush from the mouth of the president.

Long before the fall of what had once been the greatest nation on the face of the earth, liberals saw to it that cops could no longer effectively enforce the law. Sensitivity training was the order of the day. If a court decision went the wrong way (to the viewpoint of some), certain minority groups took to the streets in a mindless rampage of savagery and barbarism and looted and burned and killed and assaulted, and then certain minority leaders went on TV and stated that it wasn't their fault. Really? That's right. It was the fault of those of us who work seven days a week, obey the law, pay the *majority* of taxes in this country, try to raise our children right, and do everything else that we were taught was right and correct and moral. And the liberals? What side did they fall on . . . ? Well, you know the story by now; no point in belaboring it.

There were many who saw the direction in which the nation was heading. They wrote letters to their elected dunder- and danderheads in Washington (letters that were, in most cases, read by some little twitty self-righteous aide), they phoned (their calls were noted, and the elected officials went right ahead and voted party lines and to hell with the views and opinions of the people that they supposedly represented). The majority of the people demanded the death penalty for certain crimes (that sometimes happened— usually about fourteen years and millions of dollars of taxpayer money after the crime—thanks to you-know-who).

Then the gun-grab happened. It was predictable, for liberals are scared to death of guns. They pee their lace-trimmed drawers and stomp on hankies at just the thought of a gun. Liberals are so colossally ignorant, they cannot understand that guns don't kill, it's the person who pulls the trigger who kills. A gun can do absolutely, positively nothing until someone picks it up. Liberals are so stupid they actually believe that a gun has a brain (that might be because liberals *don't* have a brain).

There were those Americans who tried to point out certain facts to the liberal gun-grab people. Naturally they were ignored by the Washington crowd, belittled and scorned and depicted as nuts and kooks by TV news departments (anybody know of a true conservative who is a major news anchor?).

Toward the end of the millennium, the liberals got

their way—all guns were banned, except for those in the hands of the police and the military and certain elected and appointed government officials. Thousands and thousands of gun owners carefully sealed their weapons in airtight and watertight containers and buried them rather than give them up, even though liberals passed legislation that called for the death penalty for anyone found with a handgun or an assault rifle . . . unless you were a member of certain minority groups, an elected government official (and their families, aunts, uncles, brothers-in-law, and close liberal friends), a member of the liberal press, certain talk-show hosts, fans of Jane Fonda, and anyone who voted for President Blanton. Anyone who was found with a Reelect Nixon, Join the NRA, God, Guns & Guts bumper sticker, or belonged to the Charlton Heston fan club was to be put to death immediately.

"There now," spake Vice President Harriet Hooter and Representative Rita Rivers. One bore a remarkable resemblance to a Shetland pony and had just about as much sense, and the other reportedly actually offered to screw one for a hundred bucks (business had been sort of slow on the streets that night). "That ought to show those nasty Republicans that we mean business."

"Right on, sister!" Rita said. "Hot damn! Power to the people. Get down and boogie!" She turned up the volume on her Walkman and did a few steps while listening to her favorite rap group: I Be's Cool & You Ain't Shit You Honky Mother-Fucker.

"Isn't that cute?" the president's wife said.

"Does anybody have a Twinkie they can spare?" the president asked. "I'm hungry."

"How else can we fuck up the taxpayers' lives?" Senator Benedict asked.

"I have a better idea," Senator Arnold said. "Let's go after all these goddamned right-wing Republican reactionary writers of paperback pulp that have been belittling this administration."

"Oh, good show!" Representative Fox said.

"Right!" VP Hooter said. "Especially that right-wing, gun-loving, Republican bastard Ben Raines!"

Federal agents and agencies began putting the squeeze on any writer who dared question the administration's policies. Several adventure writers were shot to death, "resisting arrest," according to the field reports of the federal agents. But that tactic quickly backfired. Much to Blanton's surprise, the ACLU took the side of the writers and started filing lawsuits, even though many of the writers despised the ACLU and told them so bluntly.

Blanton called off his two-legged federal Dobermans.

Then federal taxes went up again, thanks to the likes of representatives and senators like Rufus Dumkowski, I. M. Holey, Wiley Ferret, Immaculate Crapums, Zipporah Washington, and men and women of equally liberal ilk.

But their reign was, thankfully, short-lived. A third party was formed, and their candidate took much needed votes away from the Republican candidate, and the nation once more had a minority-elected president. Shortly after Blanton was elected to a second term, the whole world blew apart in war. Within a few days of limited nuclear and germ warfare, there was not a stable government left intact anywhere on the face of the earth . . . especially in what had once been called the United States.

Which suited Ben Raines just fine.

The long years of combat take their toll on even the toughest men and women, and those who fought in the Rebel army were no different. Some of the men and women who had been with Ben the longest were through campaigning. They would never stop being Rebels, but they would not embark on this Canadian campaign against General Nick Stafford, a.k.a. Paul Revere. Those men and women—who for whatever reason—had elected to stay behind would train new recruits, join the Home Guard, raise families, and be good citizens of the Southern United States of America.

Ben had spent months revamping and realigning his armed forces. His air force was small but lethal, flying a variety of planes, mostly reworked and highly modified prop jobs. His attack helicopters were the fastest, deadliest, and most heavily armed of any choppers in the world.

Ben was fond of saying: "There might be larger armies in the world, but when it comes to mean, the Rebel army takes the prize hands down."

He was right. When it came to mean, there wasn't an army on the face of the earth that came anywhere near the capabilities of the Rebels. Each Rebel was trained in a dozen different schools by instructors who were experts in the dirtiest, most savage, low-down mad-dog mean fighting tactics known anywhere. The Rebels were all jump-qualified. They could climb mountains, live in the swamps, jungles, deserts, or timber, drive a dog sled, and strike from land, sea, or air. Each was qualified with dozens of weapons, from crossbow to machine gun.

There was a good reason for the readiness and willingness of the Rebels: The SUSA was their home. They believed in the Southern United States of America, they believed in the concepts set forth by Ben Raines, and they believed in Ben Raines.

Many of the Rebels were too young to really remember when liberals took command of the government and began what many Americans believed was their unconstitutional legislative rampage toward total control of every aspect of every American's life, from cradle to grave. But many Rebels were old enough to recall the insidious takeover, and they vowed never again to return to that form of government. They would die first—and many had over the bloody years since worldwide collapse and the formation of the Rebel army. Thousands had died fighting for the Rebel cause. But for every one that died, three stepped forward to take their place, thus ensuring that the Rebel dream would never die.

Many people believed, and liberals fervently prayed, that Ben Raines would never live long enough to see his dream come true. But Ben Raines proved very hard to kill and the Rebel concept of government even harder to destroy. Both survived and flourished, and the Southern United States of America was built out of the ashes of war and over the wild, ranting objections of the nation's liberals.

What many fair-minded people could never understand was why liberals despised Ben Raines. For even though Ben was hard-line in some areas of his philosophy, he was more liberal than a liberal in many others. People who came into the SUSA with some trepidation soon discovered that living in the SUSA was much easier and simpler than living outside of it.

In the SUSA law-abiding citizens had almost complete control over their lives and destinies, with very little government interference. The average life expectancy of a criminal in the SUSA was about an hour, for the SUSA—which took in the states of Texas, Oklahoma, Louisiana, Arkansas, Mississippi, Tennessee, North and South Carolina, Alabama, Georgia, and Florida—was an armed camp. In the SUSA a citizen had the right to protect self, family, pets, and property by any means at hand, including deadly force, without fear of criminal prosecution or civil lawsuit by the dead punk's family. Consequently there was no crime. None. It just wasn't tolerated. The same thing could have been done years before when the United States was whole, but the liberals wouldn't permit it. Ben Raines had always believed that liberals placed more value on the lives of punks than they did on the lives of decent, tax-paying, law-abiding citizens. Within the borders of the SUSA, it was decidedly the other way around, which didn't take the criminal element long to discover.

Lawyers who came into the SUSA learned quickly

that legal mumbo jumbo didn't cut it there. Everything was straightforward and aboveboard, spelled out plain and simple. Medical attention was free and offered to all residents. People who once clogged emergency rooms with bullshit ailments quickly learned not to do so in the SUSA. Ben Raines set up aid-stations all over the SUSA for the treatment of minor injuries, and no town was without medical facilities.

Ben destroyed hundreds of smaller towns in the SUSA and pulled people into workable-sized communities—not so large that a person could get lost and not so small that a person could not have privacy. There were many very good reasons for that, one of which was that they were easily defended.

Ben began destroying the cities and bulldozing the rubble. There were no slums in the SUSA. There was not a neighborhood in any town that was not safe to walk in at any time of the day or night. It was not that difficult to accomplish—Ben just got rid of the people whose propensity was toward breaking the law.

In the SUSA the educational system was the finest in the world, with emphasis on learning. Verbal and physical attacks on teachers were nonexistent because kids were taught at home to respect their elders, and teachers led exemplary lives, on and off campus. Kids had ten hours of hard physical exercise each week, and games were intramural, with emphasis placed on teamwork.

Everybody over fifteen and under sixty who lived in the SUSA was in the army. Everybody. If people didn't like that, they got out of the SUSA. Some military unit, somewhere within the eleven states, was in training at all times. Hundreds of thousands of people, men and women, were fully trained and combat ready.

Many of President Blanton's senior people had left him, opting to live and work in the SUSA, and Blanton was decidedly shorthanded when it came to people with any degree of common sense. Dick Penny had left him and sought asylum in the SUSA. Ben immediately named the career diplomat as secretary of state. Senator Hanrahan, a reconstructed liberal, and several more senior people had left Blanton's administration and joined the growing number of people in the SUSA—Blush Lightheart included. His decision had come when Rita Rivers insisted upon replacing "The Star-Spangled Banner" with "God Bless America." Blush had no objection to "God Bless America" . . . but not sung in Rap.

Visitors were amazed at the number of minorities who chose to live in the SUSA. Cecil Jefferys, a black man who had been overwhelmingly elected as president of the SUSA, cleared that right up.

"Black people are beginning to realize that here is the only place they can truly get a fair shake if they are willing to conform and work hard—expecting no free rides or handouts. Racism isn't tolerated here. From either side of the color line. Liberalism didn't help the blacks. It made too many excuses when the black man needed equal footing, not a pat on the head or the bending of laws. Here the law applies equally to all, probably for the first time in the history of the world. In the SUSA skill and the ability to get along with others is what gets you a job and keeps you working, not color."

"President Jefferys is a white man's nigger," Rita Rivers was fond of saying to President Blanton.

President Blanton had to resist the temptation to tell the woman to get fucked. Last time he said that to her, she offered to take him on.

Blanton shuddered at the thought.

Book One

One

Ben walked the long, seemingly endless lines of Rebels. Battalion after battalion of Rebels stretched out before him—and these were the ground troops. The MBTs and Dusters had long since departed the SUSA for the north, transported by Lo-Boys. Tanker trucks filled with diesel and gasoline stretched out for miles and rolled day and night toward the north.

Dan Gray's 3 Battalion, Georgi Striganov's 5 Battalion, Jackie Malone and her 12 Battalion, and Ben's son, Buddy, and his special operations group were already on the ground in Maine at the staging area.

Ben was filled with a strange mixture of pride and sadness as he passed in front of the long full ranks of Rebels. There was a time when he knew the name of every Rebel. No more. Now there were thousands and thousands of dedicated men and women ready to give their lives at Ben's command. It was an awesome feeling, and Ben had never been entirely comfortable with it.

Ben's personal bodyguard, the lovely, diminutive,

and deadly Jersey, walked a couple of steps behind him, her M-16 at the ready. Ben saluted his batt coms as he passed.

"Ike, you old bastard," Ben called in a stage whisper to his longtime friend, a former Navy SEAL and commander of 2 Battalion. "You ought to be in a rocking chair."

"Screw you, Ben," Ike returned the stage whisper. "You're older than I am, you old goat."

Both men were middle-aged.

Ben laughed and kept walking.

Ben returned the salute of the mercenary, West. "Ready to go, Colonel?"

"As always, Ben," West called. West's 4 Battalion was made up exclusively of mercenaries who had come over to the Rebel side. To say they were mean dirty fighters would be a clear understatement.

Ben gave a thumb's up to Rebet, commander of 6 Battalion, and returned the salute from the French-Canadian, Danjou, commander of 7 Battalion.

He winked at his daughter, Tina, who was in command of 9 Battalion. Pat O'Shea, commander of 10 Battalion, gave him a salute that was indescribable at best. Ben laughed and waved at Greenwalt, commander of 11 Battalion. Raul Gomez, commander of 13 Battalion, snapped to and Ben returned the crisp salute. Jim Peters, whose 14 Battalion was filled with men from the New Texas Rangers, saluted as he walked past. Buck Taylor was the new CO of 15, Mike Post CO of 16, and Paul Harrison the CO of 17 Battalion.

Ben walked back to the center of the huge parade

field, where his personal team was waiting: Beth, the record keeper and the person who kept the team running; Cooper, the wisecracking driver; Corrie, the radio operator.

There was nothing left to say. Everything had been said the afternoon before this dawn. Every Rebel had said his goodbyes to family and friends. Many would not be coming back except in body bags—whenever that was possible—providing all the pieces could be found. Many others would be buried in lonely graves in faraway places—lonely but never forgotten by the men and women who served with them.

Ben looked at Corrie. "Mount 'em up, Corrie."

Some of the Rebels went to trucks for the long ride north, others would be off-loaded at waiting planes at the airport. Thirteen thousand men and women heading north to join four thousand more at the staging area in Maine.

"You want me to have communications radio Blanton that we're moving?" Corrie asked.

Ben shook his head. "He'll know it soon enough. He may be a liberal, but he's not a fool."

The team members exchanged glances, and Ben caught them and smiled but said nothing. It was highly unlikely that any resident of the SUSA would have anything good to say about President Homer Blanton—for they knew that even though Blanton had officially recognized the SUSA as a separate and sovereign nation, and had signed treaties, Blanton and those in his administration hated Ben Raines and anything, everything, and anybody associated with the Southern United States of America. They were also well aware that given the slightest opportunity, Blanton would destroy the SUSA if he thought he could.

But as Ben had just said, Blanton was no fool. He knew that Ben Raines had nuclear weapons, and many of them were pointed directly at Charleston, West Virginia, the new capital of the United States. Blanton was also very much aware that another president a few years back had tried to destroy Ben and his Rebels. Ben had sent K-teams out after that president and his close associates and killed them all.

Homer Blanton reckoned that General Raines was about the meanest son of a bitch he had ever encountered.

Ben stopped by his house for a moment to play with his dogs and say goodbye to them . . . for he did not know if he would ever see any of them again. His husky, Smoot, would not be going on this trip.

There was no woman in Ben's life. Not lately. Ben was certainly not celibate, for there were women he visited from time to time to "take the edge off," as Jersey put it. But since Jerre had died, Ben had been unable to sustain a relationship more than a few months.*

"They'll be well taken care of, General," one of a group of Rebels standing in the yard told him as he was leaving.

Ben nodded and kept on walking, trying to ignore the frantic and sorrow-filled barking coming from his pets. He got into his Hummer and told Coop, "Go!"

Late that afternoon, Ben and his team stepped off

---

*SURVIVAL IN THE ASHES.

the plane in Augusta, Maine, and were met by Colonel Dan Gray.

"Everything quiet up here, Dan?"

The Englishman smiled. "Except for our occasional forays across the border into Canada to harass Revere's troops, yes."

"Buddy?"

"He's up there now with some of his special ops people. As a matter of fact, he's rather deep into enemy territory. He just reported this morning."

Ben started to say that he hadn't given any orders for any of his people to cross borders. Dan anticipated that and held up a hand.

"Revere's troops crossed over first and attacked us at our listening posts, Ben. They hit us five times at five different locations before I gave the orders to cross and pursue."

"Fair enough, Dan. The bridges still intact across the Saint John?"

"Surprisingly, yes. Plans, Ben?"

"We start our move into Quebec day after tomorrow. I want to give Buddy time to get into place. Let's go to your CP, I want to look at some maps."

In the command post Ben shook hands with Georgi Striganov and Jackie Malone, then studied the maps of Revere's strongest points for a time.

"Georgi, you spearhead the western attack. Dan and Jackie will be right behind you. Take tanks and artillery and head out at first light. Go up here to 201 and take it straight up to the border." He did not have to tell the old soldier to take all the supplies his people could stagger with, for the Rebels almost always outdistanced their supply lines.

"Ike and Rebet will come with me into New Brunswick. We'll clear that and cross over into Quebec. By that time the rest of our people will be in place and ready to smash through at these locations." Ben X'ed them out on the map and smiled. "I've sent small contingents of Rebels into Manitoba and Ontario with enough things that go bang to confuse the hell out of Revere's scouts. If it all works, he won't know where in the hell to shift his people. They'll start diversionary tactics at my signal." Ben tossed the grease pencil on the map table. "Let's get something to eat. I'm starved."

Several hundred miles to the north, General Revere sat in a lovely old chateau, meeting with his officers. The overall mood was not good. Revere broke the glum silence after his intelligence people read aloud their assessment of meeting the Rebels head-on.

"There is no point in us sitting around here looking like Chicken Little waiting for the sky to fall," Revere said. "We've got the Rebels to fight, and that is that. We know that Raines asked Blanton's armed forces—such as they are—to form up a line behind his own, but to stay in the States. Even if our people did manage to break through the Rebels, we'd have the American army to deal with, and we'd be in such weakened condition, plus outrunning our supply lines, that we wouldn't stand a chance. So we have no choice, gentlemen: We have to stand and slug it out with Raines."

"General—"

Revere waved him silent. "I know, Karl, I know. Our losses are going to be unacceptable. But let me tell you all something—if we were to attempt to fight Raines's Rebels in an unconventional type of war, we wouldn't stand a chance. I *know* Ben Raines. I've known him for years. I've personally watched him fight guerrilla wars and know how he thinks. Believe this: The Rebels are the finest guerrilla fighters in the world. Raines would just love that. No way, people. No way. It might come to that for us to save our own asses, but only as a last resort."

"Paul," a senior officer said, "is it true that he's got factories down in the SUSA cranking out models of the old P-51?"

Revere nodded his head. "Incredible as it may seem, yes. It's a version of the old Mustang. This new one is called the P-51E. Has a top speed of around five hundred miles an hour and carries an enormous payload of rockets and bombs, plus it has six .50-caliber machine guns. Bear in mind that during the Korean War, the P-51D shot down Russian MIG jets!"

"But we have SAMs," another officer protested.

"We have reason to believe our SAMs will be of very little use against the P-51E," Revere's intelligence officer said.

"Why?" Revere asked.

"They come in right on the deck," the intelligence officer said. "Far too low for our SAMs to be of use. They stay low until they've done their work—and that will be very fast—and then they're gone, staying at treetop level until they're out of range of anything we can throw at them in the way of missiles."

"Wonderful," Revere said sarcastically. "That goddamn Ben Raines has brought the art of warfare back to World War Two levels." He shook his head. "P-51's for Christ's sake!"

Rebels continued coming in all that night, off-loading at the airport and quickly forming up. The Rebels started moving out at dawn, and Revere's troops along the border tensed as they got the word from recon. So far, in Canada, these men had faced only small groups of civilian resistance fighters. Although many of the men in Revere's army were professional soldiers, mercenaries, and combat tested, they all knew they had never faced anything like what was now coming at them. For the Rebels were known all over the world as the toughest, meanest, hardest soldiers to be found anywhere. And they weren't known for taking many prisoners.

For two days and two nights, all along the western border, Revere's troops waited and waited. But nothing happened. What they did not know was that Striganov had halted his people many miles from the border and was sending them across on foot in tiny groups. Those crossing the border on foot were carrying, in addition to their regular equipment, blocks of C-4, silenced pistols, and some were equipped with Haskins long-range .50-caliber sniper rifles. In the hands of a skilled marksman, the Haskins rifle is accurate up to a mile and a half. The 1.5-ounce bullet leaves the muzzle with more than five times the energy of a 7.62-mm round. Depending on the type of round used, the rifle is also capable of penetrating four-inch-thick armor. The tip of the bullet, loaded with incendiary material, detonates high explosives right behind the tip, shattering the steel body into shrapnel. The Rebels were flitting into tiny villages—most of which were deserted except for contingents of Revere's troops—and taking up position. A few unsuspecting throats had already been cut.

Meanwhile Ben was moving his people toward New Brunswick. Ben had ordered Buddy and his special operations group into the Gaspé Peninsula to prevent Revere's men from escaping that way.

"They're scared," Corrie said, after receiving word from communications. The Rebels had tapped into Revere's frequencies and were monitoring everything. "Revere has only two or three battalions here in New Brunswick, and they're all running north on Highway 2, heading straight for Edmundston."

"North?" Ben questioned, looking at a map.

"Yes. Stupid move if you ask me."

Ben was silent for a moment. "They don't know about Buddy and his people. They're scared to come into northeastern Maine because of the terrain . . . and us. How big a town was Edmundston?"

"About thirteen thousand."

"They'll have some sort of airport. Revere might have transports there; probably does. That's why they're running. Order the 51's up and tell them to go to work."

It was a scene right out of World War Two as the

newly built and highly modified P-51E's roared through the skies at almost 500 miles per hour. Coming in right behind them, although much slower at about 180 miles per hour, were the Rebels' attack helicopters, Cobras and Apaches. The Apache packed a heavier, more devastating load of firepower than many World War Two attack bombers. What the P-51's didn't kill or destroy, the Cobras and Apaches would.

The souped-up and highly modified P-51's caught Revere's old transport planes on the ground and cut them to smoking shards of twisted metal. The Apaches and Cobras found the retreated troops of Revere's army and chopped them to bloody bits. The 51's circled back and came in right after the attack helicopters and finished the job.

Revere lost three battalions of men, about a fourth of his planes, and the Rebels suffered not one scratch.

Revere sat in his chateau and stoically took the news from communications. He turned to one of his senior officers. "Raines might well take Montreal, but he'll pay in blood for every inch of it."

"Orders, sir?"

"Dig in."

Two

Before the Great War Canada had even harsher and more restrictive gun laws than the United States, so takeover was easily accomplished. And after the war, just like what happened in the Lower Forty-Eight, gangs of street slime and punks and others of that particular odious and utterly worthless ilk surfaced and formed their own mini-armies, making life miserable for the heretofore long-suffering, tax-paying, law-abiding citizens, who found it hard to defend themselves against large heavily armed gangs when the only things they had to fight with were bolt-action rifles and duck guns.

But it made the liberals on both sides of the border happy. Bless their little pointy heads.

It also made the lawless very happy, once the thin blue line of authority was no longer there.

As the Rebels had done in every state in the Lower Forty-Eight and in Hawaii and Alaska, they moved into the smoking wreckage caused by the P-51's and the attack choppers and gathered up all the ammo and every serviceable weapon. Then they began passing them out to the citizens who had endured years of abuse at the hands of the lawless.

In Edmundston Ben told a small group of survivors, "You have both rights and obligations when it comes to firearms. You have the right to possess arms to defend yourself, and you have the obligation to keep these weapons from the hands of the lawless, and you can do the latter any damn way you see fit. Personally we shoot them and have done with it."

The citizens of the town, and many citizens from outlying areas, who had come into the battered town after Revere's people were destroyed, sought an audience with Ben. Among the people were the lieutenant generals of New Brunswick, Newfoundland, and Nova Scotia. They came right to the point.

"We would like to be a part of your government, General. If you'll have us."

"You mean you want to join the United States?"

"No, sir. We want to join the *Southern* United States of America."

Ben gave that a few moments of thought. Personally he was delighted at the prospect of finding another way of sticking it to Homer Blanton. "I have an idea," he finally said.

The three men leaned forward.

"He did *what?*" Homer Blanton screamed at the aide who stood nervously before him.

The aide repeated the news.

"That son of a bitch!" President Blanton said. Then he cut loose with a long string of cuss words.

New Brunswick, Newfoundland, and Nova Scotia had formally broken away from the Crown and signed an alliance with the Southern United States of America. They would hereafter and forever be known as the Northern United States of America—the NUSA—and their constitution would be patterned after the constitution of the SUSA.

"Goddamn him!" Blanton screamed.

"That's not all," the aide said. "It gets worse."

Blanton glared at the young man.

"Wyoming, Montana, Idaho, Alaska, and Nevada have officially broken with the United States and formed what they call the WUSA."

"Let me guess," Blanton spat out the words. "The *Western* United States of America—aligned with Ben Raines and the SUSA."

"Yes, sir." The aide laid a folder on the president's desk and got the hell out of the new Oval Office.

Blanton opened the folder and read the papers. He closed the folder and sat for a moment, quietly cursing. His liberal empire was rapidly crumbling all around him. Thanks to Ben Raines. God, how he hated that man. He could not find the words to fully describe his hatred. The United States of America was being torn apart . . . and it was all the fault of that damned Raines.

VP Harriet Hooter came rushing into the room at full gallop, followed by Rita Rivers and several other representatives and senators. "Is it true?" Harriet bellowed, rattling the coffee cup and saucer on Homer's desk. "Parts of Canada and five more states have broken away and joined Ben Raines?"

Homer nodded his head.

"That goddamn filthy racist honky Republican pig!" Rita Rivers squalled.

"We have an eroding tax base," Representative Dumkowski said. "We can't fund our wonderful marvelous everything-for-everybody programs if we lose another state."

"We'll have to cut," I. M. Holey said somberly.

"Cut the budgets of the military and the cops," Immaculate Crapums suggested.

"Put a ten dollar tax on a pack of cigarettes, a gallon of gasoline, and a fifth of whiskey," Wiley Ferret said. "That'll do it."

"Raise the income tax on the rich," Zipporah Washington suggested. "It's only seventy-five percent now. Soak 'em some more. Make 'em pay."

Homer lost it. "Goddamnit!" he yelled, slamming both hands on the desk top. "We don't have any rich in this nation. Unemployment is running about ninety percent. Our currency is worthless. There's nothing to back it except faith." They certainly couldn't use gold, because Raines and the Rebels stole all the gold in the United States several years back, in addition to everything else they could get their hands on. They couldn't use silver, because Raines and the Rebels stole that, too. The Rebels controlled all the gold and silver mines and most of the nation's oil.

Blanton stared at the others, who were staring back at him in shock after his outburst. The words of Ben Raines came back to him. He remembered them clearly, although their last face-to-face meeting had been several months back. Ben's words kept haunting him. Blanton had a good mind and nearly total recall. Ben's words again filled his head.

"President Blanton, much of what you and all the other liberals in government tried to do before the Great War was admirable. Only a very callous or shortsighted fool would deny that. It was very impractical, but admirable. You were trying, and will probably in all likelihood, continue to try to buck human nature.

"There will always be poor people, Mr. Blanton. That's the way life is—in any land, on any continent. It has been that way since the beginning of time, and will remain that way until God fulfills His promise to destroy the earth and all on it.

"There will be those who will work brutally hard all their lives and never have anything to show for it. There will be hopelessness and despair, tragedy and misfortune, needless suffering of good decent people, and in your society, many terrible and heinous crimes committed against the weak." Ben smiled, adding, "But not in our society.

"There will always be winners, Mr. Blanton, and there will always be losers.

"We as leaders can only point people in the right direction, perhaps provide them with some incentive and material, and then turn them loose and hope for the best. We cannot be all things to all people all the time. Not at the expense of others who can ill afford to foot the bills.

"When people take away from society more than they give, in the form of criminal acts, and do it time and time again, I see no point in keeping those people alive. Not at taxpayer expense. This time around we didn't kill them. I just ran them out and handed them to you."

"I know," Blanton said dryly.

"What you do with those people is your problem. You and the rest of the old hanky-stomping, weepy, kissy-kissy, take-a-punk-to-lunch bunch, soft-line liberal party helped create them, so you can have them. But if they come back into the SUSA with anything on their minds other than obeying the law and working hard and respecting the rights of others, we'll bury the bastards.

"Mr. Blanton, I'm telling you this not to chastise but to warn you that if you don't adopt some domestic policy very similar to ours, your emerging nation is not going to make it. You see and hear all those protestors outside this office, demanding this, that, and the other thing? Why in the hell aren't they out working on a home to live in? There are hundreds and thousand of nice homes out there that are standing empty, the owners dead—long dead. Why aren't they gathering up firewood to burn against the cold and to cook their food? There are millions of head of cattle running loose all across this nation. They belong to no one. Why don't they start a farm or ranch? There are millions of chickens running around loose, laying eggs everywhere. There is no reason for any of those people out there to be hungry. But they're waiting on the government—your government—to provide the food and put it on their plates.

"There are old people out there who do need help, and they needed it before the Great War, but they didn't get it because you and the rest of the liberal crowd were too goddamn busy providing drugs and halfway houses for junkies, free legal aid for punks, free housing for the undeserving, endless appeals for convicted murderers, pork barrel projects, free junkets . . . hell, the list is endless and depressing. There are very young people who need help, and disabled—excuse me, what is the politically correct term?—I forget—but they do need help. And you don't need forty-seven committees to provide it.

"The rest of those people out there, Homer . . . they're losers. They've been losers all their lives and they'll die losers. They're whiners and complainers, and we've kicked many of them out of the SUSA.

"I feel sorry for you, Mr. Blanton, because we've handed you the dregs of society. And the dregs of society—those who want something for nothing—are attracted to your form of government. We also gave you the idealistic and out-of-touch-with-reality people. They have lots of book sense but no common sense. They will fill your think tanks and write your pretty speeches and pass the legislation and implement all the glorious and totally unworkable social programs that will take your government right back to the way it was when you first took office a decade ago. And you know where that led.

"So, Mr. President, here we are. The Eagle and Dove. The nation that I helped create is going to fly. We're going to soar. We're already so far ahead of your nation that it's doubtful you'll ever catch up, not unless you start to copy our ways. And I urge you to do that."

Ben rose from his chair and looked at Homer Blanton. Then he shook his head. "Right now, Homer, you'll have to excuse me. I have a war to fight."

"My war, you mean." Blanton's words were softly spoken.

"That's about the size of it, Homer." Ben walked out of the office.

Blanton's wife broke into his thoughts. "What are you thinking, Homer? Why are you so still and silent?"

"Maybe he's right," Blanton muttered in tones so low no one else could hear them. "Maybe I'm wrong."

Ben sat in the long-deserted home his team had found for him in a small village in Quebec Province and studied the maps. He couldn't figure out what Revere was up to. Paul had pulled his people back to the west side of the Saint Lawrence River without firing a shot at the Rebels. He'd ordered all his tanks and troops back in a headlong retreat. But Ben knew that retreating was not Paul's style. He leaned back in the old chair for a moment, his hands clasped behind his head.

Then he smiled. "Trying to pull a fast one, aren't you, Nick, ol' buddy."

Ben felt sure that Revere would know by now that the three easternmost provinces had aligned with the Rebels. And Paul would also know how temperamental the French-Canadians were and how proud they were of the cities of Montreal and Quebec. They would not look with favor if Ben destroyed those cities.

But Ben knew that many of the towns and cities in Ontario Province had been hard hit; Toronto was a haven for gangs and for some of the last vestiges of the Night People. The Canadians would be most happy if Ben and the Rebels cleared out the scum from that province . . . and they wouldn't be much concerned about how much damage he did in doing so.

"It won't work, Nick," Ben muttered. "I'll starve your asses out of there and push you west and leave the cities virtually untouched."

Ben went to bed chuckling.

"What the hell's he waiting for?" Revere was asked a couple of days later.

Revere said nothing, just sat staring into his empty coffee cup.

"He's moving troops around," another senior officer said, walking to a huge wall map. "He's blocked every bridge from Quebec all the way around to Sault Sainte Marie. There is no way we could push across the few bridges left. He's wired them to blow. He's massed his troops east and west and put troops up here around Sudbury and North Bay in Ontario. Why?"

"He figured it out," Revere said softly. "I didn't think he would, but he did. The son of a bitch!"

"Well, when the hell is he going to launch his assault against us, Paul?"

"He isn't."

That brought the room to total silence, all eyes staring at Nick Stafford, a.k.a. General Paul Revere.

"He's going to starve us out of this city and push us into southern Ontario. That's where the fight is going to take place. We'll be running out of supplies in a few weeks. Raines has an inexhaustible supply line. Shit!"

"What are we looking at, Paul?"

"The end."

Three

Ben thanked Corrie for the fresh cup of coffee and busied himself carefully rolling a cigarette. Bad timing. Doctor Lamar Chase strolled into the office just as Ben was licking the paper and rolling it tight.

"Goddamn things are going to kill you, Raines," the chief of medicine said.

"Mind your own business, Lamar. Smoking an occasional cigarette is one of the few vices I have left to me. What the hell are you doing up here?"

"You're going to need all the medical people you can get, Raines. I sense a big push in the offing. Besides, yesterday morning I was in comm central. Revere is bugging out for Ontario and you're letting him go."

"So?"

Chase poured a cup of coffee from the ever-present pot and sat down. He smiled at Ben. "You're more of a politician than you care to admit. You spared Montreal and Quebec, knowing that single act would ensure the province to come in squarely on the side of the

SUSA. Toronto is in virtual ruins anyway; filled with gangs of street slime and creepies. People will applaud when you bring it down."

Ben grunted. He swiveled his chair and thumped the wall map. "It's not just Toronto. It's the whole area from Windsor in the west all the way up east to Toronto. The area is stinking with street gangs and creepies. And they've had years to get ready for this."

"Intelligence?"

"None. We really don't know the strength, armament, nothing. But we know they're ready for us. I've had communications monitoring everything that comes out of that area for days. It isn't good. You taking charge of all the MASH units?"

The doctor shook his head and smiled. "Nope. That's what officers junior to me are for . . . and they all are. I'll just bounce around from one to the other and make sure they're running at a hundred and ten percent."

"Aggravating everybody and getting in the way, you mean."

Lamar only laughed. The two men had known each other and been friends from the very beginning of the Rebel concept. If they didn't insult each other eighty times a day, one would think the other ill.

"When do you launch the attack against Ontario?"

Ben shrugged. "There's no hurry. I want all our people up here and ready to go. All supplies stockpiled and supply routes gone over carefully. Roads and bridges repaired. I want to leave Quebec as neat as possible."

"Then when it's over, you'll send people up to clear

out the rubble of Ontario and help with the rebuilding, right?"

Ben smiled.

Chase finished his coffee and stood up. He glared down at Ben. "You're going to box Blanton in, aren't you, Ben? You're going to surround him. You're not going to be satisfied until there isn't a liberal pocket anywhere in what used to be the United States of America."

"No, old friend, this time you're wrong. I sure as hell want a place for one hundred percent, dyed-in-the-wool liberals. I don't want to have to live in the same country with a whole bunch of them. Having a few around is fun; makes for very spirited arguments."

"Hell, Raines," Chase said, moving toward the door and as usual preparing to get in the last word. "You don't need anyone to argue with. I've seen you argue with a stump!" Then he quickly left before Ben could retort.

Jersey looked up from the old magazine she was reading, her dark eyes twinkling. "Got you again, didn't he, Chief?"

Ben grinned. "Never fails, does it, Little Bit?"

Two weeks later Ben stood on the north side of the Rideau River in Ontario Province, just east of the town of Smith's Falls.

"I bet that was a nice little town at one time," Cooper remarked, lowering his binoculars after viewing the ruins for a moment.

"Nothing there now," Ben said, casing his own binoculars, just as the scouts reported back by radio.

"Town is empty," Corrie said.

For a time Revere had his men booby-trapping towns. After the third town Ben switched his convoy north, away from 401 along the coast, up to Highway 7. Since doing that, the Rebels hadn't encountered any booby-trapped towns, but they still entered them cautiously.

"Several hundred square miles of metropolitan Toronto," Beth said, reading from an old travel brochure. "That probably means the punks and Revere's people are in the suburbs and the creepies in the city. Oh, whoopie!"

Ben laughed at the expression on the face of the usually serious Beth. He patted her shoulder. "Here we go again, Beth."

"You bet," she replied. "I can't tell you how much I've missed the smell of those filthy cannibalistic bastards."

No one was really sure how long the Night People— creeps, as the Rebels called them—had been around. At first it was thought the germ and limited nuclear warfare had created them. But that was later proven to be incorrect. Most early theories about the destruction caused by the Great War had proved to be inaccurate. Only a few U.S. cities had been hit by nuclear strikes, the rest by germ or "clean" bombs that killed the people and left the buildings intact. The same for the rest of the world. Only a very few things about the devastation wrought by the Great War were actually known. What was a fact was that it had left the entire world in a state of anarchy that still prevailed . . . There were only about ten more-or-less-stable governments in the world. And Ben was under the impression that no one even had a remote clue how to stop it.

He was wrong.

The newly formed UN, now meeting only a few miles from the new White House, in Charleston, West Virginia, had come up with what they thought was a workable solution to the world's problem. What they needed was a tough-assed force that could go in any-where and put down anarchy and set up some form of government. The Security Council just hadn't told Ben Raines or Homer Blanton—yet.

In and around Toronto, Revere and his men had struck an uneasy peace with the street gangs, warlords, and creepies. Uneasy, because the Night People and Revere and army realized they had come to the end of their rope; there was simply no place left for them to run. The street punks and slime swaggered about, su-premely confident that they would defeat Ben and the Rebels. They did not take into consideration that no one had ever done that.

As the Rebels had pushed deeper into the province, the citizens began to surface. They had been staying alive by their wits alone; the weak and those who would not take up arms against their fellow man had been killed by gangs or taken and eaten by the creeps. Those that remained were the tough ones, men and women whose will to live far surpassed any man-made laws. They had managed to procure arms for themselves and killed anyone who tried to take by force what little they had. They had banded together in small communities and survived. And they had also learned, by listening to shortwave broadcasts, of the easternmost provinces throwing in with Ben Raines.

"You can count on us," the Canadian survivors told Ben in no uncertain terms. "Goddamn a government that takes away people's right to defend themselves and the means to do so. It will not happen again."

Perfect candidates for the Rebels.

Ben smiled a lot as the convoy slowly headed west through Ontario Province.

"We'll hit our first strong resistance at Peterborough," Ben told his people. "From there on into Toronto is in enemy hands. The easy ride is over." He turned to Corrie. "Bring the artillery up and start bringing the town down."

When the first 155 round landed in the town, Revere, miles away in Toronto, smiled a grim soldier's smile and felt a grudging admiration for Ben Raines. Many of Revere's men had deserted as they realized the end was near. In tiny groups they changed into civilian clothes and slipped away rather than face the Rebels. It was a wise choice on their part. If they would find a piece of ground and plant a garden and raise a few chickens and keep their heads down and stay out of trouble, Ben would leave them alone. If they returned to a life of crime, their life expectancy was nil.

For twenty-four hours—from the north, the east, and the south—Ben's artillery hammered the town of Peterborough. Before the first round dropped in, Ben had checked with his new Canadian friends and was assured the town held nothing but criminals and their equally worthless women. Many of the women had surrendered at Ben's demand, bringing out their children. Those that stayed, died. The young children were immediately taken from the women and transported to MASH units to be checked over. Then they would be placed in foster homes.

"What about us?" one defiant woman made the mistake of asking Doctor Chase.

"Madame," he told her, "these children are suffering from malnutrition, they've been beaten, some of them have been sexually abused, they have been neglected, many are suffering from childhood diseases that could have been prevented by simple home remedies, and they have head lice. As for you and your ilk, if you are standing in my presence one minute from right now, I will have the guards shoot you. Is that clearly understood?"

"Loud and clear, Doctor."

"Quebec and Ontario provinces have aligned with Ben Raines," President Blanton was informed. "Analysis believes that before it's all over, all of Canada will join with Raines. Malcontents and whiners and the dregs of the earth are pouring across the border into the United States, demanding that we take care of them."

"Those poor, poor people," Homer's wife said. "Fleeing from the injustice foisted upon them by the cruel advance of Ben Raines and his Rebels. We must take them in, Homer. It's the Christian thing to do."

Before Homer could give any thought to his words, he asked, "But why are they so afraid of Raines? I knew

Claude LeBeau and Charles Garrison before the Great War. They're both good decent men and very capable leaders. If they have aligned their provinces with Raines, they both see something there that we have missed."

"What are you saying?" his wife shrieked in horror. "Ben Raines is a barbarian!"

"Horseshit!" Homer said.

His wife was so shocked by his reply that she was momentarily speechless—a condition that had not occurred since her junior high school days, when Mule Busbee took her out behind the schoolhouse and showed her his dick. When she recovered her voice, for fifteen minutes afterward, the principal thought a hog had gotten loose from the Future Farmers of America workshop. He'd never heard such grunting and squealing in all his life.

"Have you taken leave of your senses?" Homer's wife squalled, her voice on a par with Rita Rivers when she sang "God Bless America"—in Rap.

When Homer's hearing had sufficiently recovered for him to respond, he said, "No, dear. Perhaps I've just *found* them." The president of the United States jumped up from his chair, stalked to a window in the new Oval Office and flung it open. He stuck his head outside and shouted to the gangs of protesters below: "Go find a damn job, you goddamn lazy good-for-nothing worthless motherfuckers!"

He slammed the window down just as a thump came from behind him. He turned around. His wife had hit the floor in a dead faint.

* * *

"How many men have deserted us?" Revere asked his senior officers.

"About twenty-five percent."

Revere tossed a pencil onto the desk and stood up. He walked around the large room for a moment, his hands behind his back. "Hell, it's over," he said.

"What?" his most senior officer shouted, lurching out of the chair to his boots.

"You heard me. It's over. We're finished. Done." He pointed to the east. "Ben Raines won, we lost. I'm not going to stay here, aligned with cannibals and street punks and die for nothing. That's foolish. We can't win. Raines has us in a box, and he's going to destroy us if we fight. I know Ben Raines. He will accept an honorable surrender, and that is exactly what I intend to do."

"But all our equipment, our—"

Revere waved him silent. "Raines can have it as far as I'm concerned. I'm certainly not going to leave it for the cannibals and the street punks. My God, men, aren't we a cut above them? Think about it. Gentlemen, Ben Raines won. Get it through your heads. We're finished."

"Living does seem much more precious to me now," a battalion commander said. "But the thought of facing a firing squad does not appeal to me."

"Nor to me," the others in the room echoed.

"We'll face no firing squad," Revere said. "I've known Raines for thirty years. He has something that we don't. Or that we've managed to hide very well."

"And that is?"

"Honor."

Four

Ben looked up as two of his forward recon people walked in, a man between them.

"Says he's from General Revere, sir. Has an urgent message for you."

"Cut his bonds and get him some coffee," Ben said. "Have you eaten?" he asked the prisoner.

"Not since yesterday, sir. Our own rations are a bit thin in the city. And we haven't developed a taste for human flesh." He shuddered, then accepted the cup of coffee with thanks. A plate of food was placed in front of him, and Ben could tell the man was hungry. "But the gangs have plenty of food," he added.

"Eat and then tell me what's on your mind," Ben told him.

"I can do that while eating, General. Paul wants to pack it in. An honorable surrender. But he doesn't want the punks or those goddamn cannibals to get our equipment to use against you." He dug in his shirt pocket and handed Ben a sealed envelope. "From Paul, sir."

Ben put on his reading glasses and before reading glanced at the young officer. He caught a quick smile on the man's lips.

The messenger said, "Paul wears them, too, sir. But he doesn't think we know it."

Ben read the short note and grunted. "Are you expected to return?"

"No, sir."

Ben handed the note to Corrie. "One short word on that frequency, Corrie. At 1800 this evening."

"Yes, sir." She hesitated for a moment. "You think he's on the level, sir?"

"Oh, yes. Paul may be many things that we don't approve of, but he is a realist. He'll surrender."

"Are you going to inform Blanton, Ben?" Chase asked later that day, just a few moments before the surrender was to take place.

"No. We'll keep all his surrendered equipment and spread it around to our new allies."

"You really don't trust Blanton, do you?"

"Not yet, Lamar. I think basically he's a decent fellow. But until he gets some of that liberal pie in the sky knocked out of him, no, I won't trust him."

"Then you haven't heard?"

"Haven't heard what?"

Chase chuckled. "The president of the United States leaned out of a window in the Oval Office and gave a group of demonstrators outside a good cussing."

Ben's eyes widened. "Homer Blanton did that?"

"Yes. A few days ago, so the scuttlebutt goes."

"Maybe there's hope for him after all."

Cooper came into the office. "Scouts report Revere and troops leaving the suburbs, General."

Ben pushed back his chair and stood up. Lamar said, "He's sure to have wounded who need assistance. I'll get busy."

A few moments later, Corrie, who was monitoring transmissions, said, "He's clear of the city and ordering his men to unload their weapons."

Ben nodded and glanced at Jersey. "Relax, Little Bit. They won't try anything. They know we've got every gun trained on them. One screwup and they're all dead meat."

"Right," Jersey said, with about as much enthusiasm as a person digging at an ingrown toenail.

Nick Stafford, a.k.a. Paul Revere, was the first one to step out of a Jeep and walk toward Ben, his hands held slightly up in the air and out from his body. He wore a sidearm. "What do you want me to do with this pistol, Ben?" he called. "It's not loaded."

"Keep it," Ben told him. "You'll need to be armed because of all the roaming gangs still in the area. Come on in the house."

Seated in front of Ben's desk, Nick said, "It'll be after midnight before all my people get clear of the city. And they'll be shooting as those damn cannibals and the street punks try to stop us."

"I expected that." Ben poured them both coffee. "You hungry, Nick?"

"I could eat. But I'd like for my men to be fed first."

"They will be. What now, Nick?"

"That's rather up to you, isn't it, Ben?"

"Why did you surrender?"

Nick smiled. "I finally realized the futility in fighting you. And quite frankly I don't care much about dying."

Ben was thoughtful for a moment. "Nick? You want to join my Rebels?"

Nick was so startled he almost spilled his coffee. He stared at Ben for a moment. "Are you fucking *serious?*"

"Yes. A lot of your men are nothing but killers and psychos. But I would imagine there are lots of good men scattered among your ranks."

"Oh, sure. I have all their personnel files. Your people can go over them; weed out the bad ones. You really mean this, don't you?"

"Yep. Hell, Nick, Striganov and I were once bitter enemies. West fought against me for a time; now he's engaged to marry my daughter. What about it? You want in?"

Nick smiled. "Fighting is what I do best, Ben. I've been a soldier since I was sixteen years old. Count me in."

Ben's smile was cold. "Warn your people that the psychological testing to get into this army is rough. And you won't be exempt from it, Nick."

"I wouldn't expect to be. When does it start?"

"Tomorrow morning."

At the end of the week, about 60 percent of Nick's army had been tested and rejected. At the end of the second week, the Rebel doctors and shrinks had five full battalions of Nick's men tested and ready to assimilate into the Rebel ranks. Ben personally went over the records of the men Nick wanted to serve with him in his own battalion, which would be 21 Batt, and okayed all of them. To a man, all the former mercenaries now in the Rebel ranks said they *never* wanted to go through that mind-probing experience again.

As was Rebel custom, Nick and his men were welcomed warmly once the testing was over. Ben called for a meeting of all batt coms.

Nick took one look at Ben's son, Buddy, and shook his head. "Looks like Rambo," he whispered to Ben.

Ben smiled and whispered, "I made the mistake of telling him that once. Now he has all the movies and watches them in his free time. I think I created a monster."

Laughing, Nick took his place among the batt coms and waited for Ben to start the meeting. Ben pointed to a blowup of the area controlled by the creeps and the street gangs. "This is going to be another L.A., people, albeit on a smaller scale. But it's going to be a rough one. Nick has confirmed that the punks and creeps have a large force, they're well armed, dug in deep, and ready for a fight. This is their last large bastion in North America, so they'll be defending it with all they've got, right down to the last man. You are all well aware of the fact that Night People don't surrender. Nick, what you may not know is that we have never been able to rehabilitate a creepie child. God knows, we tried. At first."

"What the hell do you do with them, Ben?" Nick asked.

Ben just stared at him for a moment.

"Shit!" Nick said. "I've done a lot of things in my life

that I'm ashamed of, but I never went in for that, Ben. Not even in 'Nam; you know that."

"If we had the time, Stafford," Lamar Chase said from the back of the room, "I'd take you down to what we used to call Base Camp One and show you the kids—who are now adults—that we tried to rehab. They're monsters. They'll attack anybody if given the slightest opportunity. They will spend the rest of their unnatural lives locked in specially built cells. We no longer take creepie prisoners . . . unless they are tiny babies. We've had some success with them. But nothing is guaranteed, even with them."

Nick had twisted in his chair to look at the chief of medicine. "Is it in the genes?"

"We don't know," Lamar admitted. "What we do know is that they've been around for many, many years. Decades before the Great War. And the consensus is we'll never completely wipe them out."

"All right, people," Ben called. "Here it is. Ike, you take your battalion, along with Tina, O'Shea, Malone, and Gomez, and take the westernmost sectors. You'll take Windsor, then turn and work east. Georgi, you take Dan, Rebet, Danjou, and Greenwalt and drive down from the north. I'll take Buck, West, Nick, and Jim and hit them from the east. Everybody else will stay in reserve. When everyone is in position, let me know. That's it."

Nick eased up to Ben as the others were filing out. He grinned and said, "You keeping an eye on me, Ben?"

Ben returned the smile. "Not really, Nick ol' buddy.

You see, you and your boys are spearheading the push west into the suburbs."

Ben walked away chuckling, leaving Nick with his mouth hanging open.

Ben massed his troops north and south along Highway 7/12, with two battalions of reserves running east to west along Highway 48. Georgi was strung out west to east along Highway 9, with a small force of tanks and ground troops making a turn at Arthur and heading south down to just north of Waterloo. Ike had the hot spot, for when the creeps and the punks started running from Toronto, they would have only one direction to run, straight toward Ike and his people in the west. But Ben was betting they wouldn't do that.

At 0600 Ben glanced at Corrie. "Start the shelling of Windsor, Corrie."

From across the river in the rubble of Detroit, Rebel 155's opened up with a mixed bag of rounds and started the job of leveling Windsor, Canada.

"All units push off," Ben said.

"All units on the move," Corrie replied a moment later.

Lamar Chase appeared at Ben's side. "Not going in with the first wave, Ben?"

"No. I'll leave that to Nick and the other batt coms."

"Finally getting smart," the old doctor said. Ben smiled.

In the littered, trashed, and filth-strewn city of Toronto and the suburbs, the warlords and gang leaders and creepies knew their time had finally come.

They had names like Fast Eddie and Technicolor Joe and I. B. Kool and the North York Ramblers and the East York Dudes. Pure punk shit any direction one wished to look.

And well-armed punk shit, for when the world went into chaos, the punks broke into armories and police stations and army depots and stole the best of weapons. But they were not well trained and had no real discipline.

North, west, and south of the city, the land had been raped by the punks and the creepies in a never-ending search for food. It was void of people, thanks to the creeps, and trashed and looted thanks to the street slime. Georgi and Ike had reported to Ben that they never expected such devastation and lack of human habitation. From Owen Sound down to Waterloo, and from Parkhill east to Kitchener, the Rebels had encountered very few people. Most of those had run away when they saw the Rebels.

"Can't blame them," Ben said. "They don't know who the hell we are." He smiled. "Let's get a bit closer, gang."

Cooper hid his smile and stepped on the pedal. He had been Ben's driver for too long not to know that Ben Raines wanted to be right in the middle of the action. Cooper glanced in the rearview. Ben's personal company of Rebels, including several MBTs, were right behind him.

"Take the next road to the south, Coop," Ben said, after he consulted a map.

"That's taking us away from the main force," Cooper reminded him.

"Yeah, I know. Turn here. We might get lucky and run into a few surprises."

Ben's way of saying they might see some action—soon.

Cooper slowed when he spotted a half dozen running figures darting across the road in a small village about a quarter mile ahead.

"Company, General."

"Yeah, I see them. Get closer."

"Used to be about four hundred people living in this town," Beth said.

"Colonel West is rattling the air," Corrie said. "Demanding to know where we are."

"Tell him we're fine. I'm just taking a shortcut."

"He says that is totally unacceptable."

"Tell him he's breaking up and we'll try to reestablish contact in a few minutes."

Corrie did. "He says that's bullshit."

Cooper spun the wheel hard just in time to avoid getting the windshield pocked by heavy machine-gun fire. He roared in between two old buildings.

"Tell the company to dismount and spread out, west to east," Ben said, stepping out of the Hummer. "Slow advance toward our position."

Since ammunition had proven hard to come by for his Desert Eagle 50, Ben had once more returned to his Colt government model .45 autoloaders. He picked up his Thompson and walked to the edge of the building, stealing a quick peek around the corner. He ducked back to his team and said, "Whole bunch of punks massing on both sides of the street, gang. All the way to the other end of town. I think we're outnumbered."

"Why does that not come as any surprise to me?" Corrie said.

Jersey smiled. "Kick-ass time!"

Five

The punk leader of this particularly odious pack of slime called himself Mahmud the Terrible. His name was accurate to some degree, since his body odor had been known to overwhelm even the most serious of nasal blockages.

"I comes from a long line of desert warriors," Mahmud was fond of saying. Supposedly that explained his aversion to bathing. "I can trace my ancestors back to Gandhi. I am the Lion of the Desert." One could only assume he meant Haile Selassie, but what the hell? What's a continent or two when nobility is involved? Anybody can make a geographic mistake.

Mahmud was also fond of saying that he was bulletproof. He was about fifteen minutes away from having to prove that.

Mahmud stuck his head around the corner of what used to be a Mom and Pop grocery store. He was wearing a real nifty hat made of fake tiger skin. Said the hat had been in his family for centuries and had once been worn by Lawrence of Somalia. Geographically, he was getting closer.

Ben gave him a short burst from his old Chicago Piano, the .45-caliber slugs knocking bits of brick off the wall and peppering the face of the Lion of Jackson, Mississippi, son of a hard-working police officer who (after forty-seven arrests) finally gave up on his son and booted him out of the house at seventeen and told him to hit the road and don't come back. Mahmud knew better than to mess around with his daddy, for his daddy was one mean law-and-order cop. Mahmud barely made it to Canada before the world blew up.

Mahmud, the Lion of the Desert, if he didn't smarten up, was only moments away from meeting the biggest cat on the block.

"Hey, asshole!" Ben yelled. "You with the stupid-looking hat. You hear me?"

Two short blocks away, Mahmud frowned.

"I think he talkin' to you, Mahmud," one of the Lion's men said.

"Yeah, I think he just insulted your hat," another of the Lion's men said. "You gonna let him get away wit' that?"

"You leave my hat out of this!" Mahmud hollered. Again he frowned, as the sounds of a tank clanking into position reached him. "Ummm, shit!" Mahmud said. He and his men had the opportunity, years back, to steal several tanks that had been abandoned. Trouble was, the modern tank had so many computers in them, none of the Lion's kitties could figure out how to drive the goddamn thing. One of his men had flipped a switch or pulled a lever or done some damn thing and the turret swung around, the barrel of the 105-mm main gun knocking the Lion to the ground, sprawling ass over elbows. That was the last time any of them ever fooled around with a tank. Too complicated, man.

The tank that was clanking into position for a shot was a M60A3, with a 105-mm main gun. Mahmud peeked around the corner of the building just as 105 was lowering.

"Hit the trail!" Mahmud hollered, and took off at a lope just as the 105 belched fire and smoke and one side of the old building blew apart.

"Shhiittt!" Mahmud's second in command, Abdul, squalled as bricks rained down on him.

The sounds of car and truck engines roaring laboriously away drifted to Ben and his people. Rebels worked their way up the street to check it out. Ben leaned up against the Hummer and rolled a cigarette.

"Sorry-assed firefight," he bitched.

"It'll get better," Jersey said. "I got a hunch this bunch was way off their turf—just checking things out."

"West wants to know where in the blankety-blank, blankety-blank, blankety-blank hell we are," Corrie said.

"Tell him we're all right," Ben said. "Mount up, everybody. Let's stay on this old road until we reach the expressway and take that on in. I think things will begin to pick up very shortly."

They certainly did pick up, just about three miles farther down the road.

"Pull over and duck in between those old buildings

over there, Coop," Ben said, pointing. "That intersection up there just looks too clean to suit me."

Corrie was busy telling the company of Rebels and armor behind them what was happening. When she finished, Ben said, "Get me Nick on scramble, Corrie."

"Nick, I'm not far from the expressway on Lake Ontario. I don't even know what road this is. What can you tell me about it?"

"What the hell are you doing down there, Ben?" Nick came back. "From Pickering on in is strong creepie country. Get the hell out of there!"

"He's beginning to sound like all the rest of the batt coms," Copper remarked.

"Yeah," Ben said with a grin. "I do believe Nick has finally found a home." He keyed the mic. "Negative on pull-back, Nick. We're too far in for that. How is your advance?"

"Slow, Ben. The punks and the creeps smartened up and are giving everybody one hell of a fight. I just got off the blower with Georgi. He's stopped cold for a time. You watch your ass down there, Ben."

"Will do. Eagle out."

Ben studied the scene in front of him for a moment. "Corrie, bring the tanks up."

The lead tank commander popped the hatch and said, "What's up, General?"

Ben pointed out the buildings ahead. "Just for luck, put three or four rounds into each of those buildings."

"Will do."

Another tank pulled up, and a few seconds later great holes were blown into the old buildings.

All hell broke loose.

"Mortars coming in!" a Rebel shouted, then dove for cover.

The mortar rounds didn't do any harm, but they caused everybody to hunt for cover. Ben dashed for the phone on the tank and told the commander, "Bring those goddamn buildings down, son."

In seconds 105 and 155 rounds began knocking holes in the building. The third rumbled up and began pouring HE rounds into the buildings. Whoever was in the building on the north side of the road—and no one was sure whether it was creepies or punks—must have used the place for an fuel dump, for about a minute after the firefight began, the whole building blew up in a wall of flames and smoke. The explosion shook the ground for a mile in any direction and sent debris flying high into the clear blue sky. And that debris included various body parts.

"They're probably not creepies," Jersey said matter-of-factly. "The parts I can see aren't wearing robes. Although we have fought a few who dressed like normal people."

But the punks weren't anywhere near through. Heavy machine-gun fire began coming from concealed gun emplacements on both sides of the old cracked road.

Several Rebels had climbed up onto roofs and were surveying the scene through binoculars. One yelled, "Back those tanks up! The bastards have Dragons!"

The tanks quickly sought protection behind buildings.

"Mortars up," Ben said. "Let's zero in and neutralize those people."

The rooftop FO's began calling out range and the Rebel mortars began dropping in short and walking in. The heavy machine guns were well hidden but not bunkered against mortar attack. One by one the machine guns fell silent as the mortar crews used a wide variety of rounds to still them.

While all that was going on, two platoons of Rebels had been flanking the ambush site. As soon as the mortars ceased their bombardment, the Rebels moved in for the kill.

"Neutralized," Corrie said to Ben when the rattle of gunfire had ceased.

"Let's go see what we were up against."

Lieutenant Bonelli met Ben at the crossroads. "Mixed bag of punks, sir. We've got several prisoners over there." He pointed.

Ben walked over to the ditch and looked at the prisoners, their hands tied behind them. He guessed they were in their mid to late twenties. They would have all been in their mid to late teens when the Great War blew the world apart and toppled all vestiges of law and order.

"Talk to me," Ben told the small group.

"Fuck you," one said.

"Stick it up your ass, man," another said.

"Death to all niggers and Jews," yet another popped off.

"Long live the Movement," the last one said.

"What movement?" Ben asked.

"The Movement, man. Ever'body knows about the Movement."

"Sorry. I never heard of the Movement. Why don't you tell me about it?"

"Don't tell him nothin'!" the first punk shouted defiantly.

"Recon reports it's clear all the way down to the expressway," Corrie said. "But from there on into the city, the place is crawling with punks."

"Barney Holland," the last punk said. "He's the leader of the Movement."

"Shut your damn mouth, Eddie!"

Ben turned to Bonelli. "Take Eddie and see what you can get out of him."

Eddie was jerked to his feet and marched off, while the other three shouted obscenities at him. Then they turned their vulgar mouths on Ben and let him have it. They cursed Ben until they were breathless.

During the cussing, they managed to give away quite a lot about Barney and the Movement. The Movement, so it seemed, was directed toward the total annihilation of all minorities and anyone else who didn't agree with the preachings and teachings of Barney Holland.

"Same old song, different jukebox," Ben said.

"What do you want to do with these bastards?" Ben was asked.

Ben looked at the Rebel for a moment.

"Right, sir."

Eddie had been taken to a small building that had suffered only minor damage during the shelling. Bonelli was stepping out of the building as Ben approached. He shook his head.

"We untied Eddie to treat his wounds and he swallowed some sort of pill, General. He was dead a minute later."

"Well, members of the Movement obviously have enough sense to manufacture pharmaceuticals. So we're not dealing with total idiots. Did he say anything of value?"

"The Movement is one of the largest gangs in the area. The other large gang is the Mau Maus."

"Oh, shit!" Ben said. "Let me guess: They hate all whites."

"Right, sir. That first bunch we ran into is a part of the Mau Maus. A group headed by a guy who calls himself Mahmud the Terrible. The Lion of the Desert."

"If he's the Lion of the Desert, what the hell is he doing in Toronto?"

"Beats me, sir. Mahmud claims to be a direct descendant of Gandhi."

"Gandhi?"

"Yes, sir. Gandhi."

"How wonderful for him. Let's move out."

The punks and creeps were leaving Windsor like rats from a sinking ship. The guns of the Rebels across the river, using HE and WP, in addition to the Rebel planes dropping napalm, had turned the city into an inferno. The winds were blowing west to east at about twenty miles an hour and that only served to fan the flames. The punks and creeps ran toward the east and ran right into roaming P-51's. The souped-up fighters turned the highways into death pyres. Cobras and Apaches came in behind them and finished the job.

Those gangs in London monitored shortwave sets and went into a panic. They began fleeing toward Toronto.

"Give them a clear corridor," Ben ordered. "Planes and choppers are not to fire on them. They're heading for the city, so let them. They'll be easier to handle there. Let them all bunch up in the city. Let every gang and creepie in every city west of Toronto get to the city. Then we'll close off the corridor and finish it."

The creepies already knew how ruthless Ben Raines was. The gangs of punks were about to find out.

At Ben's orders, Ike began slowly swinging his battalions south, closing off any escape to the west. It was the classic pincher movement, and the creeps and punks ran right into the trap.

Ben halted his battalions' forward movement at noon. "Hold what you have," he radioed. "Give Ike and Georgi time to close it up."

Ben's northern battalions had moved down into East Gwillimbury, the westernmost battalion linking up with Georgi's easternmost troops.

Ike was driving hard, pushing his people to the max, nipping at the heels of the retreating punks and creeps, herding them into the trap.

Ben had sealed off everything north to south, running from the intersection of Highway 11 down to the lake. By midafternoon, Ben told his people to secure for the night and get some food and rest.

Inside the city it was chaos. Thousands of creeps and

punks and warlords and assorted street slime had converged in Toronto.

"I was 'bused as a child," one gang leader bitched to Mahmud the Terrible, the Lion of the Desert. "My daddy whupped me and whupped me somethin' awful. I didn't have no choice 'ceptin' to turn to a life of crime. Dat's what de social workers tole me over and over. Dey be right, I'm shore."

"My daddy whupped me, too," Ahmed Popov said. It was rumored that Ahmed got his last name from a vodka bottle . . . after he killed a tourist in Miami to get it. "He whupped me 'cause I wanted to hang wit' the homeboys 'stead of goin' to school and listen to a bunch of shit."

Actually, when the Great War struck, Ahmed was eighteen years old, had been arrested 122 times—for everything ranging from rape to grand theft auto, but thanks to liberals, he never served more than two hours at a time behind bars.

"We got to make peace with the niggers," one of Barney Holland's lieutenants said. "We got to stand shoulder to shoulder with them jungle bunnies and fight the Rebels."

"I'll be goddamned if that's so," Barney said. "They can stay on their side of the city and we'll stay on ours."

"We got to talk about makin' peace with them goddamn honkies over there," Ahmed said to Mahmud. "We can't win fightin' Ben Raines separate."

"There ain't no way I'll shake hands with that cross-burnin' fool!" Mahmud said.

"Then we got to fall back into the city and make friends with the cannibals, Barney."

"Shit no!"

"We gots to make friends with the Night People, Mahmud!"

"Is you *crazy?* You want to end up on their supper table along with the greens and the grits?"

"Then we gonna lose, Mahmud, an' that's a fact."

"We ain't never lost no fight yet, has we?"

"No."

"Then what you so worried about?"

"We ain't never fought Ben Raines."

Six

All that afternoon and all during the night, the sounds of tanks and self-propelled artillery being moved about was heard north, east, and west of the city. The Rebels knew exactly what Ben was doing; they'd seen this played out many, many times.

The punks didn't have any idea what was about to happen. But the creeps did.

"We must flee," the leaders were told.

"There is no place to flee," was the response from the Judges. "Every exit has been sealed tight. We will die, but our movement will live on. We are finished here, but all over the world our kind flourish. And Ben Raines does not know that others like us have adapted to modern ways. They have tanks and heavy guns and almost everything that Ben Raines has. We must accept our fate and fight to the finish."

"As you say," the combat leaders said, and bowed and left the stinking lairs of the Judges.

* * *

Ben slept well and rose refreshed; he never needed more than a few hours of sleep. It was still several hours before dawn, and the morning was cool. Ben got his coffee and walked outside. He did not have to look to see if Jersey was with him. She always was. Ben sat down in an old chair on the front porch, sat his coffee mug on the floor, and rolled a cigarette.

Corrie stepped out, a steaming cup of coffee in her hand. "Artillery is in place," she spoke softly. "The crews are catching a few hours sleep."

"We'll commence the barrage at good light. That should be about 0700."

"Where do we go when this is over, boss?" Cooper asked, stepping out of the house.

"I guess we go back home and settle down for a time. This has been the shortest campaign I can remember."

"It's gonna be kind of dull, isn't it?" Beth, the last of Ben's personal team, said as she joined the group in the darkness on the porch.

To many people, combat produces a high unlike any other sensation. Stay in it long enough, and one either cracks, learns to live with it, or begins to enjoy it in a strange way. Many of the Rebels, including Ben, enjoyed the high of combat.

Ben finished his first mug of coffee and stood up. "Let's wander down to the mess tent and get some breakfast."

The camp was beginning to stir as Rebels rolled out of beds and blankets and cots and sleeping bags. The shower area was sending up clouds of steam in the cool air. Ben had to smile as he recalled how the Rebel army began to rebuild after the fall of the Tri-States.

Only a tiny handful of men and women had, over the years, turned into thousands.

Ben spoke to a few of the Rebels as he walked. Most gave him a wide berth, both out of respect and out of fear, for many Rebels still believed that Ben was very nearly a god. Ben had tried for years to dispel that nonsense but soon learned that the harder he tried, the less successful he was. And the old Thompson he carried was right up there with Ben. Many Rebels refused to touch it, even though there was not a single piece or part of original equipment left. Ben had tried other weapons, but always returned to the old Chicago Piano. It took a man to control the .45-caliber spitter, especially with a fully loaded drum hung under it, but even at middle age, Ben was still very much one hell of a man.

Ben lingered over breakfast, then refilled his coffee mug and returned to his CP. The sky was beginning to lighten in the east when all his batt coms began radioing in.

"We're sitting on ready," Corrie called to Ben.

There had been no mention of calling for the surrender of the punks and the creeps in the city. That time had passed. Ben could not ask for the women and children to come out, for the Rebels had learned that the creepies had a nasty habit of including their own perverted women in the bunch. But many women who had aligned themselves with the punks and thugs and street slime had left the city, and the Rebels had let them go . . . after taking the younger children from them. The surviving Canadian people had opened their arms to the young.

Ben looked at the luminous hands of his watch. "A few more minutes."

Cooper sat on the steps of the porch, his eyes closed, dozing. Jersey sat on the porch with her back to the front of the house, her M-16 across her knees. Beth was inside, writing in her journal. Corrie was at the radio.

Ben drained his coffee mug and placed it on the floor of the porch. "All right, Corrie," he called. "Bring the city down."

Fifteen seconds later the sky was split with bright flashes as the big guns roared. The first rounds began landing on the city, and they included everything from the 105-mm rounds to the huge projectiles from the M110A2, the big 203-mm (8-inch) self-propelled howitzers, which could lay back some 24,000 yards and lob conventional rounds in and put rocket-assisted rounds in from a distance of nearly 34,000 yards. But its rate of fire was slow, about four rounds every three minutes, due to the weight of the projectiles, since each round weighed just over two hundred pounds. But the damage it caused was awesome.

President Blanton had sent several civilian observers up to Ben's position (they had arrived the day before) and were still sleeping in their quarters when the big guns began to roar. They rushed outside to see the gray horizon pocked with fire and smoke. The three women and three men ran out into the street, slightly disoriented, and walked the short distance to Ben's CP. They were startled to find him sitting calmly on the front porch, reading a Dan Parkinson novel of the West and sipping coffee.

"What is happening, General?" Catherine Smith-

Harrelson-Ingalls asked. It had taken those subtle man-haters about a generation to figure out that when they married and kept their maiden names, they were not shedding the despised man-names but instead just keeping their father's name. Now with the nation once more emerging out of the ashes and re-forming, it was chic in some circles to go one step further and add their *mother's* maiden name as well.

Ben looked up at her. "Artillery, Miss . . . ah . . . what is your name?"

"Catherine Smith-Harrelson-Ingalls. And it is *Ms.*"

Ben blinked. "Did your mother have a grudge against you when you were named?"

"I beg your pardon?"

"Never mind. We're shelling the city."

"Whatever on earth for?"

Jersey was sitting on the steps, staring in disbelief at the woman. Beth looked at Corrie, who winked at Cooper, the silent gesture stating clearly that things were about to get lively.

Ben carefully marked the page and laid the book aside. "Ms. Whatever-your-name-is, it is common practice during war to use artillery from time to time. It not only is very destructive, but it also demoralizes the hell out of those being shelled."

"Do you have the president's permission to do this?" another woman piped up.

"Lady," Ben said, mustering all the patience he could, "I don't have to have Blanton's permission to do a goddamn thing. Now why don't you people go on down to the mess tent—it's that way," he said, pointing, "and have some breakfast. After that, stay the hell out of my business."

"Well!" Ms. Smith-Harrelson-Ingalls said.

"Where are you holding the prisoners?" a man asked.

Jersey giggled, which was something that Jersey rarely did.

"Did I say something funny?" the man asked.

"If we take any prisoners, they'll be held over there." Ben pointed. "Somewhere."

"What do you mean, *if* you take prisoners?" a woman asked, looking around her at Ben's personal team.

"Creeps don't surrender," Cooper said. "Never. As for punks, who the hell wants them?"

"They're human beings, for God's sake!" a man said.

"Cooper, please escort these people to the mess tent," Ben said.

"How long is this barrage going to continue?" the woman with three last names asked.

"For twenty-four hours, lady," Jersey answered. "I recommend the scrambled eggs. They're pretty good. Goodbye, Cooper. Have fun."

"My name is Ralph Galton, General," a young man said. Ben figured him to be about thirty-five. About the same age as the others. "I report directly to ex-President Timmy Narter."

"How wonderful for you," Ben said.

Galton ignored the sarcasm. "We are all concerned about the humanitarian aspects of this operation."

"It's none of your goddamn business, sonny."

"I beg your pardon, sir, but it most certainly is our business. As you may know, President Narter has re-emerged from hiding and is chairperson of the——"

Ben waved him silent. "I don't want to hear about it, sonny. Tell him to go build a house."

"You're very disrespectful, sir."

"I've had it," Ben said, and stood up and turned, facing the group. Both his hands were balled into big fists. Beth quickly stepped between them and said, "Breakfast is being served at the mess tent. I would suggest you go there, right now. Cooper? Take them. Now!"

After the group had left, Jersey said, "Where are all these damn people coming from? Where have they been hiding for all these years? What have they been doing all the years since the Great War?"

"Waiting for us to do their dirty work, Jersey," Ben said. "It's typical of a certain type of mealymouthed liberal. They knew if they stuck their heads out of their holes, the thugs and street slime and creepies and out-laws would have them for lunch. So they waited while we did all the work—and they knew we were doing it. That's what pisses me off about that bunch. Blanton admitted it. They knew all along we were killing punks and thugs. They knew we weren't cutting any of them any slack. And they let us do it. But now, oh boy, but now . . . this is the last great gathering of slime in the Northern Hemisphere. The liberals are safe now, for a time. Now the liberals can come out of hiding and strut around puffing out their chests and weeping and piss-ing and moaning about how harshly we're treating the poor unfortunate criminal element." Ben smiled. "But their safety will be a very fleeting thing as we keep shoving more and more punks across our borders into their territory. They're going to open their eyes one morning and find they're right back where they were before the Great War: smack in the middle of a growing epidemic of lawlessness. And I am going to be very amused when that takes place."

Ben stood silent for a moment, leaning against a porch support post, listening to the steady rolling thunder of artillery. "Very amused."

The pounding of the artillery did little to harm the Night People, for they were bunkered deep underground, with dozens of exit holes once the barrage stopped—if they chose to exit and face the wrath of the Rebels.

However, things were not going nearly so well for the gangs in the city. They had stored provisions for a long siege. They had plenty of food and water and ammo and bedding and medical supplies. But they hadn't counted on the Rebels destroying the city; didn't take into consideration that the Rebels might lay back several miles and bring the concrete and steel crashing down on their heads.

They should have asked the creepies about the ruthlessness of Ben Raines.

As far as actual physical casualties, the gangs fared pretty well; it was the psychological aspect of the barrage that was taking a heavy toll on the criminal element in the city. Nothing is more mentally debilitating than a steady artillery barrage, for there is no place to run to escape it. After a time many break under the strain and are reduced to babbling, slobbering idiots. Others run headlong into the streets, to be crushed and killed by falling debris or shrapnel from the rounds. Others seek shelter in basements of buildings and are forever trapped by tons of concrete and steel, entombing them for eternity. A few stick the muzzles of their weapons into their mouths and end it. Pretty extreme, but it works.

A few minutes before dusk of the first day of the bombardment, Ms. Three-Last-Names came to see Ben.

"Here comes that woman who isn't real sure who she is," Jersey said. "And that jerk who represents Timmy Farter is with her."

"Narter," Ben corrected.

"Whatever."

"I remember reading something about him," Cooper said. "But I can't recall whether it was good or bad."

"Don't get me started," Ben said.

"I think he drank a lot of beer," Corrie said.

"That was his brother," Ben said. "That's the one we should have elected."

"Hey!" Cooper said, standing up. "A whole mob is right behind those two flakes. It's the press."

"Shit!" Ben said. "That's all we need. How in the hell did they learn of this operation?"

"Three guesses," Jersey said sourly.

"The Red Cross is with them, too," Beth said.

"I hope they brought some doughnuts," Ben muttered.

"General Raines," Ralph Galton said. "I have been asked to be the spokesperson for this group."

"So speak."

"We wish permission to enter the war zone."

"You know where it is. It's kind of hard to miss, I would say."

"Yeah, we've been pretty accurate so far," Jersey said with a smile.

"This is no time for levity, General," Ralph said, after giving Jersey a dirty look. "There are wounded in that city who need to be evacuated for medical treatment."

Ben looked at the group. All in their early to mid thirties. *The new breed of liberal,* he thought. *All earnest and forthright. Earnest and forthright . . . sounded like a vaudeville team.*

"Well?" Ms. Three-Last-Names demanded.

"Well . . . what?" Ben asked.

"Do we have your permission to enter the city?"

"Sure. Go right ahead. Don't let me stop you."

"When may we assume the bombardment will cease?" Ralph asked.

"At 0700 hours tomorrow."

"My God!" another earnest and forthright person said, standing with several cameras hanging off his person. He was wearing a jacket that appeared to have about eighty pockets. "That's thirteen hours away."

"Congratulations on your ability to tell time," Ben replied.

"That's a neat jacket," Beth said. "Where'd you get it?"

"If you don't mind," the young man said to her. "General, we demand to be allowed to enter the city."

"I told you, go right ahead. None of my people will stop you." Ben smiled. "As a matter of fact, I'll even open a corridor for you." He opened his map case, which he had been studying until the light began to fade, and used a penlight to look at it. "Corrie, order batteries 17, 18, and 19 to cease firing at—" he looked at his watch "—1830 hours. They will not resume until 1900. Tell Batts 4, 21, and 14 to cover that corridor; these people are to be allowed in, but no one is allowed out."

"Right, sir."

"Well, now," Eighty-Pockets said smugly, "the power of the press is alive and well."

"Not for long," Jersey muttered under her breath. She knew perfectly well what Ben was doing.

"Well, let's be off!" Ms. Three-Last-Names said.

"You sure are," Beth muttered.

The representatives from the Red Cross hesitated; they were not nearly so full of themselves as the press corps and the men and women from the offices of Blanton and Narter.

In their rush to get into the smoking city and report all the atrocities committed upon the poor misunderstood and much-maligned punks and thugs and street slime by Ben Raines and his horrible, nasty, right-wing Republican army, the others left the Red Cross behind.

"You opened a corridor to let them in, General Raines," a very attractive lady said. "But when will you reopen the corridor to let them *out?*"

Ben smiled. "At 0700 hours tomorrow."

Seven

The press and the nosy liberals (not that there is a modicum of difference between the two) made it safely into the smoking and burning city. They were positively aghast at the devastation. When they finally stopped their vehicles, they realized the Red Cross people were missing.

"Hell with them," a reporter said. "I didn't like them anyway. I don't trust them. They probably secretly support Ben Raines. They're holdovers from before the Great War. Old-timers. I heard one say he voted for George Bush. My God, who would willingly admit *that?*"

They were all still reasonably young, but had managed to get quite a liberal education before the Great War knocked the world to its knees, and had been living (groveling) at the feet of people like Blanton and Narter and their ilk ever since.

Because they had lived through the Great War and the bloody aftermath, the sight of bodies did not disturb them all that much. But since reporters were present, with cameras rolling and clicking (more clicking than rolling, for while many newspapers were coming off the presses across the nation, TV stations were rare in the still-recovering nation), they did occasionally manage a tear and a sniffle for effect.

"I wonder where everybody is?" Eighty-Pockets asked, glancing at his watch. It was 1900 hours. He looked up into the rapidly darkening sky. "What is that noise?"

"Incoming!" an older reporter yelled. "That bastard Raines has resumed the shelling."

"Head for that building over there!" Ms. Smith-Harrelson-Ingalls shouted, pointing.

The group took off at a flat lope, heading for what they hoped would be safety. Eyes watched them approach. Cruel, greedy, and hungry eyes.

The Red Cross representatives stayed for supper at Ben's suggestion. They were surprised to find that Ben ate the same thing his troops ate, and consequently, so did they. During dinner the lone woman in the group of four said, "That was a very unkind thing you did, General."

"And what is that, Ms. Petti?"

"It's Julie, General. And you can drop the Ms. business. I never cared for it back when the nation was whole. Sending those press people in the city knowing they would be trapped."

"That's their problem."

Julie Petti, Ben guessed, was in her late thirties or

early forties, and aging very well considering what the nation had gone through over the past decade.

"Where have you people been hiding over the years, Julie?"

"In very small groups all over the nation, General—"

"Ben. Call me Ben."

"Ben. All right. Speaking quite frankly, none of us knew what you and your forces were up to. The underground government put out so many stories about you and your Rebels, we didn't know what to think."

"I have no difficulty accepting that," Ben said.

Julie looked at Ben with amusement in her hazel eyes. She brushed back a lock of dark brown hair from her forehead. "You will have to admit that your form of government is, ah, quite novel."

"It works for us," Ben said. "Now several more states in the Lower Forty-Eight have joined us. The entire eastern section of Canada is on board with us, and I suspect that before it's over, most of Canada will join us. Liberalism is dead, Julie. It doesn't work and never has. Many Americans knew that before the Great War and wanted change, but the liberal Democratic party blocked our every move. Now we're too strong for them to stop, and it scares them to death."

Julie listened to the roar of the big guns for a few seconds. "How much of the city is going to be standing after that stops?"

"More than you think," Ben told her. "And casualties won't be as heavy as you might imagine. We'll start entering the city at 0701." He smiled. "You folks want to come along?"

"That's why we're here," one of the men in the group said.

It seemed to the victims that the rape and sodomy and degradation would never stop. Ms. Smith-Harrelson-Ingalls—along with the other women in the group—had been passed from punk to punk so many times they lost count of the number of men who raped them. Ralph Galton had gotten very indignant and quite lippy, at first. That stopped when he was bent over a table and repeatedly buggered. Another man was forced to have oral sex with his captors.

"But we're here to help you!" Ms. Smith-Harrelson-Ingalls cried. "We love you!"

"Yeah?" Tony Green, a.k.a. Big Stomper, said. "Well, we love your ass, Ms. Big Tits. Like, literally, baby."

Ms. Smith-Harrelson-Ingalls began screaming as Big Stomper sodomized her. Her cries were lost in the thunder of the artillery barrage.

Later, when the punks had sexually exhausted themselves, Ms. Smith-Harrelson-Ingalls heard one of Big Stomper's lieutenants ask, "Do we take them to the Night People?"

"Naw," Tony said. "They're bunkered in underground. No way to get to them."

"Wanna give them to the niggers?"

"Hell, no! Just burn all their clothes and leave them here. We gotta get ready to fight." He looked at Ralph Galton, huddled naked in a pain-filled ball on the dirty floor. "But first I'm gonna teach that big-mouth over there a lesson." Tony then proceeded to show the others why he was called Big Stomper. He stomped Ralph Galton to death.

The punks then vanished into the explosive night.

Gina Zapp found a rag and began wiping the blood from her thighs. "Nice people," she said sarcastically. "Really worth saving." She looked over at Eighty-Pockets, who was sobbing in a corner of the darkened room. Eighty-Pockets had taken several dicks up the ass. "Oh, stop your whimpering, Greg! Women get sodomized all the time, and you men sit on juries and won't convict. So just shut up!"

"Look around for some rags or cardboard to cover ourselves with," a man said.

"And something to defend ourselves with," Ms. Smith-Harrelson-Ingalls said, a hard note in her voice. "Clubs or bricks or boards or something. I'm going to bash that son of a bitch's brains out if he comes back here."

"Has anybody got any mouthwash?" another reporter asked.

Ben entered the eastern edge of the city just behind the first wave at 0730. Georgi's people were pushing in from the north, and Ike was advancing from the west.

"Recon's found the group who went in last night, General," Corrie said.

"Alive?"

"Oh, yeah. Some punks grabbed them and raped them—men and women. Two blocks ahead, on the left."

An angry group of reporters and human rights representatives met Ben. They were dressed in a mishmash of spare Rebel clothing from the Rebel's packs.

"I want you to find that goddamn Tony Green, General Raines," Ms. Smith-Harrelson-Ingalls squalled in Ben's face. "I want you to castrate that slimy son of a bitch with a dull knife and then shoot him!"

"I was under the impression that you didn't believe in capital punishment," Ben said. "Did something happen to change your mind?"

Julie Petti stood off to one side and listened to the exchange.

The blood drained from the woman's face and she glared daggers at Ben. "Fuck you!" Ms. Smith-Harrelson-Ingalls said, then marched off toward a waiting team of medics.

Ben glanced at Nick Stafford, sitting in a Hummer, looking at him. "I haven't started going to church, so don't worry about that. And I've abused too many women in my life to tell you that you should have been a bit more understanding with her, Ben," Nick said. "But I will anyway." Nick put the Hummer in gear and drove on down the debris-littered street.

Ben looked at Julie Petti, who was watching him. "You have anything to say about it?"

She shrugged her shoulders. "What rape does to a woman is something that men will never fully understand, Ben."

"Perhaps I was a bit cold, at that. But she had no business coming in here unarmed. But then, you were coming in here unarmed, weren't you?"

Julie and the men with her smiled. The men opened their jackets, showing Ben their sidearms nestled in shoulder holsters. Julie reached into her purse and hauled a big 9-mm Beretta, model 92S.

Ben said, "Those would have helped . . . but not much." The Red Cross people had told him at supper the night before that this was their first real outing since the Great War. Mostly they had been helping provide food and medical care to civilian survivors, not criminals.

"Got a real firefight shaping up about four blocks ahead," Corrie said.

Ben outran the others in getting to the Hummer.

Rebels halted the HumVee a block from the sounds of very heavy gunfire. "No vehicles past this point, General. We've got at least a thousand punks stretched out along a five or six block line, and at least that deep. They're dug in hard, and they're well armed. Machine guns, rocket launchers, and mortars."

"Park over there, Coop," Ben said, getting out of the Hummer. He looked back at the Red Cross vehicle. "Stay here," he told them. "Come on, gang."

The Rebel MP had the authority to stop any vehicle from passing his checkpoint, but he sure as hell wasn't about to tell the general he couldn't proceed on foot.

Lieutenant Bonelli was frantically waving people forward, several of them carrying M-60 machine guns and ammo cans. They were trying to keep up with Ben and his team.

Exasperated, Lieutenant Bonelli finally yelled, "Goddamnit, General, slow down!"

Ben grinned and ducked into an old apartment building, his team right behind him.

Two blocks away Julie was watching through binoculars. "Does he do this often?" she asked a Rebel sergeant. "My God! That's the commanding general of the entire army!"

"As often as he can, miss. Nobody has yet figured out a way to keep him from it."

"Incredible," she said.

"Yes, ma'am."

Ben could hear the rattle of machine-gun fire coming from the room directly above him. He could hear the clink of expended brass bouncing off the floor. Ben pointed toward a door and Cooper nodded. He pointed toward another door and Beth nodded and got into position, covering it. Ben walked around the room until he was certain he was directly under the machine-gun crew. He lifted the Thompson and perforated the ceiling with .45-caliber slugs. The firing abruptly ceased, and the sounds of badly wounded bodies flopping on the floor was clear. Dust rained down on those on the ground floor, just as drops of blood began leaking through several of the holes.

The sound of a heavy metal object bouncing down the stairs was loud.

"Grenade!" Ben said.

Cooper reached out and slammed the door closed and hit the floor with the others just as the grenade blew. The door disintegrated, blowing splinters and bits of paneling all over the ground-floor room.

"That was unkind of them," Beth said, just as Cooper stuck the muzzle of his M-16 around the door jamb and gave the second floor landing a full clip. There was a scream of pain, and a body came rolling down the steps to sprawl dead at Cooper's feet.

Just as Ben was moving toward the blown open door, Lieutenant Bonelli yelled that he was coming in. A half dozen Rebels burst into the room.

Bonelli quickly surveyed the scene and said, "We'll take care of this now, General. The Red Cross people want to see you back at your Hummer."

Ben hesitated for a few seconds. He was very weary of having nursemaids around him twenty-four hours a day. "I have a better idea, Lieutenant."

"What's that, sir?"

"Follow me!" Ben yelled, and charged up the grenade-shattered stairs.

Eight

President Homer Blanton was furious at the suggestion from the UN Security Council. He had regained his composure after leaning out of the window and cussing the demonstrators and had ordered hamburgers to be cooked on the White House lawn every day at noon and fed to the demonstrators.

Now this . . . *insanity* from the UN.

Name Ben Raines and the Rebels as the group to go in and stabilize governments around the world? *Ridiculous!*

"No goddamn way will I go along with that," Homer said bluntly.

"You're outvoted," the secretary-general of the UN said. "And since America is, for the first time, paying only its fair and equal share of the bills, majority rules. Raines and the Rebels will be the stabilizing force of the United Nations."

"Over my dead body," VP Harriet Hooter said.

The Korean diplomat smiled. His reply sounded

very much like a man clearing his throat and getting ready to hawk snot.

"What's that?" Homer asked.

"You have been advised of our decision. Ben Raines will be notified in due time." He walked out of the Oval Office.

"*Shit!*" Homer Blanton screamed.

Ben was on the second-floor landing, his team right behind him, before Lieutenant Bonelli could react. For a middle-aged man, the general could move damn quick.

Ben kicked open the first door he came to and sprayed the room with .45-caliber slugs, sending several oddly dressed men to that great punk heaven in the sky . . . or wherever it is. The rest of his team was busy kicking open doors and letting the lead fly. By the time Bonelli and his people had reached the second floor, the hall Ben was in was clear of unfriendlies.

"Check that one," Ben said, pointing to a hall that angled off.

On this run Ben had opted for clips instead of drums, not so much as to lessen the weight but to make the weapon easier to handle. He ejected one clip and slipped another in.

"Clear!" Bonelli yelled.

Corrie said, "Counterattack, boss! We're cut off."

"Now it gets interesting," Ben said. "Bonelli! Take the ground floor. We'll take this one. Leave one of those M-60's with us."

Without having to be told, Cooper laid aside his

M-16 and took up the M-60 and a can of ammo and moved to a window. "Look at them come," he called, bi-podding the weapon.

"Give them a squirt, Coop," Ben said, picking up Cooper's M-16, for its range was better than his Thompson.

Cooper braced the stock and held the trigger back. Ben watched a line of charging punks kiss the ground as the 7.62 rounds tore the life from them.

Ben sat down behind a shattered window and began picking his shots, watching the advancing punks fall with each shot. The line broke under the unexpected barrage and then took to the ground, hiding behind junked and rusted old cars and trucks, and mounds of rubble and debris.

Ben eyeballed the range for a moment. "Corrie, call in two hundred meters from this building. Somebody else can calculate the distance from this building back."

"Negative, boss," Corrie said a moment later. "They say it's too close to use."

Ben crawled over to her and took the phone. "This is General Raines. Start dropping those eggs down the tubes right now, or I will personally get all up in somebody's face so long and so hard their hair will look like they stuck their finger in a light bulb socket. *Now*, goddamnit!"

Fifteen seconds later the rounds began dropping in.

"Nick on the blower, boss," Corrie said.

"Go, Nick."

"You do have such a nice way of giving orders, Ben. I had forgotten how eloquent you can be."

"Yeah. Right. What's your situation?"

"Bogged down. The punks are really throwing everything at us. I'm waiting for Buck and West to get into position, and then we'll crash through."

"That's ten-four. Keep me informed. Eagle out."

The mortar rounds stopped the line of advancing punks cold as the crews went to work, creating a wall of death between the building the Rebels were trapped in and the street punks. Then they began dropping them in right on the punks' heads. The line broke, and those punks who were not too badly injured quickly retreated back to the looted and trashed buildings on the far side of the clearing.

"Nick says 15 and 4 Batts are in position to push in," Corrie called.

"Tell them to hold what they've got and call for artillery and mortar to soften up the punks' position up and down the line," Ben said. "Tell our people to have smoke ready to pop at my signal."

From three sides the artillery once more began to boom, with those capable of doing so hurling in incendiary rounds and willie peter. There was no place for the punks to go except back, cursing as they retreated.

By late that afternoon the Rebels were firmly entrenched, well into the suburbs of the city, and Ben called a halt to the advance.

Ben was sitting in the den, in an old chair in a reasonably clean home, reading what was left of a yellowed and tattered years-old copy of a Toronto newspaper, when Chase strolled in.

"Anything interesting in there, Ben?" the doctor asked.

"We're bringing our troops home from Somalia and sending them into Bosnia and Haiti."

"I seem to recall something about those exercises in futility," Chase said, pouring a cup of coffee and sitting down in a chair that was leveled with bricks on one side.

Ben laid the paper aside and Jersey picked it up.

"What's up, Lamar?"

"Boring, Ben. Boring. Not that I am complaining about the lack of wounded, for I certainly am not. But I heard even you bitching on the radio today about no real action. Why not just throw up a cordon around the city and starve these miserable miscreants out? It wouldn't be long before the creepies and the punks would be at each other's throats—literally."

Ben chuckled. "I've just given the orders to throw a cordon around the place and wait them out, Lamar."

"Good, good. I see no point in losing good men and women fighting this last bastion of thugs and creeps in the Northern Hemisphere."

Corrie walked into the room. "All batt coms have been notified of your decision, boss. They're standing down to wait them out."

Ben nodded and said, "Now it really gets boring."

The Rebels circled the city and waited. A few of the more industrious gangs of punks tried to slip out by boat. But Ben had thought of that, too, and they didn't get far before Ben's fledgling navy, patrolling Lake Ontario, blew them out of the water.

At the end of the third week, several warlords walked out under flag into Ike's sector.

"Happening sooner than I thought," Ike radioed to Ben. "I got one street gang leader says his name is Tuba Salami."

Ben started laughing so hard he could not speak for half a minute. "What did you say, Ike?"

"You heard me. Tuba Salami."

Ben wiped his eyes and keyed the mic. "How many in this bunch, Ike?"

" 'Bout eight hundred. Still going to turn them over to the Canadians?"

"It's their country."

Julie Petti, who had been keeping close company with Ben since their first meeting, said, "They'll hang them, Ben."

"The Canadians are a fair people, Julie," Ben replied. "They'll give them a fair trial, then they'll hang them. Some of them."

Julie smiled and shook her head.

"As soon as the creepies learn of any talk of mass surrender, they'll start taking prisoners of the punks, for food," Beth said. "We can count on that."

Ms. Catherine Smith-Harrelson-Ingalls paled, but for once she offered up no objections. If the Night People had a friend on the face of the earth—other than fellow creepies—Ben was not aware of them.

"You're certainly correct in that, Beth." Ben looked at Blanton's representatives. "You want any of these prisoners to take back with you?"

"This is amusing you, isn't it, General Raines?" one of the reporters who had not been sodomized or forced to suck a dick that long night of captivity several weeks back asked.

"I suppose it is," Ben said. "In a perverse sort of way. Whenever the Rebels have to come in and clean up the goddamn messes you liberals made of a formerly workable society, it pleasures me a great deal."

The reporter stared at Ben for a moment but wisely made no rebuttal. Even though Ben, at the moment, was unarmed, and giving the reporter about fifteen years in age, the man was not about to risk mixing it up physically with Raines.

Liberals hate the military; always have, always will. But they are very afraid of the military. It's all those guns and discipline and marching and flag-waving and all that other right-wing stuff makes them want to do the hoochie-coochie on their hankies.

"But don't worry," Beth said, always ready to stick the needle into a liberal . . . especially the newly emerging press. "You'll have plenty to write about—criticizing us, I'm sure."

Another reporter turned to the usually soft-spoken Beth. "Whatever in the world do you mean?"

"The creepies, pal," Beth said. "They don't surrender. So that means we'll have to go in and dig them out. So you people will have lots of opportunities to piss and moan about the harsh treatment given them by the Rebels."

"I find that remark both insulting and offensive," the reporter said.

"Yeah?" Beth said, standing up. The quiet, very pretty, and very intelligent historian of the group smiled. "Well, try this one: I don't give a flying fuck what you find offensive or insulting." She walked back into the house.

The reporter's face tightened in anger. "Someone needs to teach that young lady some manners."

Cooper laughed. "Anytime you feel lucky, pal, you just jump right in there and grab a handful. Me—I'd rather walk into a roomful of rattlesnakes than mess with Beth."

The reporter scoffed. Beth was about five feet four inches and weighed maybe 120 pounds. The reporter was six feet two inches and about 190. Besides, he'd played football before the Great War, and his coach had told him he was bad to the bone. His coach had lied. "You people certainly have a rather high opinion of your prowess, don't you?"

Little Jersey stood up and laid her M-16 aside.

"Oh, shit!" Cooper muttered, quickly getting out of the way.

The reporter towered over Jersey. He glared down at her. "I don't want to hurt you. So don't be foolish, baby."

"I'm never foolish," Jersey told him. "And I'm not your baby." Then she openhandedly slapped the piss out of him.

The reporter, whose name was Harold, cursed and took a swing at Jersey. Jersey put a bit of applied judo on him, and Harold found himself flat on his back on the porch. Jersey smiled and stepped back, allowing the man to get to his feet. Harold assumed a boxer's stance, and Jersey kicked him on the kneecap. Harold screamed in pain, bent down, and grabbed for his knee. Jersey brought up her knee and smashed it into the man's face. The blood squirted and Harold hit the boards.

"You rotten little bitch!" Harold hollered, blood streaming down his face.

"Now, now," Ben said with a smile. "That's not politically correct."

Julie studied Ben during the brief fracas. He seemed amused by the entire matter. She cut her eyes to Lieutenant Bonelli, who had walked up just seconds before the incident. He yawned. Cooper had gotten out of the way and was petting a stray dog who had wandered up the day before and who the Rebels were feeding. Beth and Corrie hadn't even bothered to come out of the house.

Julie was beginning to understand Rebels. She had been told, and had originally rejected as myth, that unarmed combat was taught in Rebel schools—beginning at a very early age. Now she knew that it was not myth but hard fact.

Harold was getting to his feet. "I'll tear your goddamn head off, you Indian bitch!" he shouted.

"Oh, my," Ben said, rolling a cigarette. "An ethnic slur from the press. Surely I misunderstood."

Harold rushed Jersey and she sidestepped, sticking out a boot and tripping the bigger and heavier man. Harold crashed through the old porch railing and went rolling ass over elbows on the ground. Jersey stepped off the porch and hit the man about fifteen times as he was attempting to get up. Hard blows to the kidneys, the back of the neck, the side of the neck, and finally, two hard blows directly over the heart.

Harold's face turned chalk white and he began gasping for breath as his heart faltered.

"Take the stupid son of a bitch down to the hospital," Ben said, lighting his hand-rolled cigarette.

"We'll sue you!" another reporter yelled at Jersey, then looked around in confusion as the Rebels broke up in good-natured laughter.

"Did I say something amusing?" the reporter asked.

By the end of the month, only the hard-core gangs and the Night People remained in the city. Hundreds of gang members had surrendered to the Rebels, choosing to face a Canadian judge and jury rather than starve to death or be eaten by the creepies.

Rebels began gearing up to enter the city and root out those remaining.

Huge tanker trucks began rolling in, and Julie questioned Ben about that. All around the edges of the central part of the city, Rebels had begun welding manhole covers closed (excuse me, *people*hole covers).

"That's one of the ways we flush creepies out of their holes. We pump gasoline into the sewers and underground chambers and burn them out."

"Barbaric," the press said, safely out of earshot of any Rebel.

Ben had received the communiqué from the UN's Security Council and was studying the suggestion; discussing it with his people.

"Once again, we get to do the dirty work," Ike said. "But what do we get out of it?"

"That's what I'm discussing with Son Moon now,"

Ben replied. "I want fully recognized sovereign nation status for the SUSA and those aligned with us. Voted on and accepted by the full UN or it's no go. And that's got to include the U.S. ambassador. The UN has my demands."

"I wonder what Blanton has to say about this?" West asked.

"That rotten son of a bitch!" Homer Blanton said.

"The nation is torn apart," VP Harriet Hooter said. "We have to find some way to bring all the states back into the fold."

"Wait until Ben Raines and the Rebels leave, then we invade the SUSA," Senator Benedict said.

"Good show!" Senator Arnold shouted.

"I love it!" Rufus Dumkowski said. "More people to tax the shit out of."

"Sock it to those rich honky bastards!" Rita Rivers yelled.

"Hey, stupid!" Wiley Ferret said. "*I'm* a honky and I'm rich!"

"Yeah," Rita said. "But you got yours by fucking it out of the taxpayers, the same way I'm gettin' mine."

"Oh," Wiley said. "You're right. That's okay then."

"Let's add an amendment to the Constitution," Zipporah Washington said. "Let's outlaw the Republican party."

"Good show!" Senator Benedict shouted, looking around for his bourbon bottle.

"I concur," Representative Immaculate Crapums agreed. "Don't you think so, Representative Holey?"

President Blanton tuned them out, wondering, not for the first time, how in the hell he ever got mixed up with such a pack of nitwits.

Blanton let the ninnies blither and blather, then cleared his office and sat for a time behind his desk. Slowly he picked up the phone and told his ambassador to the UN to vote in favor of sovereign nation status for Ben Raines and the SUSA.

Nine

But Ben had other wrinkles up his sleeve that had to be ironed out before he and President Cecil Jefferys would sign anything binding. And while Cecil Jefferys was the elected president of the Southern United States of America, everyone knew that Cecil would not go against Ben Raines—for more reasons than one. They had been friends for too many years. Ben and Cecil thought exactly alike. And while the Rebel army adored Cecil Jefferys, they revered and idolized Ben Raines.

Ben ordered his troops to maintain their starving out of the punks and the creepies in the city and flew down to Charleston, West Virginia, where Cecil was waiting.

The two old friends shook hands warmly and then embraced like brothers. Chase had told Ben that Cecil had recovered very nearly 100 percent from his multiple heart bypass surgery, and while he could never again go back into the field and endure the stress of combat leadership, he was fine right where he was in the SUSA.

"You sure you want this job, Ben?" Cecil asked.

"I'm sure. And so are my commanders. We're all soldiers, Cec. Can you see me spending the rest of my life shuffling papers?"

Cecil laughed. "Truthfully, Ben, no. You ready to go see President Blanton?"

"No. But it's something I have to do."

Actually, Ben sort of liked Homer, more so since he sensed Homer was beginning to understand that pure liberalism in government simply would not work; never had, never would. Many countries in the world had either adopted or flirted with socialism and/or communism . . . just before the Great War, nearly all had abandoned those forms of government. But the liberals continued to want to move America toward a time-and-again miserably failed form of government. Ben could never understand the workings of a liberal mind. But while he was beginning to warm to Homer, he doubted they would ever be more than acquaintances. The political breech was just too wide.

To his credit Homer Blanton stuck out his hand, and Ben smiled and shook it.

"Well, that's a start," Homer said, returning the smile.

"A pretty good one, Homer," Ben replied.

The secretary-general of the United Nations was present, as was the Speaker of the House and VP Hooter. Neither one of them offered to shake Ben's hand. Holey was dozing.

Rita Rivers, Immaculate Crapums, Zipporah Washington, Rufus Dumkowski, and several others had joined the line of ever-present protesters outside the new White House, carrying signs denouncing Ben Raines and the SUSA.

"I apologize for that," Homer said, pointing to the group on the street.

"It doesn't bother me in the least," Ben told him. "But it will bother them a great deal if they try to stop my vehicle from leaving."

Homer silently prayed that Hooter would not ask what Ben would do should that happen. It was a wasted prayer.

"I'll run over them," Ben told her.

"Dirty, rotten, filthy, right-wing, Republican bastard!" Hooter hollered. It jarred Holey out of a slight snooze.

"Can we get on with this?" Ben asked.

"Tax 'em some more," Representative I. M. Holey mumbled, slightly addled after his snooze.

"The first thing a Democrat thinks of upon waking," Cecil said. "Taxing the public."

That got him a dirty look from Hooter.

Secretary-General Moon said, "I believe you will find that everything is in order, General Raines, President Jefferys. All UN members have signed this document. Once both of you have affixed your signatures, the SUSA will be officially recognized as a sovereign nation, with all the guarantees and rights accorded such by the United Nations."

"This is a sad day for democracy," VP Hooter said.

"But a great day for those who love liberty," Cecil said, after scanning the document and signing his name.

Ben signed the paper and it was done.

Hooter got up and stalked out of the room without another word.

"Not one of my biggest supporters," Ben said with a smile as the door slammed.

Holey had gone back to sleep.

"Let's have some lunch, and then we'll work out exactly where your troops will go first," Homer said. He smiled and quickly held up a hand. "Not that I have anything at all to say about it."

"What about him?" Cecil said, looking at Representative Holey, who was snoring softly.

A quick flash of irritation passed through Blanton's eyes, and it was obvious to all who caught it that the president was not a big fan of I. M. Holey. Ben wondered what had happened to change that.

"Let him sleep," Homer said, pushing back his chair and standing up. "Let's get out of here. There is a meeting room over there."

After coffee and sandwiches had been served, Secretary-General Moon said, "You restore order in every country you enter, General Raines. That is the bottom line."

"My people are not peacekeepers, Mr. Secretary," Ben said. "You can keep your blue berets."

The secretary-general smiled. "We don't expect you to be peacekeepers, General. Just restore some semblance of order around the world."

Ben nodded. "Just as long as everybody concerned is fully aware of what we are and what we are not."

"We are that."

"Europe is going to be bad enough," Ben said. "As far as I am concerned, from what little I have been able to read about the situation, Africa is very nearly hope-less."

"I concur."

"I want it known up front, no matter what country my people go into, we aren't going to fuck around with two-bit warlords and punks and thugs. If they oppose us, they're dead. Do all concerned understand that?"

"We do," Son Moon replied softly.

"How many observers am I going to be saddled with?"

"There will be representatives from the Red Cross," Blanton answered. "A Miss Julie Petti is heading that group. And of course there will be medical people to assist your own. But you are in full command of the entire operation. Your orders are to be obeyed without question. You have full authority to relieve anyone you choose, anytime you deem it necessary."

"Do you have a choice as to your initial landing in Europe, General Raines?" the secretary-general asked.

"Yes," Ben said. "France." He smiled. "Nor-mandy."

Ten

Since the Rebels were used to fighting under the most adverse conditions—summer, winter, spring, or fall, it made no difference to them—Ben started making plans to get under way just as quickly as possible. That would put them in England in early autumn and hitting the coast of France by late fall . . . providing all went well.

Britain had begun to establish some sort of order in the country, as had Ireland, at least the southern part of it. There was not much left of Northern Ireland except rubble and death, for ever since the Great War, diehard Catholics and Protestants had been at each other's throats in open warfare. Southern Ireland had sealed off the borders to the north, and no one really knew what was going on in Northern Ireland . . . and no one really gave much of a damn. The overwhelming consensus was if they all killed each other off, the world would be a much better place.

"They stopped knowing what they were fighting for years ago," Dan Gray said. "All they know now is hate and they don't even know why they hate each other. It's pathetic."

Ben and his team, along with his personal company of Rebels, flew to England to meet with the prime minister and with the head of the French Resistance to get some sort of picture of what the Rebels would face when they hit the beaches at Normandy.

"Chaos," Rene Seaux told Ben. "Europe is aflame. Slavery abounds. We have reverted to the days of barbarism. It's the Dark Ages revisited. It is absolutely unbelievable. After the sickness swept through a few years ago—which did not do as much damage as the rest of the world was led to believe—Europe exploded in war. Those horrible goddamn Night People are in control of the cities; warlords and thugs control the countryside. From France to the Ural Mountains in Russia is one huge war zone. Past the Urals," he shrugged, "who knows? We are getting only a few radio transmissions out of Russia and they are nothing but garble. I have but three hundred men and women fighting with me. We have tiny toeholds here and there." He slapped the wall map. "But they are constantly changing as my people are overwhelmed."

"Can you lay out and hold a DZ for my people?" Ben asked, studying the map.

"Oui," Rene said. "To the last person if we must."

"The port at Le Havre?" Ben asked, not taking his eyes from the map.

"Impossible," Rene said. "The thugs control the outer edges, the cannibals the city. It will be Omaha, or nothing."

Ben smiled. "Rene, I want you to ask for volunteers

to act as pathfinders." He paused. "Do any of them know how to lay out a DZ?"

"Oui. I have several ex-legionnaires with me."

"Good. At my signal, they'll lay out a DZ . . . here." He pointed to the map. "The first of my people should be arriving in about ten days. But we're going to be short on armor."

Rene shook his head. "It is men we need now, not armor. The thugs are loosely organized and do not have much in the way of tanks. What they have is many miles inland, and they are short on shells. Most of the armor is stretched out on a line from Rennes to Le Mans to Orleans. But the thugs are quickly coming together to fight you. They know that alone they cannot stand. But together, General Raines, they will be a formidable force."

Ben nodded his head while he studied the map. "We have to take the towns of Cherbourg, Caen, and Le Havre. Once those are taken, we'll begin our push inland. Are the citizens armed?"

Rene shook his head. *"Non.* The thugs seized all privately owned weapons. All they had to do was go to the official records to find out who owned what and then take them. It was a simple matter. I do not think the people will ever again stand for government registration of weapons."

"They won't in America either," Ben said. "At least not in Rebel-controlled territory."

Rene smiled. "You and your people are making history daily, General. But of course, you are well aware of that, *non?"*

"So I've been told," Ben said dryly. "Sometimes quite profanely."

England now was a far cry from England before the Great War. Before, privately owned weapons were rare; now it was the norm, and the people had bluntly told the government if they tried to seize them, there would be blood in the streets. Parliament had wisely voted to allow the private ownership of weapons. Gangs of thugs still roamed the countryside, but with each day, their numbers diminished. The death penalty had been brought back, and killers got quick trials and a hangman's noose. The days of weeping and blubbering and excusing the behavior of criminals were over, and it was highly unlikely they would ever return.

Ben and the Rebels had swept through Britain and Ireland a few years back, arming the citizens as they went, making certain that even if the government had wanted to collect all privately owned weapons, it would be very costly in human terms.

"Get our people over here as fast as possible," Ben told Corrie. "I want Ike and Dan Gray over here first with their battalions. Every day we delay makes the enemy stronger."

Corrie paused, then turned to face him. "Toronto?"

"We don't have time to wait them out. Radio them to flood the sewer system with gasoline and flammable tear gas and flush them out."

"Explosive mixture, boss," Jersey commented. "But

they're the ones who wanted to dance. Now it's time to pay the band."

The big transport planes began landing in England and Rebels stepped off, glad to stretch their legs after the long boring flight. Ike and Dan were hustled over to Ben's temporary CP, located about halfway between Brighton and Portsmouth, on the coast road.

"Georgi and Rebet are a day behind us, Ben," Ike said. "Five other battalions are on their way by ship. Tanks and choppers and planes on ships with them. Cecil pulled in the reserves to take over at Toronto. He said they needed to get bloodied."

"So everyone is free?"

"Eighteen battalions on their way," Dan said. "That leaves five battalions back home, plus the reserves when they get through in Toronto, and the Home Guard."

"You think Blanton is going to pull something, Ben?" Ike asked.

"No, I don't. Some of those around him would like to. But I think Homer is on the level. For his sake he'd better be," Ben added grimly.

Years back, shortly after the Rebels were formed, a sitting president and certain members of Congress tried to pull a fast one and have Ben Raines assassinated. After the Rebels discovered the scheme, none of those involved lived long enough to have second thoughts about the plot. Including the president.

American politicians had learned over the bloody

years that Ben Raines was totally ruthless in dealing with his enemies.

Ben used a pointer and began laying out the assignment. "Ike, you and West and Pat O'Shea will take Cherbourg and then spread out and start cleaning out the countryside. Dan, you and Rebet will jump in behind Bayeux and hold, awaiting my signal. Georgi, Danjou, and Tina will hit Le Havre."

"As if I couldn't guess, where will you be, Ben?" Ike asked.

"I'll take Greenwalt, Jackie Malone, Raul, and my bunch, and go ashore at Omaha Beach."

"Goddamnit, Ben!" Dan Gray said. "They'll be waiting for you. It'll be a replay of sixty years ago! The only difference is you won't have divisions left and right of you at Utah and Juno and Sword."

"No," Ben said with a smile. "But I will have a lot of air support, and you and Rebet driving hard to meet me at Bayeux. Rene said the defenders have no artillery and only light mortars. He and his people are going to lay out the DZ's and then join up with you on the ground."

Ike was studying the huge wall map of France. He knew that arguing with Ben was useless, once Ben made up his mind. "The sickness that was reported sweeping the Continent a few years back . . . ?"*

"Vastly overstated. Just like all the nuclear strikes that we believed devastated the world until a short time ago. A grand plan that almost worked."

"What a terrible hoax to play on decent people," Dan said softly. "I wonder how many thousands have

*TERROR IN THE ASHES—Zebra Books.

died because of that, and how many thousands of others have lived for years in terror and slavery?"

"I wonder whose idea it was?" Ike asked, sitting down in the comfortable office of the once grand old home on the sprawling English estate.

"I doubt we'll ever know," Ben said. "Perhaps it wasn't a single person's plan. More than likely it was a rumor that caught fire. But it worked for a time." Ben put down his pointer. "Let's get something to eat and then get down to work. We've got a lot of maps to study and hours of debriefing of Rene's people ahead of us."

Supplies began coming in, thousands of tons of them, by plane and by ship. Those on the Continent had spies in England, and they reported to their various commanders throughout Europe that it looked like the whole damn American army was landing on England's shores. Huge C-130's were flying in hourly, their cavernous bellies filled with Rebels and equipment. The P-51's were rolled out, and mechanics went to work reattaching wings. Tanks rumbled and snorted about the tarmac. Millions of rounds of ammunition, ranging from shotgun shells to 223's to 203-mm artillery shells were off-loaded. Crates of boots and socks and T-shirts and shorts and panties and bras were trucked away. Medical supplies and packets of field rations were flown in to various parts of England.

It seemed to the spies watching and reporting back to the Continent that the supplies would never stop arriving. A shortwave broadcast from America was taped, the contents chilling the criminals. The last bastion of lawlessness in the North America had fallen. The Rebels had burned the lawless out of Toronto and shot them down as they tried to escape the searing flames and choking and exploding tear gas. Very few prisoners were taken.

"Jesus H. Christ!" Duffy Williams, a two-bit punk from Liverpool, and leader of one of the largest and most vicious gangs in France, said after listening to the message. He opened a map of Europe and studied it for a few moments, while his top henchmen stood around waiting for orders.

But Duffy was merely stalling for time. He knew the map. Like many lawless, Duffy possessed intelligence far above the average. And like 99 percent of the lawless, he had not been abused as a child—he came from a good, caring home. He had not been born into terrible poverty, had not suffered taunts and derision at the hands of his peers, had not been a stutterer or a bed wetter. He did not have some terrible physical affliction. He was simply a rotten, miserable punk and had been one all his life. Like all the major gang leaders in France—Tom Spivey, Dave Ingle, Robert Fryoux, Ned Veasey, Eddie Stamp, John Monson, Paul Zayon, to name but a few—Duffy came from a solid middle-class home. He was just a punk. First, last, and always. Period.

Ben closed the file folder on Duffy Williams and tossed it on his desk. It landed on top of a dozen others provided by British authorities. He took off his reading glasses and said, "Just like all the others in that stack. No excuses. He's just a goddamn worthless piece of shit and has been all his life. But like so many of his ilk, he's a smart one. I.Q. of 150 but lousy in school. Rebelled against any type of authority. Abused small animals. A smart-ass. Put all those gang leaders in a bag, shake them up and dump them out and you can't tell one from the other."

"We know all the signs," Jersey said. "How come society can't see them?"

"Oh, they can, Jersey," Ben said, standing up and stretching his tall frame. "They've been able to identify potential troublemakers for decades. It's always been a question of whether society had the right to go into a home."

"We do," Beth said. "Occasionally."

Ben smiled. "Yes. And usually we can turn a kid around. But those tactics are controversial even among our own people. It's a matter of educating the parents along with the kid." Ben walked to the window and looked out at the chilly and overcast day. He stared at the gray waters of the Channel for a moment. "Are we on timetable, Beth?"

"Ahead of it, boss," she replied. "But the riggers are having to dry out the chutes because of this weather. Ike is still pissed because you nixed that SEAL operation he dreamed up."

"I didn't nix the operation," Ben said with a grin. "I just nixed Ike going along. He's too damn old and much too large. Somebody would mistake him for a whale. But he's going in with the teams anyway, isn't he?"

Ben's team exchanged glances and smiles. "Yes," Cooper finally admitted.

"Old goat," Ben muttered. "They'll probably have to tie a submarine to his ass to keep him underwater."

"Speaking of old goats," Corrie said.

Ben turned around, disbelief in his eyes. "You can't be serious!"

"Stepped off the plane this morning," Jersey said. "Says he's going ashore with the rest of us."

"Lamar is seventy-five years old if he's a day!" Ben shouted.

"I'm seventy-six," the chief of medicine said, walking into the room. "But I'm still going to put my boots on Omaha Beach."

"I forbid it!"

"You can't forbid me from doing anything. But I can forbid you," Lamar reminded the commanding general of all Rebel forces. "I just might schedule your annual physical on the morning of D-Day if you aren't careful."

Ben knew when he was licked. As chief of medicine, Lamar could slap anyone in the hospital anytime he so desired . . . including Ben Raines.

"It's your ass," Ben told him.

"That's right. And I'm rather fond of it. Now let's talk about projected casualties."

"Less than five percent going in."

"That's all LZ's combined?"

"Yes."

"What wave will you be in, Ben?"

"The first one."

"No goddamn way!" the doctor said.

"You have no say in the matter, Lamar. Just have your people ready to patch up the wounded."

Lamar shut up about it. He and Ben had been friends for too many years, and both knew when the other would not budge on a decision.

"When are we going in?" Lamar asked.

"At 0600. Day after tomorrow."

Eleven

For two days the pilots flew their modified P-51's over selected areas of the coast of France and did nothing except look. They had a few SAMs fired at them; but since they were flying practically on the ground, the SAMs were impotent against them. The reports the pilots brought back confirmed what Rene Seaux had said. The thugs and punks and warlords had a few mortars, a lot of heavy machine guns, some SAMs, but no artillery anywhere along the coast.

The defenders along the coast were getting nervous. For the past week the weather along the coast had been unusually calm and lovely, with clear skies and warm temperatures. The Rebels did nothing except fly those damn ol' planes back and forth. What the punks did not know was that while their eyes were on the P-51's, other planes had been dropping supplies just beyond the cliffs around Etretat—which, because of their steepness, were undefended.

Bad mistake. The sheer cliffs were just the spot for Buddy Raines and his special ops people to scale and then force-march down the coast toward Le Havre, which would be under attack by the battalions of Georgi Striganov, Danjou, and Buddy's sister, Tina.

Rene's resistance people had been collecting the air-dropped supplies and caching them.

Ben had been uncommonly blunt with Rene Seaux. "Get your people to round up men and women who will fight. The ones who will stand shoulder to shoulder and fight with us are the ones who are going to be in charge of France once this scrap is over."

Rene smiled. "And those who will not? Those who have collaborated with the enemy?"

"Deal with them any way you see fit."

"It will be my pleasure, General. Do you have any objections to a firing squad?"

"I prefer a noose for traitors."

By 0500 of the jump-off day, the fog had rolled in, the seas were rough, and it was pouring rain.

"Perfect," Ben said from the deck of the ship.

Dan and Rebet had made the night jump just moments before the rain set in, and they were down and safe, with only a few minor injuries. Buddy and his people had scaled the cliffs at Etretat, and Ike and his people were set to strike at Cherbourg.

"I can't see a goddamn thing!" one of the sentries above the beach said. "Can you, Charles?"

"There is nothing to see," the Frenchman to his right said. "This is very stupid. The Rebels will not land here. Especially in this weather. They will be

landing in Calais or Dunkerque. Not here. Those
planes were a ruse, nothing more."

The worried sentry was not convinced. He started to
lift his binoculars to his eyes, then gave that up as a bad
idea. The visibility was zero. He could not see five feet
in front of him. He cussed and lowered his binoculars.

"Launch boats," Ben said. The boats were small,
with muffled engines that could scarcely be heard a
dozen yards away.

Ben was in the first boat, over the very loud and
often profane objections of his batt coms. He had given
orders for his people to inflate life vests as soon as they
were in the boats, for the water was very cold.

Ike's SEAL teams were already ashore, guiding the
boats in with tiny flashes that could be seen only
through special lenses.

"Almost there," Ben said. "That water is going to
take your breath away when you hit it, so be fore-
warned."

Since Jersey was barely five feet tall, Ben had, without her knowledge, arranged for a tall Rebel to stay
with her and make certain she didn't flounder in the
deep water. "Just don't grab her by the butt," Ben
cautioned the man. "She'll think it's Cooper and knock
the piss out of you."

The fog was just beginning to clear when Ben and
his Rebels touched French soil and made a dash for the
dunes on the beach. But the rain had intensified, and
that saved them from being spotted. They ditched their
life vests and began crawling toward the low dunes.

The SEAL teams, as soon as they had guided the
boats in, began their deadly work on the sentries. They

could not take them out prior to the boats landing because the Rebels' communications people had found that each sentry was checking in with somebody by radio every five minutes. Failure to report would have spelled disaster for the entire operation. As it was, Ben felt that luck was fast running out for them. It was going too smoothly. Something had to break.

It did. Just as a special op made his knife thrust, the sentry turned and the blade struck jawbone and glanced off. The sentry screamed, and the cold rain was suddenly warmed up considerably with gunfire.

Ben pulled himself to one knee and gave the flashes from a machine-gun nest a full clip of .45-caliber slugs. The machine gun fell silent. Ben rolled behind a small dune and slipped in another clip. Corrie flopped down on the wet sand beside him.

"Ike is facing heavy resistance in Cherbourg," she panted. "Dan and Rebet just blew through Bayeux and are pushing hard to get here. General Striganov reports he has a toehold in Le Harve."

Ben leaned close to be heard over the rattle and roar of gunfire. "Tell Raul to push in from the right flank, Jackie to push in from the left. Just as soon as the flanking maneuver is complete, tell Greenwalt we're going over the top at my command."

"That damn Scolotti grabbed me by the ass," Jersey bitched, falling down between Ben and Cooper.

"Felt good, didn't it?" Cooper said, coughing up seawater.

"Cooper," Jersey said, shaking the sand off her M-16, "one of these days . . ."

"Promises, promises," Cooper said.

Fire from a heavy machine gun stopped the conversation for a moment. A Rebel tossed a Fire-Frag grenade and the machine-gun nest went silent.

Ben was up and running, zigging and zagging, his team right behind him. Those Rebels who could see Ben surged forward, gaining another twenty or so yards.

"If we're on this beach at sunrise, we're dead meat!" Ben shouted over the gunfire and explosions.

"Jackie and Raul are moving inland, flanking," Corrie returned the shout.

"Getting light in the east, boss," Beth said.

Ben rose to his knees. "Let's go!" he shouted. "Follow me. Go, go, go!"

With a roar of defiance, the Rebels moved forward. The defenders of the coastline must have thought there were many more Rebels than there really were, for when they saw the misty shapes moving toward them, many of the defenders broke and ran. They crossed the coastline highway and hotfooted it to the east.

Those that stayed died.

When the rain had changed to a drizzle and then finally stopped, and first faint rays of the sun broke through the grayness, the Rebels were in command of Omaha Beach.

Before the Great War, Cherbourg had been a busy town of about fifty thousand people. Most of the population had been driven off, and it was now a haven for modern-day pirates and slavers. Ike and his people established a toehold in the harbor and began driving inland, with Pat O'Shea cutting away from the main group to take the airport a few miles outside of the city.

Dan Gray and Rebet had roared through the town of Bayeux, putting the few defenders there into a rout. They had commandeered anything with wheels on it, including motor scooters and bicycles, and were now driving, rolling, and pedaling toward Ben's position on the coast.

Georgi Striganov and his forces were in a hard battle with creepies. Le Harve, once the second largest port in France, and a major city of more than two hundred thousand, was proving to be a tough nut to crack. Buddy and his special ops people, at Striganov's orders, had angled off and set up just outside the town of Bolbec, and spreading down to the small town of Pont de Tancarville, closing off any escape by the creepies. For the next two days it would be search and destroy for Georgi's 5 Batt, Danjou's 7 Batt, and Tina's 9 Batt.

Ben and his people had moved inland and were nearing the town of Bayeux, linking up with Dan and Rebet and members of the French Resistance Forces. The FRF. Greenwalt and his 11 Batt had stayed on the beach to oversee the off-loading of tanks and trucks and other supplies from ships now approaching the coast.

"We'll push down to within a few miles of Caen and hold up there," Ben told his people. "We don't want to get too far ahead of the others. Caen is filled with creeps, so we'll have to dig them out. But we'll wait for armor before we do."

"Ike and Georgi have taken the harbor areas and are ready for supplies," Corrie said. "The airports at both cities are ready to receive planes from England."

"Get them airborne. I want all battalions on the Continent as quickly as possible. I want every MASH unit we've got set up ASAP. I want to know what types of diseases we're facing over here and our people inoculated. Where is Doctor Chase?"

"He's ashore and should be here in a few minutes."

"Make sure every Rebel has a Pro-kit. I'll court-martial anyone who comes down with a venereal disease. Make goddamn sure they all know that."

"Right, boss."

"There are venereal diseases over here that our medical people have never even *seen* before. Make sure that everybody knows that!"

"Right, boss."

"In other words," Cooper said, "all the men keep their peckers in their pants and all the ladies keep their legs crossed."

"I couldn't have stated it better, Coop," Ben said, to the groans of Beth, Corrie, and Jersey.

Duffy Williams had argued for months for the major gang leaders to come together. It took a Rebel invasion to finally accomplish that.

The leaders of the eleven biggest gangs in France and several dozen leaders of smaller gangs met in Tours to attempt to map out some sort of strategy. Just a month before, they had been a swaggering, arrogant bunch. Now they sat silent as Duffy walked to the front of the room.

"We can do one of three things," Duffy said. "We

can run, we can surrender, or we can fight. But we'd better, by God, make up our minds one way or the other today. Because we're running out of time."

"Run where?" Tom Spivey asked.

"That will be a problem," Duffy said. "I've learned that members of the FRF have already begun printing up wanted posters on all of us. Quite frankly, we're not going to have any place to run."

"If we surrender, they'll hang us," Guy Caston said. "That is something we'd all better fix in our minds right now."

"But we'll get a trial," a gang leader said, standing up. "Won't we?"

That got him a lot of dirty laughter. He sat down.

Marie Vidalier, a man-hater from years back, who ran one of the most vicious gangs in all of France, stood up. "I cannot surrender. I was wanted by the *gendarmes* even before the Great War. I have no choice but to fight."

"The same for me," Eddie Stamp said. Eddie was a former IRA member who was wanted for murder in a half dozen countries.

Most of the other gang leaders reluctantly admitted that for them, surrender was also out of the question.

"We outnumber the Rebels," Duffy said. "We have thousands more fighters than they do."

"They also have tanks, planes, attack helicopters, and long-range artillery," Paul Zayon pointed out. "We have machine guns and rifles and grenades. Those damned prop planes are flying so low our SAMs are useless against them. And they're flying about 550 miles an hour. By the time our people get machine guns to bear on them, they're gone."

"And what has happened to our informants in the FRF?" Ned Veasey asked.

"Rene Seaux polygraphed everyone in his groups and ferreted out the plants. He shot them. All of them," Duffy said. "Personally. I hate that ex-foreign legion son of a bitch."

Everybody present took a few moments to give Rene Seaux a sound cussing. It didn't help their situation a bit, but it did make them feel better for a few minutes.

"We fight with what we have," Duffy said, when the hubbub had died down. "A lot of us are ex-military. We know organization. And I think I have a plan that will buy us some time. Let the Rebels have everything north of a line from Chateaulin to Paris. They'll spend weeks digging out the cannibals in that city alone. That will give us time to form up battalion-sized units and put together a plan of action. We've got to separate the Rebels. We don't have a chance if we face them en masse. But if we can meet them unit to unit, spread out all over the country, we might have a chance. All right. There it is. What do you think?"

"Do we have a choice?" John Monson asked. "I think no. So I say we band together and fight. Now we must elect a leader, and we must agree to follow his or her orders. Duffy, you have successfully fought the FRF for years. I cast my vote for you."

"I'll go along with that," Robert Fryoux said.

"*Oui,*" Philipe Soileau said. "I vote for Duffy Williams to command this army."

Duffy was expecting Marie Vidalier to put up a howl

over his nomination to lead the forces. But she was the next person to vote for him. When the voting was complete, the count was unanimous. Duffy Williams found himself the commander of thousands of punks, thugs, rapists, murderers, thieves, and worse.

Duffy's chest swelled with pride. It was quite an honor.

Twelve

"Scouts report nothing," Corrie called to Ben, after receiving the last of field reports from recon.

Ben wasn't surprised at the news. But Rene Seaux was. "What are those worthless bastards and bitches up to?" the leader of the FRF asked.

"They got smart," Ben said, swiveling in his chair to look at the wall map of France. "They elected themselves a leader and banded together. How far out did our people go, Corrie?"

"From Avranches over to Dreux, and from Rouen over to Beauvais then down to the outskirts of Paris. They hit no resistance at all. Nothing."

Ben looked at the map for several moments. "Have our pilots start fly-bys over this line." He took a grease pencil and drew a line from Chateaulin over to Rennes, then from Rennes to Le Mans. He added another line from Le Mans up to Chartres and then to the outskirts of Paris. "If I'm right, whoever is now commanding the punk army is not stupid. But he's still a punk. Divide and conquer. He's going to split us up and take us that way." Ben smiled. "He thinks."

Ben started battalion numbering the map, starting with Rebet at the coastline above Brest, and ending with Pat O'Shea at Dunkerque. "When we get these battalions shifted around, have Pat and Tina start a push down to Highway 29 and stop. Danjou and Georgi have already secured their sectors. When that's done, Ike's 2 Batt and my 1 Batt will move down to this point, Caen and Saint Lo. Dan, West, and Rebet will hold what they have. When everything is clear behind us, we'll start our major push inland. When Rebet reaches Quimper and West reaches Rostrenen, they'll cut east and eventually link up with Dan's 3 Batt, which will be holding, hopefully, at Montauban. By that time, Ike will have advanced down to Avranches. The opposition will either have been destroyed or backed up to Rennes. Then we'll start squeezing them as we move toward Paris."

"But Paris is under the control of the cannibals," Rene said.

"That's right. The punks won't dare enter the city. They'll be forced to cut south or retreat eastward. If they head south, they'll be stopped by the Spanish army at the border. I'm betting they'll opt to back up toward the east. That's where our other battalions will be. Waiting for them."

Rene looked at Ben in amazement. "How long did it take you to devise this plan, General?"

"About a minute and a half," Ben said. "Count on punks to always do one of three things: the obvious, the illogical, or the totally absurd. It comes down to a game of point/counterpoint." Ben grinned. "Besides, our people are fully prepared to fight in winter's cold. I'm betting the punks are not. Let's see how they do in the snow and ice and below-freezing temperatures trying to fight with frozen feet and hands."

Rene grunted. "I have to say that you are not a very nice man, General."

"You'd be right. Let's start shifting those battalions around, Corrie."

"What is that son of a bitch doing?" Duffy muttered, standing in front of a huge wall map. "I can't figure out what the hell is going on. He's not attacking."

"Our spies say the Rebels are liberating all these towns and villages north of us," Guy Caston said. "They appear to be in no hurry. They are providing food and medical aid to the people."

"Goddamnit! It's going to be dead-ass winter in another six weeks. We're not equipped to fight in snow and ice."

"But the Rebels are," Marie Vidalier said. "That's Ben Raines's plan. That rotten bastard!"

"I have an idea," one of Duffy's henchmen said. "Let's kill Ben Raines."

"Jimmy," Duffy said, "people have been trying to do that for years. No one has even come close." Duffy did not tell any of those present that many believed Ben Raines was a god. That he possessed supernatural powers. Many of Duffy's followers were jumpy enough without adding that.

"Maybe they didn't have the right plan," Jimmy said.

"And you do?" Marie challenged him.

"I don't know," Jimmy admitted. "But it might be worth a try."

"I'll listen," Duffy said. But he suspected that nothing would come of it, and as it turned out, nothing did.

Back stateside, Emil Hite, the little con artist who had turned Rebel, was still miffed at being left behind. He was sure it had not been done on purpose. Purely an oversight on the part of somebody. Emil had been a part of the Rebels for years, ever since Ben Raines had found him and his followers along the bayou banks of Louisiana (where Emil had convinced a large number of people that he was the earthbound representative of the great god Blomm).*

Emil had gradually slipped out of his role as part-time snake oil salesman and con artist and had become a pretty good Rebel. But he was still full of shit.

Emil knew one thing for a fact: He was not going to sit around on his ass here in Arkansas with Thermopolis and his hippies listening to that godawful music. He had to get to France and join up with Ben and his people.

Thermopolis and his bunch ran the northernmost listening post for Cecil, the listening post located high up in the mountains of Arkansas. It was a very impor-

*VALOR IN THE ASHES—Zebra Books.

tant job, but not for Emil. He wanted back in the action.

Somehow he had to get to France. He'd find a way. He always did.

"About ten of those punks from Toronto escaped from the holding facility," Corrie informed Ben. "Half of them are on their way over here to join up with the French warlords."

"Wonderful," Ben said. "That's all we need. *How* are they getting over here?"

"Ship," Mike Richards, head of Rebel intelligence, said, walking in. "And it's not 'getting over here.' They're here." He consulted a clipboard. "Barney Holland, Tony Green, a.k.a. Big Stomper, Mahmud the Terrible, some punk with him called Abdul, and Ahmed Popov, and another called Tuba Salami."

"Oh, no," Ben said, struggling to maintain a straight face. "Not him!"

" 'Fraid so," Mike said. "They commandeered a freighter and forced the captain to bring them to France. Then they shot the captain and all the crew. Dutch resistance fighters found the ship yesterday smashed up on the coast. Two of the crew members were still alive."

"Were?"

"They died."

"How many of their bunch did they bring with them?"

"From what our people could gather from the

Dutch, about five hundred. Real bad ones. It was a large freighter," Mike added.

"Too bad it didn't sink," Jersey said.

"I thought that Barney Holland hated blacks and Mahmud hated whites," Ben said.

"They kissed and made up. A dubious marriage of convenience, you might say."

"Who kissed and made up?" Julie Petti asked, entering the room. She and the other Red Cross reps had been out and about for several days, doing their Red Cross business.

"A bunch of damn punks," Ben told her. Julie looked very tired. Julie, as both a registered and surgical nurse, had been working closely with Lamar Chase, and the strain of seeing the terrible results of years of medical neglect on the French people was telling on her.

"What about the Dutch Resistance?" Ben said, turning his attentions to Mike.

"They're small in number but good fighters. But like all the countries in Europe, Holland is being run by the gangsters and creepies. They desperately need our help."

"Name a country that doesn't," Ben replied, sitting back down behind his desk. "Mike, our agreement with the United Nations wasn't all take on our part—we had to give some, too. We're under mandate; a fixed schedule. I have some leeway as to what countries to assist in what order, but not much." Ben was conscious of all ears and eyes in the room on him. "We've got to establish a firm and solid hold in Europe. We've got to penetrate deep enough so that we can't be pushed back to the sea." Ben thanked Jersey for the mug of coffee she placed on his desk and took a swig. He carefully set the mug down on some paperwork he'd been putting off. He rubbed his temples, sighed, and said, "Ask for volunteers, Mike. Up to twenty-five people from each battalion. We'll send them into Holland by boat. Their orders will be to link up with the Dutch Resistance fighters and start working inland. That's the best I can do, Mike. Now get out of here."

Smiling, Mike Richards left the room.

Ben looked at a small map of Europe on his desk. "It's not a bad idea, really," he said, more to himself than to anyone else. "We've got contingents of the Spanish army guarding the passes down along the border, but up north is vulnerable. We're going to be fighting on enough fronts without having to worry about hostiles coming out of Holland."

Ben took another swig of coffee and asked, "Where in the hell are those companies of troops from Ireland and England? Can somebody tell me what the damn holdup is?"

"Food riots, Ben," Julie said. "That's what I came in to tell you."

Ben looked at her. "Food riots? But they have ample food. President Blanton and I met and personally saw to that. We sent them hundreds of tons of surplus food we had in storage."

Julie shook her head. "Saboteurs, Ben. Black market. Greed. Desperation. The food is not getting to many of the people. And—" Julie bit back the rest of it.

"And . . . what, Julie?" Ben pressed. "Come on."

Julie took a deep breath and said, "Many people are complaining the food is not ethically and religiously prepared."

Ben held his temper in check . . . barely. When he felt he could speak without blowing his top, he carefully said, "Ethically and religiously prepared?"

Cooper quietly exited the room, as did several other Rebels. Corrie clamped her headphones tighter and began studying the various dials and VU meters on her set, and Beth busied herself with her journal. Jersey braced herself for the blow.

"That is correct, General Raines," one of the human rights representatives who was tagging along said. "Many of these people are of religious persuasions that specifically forbid them from consuming certain foods. They—"

"Shut up!" Ben roared. "I don't give a flying fuck for their so-called religious persuasions. Starving people should be grateful if they get a can of dog food. And it's not that bad. I've eaten it before and was damn glad to get it. Now I don't blame a starving person for fighting to *get* food. But I have no patience for anyone who *rejects* food when it's offered to them." Ben pointed a finger at the human rights spokesperson, who was decidedly ill at ease standing in front of the man who many said was a cross between the devil and a saint. "You pass the word, mister. And here it is: I will personally shoot the first son of a bitch in this country who starts a riot over the quality of food that we are passing out—free with no strings attached. We're over here busting our asses to help these people. And we will do everything that is humanly possible for them. But my threshold of patience for certain types is very low. Now close your mouth and take your bleeding heart and get the hell out of this office before I really lose my temper."

Julie had taken a seat and was studying her finger-nails while Ben blew his top. When the office had cleared, she looked up and said, "Some people take their religion very seriously, Ben."

"Yeah, right," Ben said sarcastically. "You bet they do. You tell me this, Julie: What were they eating during the long years before we got here with hundreds of tons of freebies? I'll tell you. Anything they could get their hands on, that's what. No one in their right mind is going to starve to death over words that may or may not have been handed down from a higher deity. Oh, but now that Uncle Sam and Uncle Ben are here, with ships filled with food, oh, now they can fall back on their religious beliefs and get all righteous about it. Screw 'em! And that's my last word on the subject."

Julie rose from her chair and left the room in a huff.

Corrie turned to Ben. "You through, boss?"

"Yes. What it is?"

"All battalions in position and ready to jump off."

"Good." Ben stood up. "Pack it up, gang. We push off at first light in the morning." Ben walked out of the room muttering, "Ethically prepared—*shit!*"

Nine battalions of Rebels, backed by armor and artillery, rolled out at dawn the next day. Some of the other nine battalions would stay in reserve, others would trail along behind those spearheading in the hotter spots, to act as a buffer in case Duffy tried an attack from the rear—which was unlikely; but in war anything is possible.

Caen was very nearly a ghost town, with only a few thousand painfully thin and malnourished people living in the once-thriving city of over 125,000. Ben ordered the columns halted and ordered the medical people up. Chase was traveling with Ben's 1 Batt and immediately set up shop and went to work.

Ben wandered the small city, which now was a shambles, having been picked over and looted many times during the past decade. The churches had been trashed and desecrated.

"They made it through World War Two, but not the reign of punks," Ben said.

"My God," Beth said, reading from a tattered old tourist book. "This is the Church of La Trinite. It was built in 1062 by William the Conqueror's wife, Matilda."

"Let's go inside. This is the cathedral part, I think."

The others noticed that Ben removed his helmet upon entering the old church. Inside, they stood in shock for a moment. The interior had been torn apart, everything of value taken. Obscene words had been painted on the walls. A better than average artist had painted various pornographic scenes of Jesus screwing different women . . . among other sexual acts.

"Why?" Cooper asked, after looking all around him.

"Because they're punks," Ben said. "Worthless punks." Then he jumped toward Beth and rode her down to the floor just as several people with automatic weapons opened up from the rear of the building.

The team scrambled for cover and Ben said, "Corrie, get some people to the rear of the church. We'll take care of the inside."

While Corrie radioed for help, Ben belly-crawled to a better position and got behind some overturned pews just as a punk opened up out of the gloom of the far interior.

Ben gave him returning fire and the punk's weapon clattered to the floor, followed by the punk. Ben had stitched him from left to right, hip to shoulder. He was dead when he hit the floor.

"All of us on my signal," Ben whispered. "Now!"

Four M-16's and one Thompson opened up on full auto, scattering lead all over the rear of the cathedral. There was one howl of pain—just one—and the wounded punk crawled out of the gloom to flop on the floor, both hands holding his bullet-perforated belly.

He lay there amid the litter and cussed Ben and the Rebels in French, until he was out of breath. Then he switched to English and let them have it again.

"Coming in!" a Rebel yelled from the back of the building and then kicked in a door. The place filled up with Rebels.

One Rebel stepped up two steps and fired one shot, and that ended the resistance in the old abbey. The Rebels were not known for taking many prisoners.

A very old priest, his clothing tattered and impossibly patched, walked out of the rear of the building, leaning heavily on a cane.

The wounded punk saw him and cried out for him to come give him some blessed comfort.

Ben and the others stood up in silence and watched as the priest limped over to the punk.

"I have sinned, Father!" the punk said. "Many times."

The old priest nodded his head. "You damn sure have," he said, and then extended the middle finger of his left hand to the punk and walked away.

The punk died on the church floor, absolute disbelief on his face.

Ben looked at the shocked expressions on the faces of his team. "Priests are human first and men of God second," he said, then walked out into the sunlight.

Thirteen

While the Rebels were hauling out and disposing of the bodies in the old abbey, Ben walked around and found the old priest sitting on a bench.

When he saw Ben, and recognized him for what he was (it never failed to astonish Ben that the whole world knew who he was), the old priest said, "I lost my faith, General. At first I blamed it on God. But it wasn't God's fault. I simply lost my faith."

"Bullshit," Ben said, startling the man. Ben sat down beside the old man. "Did God speak to you and tell you of this loss?"

The priest looked at him. "Hardly. Are you a religious man, General?"

"No. I believe in God. I believe in some form of heaven and hell. But I don't believe that a person can live a life of crime, engaging in the most unspeakable and perverse acts all their life, then, on their deathbed, a human being can say a few words and absolve them of all their sins."

For the first time since Ben had seen the priest, the old man smiled. "Spoken like a true Protestant."

"Or a realist who was brought up in a Christian home and a man who has been reading the Bible for forty years. You didn't lose your faith. If you had lost your faith, you wouldn't be hanging around here. Maybe, Father, you just finally realized that it's the good people of this world who need you, not the punks and crud. The good people need to be reminded of their duty every now and then. The punks and crud and crap don't have what it takes to be a good person . . . much less a Christian. Never have had and never will. Stop worrying about them and concentrate on the people who are struggling to bring order to a world filled with chaos."

The priest looked at Ben, amusement in his eyes. "End of sermon, General?"

"Yep. Now let's have you checked over by the medics and get some hot food in you. I know a priest who'll be glad to see you."

The people began returning to the city. They crawled out of caves and dugouts and little hidden places and returned to the city they once called home. And they were a pitiful-looking lot, with very few young among them; most of them were middle-aged and up.

"The thugs and degenerates took the young people," Ben was told. "Some were made slaves, some forced into prostitution, others traded to the Night People."

Ben pulled in Paul Harrison's 17 Batt to see to the stabilizing of Caen and moved his 1 Batt on. Ike had barreled through the countryside and had pulled up and was waiting at the intersection of Highway 174 and 175 for Ben to pull even. Rebet had secured his sector down to within a few miles of Chateaulin. West was waiting at Corlay. Dan was within a few miles of Highway 164 and holding. Georgi was holding outside of Orbec. Danjou had taken Rouen and was bivouacked a few miles south of the city. Tina was waiting near the town of Gournay-en-Bray, and Pat O'Shea was just outside of Beauvais.

South of the clearly defined battle lines that stretched from Chateaulin over to Paris, Duffy Williams's people waited.

Ben rolled up to the outskirts of the town of Falaise and sent his scouts in to check it out.

"Well, sir, at first glance, we're being welcomed with open arms," the scouts reported back. "Looks like the whole town turned out. Food, wine, banners, and music. They plan on tossing us quite a party."

Ben stared at the young man for a moment. "Now tell me what you really think about it."

"I think it's a trap," the scout said, his combat-hardened eyes cold.

"Duffy's people?"

"No, sir. I think it's those goddamn creepies."

"Why?"

"Too well fed, General. They're fat and sassy."

Ben was silent for a moment. "They pulled this a couple of times back in the States. Our intelligence showed that there are different sects of the creepies. This is one that shuns the robes and the underground. Well, to hell with them. We won't play their game.

We'll split the column and throw a loose circle around the town, staying well back, off the road. Let's lay back and see what they do."

When Corrie radioed Ben's orders, the column buttoned up and split up, engines roaring. The town was soon circled. The Rebels settled down to play a wait-and-see game.

Inside the town the creepies were furious. A young Judge smiled ruefully and said, "They made us. I don't know how they did it, but that is no matter now. Take the children and the young men and fertile women to the tunnels and get them clear."

"And you, Judge?" he was asked.

"I will die here. When those fleeing are clear, take up positions."

The escape tunnels had been dug over a period of many years; long before the Great War tore the world apart. Years before the existence of the Night People was widely known. And now they had been greatly enlarged. The escape mouth exited out more than a mile from the town.

"Too easy," Ben muttered, standing by the side of his Hummer. "Corrie, how far back is Buck's 15 Batt?"

"Holding three miles behind us."

"Tell him to pour on the coals and get up here. Throw a loose circle around us, a mile between our two batts. Something fishy is going on." That done and Buck on the way, Ben said, "Tell our people not to open fire until they are fired upon. Then get Lieutenant Bonelli up here. We're all going for a walk in the countryside."

"We are?" Jersey asked.

"We are."

"What are we looking for?" Cooper asked.

"Rabbit holes," Ben said.

Cooper and Beth exchanged glances, and both shrugged their shoulders just as Bonelli ran up.

"Break your people up into squads," Ben told him, opening a map. "First and second platoons do a half-circle on this side of the highway. The rest start working the other side. Work about fifteen hundred to two thousand meters out. There may be escape tunnels leading from the town. Go."

"Buck on the horn," Corrie said.

Ben took the mic. "Buck? Eagle. The town is full of creepies. But something is all wrong with this situation. They know we've smelled them out, yet they're holding fire. I think they may be buying time, sending people out through tunnels. Watch yourselves."

"Prisoners, sir?" Buck asked what Ben knew was coming.

Ben sighed. He did not relish the idea of shooting kids anymore than the next person. "You can try," he finally said. "We all can. For all the good it will do." He didn't have to explain that. Every Rebel knew that the Night People could not be rehabilitated—from the oldest to the youngest. The why of that was something that still eluded the Rebel doctors and shrinks, even after all these years. They all had seen Rebels try to befriend the children of creepies, only to have the young kids suddenly turn on them savagely with any weapon at hand . . . and then dine on the raw and still-cooling human flesh. It was disconcerting, to say the least. "Bring some explosives," he added.

"Right, sir."

No fire came from the town as the searchers spread out and worked slowly, carefully checking out every stand of trees and anywhere else the mouth of tunnels might be hidden. It was Cooper who first spotted movement.

"Up ahead," he called softly. "Two o'clock."

The Rebels immediately dropped belly down to the ground and waited and watched.

Ben watched as two women and a half dozen young kids sprang out of the ground and raced toward the woods. He silently cursed. Even if they had been in range, he still could not bring himself to shoot kids.

The squad leader from Bonelli's company looked at Ben. Ben refused to meet the young woman's eyes. "Let them go," Ben finally said. "Get up there and blow that hole closed."

It amounted to the same thing, but this way was far less personal.

Two Rebels leaped from the ground, each carrying heavy rucksacks filled with C-4. "Warn the others what we're doing," Ben said.

A few minutes later, the ground shook as the C-4 blew. "One hole closed," Ben said. "But they'll be others. Let's go."

Fifteen slow minutes later Corrie said, "Buck found another hole. He's blowing it."

Inside the town the creepies could accurately guess what was happening, and it filled them with rage.

"Take a break," Ben ordered. He sat on the ground and took a sip of water, then rolled a cigarette and leaned back against a tree, his brow furrowed in thought. "There might be one more short hole," he said. "Probably is. We'll all work closer to town and see if we can find it."

The second hole was blown, and from the sound of it, it was a good mile from Ben's location. Ben remained where he was after the sound of the explosion had long died away. The Rebels knew why he was not moving. He just didn't want to have to kill kids . . . up close and personal.

"Some of the press has just linked up with Buck's 15 Batt," Corrie said, sitting down beside him. "That fellow Greg who wears the fancy jacket and Gina Zapp. Couple of more."

"I thought Zapp worked for Blanton."

"One of the networks that's just getting back in operation."

"Something else for Cecil to worry about back home."

Corrie knew what Ben was saying. She'd heard Ben and the others discuss what they would do once the Big Three networks got cranked back up. There was going to be some heavy signal blocking if they ran the crap they used to run back when the nation was whole. Corrie's headset crackled and she listened, grimaced, muttered several very ugly words, then acknowledged the transmission.

"What's wrong?" Ben asked.

"Buck's people just captured some creepies. Young men and women and kids."

"Shit!" Ben said.

"That isn't all. The press is there, with human rights

people on the way, and they're all raising holy hell about kids being tied up like wild animals."

Ben stood up. "Tell Bonelli to carry on here. Let's head for Buck's location."

What Ben did not know was that in the weeks since he and the Rebels had left the States, dozens of newspapers had cranked back into operation and two of the Big Three networks were back in operation. Their coverage areas were still good, since most of the transmission/relay satellites, those between fifteen thousand and eighteen thousand miles up were still operational

"This ought to be good," Coop muttered, as they approached the large knot of men and women standing outside the circle of uniformed Rebels.

Many of the press people had never seen Ben in person, but they had all studied his dossier. And they knew who he was immediately. They all started shouting questions at once.

Ben emptied half a clip of .45's from his Thompson into the air and the press hit the deck. During the rather pregnant silence that followed, Ben said, "I will answer your questions, ladies and gentlemen. But they will be asked with some decorum and respect. I in turn will reciprocate that respect. Now get up off the ground. At least you had the good sense to hit it."

"Savage!" one reporter muttered.

Ben heard it and smiled. He didn't give a damn if the press liked him or not. Just as long as they were afraid of him. Julie was there, and she was not happy with the kids being hog-tied. The expression on her face looked like she was going to cloud up and rain all over Ben at any moment.

Which wouldn't faze Ben; he'd been rained on before. He smiled at her, and the look she gave him would have melted ice.

When the press had gotten to their feet, Ben pointed at one man that he thought he recognized from the old days. He had been an arrogant bastard back then. Ben wondered if the years had mellowed him. "You have a question?"

"These small children, General Raines. Some of them are no more than seven or eight years old. Don't you think your people are overreacting by trussing them up like savage beasts?"

"No, I don't. You obviously have had little or no experience in dealing with the Night People. How you folks managed that is a mystery to me, but we have had years of contact with them. They are very dangerous. The children as much as the adults. None of them can be rehabilitated. We tried for years with no luck."

"Oh, come now, General!" a woman scoffed at him. "These are children. How dangerous can they be?"

The sarcasm came as no surprise; Ben expected it. The press hadn't changed much. They still felt they were experts in all fields and knew more than anyone else about anything one might care to name. "It's nice to know that nothing has changed," Ben said.

"What do you mean by that?" another reporter asked, hostility evident in his tone. "I demand you untie those poor little boys and girls."

"You demand?" Ben asked. Then he chuckled. He eyeballed the group of reporters and human rights observers and men and women representing various other groups. "You all feel that way?"

"Yes," several men and women said.

"Release those children!" a woman yelled. "Look at them. My God, their bonds are so tight they're in pain."

"Yes," another reporter said. "If this is the way you treat children and women, God knows how you treat adults."

"Those poor, poor babies," yet another reporter blathered. "My heart just goes out to them."

"I've seen them eat hearts that were still beating," Ben said.

"That's ridiculous!" the reporter popped back to Ben.

Ben reached into a jacket pocket and tossed the man a clasp knife. "Cut them loose. Be my guest." He looked around him. "All Rebels—do not interfere. No matter what happens—do not interfere."

"Get pictures of this," a reporter that Ben knew as Daniel said, just as the knife was opened and the man walked to a young girl.

"It's going to be all right," he said. "We'll take care of you. My, you are a pretty thing."

"Please cut us loose, mister," the girl said. "I'm in terrible pain."

"You heartless bastard!" a woman yelled at Ben.

Ben smiled at her.

The reporter cut her bonds and the girl lay still on the ground, her eyes glinting savagely. But only the Rebels recognized that brightness for what it was. The man cut the bonds of several more children to the applause of the group. Ben looked at Julie. She was not applauding. She stood with a strange look on her face.

She was very curious about the smile on Ben's face. She noticed the heavily armed Rebels were backing away from the circle, putting the civilians between them and the children of the Night People.

Julie backed up until she was standing behind two burly Rebels. She'd seen enough of Rebels to know that when they turned cautious, there was usually damn good reason for it.

The girl who was first to have her bonds cut rose to her feet. "Oh, thank you, sir," she said sweetly.

"You're quite welcome, child," the man said, as the other children of the Night People were getting to their feet. The reporter looked at Ben, now standing several dozen yards away. "Dangerous," he scoffed. "How ridiculous!"

The girl leaped at the reporter, wrapping her legs around his waist, her arms around his neck, and started eating his face.

Fourteen

The reporter dropped the knife Ben had tossed him as he was ridden down to the ground by the girl. His screaming was both wild and unbelieving. A young boy leaped at a woman and popped out her left eye, eating it with a grin as she screamed and then passed out, hitting the ground. The reporter who had called Ben a savage was on the ground, blood arching in spurts out of a hole in his neck. The girl who was sitting on his chest was lapping at the blood, grinning hideously, her face slick and crimson. The Rebels were standing back, weapons at the ready, but not interfering.

"Do something!" Gina Zapp screamed at Ben.

"You all were warned," Ben spoke over the screaming and howling. "And you all chose to ignore the warning. You want something done, you do it."

"You son of a bitch!" Gina yelled at him.

Ben shrugged. He'd been called worse.

A mini-cam operator stepped into the bloody circle and smashed in the head of a boy with his camera.

"Somebody finally got smart," Jersey remarked.

"Shoot them, goddamn you," a man yelled to Ben.

Ben tossed him a .45. "You shoot them. The bullet comes out of the little end with the hole in it. Everybody back up!" Ben yelled. "We've got a liberal with a gun in his hand."

Every Rebel there either hit the dirt or sought cover behind anything that might remotely stop a bullet.

"How do you work this thing?" the reporter yelled, holding the pistol as if it were a writhing snake.

"Oh, shit!" Jersey said. "Where do these people come from?"

Several of the creepie young men and women had managed to free themselves during the melee and were now attacking anything in sight. One of the women leaped toward Cooper and he put a .223 round right between her eyes, snapping her head back and dropping her to the ground.

Gina Zapp had picked up a club and was swinging it wildly, hitting as many of her cohorts as creepies. Eighty-Pockets Greg stepped into the circle of blood, took the pistol from the reporter, and blew a hole in the girl straddling the chest of the dying man with a hole in his throat. The other reporters and human rights reps picked up anything they could find and started smashing heads.

The blood-splattered circle fell silent. Those creepies still trussed up on the ground glared hate at the men and women around them. Ben stepped through the crowd and retrieved his .45, holstering it.

He looked at the stunned and shocked and bloody crowd. "You all should have learned a hard lesson today, but it won't keep. Many of you will go right back to being your same arrogant and know-it-all selves. But if you retain anything from these bloody moments, retain this: The next time a Rebel tells you to do something, don't argue. Just do it."

Ben pushed his way out of the crowd and walked off. "Corrie," he called over his shoulder. "Shell the town."

Ben caught a lot of bad press stateside because of the creepie incident, with most of it accusing him of allowing the attack to happen. Only a few write-ups told the entire story. Katherine Bonham, David Manor, and Paul Carson were the only ones who actually reported the story exactly as it happened. Since the Rebels monitored every transmission from the Continent, and those were given to Ben daily, Ben now knew which reporters to trust and which would slant their stories. Twelve hours after the creepie attack on the reporters and the various human rights reps, an invisible wall of silence had been erected between Rebel spokepersons and the majority of the press. Those reporters who slanted their stories now found themselves unable to get even so much as a "good morning" from a Rebel. And they also found themselves unable to get to any front.

The reporters who now found themselves unable to get a story immediately went pissing and moaning to President Blanton's reps, who immediately after hearing the sad stories went blithering and blathering to Ben.

"Truth," Ben said, after listening to the complaints.

"I beg your pardon?" one of the president's reps said.

"Truth," Ben repeated. "Tell the reporters to report the truth as it is, not as they see it. And they do know the difference."

"I . . . am not certain I understand, General."

"Since you work for a politician, I have absolutely no difficulty at all believing that. Get out of my office."

The Rebel artillery pounded the small town for eighteen hours, and then the troops began the slow, dangerous job of mopping up. David Manor was with one team, Paul Carson with another, and Kathy Bonham went in with Ben and his team. It was from Kathy that Ben learned where a lot of the emerging reporters had been over the years.

"Putting out underground newspapers," she told him. "Broadcasting the news on very short-range portable transmitters. It would be picked up and relayed from point to point."

Ben was astonished. "Why that way, for heaven's sake?"

She stared at him for a moment. "Because of you and your Rebels, General."

"Call me Ben. Me and my Rebels," he repeated softly. Then he became amused at the thought of men and women, who had once been the most listened to and watched newspeople in the world cowering underground, broadcasting the news furtively. "What in the world did you think we were going to do if we heard it, Kathy?"

"We didn't know. Blanton's people had put out so many stories about what the Rebels were doing . . .

well," she paused, "we actually thought we might be shot for treason."

Ben smiled. "Treason . . . against who, what?"

"Treason against the regime you were setting up."

"That's ridiculous!"

"I see that now. But we were running scared, Ben. Many of these reporters over here are still very wary of you and the Rebels."

"Well, truthfully, I'd like to throw them out of this country, but that's all that I would personally do to them."

"They think you would like to shoot them."

"What an interesting thought."

Kathy smiled at him. "What happens when the networks start up again, Ben? Evening news and all? Will you carry it in the SUSA?"

"I doubt it, Kathy. Cecil is in the process now of setting up our own TV news and other programming. He found some good people who want to report the news truthfully . . . for a change."

"Oh, Ben!" she said, exasperation behind the words. "Most broadcast journalists always told the truth. But the truth oftentimes, or perhaps always, is in the eyes of the beholder. You can't expect an avowed liberal to see the same thing as an archconservative. Both of them can look at the same event and see it very differently."

"Kathy, to a liberal, there is no such thing as an absolute. Everything is gray. Nothing is truly black or white, right or wrong. Conservatives, on the other hand, know the difference between right and wrong."

Both of them, along with Ben's team, left and right

of them, were crouched behind the rubble of what had once been a home, waiting for Recon to give the all-clear to advance. Ben had not wanted to destroy the old town, but he was not going to sacrifice the lives of his people for a building.

Ever the reporter, Kathy asked, "Why do you carry that old submachine gun, Ben?"

"I started out with it, years back," Ben replied, easing up to his knees and looking out over what remained of a wall to view the smoking rubble in front of him. "I'm comfortable with it."

Recon waved them forward. Ben stood up in a crouch and said, "Stay with us, Kathy, and do exactly as we do."

Kathy fell back a few meters to walk with Beth and Cooper. Jersey, as always, was with Ben, Corrie on the other side of him. "How did that cute little lady become the general's bodyguard?" she asked.

"It just happened," Beth said. "A lot of teams form up because the people work well with each other. We were all kids when we joined with the Rebels. Back in the old days, it was a family; everybody knew everybody else. There were only a few thousand of us."

"A lot of Rebels have retired from the field," Cooper said, as they slowly advanced through the town, eyes constantly moving for signs of hostiles. "Some because of wounds, some because of age, some because they wanted to raise a family." He sighed. "Some just couldn't take it anymore."

"And the four of you have been with the general . . . ?"

"Years," Beth said. "We've been all around the world and going again."

A creepie suddenly popped up out of the rubble, and Ben stitched him with a short burst. The team kept walking. Kathy glanced at the dead man, calm and peaceful looking in death. She spoke softly into a small cassette-corder.

"I hate those bastards," Beth said, cutting her eyes to the dead creepie. "We can sometimes rehab normal people. A lot of people now in the ranks once fought against us. Not these people. You can't do anything with them except kill them."

"Down!" Ben called, and the team hit the ground. "Movement at two o'clock," Ben said to Corrie. "The second floor of that building."

Kathy looked around her as best she could from her prone position. Not a Rebel was in sight. They had vanished amid the rubble.

"Bring a tank up," Ben called, and Corrie radioed in.

Within seconds, a MBT clanked through the wreckage.

"Take it down," Ben said to Corrie.

The 120-mm smooth-bore cannon elevated slightly and then began roaring, and the old building began crumbling and flying apart under the impacting rounds. A couple of minutes later, the entire top floor was gone. Kathy had seen two bodies come sailing out of the building. One had been missing a leg.

By the middle of the afternoon, the town had been cleared and the Rebels were bivouacked about two miles from the town, on the road to Argentan. Ben had offered no objections to Kathy staying with the team, and she was sitting in the front room of an old home, listening to him talk to his batt coms by radio. She looked up just as one of the most physically powerful and strikingly handsome young men she had ever seen walked in.

"The boss's son," Beth said. "Buddy Raines. He's commander of 8 Batt. The special ops group. The boss's daughter, Tina, is commander of 9 Batt."

"What the hell are you doing here?" Ben asked his son.

"Bringing you news that will surely lift your spirits," Buddy said, pouring a cup of coffee and sitting down.

"That means it's sure to depress me," Ben said. "So what's up?"

Buddy smiled. "Emil Hite is on the way."

Ben sat down and stared at his son. "You have got to be kidding!"

"Nope. He and most of his . . . ah, flock, slipped aboard a freighter and should be landing in France in a few days. Thermopolis reported them missing and discovered several trucks gone from his motor pool. He traced their movement to South Carolina and the rest is, as they say, history."

"Who is Emil Hite?" Kathy questioned.

"There is no way to describe Emil Hite," Ben said. "He's like the candy bar—indescribable."

Jersey, Cooper, Beth, Buddy, and Corrie all exchanged puzzled glances. Only Kathy was old enough to know what Ben was talking about. She smiled. "I haven't seen one of those in years, Ben."

"Neither have I. But I sure would like one."

"What are you two talking about?" Buddy asked.

"A candy bar, son. Indescribably delicious." He and Kathy started laughing at the expressions on the younger Rebels' faces.

"There is one more bit of news, father," Buddy said when the laughter had faded. "A message from Julie Petti."

Ben didn't even have to ask what it was. Julie had been avoiding him for days. Word had gotten back to him that she had been appalled at the Rebels' treatment of creepies and punks. He nodded his head. "She wants a transfer out of this front and feels that we should not see each other again because we are too far apart in our treatment of human beings."

"That's . . . uncannily close, father," Buddy said. "You never cease to amaze me with your ability to read peoples' minds."

"I can't read minds, boy. But I can read sign. And I've been reading her sign for the past week. This comes as no surprise. Tell her to stay in the rear if she doesn't like our methods." Then, under his breath, he muttered, "I ought to assign Emil Hite to be her guide."

When Emil Hite got off the ship in England, he knelt down and kissed the ground . . . or the dock, as it were. It had been a rough crossing, and Emil had been sick the entire time. Emil had come a long way from the days when he wore flowing robes, sandals, flowers in his hair, and scooted about preaching pearls of wisdom from the great god Blomm. A long way, but not that far.

When Emil felt the earth—or the dock—remain firm and unmoving beneath his feet, he rose wobbly to his full height—which wasn't all that much—and looked around him. "France," he whispered. "The cradle of liberty." He smiled. "And broads." He looked back at the faithful who had accompanied him; about thirty men and women who knew exactly what Emil was all about but liked him anyway.

Emil marched up to an official-looking person who was carrying a clipboard and said, "I am Colonel (he wasn't) Emil Hite, commander of the Blomm Brigade (no such outfit) of Raines's Rebels. I must get to France. General Raines needs me." (About like a head cold.)

The elderly Englishman gave Emil a thorough going-over, from boots to beret, taking in all the medals and ribbons Emil had pinned on his uniform, which ranged from the Burma Campaign of World War Two to Vietnam, and covered every inch of fabric from waist to neck and both sides of the jacket.

"My word!" the dock-master said. He pointed with his walking stick to a ship down the way. "She'll be sailing with the tide. You can board anytime."

Emil turned to his group. "Come, warriors. Forward into the fray. I can assure you all that General Raines will be so overcome with emotion when he sees us, he will be rendered incapable of speech."

More than a modicum of truth in that statement.

The captain of the ship, a sturdy Scotsman and a veteran of dozens of trans-Atlantic crossings, and a survivor, stood on the bridge and watched the strange collection of men and women march up the gangway and board his ship. He had never seen anything quite like them. He turned to his first mate.

"They must be some sort of secret weapon General Raines plans to use. Although I can't possibly imagine how."

The trip from Southhampton to Le Havre was uneventful, except for the captain having to retreat to his quarters with a splitting headache after listening to Emil talk for fifteen minutes.

"God is on our side," Emil said to the first mate.

"I certainly hope so," the first mate replied, then hid in a lifeboat for the remainder of the crossing.

On shore Emil commandeered several trucks, and after getting lost fifteen times, managed to reach Ben's CP about an hour before dark. The Rebels in the area saw him coming, and most managed to make themselves scarce. But they forgot to warn Ben, who was busy going over maps in the house.

A Rebel on the porch saw Emil coming and dropped a sandwich on the floor in his haste to get away. Emil leaped up onto the porch and stepped right into the peanut butter and jelly. He went slipping and sliding and flailing his arms through the open front door and into the main room, his antics resembling a cross between the frug and country line dancing. Jersey had gotten up to see what the commotion was all about, and Emil ran into her and knocked her flat on the floor.

"Goddamnit!" Jersey hollered.

Kathy Bonham, not knowing what this human Tasmanian devil was, just barely managed to get out of Emil's way.

Emil unintentionally bugalooed across the room and landed on top of Ben's desk, sending maps, notes, a mug of coffee, and Ben's fresh-baked piece of apple pie to the floor.

"Lafayette!" Emil cried, nose to nose with Ben. "I am here!"

"France might never recover from this," Ben said. He cut his eyes to Cooper, who was trying to keep Jersey from shooting Emil.

Ben had no choice but to assign Emil and his group to his own 1 Batt. That was the only way he knew to keep Emil out of trouble. There was another reason for that decision: Emil was scared to death of Jersey. The little bodyguard had threatened to shoot him more than once. As long as Jersey was around—and she was always around Ben—Emil was on his best behavior, which wasn't anything to write home about, but it was better than the norm.

"What will you do with him?" Kathy asked, the morning after Emil's arrival.

"Believe it or not, Emil and his bunch have turned into tough little fighters," Ben said with a smile. "Not that it was that way at the beginning." He laughed at some old prank of Emil's. "Once you learn to accept his rather unorthodox ways, he's really quite likeable."

"He's a prick," Jersey said, from across the room. "Why don't you send him back to Thermopolis?"

Ben thought about that for a moment. "I have a better idea. Why don't we bring Thermopolis over *here?*"

Fifteen

Thermopolis jumped at the chance. He and his crew had, at first, thought they would like to stay home and run listening posts. But Ben had guessed the other way. Combat is infectious. For many it produces a high unlike anything else. Besides, Thermopolis liked Emil and could control him.

"And bring Smoot with you," Ben concluded the broadcast.

Thermopolis and his crew would fly down to Ben's home, get Ben's husky, Smoot, and then fly out of the East Coast on a transport.

"You're full of surprises, Ben," Kathy said. "I didn't know you liked dogs."

"I don't particularly care for people who don't like dogs," Ben replied. "And I have been known to shoot people who abuse any type of animal."

She fixed serious eyes on him. "You are kidding. Aren't you?"

"Nope. People who abuse animals are sorry excuses for human beings. I don't want them around me, and I won't tolerate them around me."

"You are a complex person, Ben Raines."

"A lot of people think that's so. But it isn't really true. Animals can't help being what they are. Humans can. It's just that simple."

"You really haven't killed a person for abusing an animal, have you, Ben?"

He didn't have to vocalize a reply. The bleak look in his eyes spoke volumes.

Ben let the punks and the creeps and self-styled warlords stew for a time while he waited for Thermopolis and his bunch to arrive and take over keeping track of supplies and routes and battalion positions and all the other tedious things that Ben hated and Therm was so good at—actually it was his wife, Rosebud, but she gave her husband the credit.

When the big transport landed, Smoot jumped off and didn't even take time to pee before she leaped into Ben's arms and both of them went rolling around on the tarmac. Smoot had grown into an eighty-five-pound husky. Thankfully, she was, like many of her breed, an easygoing, good natured dog. But Smoot had a very respectable set of teeth, and when angered, she could be quite formidable.

Kathy watched with amusement as Ben played with Smoot, the husky clearly the winner as she knocked Ben down several times roughhousing. Thermopolis finally broke it up, and he and Ben shook hands.

"Good to have you back, Therm."

"Good to be back, Ben. When do we push off?"

"I figure it'll take you seventy-two hours to get organized. In a few days."

"Good enough. Let's get to work."

The Rebels were glad to see Therm and his bunch return to their ranks, for the hippies turned warriors were well liked. They preferred to handle the tedious jobs that most others detested, but could turn into vicious fighters when pressed into service.

Duffy Williams and his thousands of malcontents had waited behind their guns while the Rebels shifted around and made ready for an all-out attack . . . but they had not done so patiently. The waiting was getting to them. They were growing increasingly short-tempered and hard to handle as the weather began turning cooler and the nights were becoming downright cold.

Duffy was now beginning to fully grasp the enormity of keeping a large army in food and clothing, and morale up. He began traveling from sector to sector, talking with the leaders of the various groups, cajoling, sometimes threatening, and often making deals to keep them ready to fight.

Ben and his Rebels waited.

Kathy Bonham possessed every trait that made her a good reporter: She was highly intelligent, literate, and had the ability to see both sides of a story and report fairly . . . in that, she very nearly stood alone among her peers. As the days passed and she more closely watched Ben, she began to realize that she was observing a brilliant military tactician at work; also a very ruthless man when it came to seeing his own plans bear fruit. Ben was inordinately compassionate to the very young, the very old, and toward domesticated animals and wildlife. But he was totally without mercy toward his enemies. Ben did not believe that the Rebel way was necessarily the only way, just that it was the right way. Every Rebel she spoke with believed exactly the same. Which came as absolutely no surprise to her.

Kathy also began to realize, with some trepidation, that these men and women would *never* be defeated. As long as there was just one Rebel left alive, the fight would continue. The Rebel philosophy would never die.

Kathy felt eyes on her and turned. Ben was standing to one side, looking at her. Kathy was a tall woman, almost five feet, ten inches, and while her figure had matured, she could still cause men's heads to turn. She stood for a moment, meeting Ben's eyes.

"You ready to go to war?" Ben asked.

"Is anybody ever ready to go to war?"

"You have a lot to learn about Rebels, Kathy. The Rebels are always ready. It's what we do best."

"I see. Day after tomorrow is still firm?"

"Yes. We jump off at 0600."

She turned to look outside. It was full dark. The evening meal had been served and the mess tents cleaned and made ready for an early breakfast. But there would be hot fresh coffee and sandwiches available at all times during the night for the guards coming on and going off shift. She had quickly learned that Ben insisted that the best of food be ready for his people, whenever possible. But prepackaged field rations were field rations, no matter what country packaged them— many times they still tasted like shit.

She turned to face Ben. "It's late."

"Not that late."

They looked at one another for a moment. Kathy brushed back a stubborn lock of black hair . . . black hair now sprinkled with gray, which she made no effort to disguise. He dark blue eyes suddenly sparkled with mischief.

"You have something in mind, *General* Raines."

A smile played at his lips, and his hawkish features softened. "I thought perhaps you might like to have a brandy with me. A local family gave me a very old bottle of brandy."

"And after the brandy?"

He shrugged. "That's not up to me, is it?"

She moved closer to him. "If your reputation is to be believed, you generally take what you want."

He moved closer to her. "My reputation is grossly exaggerated. When the Rebel army was being formed, we had growing pains. Some, a very few of my men, in the early days, had their way forcibly with women. That stopped quite abruptly after two of them were tried and shot."

"There were more than two?"

"Three. The third man was found not guilty. The woman confessed she promised him sex and then allowed him to become quite aroused before she stopped it cold. That's bullshit, Kathy. Set the rules before, not during. If a man knows how far he is to be allowed to go, and then steps over that line, that's rape. If a woman promises sex, gets a man all worked up, and then suddenly pushes him away and tells him to go sit in a corner and jack off, that might not set too well with some men."

His language did not faze her. "Your views on that subject would not be popular with a great many women's groups, Ben. Past and present."

"I don't care. I haven't lost any sleep over it. There aren't many Rebel women who disagree with that philosophy. But I'm not one of those men who would turn violent if rejected. However, I might cuss a lot."

She stepped over to the desk and turned off the lantern. "Well, you won't have to cuss me, Ben."

Nine battalions of Rebels, with nine battalions coming right behind them, with full artillery and armor, MBTs spearheading, smashed through the line set up by Duffy Williams as if it were made of papier-mâché and put the untrained and undisciplined army of punks, thugs, and assorted human slime into a full-blown rout. Kathy, riding in an armored vehicle with Ben's 1 Batt, later reported that Ben didn't make any attempt to finesse this one; he just bulled through using brute force, smashing anybody who got in his way.

In a lightning-fast operation, faster than even most Rebels could recall, the battalions of World Stabilization Forces—their official United Nations designation—took everything from Quimper over to Orleans in a move that stunned even career military leaders around the world. Ben instructed those nine battalions coming up behind to take the lead and continue the pursuit of Duffy Williams and his joke of an army, with his own nine spearheading battalions to begin the circling of Paris.

But Ben knew that while Duffy's army was, for the moment, a joke, it would not be that way for long. For those hundreds of men and women who stood and fought and fell back with Duffy were, even without their knowledge, rapidly being molded into an army. And they would quickly turn into a formidable fighting force.

Many of the reporters and human rights people traveling behind the Rebels were appalled at the ruthlessness of the advancing Rebels. The Rebel philosophy of warfare was simple: You get one chance to surrender. Only one. Fight us, and you die. Period.

"Look, you stupid son of a bitch," Ben told one rather suddenly startled reporter who confronted Ben about his stabilization tactics. "We're not here to play patty-cake with these crud. That entire punk army out there is not worth the loss of one Rebel soldier. You people can piss and moan and sob and stomp on your hankies all you want to, in print and broadcast. But you better stand far away from me when you do. And something else: The first time you try to interfere with the job we've been assigned, I'll kill you. Do I make myself perfectly clear?"

"Very."

Ben and the Rebels had never been, by any stretch of the imagination, the darling of the press corps. Now it was almost as if the Rebels were the enemy instead of the roaming hordes of gangs. The press had never met anyone like Ben Raines. He refused to kowtow to them and actually had the nerve to threaten them. Up to now that had been unheard of. Didn't this tin soldier know who they were?

Oh, yeah. He just didn't give a damn.

Then, after the press launched several vicious attacks against the Rebels, accusing them of the most heinous of civil rights violations (against rapists, murderers, child molesters, and other assorted human vermin), Ben started kicking the press out of the country . . . sometimes quite physically.

"We would have won in Vietnam if the goddamn press had been kept out of the country," Ben said to Kathy one evening.

"I am the press, Ben," she reminded him.

"Yes, you are," he conceded. "But a minority member. You and about a half dozen others over here report the truth . . . without adding your own slanted opinions. You and David and Paul and a very few other members of the press have your heads screwed on straight. You understand that sometimes things have to be measured in black and white for the good of the majority. You are fully cognizant of absolutes. You know that the lives of a thousand punks is not worth the life of one decent human being. That's the difference, Kathy." He smiled at her. "Your mother and father, Kathy, belonged to what political party, back when those things mattered?"

She laughed, then shook her head. "They were registered Republicans, Ben."

"I never would have guessed," he said dryly.

While Ben prepared his people to fight on two

fronts, those members of the press who had been booted out of the country began complaining to anybody who would listen, which, of course, was every liberal Democrat in Congress. But to everyone's surprise except Ben, for he knew the man had steel in his backbone—it had just taken Homer a while to find it—President Blanton told them to shut up. In Blanton's words, "World stabilization is much more important than the lives of a few hundred, a few thousand, or a few million hard-core criminals. Those who stand in the way of a return to civilization and orderly government had best understand now that if they persist, they will be treated in the harshest manner. I fully back General Ben Raines and his Rebels."

"Well, I'll be damned!" Kathy said, after reading the communiqué. "What the hell happened to him?"

"He stopped paying attention to the screwballs in his administration, told his wife to shut up, and started listening to the majority of the American people. That's what happened," Ben replied. "If the politicians had done that years ago, worldwide, this goddamn mess we're now in, and will be in for the rest of our lives, and a good portion of our children's lives, probably would not have occurred."

"To someone who didn't know you, Ben, that remark would sound very racist."

"One has only to look at the ranks of the Rebels to know that racism is not tolerated, Kathy. From any direction."

She smiled at him. "Really, Ben?"

Ben was still puzzling over that question long after she had left the room. His team had been in the room when Kathy made the comment, and he looked over at Corrie, who was taking a break from her radio. She shrugged her shoulders.

"Beats me what she meant, boss. But reporters are weird people. I never met one yet I'd trust very far."

Ben met the eyes of each of his team members. No more than kids when they first joined him—and they picked him rather than he choosing them. Now they were all adults, in their midtwenties, and there wasn't fifteen cents worth of difference in their combined philosophies. They had taken Ben's philosophy as their own. But, as Ben remembered back over the years, not without question; and they had asked good questions and still did.

"You might be right about that, Corrie," Ben finally addressed her statement, wondering if she were trying to caution him about Kathy. "You may be right."

Sixteen

Paris was going to be a real bitch.

Ben had been studying maps for several days, while his battalions made ready for urban warfare against the creepies in the old city. Paris had to be taken and the back of the creepies broken. Once Paris was taken, Ben and his nine battalions could link up and finish the warlords and punks. But there was no way Ben could bypass the city and leave the Night People at his back, nor could he totally destroy Paris. That was part of the agreement he made with the secretary-general of the UN. There were about a dozen cities in Europe that he had agreed to leave intact . . . if at all possible. Paris was one of them.

"A real son of a bitch," Ben muttered, folding the old maps carefully and putting them away. He looked up at Jersey. "They're going to be down in the old sewers, Jersey. We've got to go in and flush them out."

"Then let's get to it," she replied.

"Indeed," Ben said, thinking, *Oh, to be that young again.* He looked up as Mike Richards strolled in. The chief of Rebel intelligence had been out in the field with some of his other spooks for the past week, and he had a grim look on his face. "You going to rain all over me?" Ben asked.

Mike nodded his head. "Yeah," he said, pouring a cup of coffee. He was unshaven and his clothes were dirty from days of working close to Paris . . . and probably inside the city as well. "Goddamn cannibals are holding several thousand men, women, and kids prisoners inside the city, Ben. Fattening them up for slaughter."

"We anticipated that, Mike. And no, we aren't going to launch a rescue mission."

Mike looked at Ben. "That's firm?"

"Yes. And you know all the reasons."

Mike nodded. Something happened to those prisoners once they were held for a long period of time, knowing they faced being eaten, some of them consumed alive. A large percentage of them lost their minds and had to be warehoused for the rest of their lives.

"The press is going to raise hell, Ben," Mike said softly.

"I can't help it, Mike. You know as well as I do they're better off dead. How did the press find out?"

"I don't know that they did. But my people tell me they're all roaming the secure areas, trying to find something they can use against you. Why don't you just run them out of the country?"

"The thought is becoming more appealing. But I keep coming up with reasons why I shouldn't."

Mike drained his coffee cup. "When do we hit Paris?"

"Day after tomorrow. Dawn."

The FRF moved in to help in the job of sealing off roads on the outskirts of the Paris suburbs. Ben was under no illusion that he could destroy all the creepies in the city; the best estimates his intelligence people could offer was that 60 to 70 percent would be eliminated. And the Rebels would suffer between 0.5 and 1 percent killed and another 2 to 3 percent wounded.

"Let's prove them wrong," Ben told his batt coms just hours before the push was to begin. "If I find anybody without body armor, I'll court-martial them."

"How about the press?" Pat O'Shea asked.

"They can get their own body armor."

The batt coms all laughed. Pat shook his head. "Are they going to be with us?"

"Some of them will be working a day behind us. Only a half dozen will actually go in with us. I just don't want to have to read about how harshly we treat these poor, misguided creepies: how they were forced into a life of cannibalism because when they were young the coach wouldn't let them play, or the homecoming queen wouldn't date them, or they had pimples, or somebody was politically incorrect with them—and because of that terribly unfair treatment, they were somehow forced into a life of crime in order to rebel against the system, or some such shit."

The batt coms and company commanders and platoon leaders were roaring with laughter. There were those among them who had personally suffered terrible deprivations as children, or knew of others who had, and who had gone on to become productive, law-abiding men and women, both before and after the Great War.

Kathy, David Manor, and Paul Carson were in attendance, sitting in the rear of the room, and the three of them exchanged knowing glances and small smiles at Ben's remarks and the laughter that followed the words. They all knew men and women in the press corps who would have done just that . . . they themselves had done it in their early reporting days, before a hard dose of reality slapped them back into the real world.

"You all know where you're going in and what to do once in there. I don't have to belabor the point. Our objective is to kill creepies and stabilize the city. Let's do it building by building, slow and easy. That's it, people. Take off."

When the room had cleared except for Ben, his personal team, and the three reporters, Kathy said, "Ben, you're really going to get some bad coverage if you don't permit the press to enter the city tomorrow."

"I don't recall ever getting good coverage from those people. It's a little late to worry about it now." He looked at Paul and David. "You know your staging areas?"

They did.

"I'll see you in the city." He took Kathy's arm, and together they walked out of the room.

* * *

Rain began slicking the streets just before dawn, a light but very cold rain, the temperature hovering in the low forties. Ben and the Rebels looked like some mad artist's drawing of people from outer space dressed in their protective gear. They stood around and sipped hot coffee from canteen cups, waiting for the first tints of gray to fill the eastern sky. Tanks snorted and rumbled around the outskirts of Paris, filling the cold air with diesel smoke.

The Rebels loathed the creepies and hated dealing with them. They despised going in and finding the creepies' fattening farms, filled with insane and half-insane men and women and young children waiting to be eaten by the cannibalistic clan. Even Jersey was nervous as she waited for Ben to give the jump-off signal. She wished Smoot was here, so she could pet the husky, but Smoot was back with Thermopolis, out of harm's way.

For once even Emil was silent, his face showing the signs of strain at the thought of dealing up close and face to face with the stinking Night People. Emil was not afraid of the creepies, he just hated dealing with them. They were savages through and through.

Ben stood by his HumVee, sipping coffee, his facial expression unreadable. Kathy stood a few yards from him, trying to guess what might be running through his mind. She soon gave that up as impossible.

The Rebels had circled the city and were miles from the heart of Paris. They were right at the edge of the suburbs, and intelligence had warned them that they were about to wage war on the most massive gathering

of Night People anywhere in the world. Paris was literally filled with them.

"So you will be outnumbered again?" Kathy said to
Beth, after giving up trying to engage Ben in conversation.

"Nothing new," Beth replied casually. "We're almost always outnumbered. It's been that way ever
since the Rebels were formed." She smiled. "The general is always like this before a big fight. It's nothing
personal. He's gearing up mentally for the fight, that's
all."

A few gunshots were heard coming from the mist-
shrouded homes and buildings that lay rain-gray ahead
of them. The shots were muffled by the rain.

"Recon," Beth said. "They're clearing out a place
for a MASH unit and communications. They're doing
the same in three other locations. We'll take some
casualties," she added.

"You say that very matter-of-factly," Kathy said.

"Can't make scrambled eggs without breaking the
shells," Beth said. "Better drink your coffee. We'll be
shoving off in a few minutes, I think. Did you fill your
canteens?"

"Yes. Both of them."

Beth nodded and walked off.

Kathy looked at her watch and turned to Cooper.
"It's past 0600. What's the delay?"

"The boss is waiting for good light. It's going to be
bad enough when we do push off; streets slick as goose
shit."

"The Rebels have a healthy respect for these Night
People, right, Cooper?"

"You bet we do. They don't surrender. Ever. They fight to the last person. They'll rush you carrying fifty pounds of C-4, or Molotov cocktails, or whatever they can get their hands on. Just as long as they can take one of us with them."

Ben gazed up at the gray sky for a moment and then took a final drag on his hand-rolled cigarette. He toed out the butt with his boot and muttered something under his breath that no one could hear and then glanced at Corrie. He lifted his right hand and began making a circular motion with his index finger up.

"Get to your vehicle," Cooper said to Kathy. "The boss is gettin' this circus on the road." He glanced at her. "Secure that body armor and fasten the chin strap on your helmet. It's gonna get real mean, real quick." He walked off toward the Hummer and opened the driver's side door. Ben's voice stopped him.

"On foot, Coop. Corrie, order the tanks to spearhead." Before Cooper could respond, Ben was off and running through the mist and rain and fog.

"I knew it, goddamnit!" the driver of the vehicle Kathy was in said, opening the door and jumping out just as Lieutenant Bonelli was yelling for his people to follow the general.

Kathy jumped out of the backseat and went running off toward Ben and his team, almost losing her footing on the slick street and busting her ass before she caught up with them.

Ben was squatting down behind a house. He glanced at her and grinned. "You sure you don't want to stay in the rear?"

"I'm sure."

He nodded and was up and running toward another house before Kathy caught her breath. Saying a few very choice words under her breath, Kathy followed, staying with Beth.

"That area is not secure!" a scout yelled, as Ben angled off and went running up another block.

"Then let's secure it!" Ben yelled over his shoulder just as unfriendly fire started yammering from a house. Ben hit the wet grass and slid on his belly for a few feet before coming to a stop behind a tree. Beth and Kathy took to ground and belly-crawled to a low stone fence.

"Is he always like this?" Kathy asked, as heavy machine-gun fire clipped bits of stone from the fence just a couple of feet over their heads.

"Yes," Beth said, setting the fire selector on her M-16 to full auto. "But you haven't seen anything yet."

"I can hardly wait," Kathy muttered.

Ben tossed a grenade toward the open window of the house where the heavy machine gun fire was coming from. The grenade fell about a foot short, but the explosion caused the old bricks to collapse and when they did, part of the roof fell in. Ben was over the fence and running toward the rear of the house. Beth was over the fence and running toward Ben before Kathy could react. Wisely she decided to stay right where she was for the time being.

The back door flew open just as Ben reached it, and a familiar stench reached his nostrils. Ben leveled his Thompson and held the trigger back, sending the knot of creepies that crowded the back entrance into that long sleep.

"Teams left and right of me!" Ben yelled to Corrie. "Let's clear this block and do it right the first time."

Ben cautiously stepped over the stinking bodies of the creepies and into the house. One of the creeps was still alive and moaned. Ben shot him in the head. His eyes penetrated the gloom of the dark interior and found the body of a young woman—or what was left of the naked being. The creepies had been eating on the carcass.

Ben glanced over his shoulder. Corrie and Cooper were right behind him. "Get Kathy and that film crew up here," Ben said. "Now. Have other batt coms pull reporters in and do the same."

Rebels were working the block, quickly clearing the houses of creepies. Kathy and a network reporter and film crew came to the rear of house and looked for a moment at the dead creepies piled in a stinking heap at the back door.

Ben stepped to one side and motioned them all inside. He pointed to what was left of the naked and eaten-upon young woman. "Film it," he said, and his tone warned them all they had better do it. "The people we're fighting eat other human beings alive. They keep them alive as long as possible. They say the flesh tastes better that way."

The top-gun network reporter gasped and stepped to the door, barely able to hold his vomit until he reached the outside. There he lost his breakfast, almost puking on the boots of several other reporters who had gathered . . . or had been herded over to the house.

Ben said, "From this moment on, I don't want to hear another goddamn word about offering these people pity, or compassion, or mercy. The first time I hear any of those words, or similar words, in conjunction with the Night People, the reporter who says them will be out of this country so fast it will take his or her breath away. Does everybody read me loud and clear?"

"We have only your word that all Night People commit these atrocities, General," a man said.

Ben did not hesitate. He pointed to two Rebels. "You and you. Escort this person to the airport at Rouen and make damn sure the officer in charge there gets him on a plane for the States. Pull his entry papers. He is not to be allowed back on this Continent without authorization from me. And that is not likely to happen."

The reporter flushed in anger and opened his mouth. "Now you see here, General. You can't—"

Ben stepped forward and hit the man on the mouth with a gloved fist, splitting his lips and loosening several teeth. The reporter's butt bounced on the blood-slick floor, and before he could recover, the two Rebels assigned to escort him had jerked him up and tossed him outside.

The other reporters present wisely kept their mouths closed and their opinions to themselves.

Ben pointed to the naked, half-eaten human carcass on the floor, the last horrible grimace of unbearable pain frozen in death on her face. "Film it!" he roared. "And from this moment on, until I feel I can trust you people to tell the truth and not slant your reports, all copy, all film, will first be submitted to our censors for evaluation before being sent back home. Is that understood?"

It was. Perfectly. Loud and clear. The reporters didn't like it, but the order was understood.

Ben turned away from the knot of print and broadcast reporters to look for a moment at the stiffening young woman on the dirty floor. "Bury her," he ordered. "Burn the bodies of these goddamn creepies."

The reporters quickly stepped to one side to allow Ben through to the outside. The rain had picked up. But it could not cleanse the earth of the stench of death and depravity and horrible perversion.

"I hate these goddamn people," Ben said, stepping under the dubious protection of the barren limbs of an old tree to roll a cigarette.

"The creepies or the reporters?" Jersey asked with a straight face.

Book Two

My opinion is that the northern states will manage somehow to muddle through.

—John Bright

One

"General Raines has thrown several reporters out of France," an aide told President Blanton.

"Lucky him," Homer muttered.

"Sir?"

"Nothing." Homer looked down at the pile of papers on his desk and pushed them away.

"Some coffee, sir?" the aide asked.

"That would be nice. Yes. Thank you." Homer waited until the aide had brought his coffee and exited the room and then rose from his desk to stand by the window overlooking the street. Despite the weather being as cold as a witch's tit, the demonstrators were still walking up and down in front of the new White House, carrying their placards and chanting about one thing or another. "Screw you," Homer said, and closed the drapes.

Homer Blanton's thinking had changed dramatically since his first encounter with Ben Raines. Had it really been such a short time ago? Yes. Seemed much longer. The Southern United States of America and those other states that had aligned with the SUSA were running smoothly. Roads and bridges being rebuilt. Factories moving in and opening up. The strongest economy anywhere in the world. And what was left for Homer and his administration to govern was in ruin. Liberal versus conservative. Same old story. It was worse now than back when Homer first took office. Now there were no bargaining chips. Hell, there wasn't anything left that wasn't rusted, worn out, broken, demolished, or burned. Ben Raines and his Rebels had seen to that. Years back Ben Raines had sworn he would smash the liberal-run government of the United States; grind it into dust under the heel of his boot. And he had done that.

All things taken into consideration, Homer should hate Ben Raines. But he didn't. He felt a grudging admiration for the man. Raines told people to go to work and they went to work. Raines said to build a bridge and the goddamn thing got built. The Rebels could build five bridges in the time it took Homer's people to drive the pilings for one. For every mile of highway that was repaired outside the SUSA, the Rebels overlaid fifty. The USA was rampant with crime. The SUSA had no crime. Unemployment was 70 percent in the USA. Unemployment was zero in the SUSA.

"Shit!" Homer said.

"Rita Rivers and VP Hooter to see you, sir," his secretary buzzed him.

"Jesus Jumping Christ," Homer muttered. "That's all I need. All right. Send them in."

One bad thing about this job, Homer thought. *There is no place to run!*

* * *

The Rebels fought for every inch of ground they covered that cold, wet day in France. The creeps slowly backed up under the Rebel assault, but they did so reluctantly and did not mind paying for it in blood . . . almost always their own. And they did not take their prisoners with them when they retreated. They hung them up on meat hooks and left them to die a slow, horrible death: men, women, and children.

"General Striganov's found another bunch of prisoners," Corrie said. She nodded her head at the silent questions in Ben's eyes. "All dead or dying."

Ben turned his head to look into the eyes of a network reporter. The man's eyes were bleak. "You don't have to belabor the point, General. I get the message. I hope you kill every one of these savages."

"I plan to do just that," Ben said. "And you may quote me."

"Rest assured I will."

"I never doubted it."

"But Duffy and his men and women are quite another matter."

"In your view. Not in mine."

"May I quote you on that?"

"Be my guest."

The rain continued to fall, mixed with tiny bits of sleet. At three o'clock that afternoon, with the weather worsening, Ben told Corrie to radio all batt coms to call it a day and to secure their positions for the evening. "Get me Greenwalt on scramble, Corrie," Ben said, accepting a canteen cup filled with steaming black coffee.

The commander of 11 Batt came on. "Go, Eagle."

"Give me a situation report, Greenie."

"Duffy's people aren't putting up much of a fight in my sector, Eagle. But they're not surrendering, either. Intelligence believes they have a definite plan, but damned if I can figure out what it is."

"Buddy has some of his people working behind the lines, Greenie. They'll do some snatching, and we'll find out. I'll be back with you."

Ben had set up his CP in a long-abandoned old home. A fire was crackling in the fireplace, and the smell of coffee was pleasant in the home. All Rebel batts were still at the very edge of the city. But they had a toehold. And once the Rebels secured even the tiniest of toeholds, they were like a bulldog; not likely to give it up.

Mike Richards, Rebel chief of intelligence and a former CIA station chief in Argentina, sat quietly in a chair by the coffee pot. Two of his people sat with him, the three of them waiting for Buddy's special ops people to bring in some prisoners. The only reporter present was Kathy Bonham. She could not remember ever being so tired. She marveled at the Rebel ability to gain ground without suffering a single fatality. They had several wounded but no deaths. On the other hand they had killed several hundred Night People. As they advanced, Rebel combat engineers welded shut manhole covers. Other teams of Rebels came in behind the main body to search each home, each building, for creepie escape holes. They either pumped them full of tear gas and pepper gas and drove them out and shot them, or sealed the hole with explosives. Ben Raines left nothing to chance. Even those reporters who openly despised him had to respect the man's genius at waging war.

"There is no way we're closing all the holes," Ben told Kathy. "But we're getting quite a number of them."

"Buddy's coming in," Cooper called from the front porch. "They've got a half dozen punks with them. Jesus! What a crummy-looking bunch."

"I would like to watch this interrogation, Ben," Kathy said.

"You really don't want to do that," Ben replied blandly.

She cut her eyes to him. "Oh?"

"No. And we do not use physical torture, so put that out of your mind. However, we do use chemicals, and they can be quite unpleasant."

Their conversation was cut off as the punks, four men and two women, were shoved into the room. The punks started shouting curses at Ben the instant they spotted him.

Kathy had stepped away from Ben. "How do they know who he is?" she whispered to Corrie.

"You knew what he looked like long before you met him, didn't you?"

"Well . . . yes. You do have a point."

"And remember this: The boss is the most wanted man in the world," Corrie continued. "And the most hated."

"I ain't tellin' you nothin'!" one of the men screamed at Ben. "You king-shit son of a bitch."

Ben sat on a corner of a old desk and smiled at the

captured punk. "Have you people had anything to eat?"

"Huh?" one of the women blurted.

"Are you hungry?" Ben asked pleasantly.

"It's a trick!" the man who had first screamed at Ben said. "Don't eat nothin'. The food is drugged."

Ben laughed at him and stood up, walking to the coffee urn, pulling himself a cup of coffee. He sugared it and returned to the desk, sitting down in his chair. He lifted the cup and took a sip. "The coffee is fine. If you're not hungry, have some coffee. It's a raw day." He looked at Buddy, who knew exactly what his dad was doing. "Remove their handcuffs, Buddy. And get them some coffee."

"Jump that bastard!" the defiant one yelled. "Kill him."

"How about this one?" Buddy asked, looking at the man who had just screamed at Ben.

"Sure. If he's that anxious to die, we can certainly oblige him."

Handcuffs removed, the others moved away from the mouthy prisoner, one of the women saying, "Shut up, Sonny. Let's just make the best of a bad situation. How about it?"

Sonny bluntly told her where she could shove her suggestion. Sideways.

She shrugged her shoulders and moved hesitantly toward the coffee urn. She drew a cup of coffee and looked first at the tray of sandwiches, then at Ben.

"Help yourself," Ben told her.

Five of the six drew mugs of coffee, helped themselves to sandwiches, and returned to their chairs. One of the men asked, "Is this our last meal, General?"

"That is entirely up to you. If you try to escape, you'll be shot dead. If you accept the obvious fact that you are prisoners, you'll be treated accordingly. If you wish to talk openly to me, you will be made as comfortable as possible for the duration of this campaign. If you do not wish to speak without coercion, you will be injected with a truth serum and questioned in that manner. It's quite unpleasant—so I'm told. Just like before the Great War, and after, your destiny is in your own hands."

"The cops was always pickin' on me," one of the men said sullenly.

"Don't hand me that shit!" Ben's voice turned hard, and all of the prisoners picked up on it immediately.

"I am French," a man said.

"Then I'll turn you over to Rene Seaux," Ben told him.

"Mon Dieu!" the man blurted. *"Non. Non!"*

Rene and his resistance people had little patience with the outlaws and warlords who had ravaged their country. They had a habit of questioning them quite savagely and then hanging them. It was not an uncommon sight to see punks dangling from tree limbs and lamp posts.

The others paled at the thought of being handed over to the French Resistance.

"He's bluffing!" Sonny said.

The others looked at Ben, sitting at his desk, smiling at them. But it was the hard and ruthless smile of a conqueror.

"No, he ain't." A man spoke the words softly. "Ben Raines don't bluff."

"I'm Marie," one of the woman said. She patted her

hair and smiled at Ben. "I could go for you, General."

"I'm very flattered," Ben replied. "But I don't believe the lady I am seeing would be very understanding about that."

"Ain't that the way it always is?" Marie said with a shrug of her shoulders.

Kathy noticed that Ben was drinking his coffee with his left hand. His right hand was out of sight. She could feel the tension in the air; the room seemed thick with it.

"Don't tell him nothin'!" Sonny yelled. "Can't you see what the bastard is doin'?"

"What am I doing?" Ben asked.

Sonny cussed Ben until he was breathless.

"You feel better now?" Ben asked him, his eyes watching the man's hand move toward his belt buckle.

Kathy was confused when Ben said, "Don't do it, Sonny. You'll never make it."

"Make what?" she asked.

"Fuck you, Raines!" Sonny yelled. Then, with a scream of rage, Sonny leaped toward Ben, a small knife suddenly appearing in his right hand.

Ben lifted his right hand and shot him.

The big .45 slug struck the punk in the center of the chest and stopped him, flinging him back and stretching him out on the floor. Kathy was stunned by the suddenness of it. One of the men prisoners started trembling.

"I don't want to die!" he blurted. "I don't want to die. I'll tell you whatever you want to know."

Buddy motioned toward two Rebels standing at the rear of the room and they dragged the dead punk out into the gloom of early evening. Kathy grimaced at the sound of Sonny's body being tossed off the porch to land on the wet earth.

Ben eased the hammer down on his .45 autoloader and holstered it. He picked up his coffee cup and took a sip. He looked at Marie and smiled. "We're all going to be very cooperative, aren't we, Marie?"

"You can bet your ass on that," the woman said, her voice very shaky.

After the blood on the floor had been cleaned up, and the others gone to bed, Kathy sat for a long time before the fire, while Ben worked at his desk. Finally she said, "You knew he had a knife, didn't you, Ben?"

"I suspected it."

"You could have ordered him searched and disarmed."

"Could have, but didn't." He leaned back in the chair. "Before you get all misty-eyed and filled with moral indignation, know this: Clarence 'Sonny' Fontaine was a warlord. He traded French civilians to the creepies in return for the safety of himself and his gang. He's been on Rene Seaux's most-wanted list for years. He dealt in human misery. If his death somehow diminishes you, then we'd better call off our relationship right now, Kathy."

"I have never in my life seen a man as cold-blooded as you, Ben."

"Then you'd better be glad Sonny Fontaine didn't get his hands on you, baby."

"Don't call me *baby!*"

Ben chuckled. "All right, Kathy. We had our little fling, and we both enjoyed it while it lasted. Now it's over. Go on back to your out-of-touch-with-reality friends. Wallow in your newly restored liberalism. It's been fun. Good night."

With her eyes flashing fire, Kathy Bonham rose from the chair and stalked out into the Paris mist, almost running into Buddy.

Buddy wisely and very quickly sidestepped her and entered the room, walking up to his father's desk. "You are hell on women, father." When Ben did not reply, he asked, "You think she'll be back?"

"I haven't any idea, son. But if you're asking for a guess, I would say no."

"Pity."

Ben shrugged that away, and his son laughed at him. "You'll never change, father. Someday you must tell me what qualities you are searching for in a woman."

Ben smiled and said, "I don't know that I have any set criteria, son. Just someone that I can get along with and who can get along with me, I suppose. Although sometimes I think God has not yet created that woman."

"Or you just haven't found her yet," Buddy said. He walked over to the closet to hang up his dripping raincoat just as Ben dropped a pencil on the floor and bent down to pick it up.

The room suddenly exploded in sound and fury and flames and Ben fell spinning into blackness.

Two

Ben never really lost consciousness, but for a couple of minutes he was addled and unable to make much sense out of what was happening, nor was he able to move his legs. He was cognizant of heavy gunfire and much yelling. Then it dawned on him that his legs were pinned under the rubble that was once his desk.

Rocket attack! His brain finally started working. The bastards must have had tunnels under us.

"Dad!" he heard Buddy calling his name through the ringing in his ears.

"The damn desk has me pinned, boy. And probably part of the roof as well. Get some people in here."

Buddy didn't wait for help. He muscled the rubble off his father and helped Ben to his feet. "Are you all right?"

"Yeah. Just pissed off, that's all. Where's my team?"

"I don't know. Probably outside in the fight." Both men had to shout to be heard over the yammering of automatic weapons and the smash of grenades.

Ben found his Thompson and wiped it clean of dust.

Fires started by other rockets tossed enough light through the blown-out windows of the house so Ben could see his weapon was not damaged.

Ben's team began to gather. Due to the construction of the home, Corrie had set up her radio in another room, and she and Beth were all right. Cooper had been outside, and he was unhurt. Jersey had just closed the door to the latrine behind the house. The latrine had blown over, trapping her inside, and except for her pride, she was unhurt. Jersey ran in the back door, cussing a blue streak.

"Talk about getting caught with your pants down," Cooper said with a grin.

Jersey gave him a look that was guaranteed to stop an angry grizzly.

"It's a coordinated attack against all battalions!" Corrie called from the radio room. "Pat, Tina, and Rebet have been forced to yield ground. The others are holding."

From memory, Ben reviewed the positions of his battalions. "Have Ike and Georgi shift some people over to help 10, 9, and 6 regain that ground, Have that special ops company with Dan's 3 Batt assist."

"They've broken through the rear!" a Rebel shouted. "Heads up inside the CP."

Ben turned to a blown-out window and fired at robed shapes running toward the house. One second later his team was firing, filling the smoky, explosive night with lead. There was no time for talk.

Buddy's weapon had been shattered by the first rocket, and he had smashed open a box of pineapples and was hurling Fire-Frag grenades into the misty night. The shrapnel-filled mini-bombs were doing terrible damage to the now wavering and broken line of Night People.

Ben burned clip after clip of .45 rounds into the night. The muddy, torn ground behind the old house was littered with the dead and dying. Any sensible commander would have ordered a pullback, but the creeps were fanatics; they kept coming, and they continued dying at the hands of the small team of Rebels in the command post.

Fifteen minutes after the first rocket was fired, the creeps pulled back from all positions, and the night slowly became silent—except for the sound of single gunshots as the Rebels moved through the carnage, shooting creeps in the head. Kathy Bonham watched in horror as Ben moved through the night, a .45 in each hand, finishing the cannibals.

"You got an audience, boss," Jersey said.

"Yeah. I know. Can't be helped. If she can't understand these people are as dangerous as bubonic plague and have to be wiped out to the last person, that's her problem."

A few minutes later he said to Corrie, "Get me reports. Let's see how hard we got hit."

Not too bad. For the Rebels were dressed head to foot in body armor and deaths were light. Most of the wounds were minor ones, but what really pissed Ben was the few Rebels the Night People had managed to take prisoner. Everyone knew what would happen to those men and women—they'd seen it before.

With the taking of Rebel prisoners, and the knowledge of what would happen to them, Lieutenant

Bonelli summed up the feelings of all the Rebels. "The creeps were standing ankle-deep in shit. Now they're in the shit up to their necks."

The Rebels had, up to this point, offered the creeps a quick and humane death. All that had abruptly changed during this rainy, bloody night. Now there would be no pity, no mercy, no compassion, no quick deaths for the Night People. The Rebels could be horribly brutal and savage when provoked—and they were provoked.

"Bring up the flamethrowers," Ben told Corrie. "And canisters of gas. Fuck these goddamn cannibals."

"The reporters?" Buddy questioned.

"They're idiots. They think war should be fought with rules. Savages don't know rules. In order to win, one has to come down to the level of the enemy . . . or very close to it. The press can stay, they can leave, or they can go to hell. I don't give a damn which one they choose."

Ben issued just one order. "Kill the enemy."

Ben viewed what was left of the first Rebel prisoner found. He knew there was no point in bringing the press in to see it. The majority of them would only come up with some excuse for the behavior of the Night People.

The woman had been with the Rebels for many years and was a platoon leader. She could be recognized only by the missing tip of her little finger, left hand.

Jersey said, "Knew her. She was a good person. Had

two kids. Her husband lost a leg during the Hawaiian campaign." Jersey spat on the ground. "I figure it took her long hours to die."

"Yeah," Ben said.

"We found a pocket of creeps that got themselves trapped," a scout said. " 'Bout a quarter of a mile from here. Part of their tunnel collapsed."

Ben's eyes were as cold as the North Sea. "Let's do it."

"We got a problem. They've been in radio contact with the press and have offered to surrender."

"And the press have gathered." It was not a question.

"All of them assigned to this operation."

The reporters began shouting questions at Ben as he walked up to the tunnel entrance, located in a small park on the outskirts of the city.

"Why is that gasoline tanker truck here, General?" one yelled.

"We're going to have a cookout," Ben said, and kept on walking.

He was true to his word. Explosives had already been placed, and the tanker started pumping gas into the tunnel. The reporters were quick on the uptake.

"That's against the rules of war!" a woman yelled.

"Idiot," Ben muttered.

The reporters were not as quick to notice the Rebels backing up. When the specially prepared explosives blew, igniting the gas fumes, about a dozen members of the press were knocked on their asses by the concussion. None were seriously hurt, except for their pride, which was considerably bruised, along with their asses.

The Rebels stood by impassively as the flames ate the life from the creepies.

"Those poor wretches offered to surrender!" a man yelled over the roar of flames coming from the seared mouth of the tunnel.

A few members of the press were standing close enough to Ben to hear him say, "Nobody tortures Rebels and gets away with it. Nobody. Not without paying a terrible price." He whispered to Corrie, "Tell the censors to let all copy from this incident go through as is. I want to see what side these people are on."

"Shit!" Corrie said, quite uncharacteristically. "I can tell you that right now."

"Let's be sure," Ben replied. "Bring me copies of all transmissions."

GENERAL RAINES DECLARES HIS TROOPS SUPERIOR TO ALL OTHER HUMAN BEINGS, one headline silently screamed.

GENERAL RAINES IGNORES ALL RULES OF WAR, another stated.

The rest were predictable. GENEVA CONVENTION TRAMPLED UPON BY RAINES'S REBELS.

RAINES'S REBELS NO BETTER THAN THE SAVAGES THEY FIGHT.

A few reported the incident without personal embellishment. They neither praised nor condemned Ben's actions in dealing with the creeps. They told it exactly as it happened—no more and no less.

"They stay, the rest leave," Ben ordered.

"That man has more cold nerve than Dick Tracy," President Blanton remarked, after reading of the expulsions of dozens of reporters.

"You can't be supportive of that racist, honky, Republican pig!" Rita Rivers hollered. "I heard he carries around a book authored by Rush Limbaugh!"

Homer almost told the woman to kiss his ass, but quickly thought better of it. Last time he'd done that, she told him to drop his drawers.

Ben began tightening the circle around Paris. Each day the Rebels gained another block or two or three, slowly closing the noose, forcing the creepies toward the center of the city.

Ike and Georgi took Charles de Gaulle Airport after a bitter two-day fight, while Rebet and West took Orly Airport. Now the Rebels could resupply by air . . . after cleaning up the runways and airing out the stink of creepies from the buildings. Ever so slowly the Rebels were pushing out of the suburbs and inching toward the city proper. Thanksgiving passed and November was gone. During the first week of December, the area was blanketed with a heavy covering of snow, and then the temperature plummeted, turning bitterly cold.

The nine battalions chased Duffy's army of thugs and punks and malcontents but could not make them close and slug it out.

"They plan to fight us guerrilla-style," Mike Richards told Ben. "Small units. Every scrap of intelligence we have, including information from the prisoners, points in that direction."

"Then they're fools," Ben said. "There are no better guerrilla fighters in the world than the Rebels."

"But Duffy doesn't know that," Mike replied.

"He soon will," Ben countered.

The Rebels began hammering at the creepies day and night, without letup. They flooded the sewers with tear gas and pepper gas and drove them aboveground, then shot them as they staggered out of their stinking lairs.

When the first battalions of Rebels hit the edge of the city proper, known as Ville de Paris, they were stopped cold by the Night People. Had the Rebels been able to use heavy artillery, the fight would have been much simpler and not nearly as costly to the Rebels. As it was, the Rebels suffered far fewer fatalities than the experts predicted, but their number of wounded was far more than first calculated. Ben had suffered a slight hand wound. Jersey had been burned on the thigh. Corrie had a radio shot off her back, and that left her badly bruised for a few days and out of commission.

The months-long campaign was taking its toll on the Rebels.

And they hadn't as yet entered the city proper.

Duffy's people had broken up into small units and were preparing to launch a guerrilla-type war against the Rebels. That act itself did not worry Ben . . . but what did worry him was that it would tie up more people in the field, and out of Paris, than he first anticipated. Duffy's people were also raping the countryside of food and warm clothing, making the already over-burdened residents pay a terrible price in human suffering.

"Your hand is healing nicely," Doctor Chase said, after changing the bandage.

"That bandage is bulky and gets in my way," Ben replied. "Take it off and put a Band-Aid on it."

"Not yet. And don't argue with me."

Fat chance of that happening.

"It was only a scratch to begin with!"

"You let it get infected, ding-dong."

"Ding-dong!"

"That's what I said. If you had gone to an aid-station shortly after it happened, a Band-Aid would have sufficed. But since you continue to believe yourself invulnerable to wounds that we mere mortals suffer . . . well, what's the point of arguing? You let it get infected."

"Ding-dong!"

Nick Stafford walked in the room just in time to put a momentary end to the bickering that had been going on for years between the two men. Nick was limping badly, and there was a bloody bandage on one leg.

"Good God!" Lamar said. "Another old soldier who thinks he is immortal. Sit down, you overage Rambo."

"I don't have time for that," Nick said. "I—"

"Sit down, goddamnit!" the chief of medicine roared. "Take off that boot and cut those fatigues away from that leg. And that's an order."

Ben was smiling, happy to have Chase direct his acid tongue toward someone else.

Chase took one look at the wound and said, "Hospital. Period. You're out of the field." He glared at Corrie. "Get an ambulance over here. Right now."

Nick started to protest and Ben said, "Don't say a word. Not unless you want a visit to the proctologist added to your chart."

That shut Nick up.

Chase smiled wickedly.

"I'll have your XO take over your battalion," Ben told the mercenary.

"Chuck Gilley," Nick said. "He's a good man. Ben, we're spread thin in the countryside. Too damn thin. Intell just reported that the Spanish army is up to their eyeballs fighting the Basques along the mountains. They're not going to be able to help us much. I personally think Duffy is planning to move his people east. Some batt coms agree with me, others don't. But I think the signs point that way."

Ben looked at map of Europe thumbtacked to the wall behind his desk. After a moment he asked, "Why, Nick?"

"They know they can't get into Spain. I think they're trying to link up with all the punks now gathering in Germany, Belgium, Holland, Switzerland, and Northern Italy. If that happens, they could put together a front that might take us months to bust through."

"The intell about Duffy's planned guerrilla war against us?"

"Pure bullshit. Duffy is not a fool. I think I know this guy. And if he's the man I think he is, he's got some good solid military experience under his belt. He came from a good, solid, upper-middle-class English family. You've read the file on him. He's got lots of smarts. And some tough paratrooper training."

"What about the gangs he's breaking up and forming into small guerrilla units?"

"Expendables," Nick said. "But they don't have a clue as to Duffy's real reason for breaking them up. It's just guesswork, Ben, that's all."

"But good guesswork. Thanks, Nick."

After Nick and Chase had left, Ben sat for a long time at his makeshift desk: an old door placed on two sawhorses. Ben didn't like to be outsmarted, and if Nick was right—and Ben felt he was—Duffy had done just that.

Problem was, there wasn't a damn thing Ben could do about it. The cities in France had to be cleared of creeps. The countryside had to be cleared of roaming gangs. And while Ben and his people were accomplishing those tasks, Duffy and his main body of fighters were going to be heading east to link up with thousands of other punks along a north/south route that ran through a half dozen countries.

"And they'll be moving in small groups," Ben muttered. "Probably at night, so that lets out strafing. Shit!"

He called in Mike Richards and Rene Seaux and laid it out for the men.

Mike frowned and then cursed. Rene stood up and paced the room. Rene was the first to speak. "They fed us false information, and we took the bait like a hungry fish. I am sorry, General. Truly sorry."

"It wasn't anyone's fault," Ben said. "The prisoners we took were the expendable ones, and they had been given false information. But to correct the mistake, we've got to move very fast."

"You have a plan, General?" Rene asked.

Ben nodded his head and frowned. "Not much of one. But it'll have to do." He walked to the door and opened it. "Corrie. Call all the batt coms in. I want them here like a hour ago!"

Three

"I can't even find the damn borders on these old maps!" the former Navy SEAL, Ike McGowan, bitched.

"You redneck ninny," Dan Gray, the former British Special Air Service officer, said with a smile. He couldn't let this pass. "Don't confuse that saltwater-logged brain of yours with international borders. It's much too much for a fat frogman to absorb."

"SEAL, goddamnit!" the Mississippi-born Ike told him for about the one millionth time. "SEAL! You tea-drinkin' Limey priss-pot. And I've lost fifteen pounds, thank you anyway." He did his best to ignore Dan's chuckling and said, "Ben, this idea sucks! We're goin' to be spread all over the damn map!" He shook his head. "But if we don't do it, that bunch of punks and thugs stand a pretty good chance of boggin' us down for months." He held up a finger. "But . . . gettin' supplies to you is goin' to be tough, and where in the hell are the pathfinders goin' to set up the DZ?"

Ben pointed to a map. "Here, here, and here."

Ike shook his head. "It's goin' to be tight."

"Not with the type of chutes we'll be using. Relax, Ike. You've jumped into tighter places."

"Ben," Ike persisted. "Those were quick in and outs. Snatch-and-grab ops. The weather can turn shitty over there in a matter of minutes and lock you people in. And," he added with enough ice in his voice to match the climate outside the room, "we both were much younger back then."

"I'll be landing on a nice, soft field of snow," Ben said with a smile. "Let's stop bickering. It's settled." He turned to Thermopolis. "Therm, logistics?"

"Are you kidding?" the hippie-turned-warrior said. "There is already snow between here and there that's ass-deep to a giraffe. You won't have tanks. You won't have heavy artillery. The list of what we can't immediately get to you is longer than a child's Christmas list. You will have to seize and clear Cointrin Airport the very first thing. And if the weather turns lousy, you just may be cut off for days."

"Swiss Resistance people are going to meet us," Ben said. "Up here," he pointed to the map, "we have German Resistance groups ready to start blocking roads. Down here, Italian Resistance groups are in place and ready to go. It's a piece of cake." He eyeballed the group. "And it's settled," Ben ended the discussion.

Ben and his 1 Batt, Jackie Malone and her 12 Batt, Danjou and his 7 Batt, Dan and the 3 Batt, Buddy and his 8 Batt special ops group, and West and his 4 Batt would be jumping into and around Geneva.

Ike, Pat O'Shea, Tina, Rebet, Raul, and Nick would

concentrate on clearing out Paris proper. Rene Seaux and his resistance people would be with Ike's command.

Georgi, Greenwalt, Jim Peters, Buck Taylor, Mike Post, and Paul Harrison would be out in the French countryside, after the dregs of Duffy's army of punks. They would start north and south of Paris and work east, toward Ben's position, working in a wedge-shaped march, with the point aimed at Geneva.

"Therm," Ben added, "Emil will stay with you. I don't want to have to put up with him on this op."

"Thank you so very much, Ben."

"You're welcome. Let's get this circus moving."

The steel wall of secrecy came down with a bang. The press knew something was up, they just didn't know what. And those in the know weren't talking.

Ben had long held the opinion that no military campaign could be completely successful as long as the press was in any way involved. His philosophy was to win the war first and *then* invite the press to visit. Ben was of the opinion that for years the majority of America's press had hated the military and would stop at nothing to criticize, belittle, and nitpick anything the military did. And so far the majority of the press had done nothing to lessen that opinion.

The head of meteorology had some good news. "The way it looks now, we feel you're going to have about three days of excellent weather, General. The next two days will show a gradual deterioration, then snow."

Ben told the batt coms who were jumping in with him, "One day to take the airport, two days to gather the air-dropped supplies, two days to get the runways in shape." He smiled at Thermopolis. "Would you like to jump in with us, Therm?"

"No, I most certainly would not!" Therm said quickly. "But thank you so very much for the invitation."

Therm beat it out of the ready room and back to his own operations building. Throwing his body out of a perfectly good airplane held absolutely no appeal for Thermopolis.

"We don't have enough planes to drop five full battalions in at once," Ben was told. "Not with supply drops as well. We can drop two battalions in with supplies, then two more that afternoon, then two more the next day. Sorry, General."

Ben had already figured that out. There was nothing he could do about it. "My 1 Batt and Dan's 3 Batt will go in first, followed that afternoon by Buddy's special ops group and West's 4 Batt. At dawn the next morning, Danjou's 7 Batt and Jackie's 12 Batt will come in. The pathfinders are in place. They HALOed in. (High Altitude, Low Opening.) They'll smoke the DZ. We go in tomorrow morning. That's it."

What press remained had gathered at both Orly and Charles de Gaulle airports. Ben and his people loaded up without a word and took off. At Ben's instruction, the pilots headed due north and then cut toward Geneva. Helicopters were originally planned to be used to land troops, but much to the surprise of the weather prognosticators, the weather turned so bad the choppers were all but useless.

"So much for modern science," Jersey muttered, sitting next to Ben in the plane.

"The weather around Geneva is good," Ben told her. "Cold, but ideal for jumping."

"Wonderful," Jersey replied with a total lack of enthusiasm. Jersey had never developed Ben's love of jumping.

Ben laughed at her and stood up, walking—waddling, with all the equipment he was carrying—to the rear door. It was not a long flight, and he was going to act as jumpmaster. He would be the last one out of the big transport.

Ben sat down and waited for the crew chief's signal.

Duffy Williams sat and stared at the message just handed him. Ben Raines and about six or seven battalions were in the process of leaving the Paris area by transport plane. The spy had said the Rebels walked funny; looked like they were loaded down with so much gear they were bowlegged. Duffy, an ex-paratrooper, knew exactly what that meant. Airborne troops had to carry so much gear they appeared to be bowlegged under all the weight. That's where the term *straightleg* came from. Any nonjumper was sometimes sarcastically referred to by paratroopers as a straightleg, or leg.

So the Eagle himself was leading an airborne drop, Duffy mused. But where? The spy said all the planes headed north. *North?* Were the Rebels going to drop into Belgium? That had to be it. Couldn't mean anything else. Good. His plan was working.

The Judge in Geneva looked at the message just handed him by a runner from communications. Rebel paratroopers leaving Paris and heading north. *North?* That had to mean the Rebels had chosen to invade Brussels. Good. That could only mean the Rebels were not going to attack Switzerland until spring. That gave his people several more months to prepare for the invasion.

The Judge looked over at the screaming, half-maddened child he'd been brought for lunch. A nice fat child. He smiled and reached for his knife.

Ben received the signal from the crew chief. One minute to red light. "Stand up!" he shouted.

The Rebels laboriously rose to their boots.

"Check equipment!"

Equipment checked. The rear gate lowered and a blast of frigid air swirled around the jumpers.

"Hook up!" Ben shouted.

The sticks on either side of the plane hooked their static lines to the wire.

"Hey, boss!" Jersey shouted. "I forgot how to yodel. Do I get to stay in the plane?"

Ben grinned at her, his eyes on the lights, waiting for the green. "Keep your feet together when you hit!" Ben shouted. "I don't want any cracked spines." It was an unnecessary command from an old paratrooper, for the chutes they were using allowed the jumpers to land easily, unlike the old models that left raspberries on the shoulders and sometimes promised a very hard landing.

The green light popped on.

"Go! Go! Go!" Ben shouted, and the lines shuffled forward toward the gaping rear of the plane.

Static lines stretched tight and the chutes popped, the grunting of the jumpers at the opening shock lost in the cold air and the roaring of engines. Ben jumped into nothing, legs together, knees slightly bent, arms folded.

The few creepies in the city of Geneva who were at street level could but stand and stare in disbelief at the hundreds of chutes that floated down to the ground— Rebels and equipment. By the time they recovered from their shock, several hundred Rebels were running through the snow toward the airport runways and terminal buildings.

Jersey spilled too much air and landed wrong, the chute collapsing all over her. "Shit! Shit! Shit!" she hollered, her voice muffled under all the panels. "I hate jumpin' out of airplanes."

Beth ran over to her and slashed at the lines with a jump knife, freeing the diminutive bodyguard. "Get me outta here, goddamnit!" Jersey shouted.

Ben landed with a grunt just a few yards away from the cussing, hollering, kicking, and flailing Jersey . . . and laughing Beth. He grabbed up his equipment bag, uncorked his .223 CAR—he had opted for the lighter weapon because of its ease of handling—and ran over to Beth and Jersey just as Jersey was struggling to her boots.

"Let's go, short-stuff!" Ben shouted, and took off for the airport, his team right behind him.

Dan and his people had landed south of the city, the River Rhone between Ben and his group.

The first Rebels had jumped in with only light machine guns, a few mortars, and three days of rations. The heavier .50's and other gear would be coming in about fifteen minutes behind them. Teams of Rebels would be jumping in just seconds behind the equipment, to unpack and set up. It was a dangerous drop, and Ben knew it, but it had to be done.

The airport was three miles from the city. It was going to be dicey. Very dicey.

"They're down!" The word was shouted to Ike. "Looks like everyone made it in okay."

"It was a complete surprise." Another shout brought a smile to Ike's lips.

But the smile quickly faded. "Estimates say there are probably eight to ten thousand creeps in and around that city," he said to no one in particular. "It's goin' be chancy as hell until Buddy and West get on the ground."

"I hope this doesn't turn out to be one town too far," Tina said, a grim expression on her beautiful face, after looking at a map and silently counting the miles between Paris and Geneva.

"Yeah," was all Ike said in reply.

* * *

Cooper was carrying a SAW (squad automatic weapon). A 5.56-mm machine gun with an effective range of about 1200 meters. The SAW utilized a 200-round magazine, and Cooper was carrying two more of those. Corrie was carrying another mag for the SAW, and Jersey and Ben each carried a full mag for the weapon. The Rebels were literally staggering under the weight of weapons and ammo.

Cooper bi-podded the SAW and fell down in the snow as a line of creeps ran toward them. The line crumpled and went down under the hail of 5.56 lead, and the snow turned technicolor. Cooper was on his feet and running before the death kicks stopped.

Bloop tubes fitted under the barrels of M-16's blooped out their 40-mm grenades, and more lines of creepies went down as the Rebels clawed their way toward the tarmac. The Rebels ran through the bloody snow.

Across the river Dan and his 3 Batt were on the edge of town and setting up a holding position. The transport planes were hammering their way back to Paris, where Buddy and West and their batts were impatiently waiting on the tarmac.

By now the press knew a big op was in progress, but they could not get a word out of anybody. They finally decided it had to be Brussels and reported it. Then they saw the transports returning from the east and started cussing. Suddenly P-51E's screamed overhead, traveling at more than 500 mph, heading east, carrying a tremendous payload.

"What the hell is going on?" Paul Carson yelled.

Kathy Bonham shrugged her shoulders. "Typical Ben Raines," she said.

The newly built and highly modified Mustangs began taking out the bridges that crossed the Rhone River. They took out every bridge except the double span that connected Place Bel-Air with Quai des Bergues. Then a squadron banked and came in low over the airport, the .50-caliber guns yammering and making a big bloody mess of the creepies trying to cross the runways to stop Ben's 1 Batt. The pilots did not use their cannon for fear of further damaging the runaways. As it stood now, it was going to be a massive undertaking for the thin ranks of Rebels to clear away all the debris now littering the runways . . . in the time Ben had alloted for them to work.

These were the traditional Night People, hooded and robed, and the pilots had no difficulty in telling the good guys from the bad guys. And as Ben quickly found out, they shared one other thing with their brothers and sisters in cannibalism: They stank like buzzard puke.

Ben ran into a building on the outer edge of the airport, his team right behind him, and came face to face with several creepies. He lifted his CAR and pulled the trigger back and held it, letting the .223 slugs howl and spit. Jersey stepped up and added her M-16, as did Beth with her CAR. The creepies flopped on the dirty floor and died.

"Phew!" Beth said, wrinkling her nose. "Some things never change, do they?"

Cooper came panting up with his SAW, and Ben pointed to a shattered window. "Set up there, Coop, and keep a good eye out. We'll toss these bodies outside." That done, Ben turned to Corrie. "Bump Dan and get a situation report."

After a few moments, she said, "Great. No one hurt and advancing on schedule. We took them by surprise on both ends of town."

"But the element of surprise is gone now," Jersey said. "Now it comes down to holding what we have."

"And here they come!" Cooper yelled.

Four

None of the Rebels had ever been able to ascertain why the Night People were so infatuated with airports. But they seemed drawn to them like steel shavings to a magnet. And this airport was no different. The creeps poured out of buildings, met the Rebels, and died in the snow and on the tarmac.

The fight for the airport was savage but relatively brief, for the other creeps in the city thought they were being attacked on all sides by thousands of troops— another of Ben's ideas. When the jumpers had left the planes, the pilots did a slow circle of the outer edges of the city with crew members tossing out canisters of smoke and napalm that exploded upon contact with the ground, sending the creepies in the city into a wild panic, running in all directions instead of beefing up the two points that were being attacked.

By nine o'clock in the morning the airport was in firm Rebel hands. Snipers armed with .50-caliber rifles were on the high ground and on rooftops, patrols were out against infiltration, and Ben was positioning his 1 Batt for an attack that never came.

Dan had dug his 3 Batt in tight just inside the city proper and was bracing for a counterattack . . . that never came in full force that morning.

"I wonder why the flesh-eating savages are waiting?" Dan radioed Ben. In the distance the sounds of delayed-action bombs boomed. About half of the bombs dropped after the jump were set to go off all during the morning, further confusing the creeps.

"I don't know," Ben replied. "I'm just glad they are." He checked his watch. Three hours max until Buddy and West dropped in.

And there was no guarantee that Duffy would take the false bait and not try an end around.

"Approximately four hundred kilometers from Paris to Geneva," Beth said. "Figuring ground time to load, the planes just might be back here way ahead of planned schedule."

Ben nodded his head. "We can always hope."

The pilots poured it on, and the second drop was ninety minutes ahead of schedule. Much to the delight of the worried Rebels north and south of the city, and much to the chagrin of the creeps in the city, just before noon the skies around the city were filled with blossoming chutes.

Buddy and his 8 Batt linked up with his father, and West and his 4 Batt beefed up Dan's troops on the other side of the river.

"Just as soon as Jackie and Danjou are on the ground tomorrow," Ben said to Corrie, "bump Ike and have him release the news to the press." He chuckled. "Then we'll see what Duffy does next."

The creeps tried several night attacks against the Rebels, but the commanders had anticipated that and threw them back with superior firepower and ruthless fighting ability.

Just after dawn, when the creepies in the city saw two more full battalions of Rebels fill the faintly blue skies, they knew it was all over for them. The Night People had never successfully met the Rebels . . . anywhere in the world.

"Well, I'll be damned," a reporter said, after reading the press release from Ike. "Eight full battalions of Rebels have linked up with resistance fighters from Germany, Switzerland, and Italy and thrown up a north/south line. They've got Duffy and his people in a box."

"We're fucked!" Duffy said, after reading the communiqué from his communications people. "That bastard Ben Raines saw through it and beat us to the punch."

"Now what happens?" another reporter asked.

"Damn good question," Ben responded to Jersey's inquiry. "If Duffy figures out this is all one big bluff, we could be in very real trouble."

"Would you believe this town was first settled by people twenty-five hundred years before Christ?" Beth said, reading from an old tourist pamphlet.

"The Celts settled here about 100 B.C.," Ben replied. "Various tribes and countries have been fighting over this area for several thousand years."

"And here we are," Cooper said. "Stone axes and

bows and arrows have been replaced by automatic weapons and airplanes."

"That's good, Coop," Jersey said. "Very good. You do have a brain after all. I've been wondering about that for years."

"Let's get this town cleaned out," Ben said, putting an end to it.

The runways were ready to receive planes: Huge transports began landing, disgorging Hummers, APCs, tanks, and all the other supplies needed to wage war. Reporters tried to hitch rides on the planes, to no avail. At Ben's orders, this new front was off-limits to the press.

Street by street the Rebels began taking Geneva from the Night People.

But to the east of Ben, there was trouble waiting that he knew nothing about—yet.

"Bruno Bottger," Mike Richards said, taking a seat in Ben's temporary CP.

"Who?" Ben looked up.

"Self-styled Nazi and head of the new Reich. Bruno Bottger. He and his followers have just overthrown the new government of Germany, and they are the powers to be reckoned with. Bruno is a former skinhead and commander of an army thought to be from 75,000 to 125,000 strong. Well armed, disciplined, and ready to fight for their beliefs."

Ben tossed his pencil to the desk and stared at Mike for a moment. "You have any more surprises for me, Mike?"

"I'm just getting started. I told you Bruno Bottger was a former skinhead. When he was twenty, he gave it all up and renounced the movement. Then he went to college, got his degree, and enlisted in the army. He was quickly chosen for the German equivalent of our OCS. Made top grades all the way through, and promotions came quickly for him. He was a captain when the balloon went up."

Ben felt a sick feeling start growing in the pit of his stomach. "Those German troops who came over to help us against Hoffman?"*

"We don't know. We think they're dead, Ben. All of them that Bruno could round up."

Ben rubbed his face with his big, hard hands. He felt suddenly depressed. He thought of those brave men of the GSG-9 who had traveled so far to aid the Rebels. Colonel Lenz, Major Streicher, Major Dietl, and all the others.

"Bruno killed them, or had them killed?"

"We think so. We think he'd taken them prisoner when he made his bid to seize power, and when he learned the Rebels had been named the World Stabilization Force, he had them all shot."

"I feel like puking."

"Yeah. I do know the feeling."

"Lenz and some of the others were going to stay with me and join up. They talked about it; they really wanted to stay and fight with us. But love of country pulled them back to Germany. They all talked with me at length. And to a man they were afraid something like this was going to happen." Ben shook his head and looked down at a map for a moment, then lifted his

*BATTLE IN THE ASHES—Zebra Books.

eyes to Mike. "I probably know the answer, but I have to ask: The Jews in Germany?"

"In hiding, Ben. And not just in Germany. And . . . a good percentage of the members of Bruno's army were not all born in Germany. His forces are made up of men and women from all around the world. But no blacks, Jews, mixed bloods. Hell, you know the drill."

"Unfortunately," Ben said, "I do." He grimaced. "What Reich is this one, Mike? Sixth or seventh?"

"Hell, who knows?" the chief of intelligence replied. "The bottom line is this, Ben: We think Bruno has agreed to help Duffy Williams." He held up a warning finger. "But before he does, Duffy has to get rid of all the minorities in his army."

"Get . . . rid of?"

"Yes. We think that means kill them."

"That suits the shit outta me," Marie Vidalier told Duffy. "The sooner we can get rid of all the niggers in the world, the better off we'll all be."

"Personally I'd rather get rid of Ben Raines," Paul Zayon said. "But if shootin' all the spades we got with us is the only way Bruno will help us . . ." He shrugged his shoulders. "Hell, let's do it."

Duffy looked at the other gang leaders: Tom Spivey, Dave Ingle, Robert Fryoux, Ned Veasey, Eddie Stamp, John Monson, Guy Caston, Philipe Soileau. To a person, they slowly shook their heads in agreement.

Duffy looked at two men guarding the door to the meeting room. "Let them in," he called.

The door was opened, and two men marched into

the room. They were blond and fair and military in bearing. Both of them about thirty years old. They were not related but could have passed for brothers in appearance, and thinking. They were from Bruno Bottger's army and had brazenly driven across country to meet with Duffy.

"Well?" one of the men asked Duffy.

"We've agreed to your terms."

"Good, good!" the other man said. "General Bottger will be pleased. Now you must show your good faith to us so we can report to the general."

"How?"

"That jungle bunny standing out in the hall," the other man said. "Call him in here, and shoot him in our presence."

Duffy stared at the man for a few seconds, then sighed and nodded his head. "Call that shine in here," he said.

The black gangster from Marseille strolled in and up to Duffy, seated at a desk. "You wanna see me, Duf?"

"Yeah," Duffy said, then lifted a 9 mm and shot the man in the center of the forehead.

"Oh, good!" one of the Aryan twins shouted, as the black hit the floor. "Very good."

"Excellent!" the other cried out in joy. "You are a man of your word, Herr Williams. You are a true believer in the superiority of the white race."

"Now," the other one said, "you must all shoot a porch monkey in our presence. Anyone who does not will be considered an enemy to the MEF."

"The MEF?" Philipe Soileau questioned.

"Yes. The Minority Eradication Force."

"Oh, what the hell!" Marie said. "I shot my own sister, and haven't lost any sleep over it. Bring in another shine."

It was to be a very bloody and treacherous night.

Mahmud the Terrible, Abdul, Ahmed Popov, Tuba Salami, Jose LaBamba, Romero Richardo, and about two dozen other gang leaders of Negro and Spanish heritage hit the air when the rumors started flying that cold winter's night. They headed for the French countryside faster than any of them had ever moved in their lives. Since Tony Green, a.k.a. Big Stomper, and several other gang leaders of dubious parental couplings weren't exactly certain of their own lineage, they hit the trail with the more obvious.

In Ben's CP, Corrie smiled with grim soldier humor as the airwaves filled with frantic messages.

Ben noticed the smile and asked, "What do you find so amusing, Corrie?"

"Panic in the ranks of Duffy's army. The purge has begun."

"I wonder why I don't feel a bit of sympathy for them," said Jersey, whose ancestors 'way back were Apache Indian. She looked up from cleaning her M-16, her dark eyes unreadable, as usual.

"What are they saying?" Beth asked.

"Some of Bruno's men met with Duffy earlier today. Made each of the gang leaders aligned with Duffy shoot a minority person to prove their allegiance to something called the MEF—I don't know what that is. About a dozen or so minority gang leaders and their followers took off, fanning out over the countryside. Wait a minute." She listened for a moment and then said, "The MEF is the Minority Eradication Force." She shook her head and took off her headset. "I lost the transmission—it's garbled. But there sure is a lot of panic going on."

"Nice folks, the MEF," Cooper said. "They're all heart. We're about to be flooded with gang members, boss."

"Probably some of them will seek sanctuary with us," Ben replied. "But they get no amnesty. If they choose to surrender, we'll accept them, but only with the condition that they must stand trial for their crimes, either here or back in North America. Corrie, have communications start broadcasting that on an open frequency. I want those punks to know where they stand, loud and clear."

"The press is going to pick it up," Jersey said.

"It'll give them something to write about. And I'm sure some of them will condemn me for this action."

With the arrival of all the battalions Ben had assigned to the taking of Geneva, the Rebels were gradually pushing the creepies toward both sides of the river. Ben was trying hard not to destroy the small city, but he was determined not to lose a single Rebel life just to save a building—not if he could help it.

Ben and his people had fought their way to the north side of the Rue de Lyon, with one detachment slugging it out to the edge of the Parc Geisendorf, and Ben and his battalion fighting their way down the Rue de la Servette.

Dan and his command had clawed their way to the

north side of the Museum d'Histoire Naturelle—which had been looted and the interior spray-painted with slogans and obscenities—naturally. Punks and other assorted street slime had a thing about cans of spray paint. Over the years liberals maintained that the poor little deprived darlings were only expressing themselves, but conservatives had quite a different opinion . . . including the fact that it cost taxpayers a lot of money to clean up what the pus-brains sprayed paint on.

"Goddamn lowlife good-for-nothing hooligans!" Dan cursed, standing inside the museum and gazing at the destruction. He had a few dozen other very choice words for people who wantonly destroyed such beauty.

Then Dan hit the deck as creepies opened up with automatic weapons. He had a few more very choice words to say about them, too, before he crawled to his knees and gave the entire line of creeps a full thirty-round clip of .223's.

"You all right, Colonel?" one of his people called.

"Just ducky!" Dan said, brushing the dirt off his BDU's. He glared at the words spray-painted on the wall in huge block letters.

FUCK YOU

"Indeed," Dan said. "How literate. How profound. The intelligence which moved the hand to create such a whimsical phrase surely must be of staggeringly high proportions." He felt a breeze fan his buttocks and twisted around and looked. Somehow he had ripped the entire seat out of his BDU trousers.

The Englishman stared at the words for a moment longer, then lifted his clenched right fist and extended his middle finger toward the words on the wall.

He ignored the laughter of his people as he marched out the front door with as much dignity as he could muster, which was considerable when one considered that his drawers were hanging out.

Five

One of Bruno's aides was pacing the polished floor of the general's office as he spoke. "General Bottger, we are missing a golden opportunity. Our spies tell us that Ben Raines has not joined with any sizeable resistance force. Those silly Swiss have only a few hundred fighters at best. We could send our vastly superior forces in and wipe out Ben Raines and his battalions in Geneva once and for all."

Bottger shook his head and smiled, the smile never reaching his cold, very pale blue eyes. "No. And the reason is obvious, my dear Claude."

"It escapes me, General."

"Simple deduction, Claude," Bottger said smugly. "It's a trap. I have studied Ben Raines extensively—for years. Every campaign. I know the man better than he knows himself. He has carefully nurtured the image of himself as a chance-taker. He is hoping we will fall for this ploy. But we won't. I think that Ben Raines has very furtively, over a period of weeks, moved several battalions of Rebels to just a few miles west of Geneva, and there they wait in hiding for us to try something like you have suggested. This is too obvious a trap—a trap set for us. We won't play Ben Raines's game this time."

"Ahhh!" Claude said. "I see. Of course. You are truly brilliant, General."

"Of course I am," Bruno said. "General Raines has finally met his intellectual match." He smiled. "Me!"

Ben looked at the map for the one hundredth time and shook his head in disbelief. "This Bruno Bottger person is not as smart as he thinks he is. He's passing up a golden opportunity by not coming in here and tangling with us. If he really has six or seven divisions of combat-ready troops, he could easily overwhelm us here in Geneva."

"That thought has occurred to me," Buddy Raines said.

"Then why doesn't he do it?" Cooper asked.

Ben smiled. "He just might believe it's a trap. That's the only reason I can come up with."

"We're sitting here with six battalions spread out across the city and Bruno has seven *divisions?*" Jersey said. "What kind of trap could we have for him?"

"One of his own making," Ben said. "Let him think it. I hope he continues thinking it."

Ben and his battalions had pushed the creeps into a downtown pocket of a few blocks on the north side of the river, and Dan had done the same on the south side. The fighting was now close up and nasty.

"One thing Bottger did was to kill every creepie he

could find in the territory he controls," Mike Richards said. "Of course he also killed every minority he could find, too," he added dryly.

Mike got along well with the minorities in the Rebel army, but he had no patience with people—of any color—who wanted something for nothing and who blamed all their woes on people not of their color. It had not always been that way, for Mike was deep-South born; but slowly, over the years, Mike had shed most of his prejudices and actually become very good friends with some blacks in the Rebel army, astounding Ben and probably himself.

Ben was silent for a moment, then again met the eyes of his chief of intelligence. "How reliable is your information about the MEF, Mike?"

"Very good. But we have no plants within his army." Mike smiled. "Bruno took a cue from you and polygraphs his people. There is no way we can penetrate any of the five circles leading to him."

"Five circles, Mike?"

"There will be a comprehensive report on your desk tomorrow, Ben. But the five circles start at company levels and work up to the inner circle. Five is company, then battalion, regiment, division, and finally the inner circle, which is one."

Ben grunted. "Bastard is smart, I'll give him that. But how paranoid is he?"

Mike smiled, snapped his fingers, and pointed his index finger at Ben. "Right on the money, boss. Bruno even has food tasters . . . when he doesn't cook himself, which is not often. He considers himself to be quite a gourmet chef. He has a dozen lookalikes, and no one aligned with us has ever been able to pinpoint his exact location—with any accuracy.''

"So that lets out any wet work on our part.''

"You got it. My people have yet to figure out a way to kill the bastard.''

Ben let that slide for the time being. If Mike's boys and girls couldn't come up with a way to kill Bruno, it simply couldn't be done.

"How long before Geneva is clean?''

"About a week,'' Ben replied. "Duffy and his people are being slowly pushed our way by Ike. The French Resistance Force is growing, and it won't be long before it will be a large enough army to take some of the strain off us. Units of the FRF are already in place north and south of us with more coming in. Just as soon as Geneva is declared clean, I'm going to take my battalion and head west for a look-see.''

Mike smiled. "Things getting too dull around here for you, Ben?''

Ben returned the smile. "My people are covering me like a blanket, Mike. I can't get into any trouble in this city. But in about a week, all that is about to change.''

Ben left Dan in charge of the nearly completed task of clearing out Geneva, and with his 1 Batt and armor pulled out and headed south toward Grenoble. Dan raised no hell about him leaving, for he knew it would do no good. Ike bitched and cussed over the air, but he knew it was falling on deaf ears and soon said, "Oh, to hell with it!'' and broke the connection.

Ben and his battalion rode for two hours over incredibly bad roads without seeing a living being. All knew what had happened to the people, but all were loath to speak the words: The creeps had ranged out many miles from Geneva, in all directions, taken prisoners whenever they could find them, and eaten them.

About thirty kilometers from the city, they left the main road when they saw smoke coming from many chimneys in the distance. Ben halted the convoy and sent scouts ahead to check it out. They came back shaking their heads.

"They're in bad shape, General. Many of them are starving to death. The gangs came through not long ago and took all the food. They don't have anything in the way of medicines, either. Many of them are awful sick."

"Mean damn country for an airdrop," Cooper commented. "And those winds are really rough."

"There is a pretty good-sized valley just over the way," Beth said, pointing. "We could use that for a DZ."

While the scouts checked the valley, Ben walked through part of the village, growing angrier by the second. These were mostly old people, unable to fend for themselves, and a few young women with half-starved babies.

"Old people don't taste good," a Rebel who spoke fluent French told Ben. "The creeps leave them alone. The gangs took all the young women to rape and then trade to the creeps . . . and some of the young boys, too," he added. "The young men are used as slaves until they're worn out and then traded to the creeps."

"Tell them we're arranging to have food and medicine flown in," Ben said. "Ask about Lyons."

"No creeps there," the Rebel said, after a moment of French too fast for Ben to follow. His French was not all that good. "They pulled out to beef up the bunch in Geneva. He says he heard that the cannibals pulled out of the entire eastern part of France. Grenoble, Avigon, Marseille, Toulon, Cannes, Nice. Some went to Geneva, but most of the others broke up into small groups and ran for hiding."

"I hate to hear that," Ben said. "The bastards will be popping up everywhere we go." He was thoughtful for a moment. Then his eyes met those of Mike Richards, who had walked up in time to hear most of the conversation. Mike spoke fluent French—and some five other languages and a dozen dialects.

Mike nodded his head. "They planned it, Ben. Has to be. They figured this was the only way to keep their movement alive. I don't think they knew we were dropping in on them in Geneva. However, I do believe the breaking up was planned the instant we hit the continent . . . or perhaps long before. That's guesswork."

"Pretty good guesswork, Mike. I agree. Shit!" Ben startled the old Frenchman, who stepped back, wide-eyed. Shit was a word recognized nearly worldwide. The other one rhymed with luck. Ben smiled and patted the elderly man's bone-thin shoulder. "You'll be all right," he said, in very bad French. "We'll take care of you."

The old man smiled and spoke in fast French. Mike laughed and gave the man a bag of tobacco and papers. "What'd he say?" Ben asked.

Mike said, "He said the Americans took care of us in '44, too. And then the French government and many of the people, as usual, turned their asses to their liberators. He was not one of those types of people. He fought with the French Resistance and has the papers to prove it."

"My God, Mike. How old is this man?"

"He's almost ninety."

Jersey walked by and the old man grinned, his eyes following her. He rolled his eyes, and said, "Oh, *la-la!*"

Jersey laughed and said, "At his age, he wouldn't know what to do with it, anyway."

"Don't bet on it, *chérie,*" the old man said, in nearly flawless English, just before his wife whacked him across the butt with a straw broom.

Several Rebel doctors and medics dropped in with supplies and immediately went to work. A small detachment of Rebel troops came in with them, and the following morning, Ben and his 1 Batt pulled out. Annecy was a looted and destroyed ghost town. The resort town of Aix-les-Bains was lifeless. They drove along the shores of the blue-watered and beautiful, mountain-rimmed Lac d'Annecy and continued on toward Chambery. This was wild and lovely country, with dark forests, deep valleys, and towering limestone cliffs. They found Chambery virtually deserted, except for a small gang of punks that had fled for their lives upon hearing of Bruno Bottger's orders of extermination.

"Carry your asses on," the punk leader told a scout,

the first Rebel to enter the city. Just as the words left his mouth, the punk, a man who called himself Junkyard Doggy Woggy Do Da Day, found himself on the ground, his mouth bloody from the butt of a rifle, and a dozen Rebels pointing various types of weapons at him and his followers.

"Shitttt!" Doggy hollered. "How come you whuppin' on me, man? You a brother!"

The Rebel scout glared down at the punk in the snowy street. "I most definitely am *not* your brother."

"Well," Junkyard Doggy Woggy said, spitting out part of a broken tooth, "I din mean no disrespect. I thoughts you was part of that mean-assed honky Duffy's army."

The scout smiled . . . sort of. "No, but I am part of the meanest-assed army you're ever likely to see."

"The Rebels?" Doggy Woggy whispered.

"That's right."

"Shitttt!" He took a deep breath. "Don't nobody do nothin' stupid!" he hollered to his people, his words echoing around the quiet streets of the old town. "Lay down your guns and step out so's these nice people can see you. And keep your hands high up in the air."

"A very wise thing to say," the scout told him.

"I figured so. Can I get up?"

"Slowly."

The scout could see that Junkyard was frightened, and he had every right to be.

Junkyard Doggy Woggy cut his eyes as the tires on Ben's Hummer slowly crunched over the snow. Doggy could vividly remember when he was a punk back in Los Angeles; back when punks had more rights than law-abiding citizens. Back when a brick used to bash someone's head in was declared a nonlethal weapon. Back when a tiny percentage of the city's population could form gangs and terrorize and intimidate an entire city. Back when liberal Democrats ran things. Back when people could riot and burn and loot and get away with it.

Back before Ben Raines.

Doggy watched the man with the salt and pepper hair get out of the Hummer and walk toward him. "That's Ben Raines, ain't it?"

"That's right," the scout said.

"I'm in deep shit, ain't I?"

"That's right."

Bathed and fumigated, dressed in old BDUs with a large white P painted on the back, and wearing clean underwear, Junkyard was brought to Ben's CP in the center of the town.

"Sit down," Ben told him.

Junkyard sat.

"What is your name? And don't give me any street-talk bullshit."

"Clarence Wilson," he blurted. "My daddy run off when I was just a little boy. My mamma din have no job, and she beat me. The cops picked on me all the time even though I was really a good boy. I din have no toys to play with. I—"

"Shut up," Ben told him.

Clarence shut up.

"You sound like a Democrat running for political office. Now you listen to me, Clarence. You're going to tell me everything you know about Duffy Williams and his army."

"I is?"

"You is. And if you don't level with me," Ben said, pointing to Mike Richards, "I will turn you over to that man."

Clarence cut his eyes and stared into the very mean eyes of Mike. The man reminded Clarence of the only L.A. cop he was ever scared of. That big honky bastard wouldn't take no shit off anybody, and it didn't make no difference what the color might be.

Ben turned Clarence and his gang over to a small contingent of French Resistance Forces and pulled out of Chambery the next morning. He did not know for certain what the FRF would do with Clarence and his followers, but he thought he could make a very good guess.

The monastery of La Grande Chartreuse, where the monastic Carthusian monks used to meditate, had been looted and desecrated, obscene slogans and phrases painted on the walls. But the old structure, built long before, still stood. There was no sign of the monks.

Only a few elderly men and women had gathered to watch the arrival of the Rebels. They stood in silence, hunger etched deeply in their faces.

Ben had his medics check them out and arranged for a drop of medicines and supplies.

The old people told him that Grenoble was filled with all sorts of thugs, bandits, and criminals.

"It won't be for long," Ben replied.

Six

Ben studied the city of Grenoble through binoculars. The scene was tranquil—Ben knew it was anything but.

At Chambery Ben had split his battalion, sending one company down Highway 520. At the junction with the main highway leading from Grenoble to Lyon, they would cut south and attack from the west side of the city. Another company would take Highway 524 at Gieres and come in from the south. Ben and two companies, with tanks spearheading, would smash through from the north, taking the old forts of la Bastille and Rabot and securing the bridges across the Isere, which led to the main section of the once-thriving city of some 160,000.

The Rebels had been fortunate in reaching Grenoble, for oftentimes during the winter months, many of the roads were snowed under. But the past two days had been warm, and much of the snow had melted in the valleys, and the roads were in passable shape.

"First we take the airport so we can be resupplied,"

Ben said, lowering his binoculars. "Baker Company, that's your job. Lieutenant Bonelli, we drive straight through and take the high ground."

"Yes, sir."

"Let's do it."

Baker Company slammed into the airport and finished the few punks and thugs there in five minutes of light fighting. Since the punks had no interest in old forts, museums, or universities, Ben and his company drove right up to the banks of the Isere, without having a shot fired at them, and secured all three bridges leading across to the Quai Crequi, Quai Stephane Jay, Quai Brosse, and Quai Jongkind.

"The airport is secure," Corrie informed Ben.

"This is the dullest campaign I have ever been on," Cooper bitched. "If it wasn't for the creeps, we could have rolled across France and had picnics every day."

Ben stood on the north side of the Isere and looked down the long expanse of Boulevard Gambetta. It was deserted as far as he could see. He turned to Corrie. "Do you know what frequency they're using to communicate with each other?"

"Oh, yes."

"Tell them I'll give them fifteen minutes to lay down their weapons and step out into the streets with hands raised high. Those who refuse to surrender will be hanged."

One minute later the boulevard was lined with men and women, most of them black and Hispanic. They stood with their hands over their heads.

The same scene was being played out all over the city, as about a thousand gang members chose surrender and a trial rather than certain death fighting the Rebels.

"This is the end of the easy trail," Ben said. "Those remaining will fight; they're the hard core. Once we've dealt with them, we've got Duffy and his people to contend with, plus ambushes from creepies."

"What do we do with this pack of bums?" Cooper asked, as the thugs and would-be toughs and bully boys and their women were marched across the bridges.

"Find every shovel in this town and put them to work clearing the airport. Let them work for a change. It might be a refreshing sight to witness."

Those who started bitching about being forced to shovel snow off the runways, clean out the hangars, and sweep out the terminal buildings were taken out of the lines and turned over to representatives of the FRF and led away. That put a quick halt to the complaining. Ben was not a man who paid much attention to legal technicalities.

Rebel teams were roaming the city, taking statements from residents and having the prisoners stand in lineups. Those who were accused of rape and murder were hauled out of the lineups and given polygraph and PSE tests. If any doubts remained after that, they were given drugs to get at the truth—both parties involved. The Rebel system of justice was harsh, but not nearly so unfair as many believed.

When the runways were ready for traffic, transports began bringing in supplies and taking back prisoners. Those wanted in America would be put on ships and taken back for trial there; those wanted in France would be tried on the Continent.

On the second day after the airport was opened, Ike flew in. On the ride back to Ben's CP, he said, "Paris is ninety percent cleared, Ben. But Duffy and his people have dropped out of sight. Mike's spooks seem to think they've slipped through and crossed the border into Austria and Germany."

"That's not all intelligence thinks," Ben said. Ike was not surprised by the statement, for Ben seemed to be on top of everything all the time. "Mike thinks the creeps hate us so greatly, they deliberately sacrificed themselves in Paris in order to give Duffy time to get clear. And also allow the other creeps scattered throughout France to get away in small groups. That's just a theory, but one I can buy."

Ike thought for a moment, then nodded his head. "Yeah. I'll buy it. What about this kook over in Germany? Any further info on him?"

Ben shook his head. "Not much. Except that he's going to damn well give us a run for our money."

They rode in silence for a time, these two men who had been close friends all through the long and bloody years after the Great War. Both had seen their dream of a separate nation flourish, almost die, then rebound with such strength and vigor that nothing could kill it. Both had lost wives and children and friends to the fury of a Democratic party controlled liberal government (spell that socialistic) grown too strong and too dictatorial . . . and so afraid of any voice of opposition they went to extreme lengths to silence any voice that cried out for reason and the return to a common sense form of government.

It had been an uphill battle for Ben Raines and his

Rebels from the very start, and for a time it looked as though they could not win. But Ben had never doubted it. His faith had never wavered.

"What are you thinking about, Ben?" Ike asked.

"Long ago and far away," Ben replied softly. "All the men and women who died getting us to this point."

"I think about them more and more," Ike's reply was equally as soft, his tone filled with memories. "I was thinkin' about Pal and Valerie the other day. Badger Harbin. Megan and Junebug. Voltan. Belle Riverson. Your son, Jack. And all the others," his voice trailed off.*

Ben smiled, putting a crack in the mood. "We're getting maudlin in our middle years, Ike."

"A lot of blood behind us, Ben."

"And much more ahead of us, friend."

With French militia now able to take over in Paris and mop up, Ben began shifting his battalions around for the final eastward push through France. What remained were the hard-core gangs who broke from Duffy after his alignment with Bruno Bottger, and pockets of creeps who had spread all over the countryside.

Ben arranged his battalions north to south, starting with Nick's 21 Batt up north in Holland and ending with his own 1 Batt pushing off from Perpignan in the extreme south of France. On a very cold but clear day, Ben gave the orders.

*OUT OF THE ASHES—Zebra Books.

"Move 'em out, Corrie."

Eighteen overstrength battalions with heavy armor spearheading moved eastward. When the news reached the cold ears of the punks, many threw down their weapons and made ready to surrender to a clearly overwhelming force. Many more vowed to fight to the death.

They did just that . . . and died.

Ben's 1 Batt hit some of the fiercest fighting they had seen in weeks in the old capital of Roussillon and the kingdom of Majorca. It was house to house, building to building. France was now very nearly overrun with press types, print and broadcast, and there was no way (short of shooting them) that Ben could keep them out of any combat zone.

"Let them in," he ordered. "But they're on their own." He smiled ruefully at his team. "And since the punks who hold Perpignan are black, get ready for the press to brand us as right-wing racists."

"Well, goddamn!" Jersey flared. "All they have to do is look around them. The ranks of the Rebels are filled with people of all colors."

"You're speaking from a logical point of view, Jersey," Ben told her. "You can't use logic when describing the reporting of many members of the press because nearly all of them are liberal. As I have said before, nothing is ever black or white to a liberal; it's all gray. You have to adopt their type of thinking: *One:* guns kill people, so all guns are inherently evil. Back when the world was more or less whole, I never, ever, heard any major reporter or anchorperson suggest that it just might be people who kill people. *Two:* just because a punk breaks into your house and threatens you or your family, that does not give you the right to defend what is yours by the use of deadly force. *Three:* if you leave the keys in your car and that car is stolen, it's your fault for leaving the keys in the ignition—not the fault of the thief. The thief, you see, probably came from a broken home and was merely expressing himself by stealing or looting. It really wasn't his fault, it was society's fault." Ben smiled and waited.

Several reporters were standing nearby listening (Ben was well aware of that), and steam was beginning to rise from several of them, and it had nothing to do with the cold weather.

"Goddamnit, General!" one reporter finally blew his safety valve.

"Yes?" Ben said pleasantly, turning to face the man.

"Just maybe, General—" the reporter said, thinking that perhaps he should have kept his mouth shut "—maybe we value all human life far more than you do."

"You probably do," Ben said. "But the problem with that is, you people wanted those who felt differently to help pay the bills for halfway houses, drug rehab programs, early release of murderers, rapists, muggers, and others of that ilk, free legal assistance, methadone handouts, welfare under half a hundred different names, and all the other dozens and dozens of giveaway programs using taxpayer money. End of discussion."

Ben turned his back to the knot of reporters and walked away, his team with him.

"I hate that bastard!" Dick Bogarde, the hot-under-the-collar reporter, said, but not loud enough for Ben to hear him . . . he hoped.

"Easy, Dick," a friend cautioned.

"Did any of you ever consider that what he says about us just might be true?" another questioned.

"Oh, get off it, Cassie!" Dick shouted, red-faced. "I'm tired of Mr. High-and-Mighty Raines questioning my integrity. I report what I see."

"Do you really?" she questioned. "Do any of us really report *just* what we see? I'm beginning to question statements like that. I've gone back and researched Ben Raines, back when he was a writer of adventure books and those few articles he did. Those articles touched a nerve in me."

Perpignan had been taken for the most part, and only the occasional gunshot was heard as the last of the gang members were routed out. The French militia moved in to take over, and the Rebels handed the mop-up over to them and were preparing to pull out for Narbonne the next morning, about sixty kilometers up the coast.

Cassie's colleagues stared at her. She had been an up and comer in broadcast news before the Great War—a woman who spoke her mind and damn the consequences. Cassie Phillips was not a breathtakingly beautiful woman, but one whose quick smile, intelligence, and wit coupled with a pretty face made her seem more attractive than she was. In addition, as one male reporter said, "Cassie's got a hell of a bod."

Cassie said, "Why didn't we say 'taxpayer money' instead of government assistance when money was handed out for this or that program, even when we all knew the majority of people were opposed to the programs?"

"Come on now, Cassie," Nils Wilson said.

"Come on . . . where, Nils?" she retorted.

None of the reporters noticed that Ben had stopped and was listening to the exchange.

"Back to the old days of slanted reporting?" Cassie didn't let up.

"I never slanted a story in all my years of reporting!" Dick shouted. "Never."

Cassie laughed and stood her ground as Ben moved closer, a deuce and a half between Ben and team and the arguing reporters. Well known for having an eye for the ladies, Ben had certainly taken note of Cassie, thinking her a very lovely lady. But he had originally pegged her as just another liberal reporter. *Could be,* he thought, *I was wrong.* This just might get interesting. Ben handed his Thompson to Cooper.

Dick pointed a finger at Cassie. "That laugh was derisive, Cassie, and I resent it. If you were a man, I'd whip your ass."

"Talk about politically incorrect," Nils said with a laugh, trying to lighten the moment.

"Shut up, Nils!" Dick popped. "And stay out of this."

"Never slanted a story?" Cassie said. "You have to be kidding, Dick. How about that series you did on L.A. gangs after the riots? That was the worst piece of pandering shit I ever heard. You invented more excuses for that pack of savages than a stray dog has fleas."

"You damn snooty bitch!" Dick yelled. "What the

hell do you know about being poor and of color. You come from old money. You never wanted for anything in your rich, spoiled life. You goddamn dyke."

Ben arched an eyebrow at that last remark. "I don't think so," he muttered.

"If she's queer," Beth whispered, "I'm Attila the Hun."

Cassie laughed at Dick and shook her head. "Dick, as usual, you're wrong. Can't you get anything right?"

Dick took two steps and slapped the woman, the openhanded pop knocking her to the ground and stunning those who witnessed the slap.

Ben stepped from behind the truck and flattened the reporter with a hard right fist. "I didn't like you before the Great War, Bogarde, and I don't like you now. Now get up, you son of a bitch!"

Seven

Dick was a good ten years younger than Ben and felt he was capable of taking care of himself in any situation. After all, he had been on his college wrestling team. Besides, he'd been a member of the most prestigious frat house on campus, and that alone automatically made him far superior to anyone else.

Dick bounced to his feet and took a swing at Ben. Ben slipped the punch and gave the man two hard shots to the belly, a left and right. Dick grunted in pain and stepped back. Ben pressed and popped him on the mouth with a straight right, the blow bringing blood. Dick came in like a windmill, both fists flailing the air. Ben sidestepped and clubbed Dick on the kidney, bringing a cry of pain. Dick put both hands to his aching lower back and Ben started his punch down around his ankles and knocked the shit out of him.

Ben stepped back and waited for Dick to climb out of the churned-up mud. The cameras were rolling, recording it all.

Cassie was sitting on the ground, the left side of her

face swelling, and a thin trickle of blood leaking out of one side of her mouth. Dick Bogarde was not a small man, and the blow had hurt.

She looked up just in time to hear Ben's punch impact against Dick's mouth and see Dick's butt hit the mud, his mouth scarlet with fresh blood. "There is justice in the world after all," she muttered.

Cassie felt hands on her arms and looked up into the faces of Beth and Corrie, pulling her to her feet. Jersey was standing with her M-16 at the ready, in case anyone tried to interfere on the side of Dick, against Ben. One of the men present would later report that just one look at Little Jersey would have been enough to scare away Vlad the Impaler.

"Enough." Dick pushed the words past loosened teeth and bloody lips.

"It better be," Ben warned. "For the next time I witness you slapping someone for speaking the truth, I'll kill you."

Dick thought plenty but wisely said nothing.

Ben turned to a couple of medics who walked up. He pointed to Dick. "One of you see to that son of a bitch," he ordered. "The other check out Miss Phillips."

Ben pulled off his gloves and walked over to where Cassie was standing with Ben's team. She looked at him; there was a frankness in her gaze that Ben liked.

"A tooth cut the inside of your mouth, miss," the medic said. He dipped a cotton-tipped swab in a bottle of solution. This will stop the bleeding. You'll be all right."

"Thank you," Cassie told him, then winced as the tip touched the small cut.

The medic looked at Ben. "You all right, sir?"

"I'm fine."

The medic smiled. "Good fight. I just hope Doctor Chase doesn't hear of it."

"Oh, he will," Ben said.

The medic laughed and walked over to where the other medic was working on a moaning and bleeding Dick.

Ben turned to look at the reporter. Cassie was staring at him through incredibly pale-gray eyes. Ben suddenly realized that while some men might not consider her attractive, he did. Very attractive.

"I would say that you are not the first woman he's struck," Ben told her. "However, that's just a guess on my part."

"A pretty good guess, General," Cassie said. "There have been rumors circulating about Dick for years. Even before the Great War."

"Ben, Miss Phillips. Call me Ben."

She smiled, and she was lovely. "In that case, I'm Cassie."

The two gravely shook hands, surrounded by the cold winds of January and hundreds of heavily armed Rebels and thousands of tons of the machinery of war.

Beth and Corrie and Cooper and Jersey looked at each other and smiled as Ben and Cassie stared into each other's eyes like a couple of junior high students suddenly struck for the first time with love-tipped arrows from Cupid's quiver.

"Nice to meet you, Cassie," Ben said.

"Very nice to meet you, Ben," Cassie said.

"Oh, my God!" The voice of Doctor Lamar Chase came from just behind Ben's team. "Has that middle-aged lothario been smitten again?"

"Looks that way," Beth said. "How long have you been here, Doctor?"

"I landed at the airstrip about half an hour ago to inspect the MASH unit attached to 1 Batt. Heard about Ben's fight a couple of minutes ago. That is a handsome woman. Who is she?"

"Cassie Phillips," Jersey said.

"The reporter?"

"Yes, sir."

"I'll be damned. Did Ben get hit during the fight?"

"No, sir," Cooper said. "That clown didn't land a single punch."

Lamar shifted his gaze over to where the medics were working on Dick Bogarde. The man's face was a mess from Ben's blows. He would carry the cuts and bruises from Ben's fists for quite some time.

The mood of the moment was broken by a shrill voice coming from some distance away.

Chase took one look and said, "I'm out of here, boys and girls. See you later."

The lines of Rebels began parting like the Red Sea under Moses' command.

"General, my General!" the voice called. "I have come to your assistance."

"Oh, my God!" Ben said.

"Who is that little man?" Cassie asked.

Emil Hite came rushing up to the recent scene of conflict, and his boots hit the churned up and muddy ground. "Whoa!" he hollered, flailing his arms as he slipped and slid across the area, looking very much like a crazed ballet dancer attempting to dance the tush-push to the mental strains of the 1812 Overture.

"Get out of the way!" Ben yelled, two seconds before Emil impacted against him, and both of them went to the ground in a sprawl of arms and legs.

Sitting on top of Ben, his helmet drooped over one side of his face, Emil cried, "Are you hurt, General Raines?"

"Only my composure, Emil. Now get off of me!"

Emil climbed off Ben, only managing to step on him about five times in the process. Cooper and Jersey finally jerked the man off Ben and helped Ben to his boots.

Cassie was nearly doubled over with laughter. Ben brushed and wiped the mud off his BDUs and said, "Emil, what the hell are you doing here?"

"To be truthful, General," Emil said, "I think I was beginning to get on Thermopolis's nerves. I got the first small inkling of that yesterday when he suddenly started screaming and chasing me around the camp with an baseball bat. I truly believe Therm was having some sort of temporary breakdown. I decided that my talents were no longer needed in that vicinity, and thought I might be of more help here."

"I can't begin to tell you how much I appreciate that gesture, Emil."

Emil beamed. "I knew you would feel that way, General. I brought my entire flock with me."

"That's . . . wonderful, Emil."

"What important assignment do you have for me, General?"

Ben thought about that for a couple of seconds, then smiled. "Emil, I want you and your . . . flock to act as rear guard for this column. I'm expecting a sneak attack as we work our way up the coast, so this is a very important move. You've got to be on guard constantly. You think you can handle that assignment?"

"With the diligence of a trained Doberman, my General."

Ben thought a basset hound might be a more apt description, but he kept that to himself. He pointed to a Rebel sergeant trying to hide behind a HumVee. "The sergeant over there will get you all set up, Emil. We move out in the morning."

"*Oui, mon General!*" Emil gave Ben a French salute, palm out.

As Emil was being led away by a reluctant Rebel sergeant, Cassie said, "You certainly have some strange people with your organization, Ben."

"Have you ever met Thermopolis?" Ben asked.

"I haven't had the pleasure."

"Hummm," Ben said with a smile.

With Rebels closing in from the west and the north, and Ben's 1 Batt coming up from the south, the thugs who had gathered along the way fled northward, paused briefly in Narbonne (very briefly, for the citizens left in the small city started shooting at them with recently dug-up rifles and shotguns), and fled on up the highway to Beziers. They received a less than warm welcome in Beziers and kept on traveling, with Ben's 1 Batt closing the distance.

At Montpellier the thugs turned and made their stand. To a person they had vowed to die rather than surrender and be tried and probably, for most of them, hanged, either in France or back in America.

"Corrie," Ben said, as his battalion waited at the edge of the old university city of Montpellier. "You have contact with this bunch?"

"Affirmative."

"What's the name of the leader, if any?"

"Mahmud the Terrible," Corrie said with a straight face.

"From Toronto?"

"Right."

"The Lion of the Desert?"

"Affirmative."

"Lawrence of Somalia?"

"Right."

"The one with the silly hat?"

"That's the one."

"The one who claims to be bulletproof?"

"Right."

"Shit!" Ben said. "This is part of the bunch who commandeered that ship and killed all the crew members."

"Affirmative."

"Tell Mudpie the Terrible he has ten minutes to surrender. If he chooses to fight, I will wipe out his entire gang of punks, and I will show no mercy."

Corrie relayed the message, listened for a moment, then said, "And the same to you, too, asshole!" She smiled sweetly and turned to Ben. "Mahmud the Terrible, Lion of the Desert, Lawrence of Somalia, and one mean motherhumper said to tell Ben Raines to kiss his ass."

"Really?"

"That's what he said."

Ben smiled. "Take the town."

By the afternoon of the second day, the punks had been forced into the downtown area, and they had suffered terrible losses in their retreat. The weather had turned bitterly cold, too cold for it to snow, and while the Rebels were equipped in the finest gear for cold weather operations, the punks were not. Dozens of bodies, frozen in the most macabre positions, littered the streets of the old city.

Most of the residents who remained had fled when the hordes of punks descended upon the city, and Ben had his people take time to clean out shelters for them and to supply blankets, food, and camp stoves for cooking and heat. Those survivors were mostly the very old and the very young, with little in between. But they were not a beaten people. They were the survivors, and Ben was proud of every one of them and told them so.

On the other side of the coin, Mahmud the Terrible, Chief Doo-Da and Poo-Pa of the Mau Mau gang was finished, and even he had sense enough to realize that. He had never been so cold and so hungry in all his life.

And like nearly all of his ilk, the thought never once crossed his mind that he and he alone was responsible for the predicament he was now in.

It was somebody else's fault. Liberals had told him that before the Great War; he'd heard countless news programs that supported their claims. All his friends said that society owed them something, and if society wouldn't give it (whatever *it* might be) then by God they'd just take it. Which was exactly what he'd been doing since long before the Great War. And it had been a *great* war to Mahmud's mind. Ever since the Great War he could rob and rape and assault and kill and all that other good stuff and not have to worry about the cops.

Then along come Ben Raines and screwed it all up.

Maybe he could use that "you owe me" approach with Ben Raines? It was worth a try.

"You can hang that shit up," Abdul told him after Mahmud suggested it a short time later. "Ben Raines don't play that game."

"Then how come all them people told us it was true years back?"

Abdul was stumped for an answer to that question. 'Cause he felt the same way Mahmud did about it. "Must be that Ben Raines was born in Mississippi or Louisiana or some other damn redneck nigger-hatin' southern state."

"That's it! Has to be," Mahmud agreed.

Actually, Ben was born in the Midwest and did not hate anyone for the color of their skin. If Ben had used the term "nigger" while living at home, his mother would have slapped him out of the chair, and then his father would have taken a belt to his behind and used it so thoroughly that Ben would have been able to heat his own bathwater simply by sitting in it.

But Ben's mother and father had no patience with people who would not work and who wanted something for nothing. They had both lived through the terrible years of the Great Depression and knew firsthand, and for a fact, that people could survive on a lot less if they would just put their minds to it.

Ben learned without being told (at a very early age) that each individual controlled their own destiny . . . and no one else. And Ben didn't give a damn what liberal sob sisters and hanky-stompers preached. It was all up to the individual. You could fritter your life away and be nothing. And if you did, that was your own fault and to hell with you. But Ben knew that one had to become somebody before they could become anybody. Work, study, learn, and continue doing that all your life. Ration your spare time. Read. Ben had little patience with people who did not read. That was why for years he had forbidden television in any Rebel-controlled area.

And Ben knew that he who stands alone is the strongest.

Mahmud stood up and walked away from the fireplace to stand by a window and look out at the cold winter's day, windy and gray and unfriendly. Death lay all around him. And death was called the Rebels.

Mahmud had never seen anything like the people in Ben Raines's army. Mahmud had always thought himself to be the meanest motherfucker in the world until he came head to head with the Rebels. These men and women put a new meaning to the word *mean*. He turned and looked back at Abdul, who was staring into the flames.

"You wanna give it up, Abdul?"

"They gonna hang us if we do."

"Yeah. I know. Prob'ly. And they gonna shoot us or blow us up if we don't."

"We ain't done nothing here in France. So that means we gonna be shipped back to Canada for trial. We busted outta jail 'fore."

"Yeah. That a truth." Mahmud turned to once more stare out of the window.

"I'm hungry. I'm cold. I'm tired. My head hurts and my feets hurt. I ain't had me a good night's sleep in so long I can't 'member when. Even my eyes hurts. I want a hot cup of coffee so bad I can taste it." He sighed dejectedly. "We was lied to somethin' fierce back in the States, Mahmud. All them years we was flat out lied to."

"How you mean?"

"Don't nobody owe us nothin'. It don't make no difference what happened to our granddaddys or such. That ain't got a goddamn thing to do with me and you. Not here and now, not back before the Great War. It was all up to us, and we was too goddamn stupid to understand it. But, brother, I see it now."

"But it be too late, don't it?"

"Yeah. I guess so." He shook his head. "Maybe not."

"What you got in mind?"

"Talkin' to Ben Raines."

"You think that'll do any good?"

"I don't figure we got anything to lose by tryin'."

Eight

"Show them in," Ben said.

He was sitting in a comfortable chair, behind an antique desk. A fire was crackling in the huge fireplace. A pot of fresh coffee and sandwiches were on another table. Mahmud and Abdul were shown into the warmth of the room, and Ben had to hide a smile. They were two of the most woebegotten-looking people he had ever seen.

The Lion of the Desert wore an expression like he'd been thrown from his camel, had his tent set on fire, and his harem had turned frigid . . . and Abdul looked even worse.

Ben pointed to the coffee pot and the sandwiches. "Help yourselves."

The pair quickly consumed about a dozen sandwiches and slurped two mugs of coffee before they sat down in front of Ben's desk. Jersey watched every move they made, and that unsettled them both.

"That's a mean-lookin' woman over there, General," Mahmud remarked.

Ben ignored that and asked, "All the gangs in the city ready to pack it in?"

"Most of 'em, yeah . . . ah, yes, sir," Abdul said.

"You understand that you all will be placed under arrest and processed? If you have committed crimes in France, you will be tried here."

"We understand," Mahmud said, defeat in his voice.

"How many gangs are represented here?"

" 'Bout eight. Tony Green, Tuba, LaBamba, and Richardo done pulled out on they own," Abdul confessed. "There ain't but about four hundred of us left. The rest is dead."

Mahmud looked slyly around the large room. Back in the old days, he had always been able to elicit a great deal of sympathy for himself from other people . . . especially from dumb-assed honky liberals. He couldn't find the first trace of sympathy from anybody in this room. Ben Raines's eyes were hard as flint. That foxy, sorta Indian-lookin' bitch had a mean light in her eyes. There were two more fine-lookin' honky cunts in the room, but fine stopped at their eyes. Mean and hard. The other man in the room was about the same age as the women, and he had the same look in his eyes as the others. Mahmud sighed and shook his head. No help here.

Then Ben Raines shook him down to his boots when he said, "It won't work here, will it, Mahmud?"

"Whut you mean?" Mahumd managed to ask through his fright. Could the man really read minds like some said he could?

"You know damn well what I mean, so don't play dumb with me. All your poor childhood crap. All that bullshit about society holding you down because of your color and forcing you into a life of crime. It won't wash with us, Mahmud. We've proven it to be what it is: pure crap invented by liberals."

"You a mean honky son of a bitch, Ben Raines!" Mahmud blurted, glaring hate at him.

Ben smiled. Sort of. "I'm a realist, Mahmud. And I can spot crap from the mouth faster than shit through a goose. Now get on that radio over there in the corner and tell your people to surrender."

"And if I don't?"

Ben picked up a .45 autoloader from the desk and pointed the muzzle at Mahmud's head. "I'll blow your goddamn worthless brains out!"

Abdul started shaking in his chair. Fear sweat popped out on his face; his eyes were wide. "He mean it, Mahmud. Do it, man. He'll kill you."

Ben cocked the .45, the cocking very loud in the suddenly quiet room.

Mahmud cut his eyes to Jersey. She was smiling at him. *Smiling!* Bitch mus' be crazy! Whole damn bunch was crazy! Mahmud had never run into nothin' like this in his whole entire life. "I be gettin' up now, General," Mahmud said very cordially. "An' goin' to the radio. I'll tell my people to give it up."

"You do that."

Ben had known all his adult life that the way to win the war on crime was to be twice as mean and nasty as the criminals. Thugs and punks and street slime did not respond to compassion, because they possessed none. It was an unknown emotion for them. They respected and responded only to brute force and strength.

Half a minute after Ben de-cocked the .45, the battle for Montpellier was over.

Ben halted the advance at a small town just about halfway between Montpellier and Nimes. He was beginning to range too far ahead of the north to south line of Rebels. Located deep in Germany, Bruno Bottger's spies were reporting all this to Bruno, and he was reviewing it through cautious and knowing eyes. He now realized that he had made a terrible blunder by not attacking the Rebels when they went into Geneva. But he made no mention of it and neither did any of his people. To question any decision of the new führer was not terribly wise.

Bruno leaned back in his chair and was thoughtful for a time. It just might work. Ben Raines was alone between Montpellier and Nimes with just one battalion of ground troops and some armor. And Bruno had the planes and French-speaking troops to pull this off. Yes. He smiled. It *would* work.

Ben figured his battalion was a full week ahead of the other battalions, so he told his people to take it easy until the other batts grew even on a north/south line.

There were still several thousand gang members roaming around France—at least that many—but the thugs had been so reduced in numbers that now they were only a minor thorn in the side of the Rebels.

The Night People were quite a different matter.

The creeps, Ben knew, unlike the gangs of punks,

were highly organized and would fight to the death. Ben was expecting some sort of attack from the creeps at any moment. And while to civilian eyes his people seemed relaxed and unconcerned, the Rebels were ready for any attack. They just *seemed* to be 100 percent at ease.

Even Emil Hite had stopped joking around and had put his little group of followers on high alert. Ben didn't worry about Emil when push came to shove. The little man and his group could be as ferocious as badgers when cornered.

But it was Bruno Bottger that worried Ben.

Mike Richards's people inside Germany had confirmed that Bruno's army was massive . . . probably at least 125,000 to 150,000 strong with another 100,000 or so civilians armed and ready to fight on the side of their new leader. The majority of Germans were appalled and disgusted by Bruno Bottger and his followers, but due to many countries blindly, and as it turned out, stupidly following the socialistic leanings of the United States under the misguided mumblings of the liberals in the ruling Democratic party they had been totally disarmed long before the Great War rocked the world and were helpless to do anything except watch in horror as Bruno purged the country of "undesirables."

"And here I sit with one battalion and some armor," Ben muttered softly. "Wide open for attack."

Sitting at his desk in a lovely old home, Ben suddenly felt that old familiar warning grabbing at his guts. Warriors cannot describe how they know danger is imminent—they just know. Perhaps it was some cultivated sixth sense, nurtured over the years. But they were usually correct.

The mood jumped from Ben to his team in a matter of seconds. Ben lifted his eyes. All members of his team had stopped what they were doing and were looking at him.

"Tonight, boss?" Cooper asked.

"Yeah," Ben replied. "Tonight."

Thousands of miles away President Homer Blanton tossed his pencil to the desk and leaned back in his chair. He supposed things could conceivably get worse in what was left of the United States, but damned if he could figure out how.

The liberals had finally gotten what they wanted: a society totally free of any type of guns in the hands of law-abiding citizens, social programs that promised to be all things to all people all the time, political correctness down to the *n*th degree, and all the other foolish babblings of the liberal wing of the Democratic party . . . and the goddamn nation was in shambles.

Factories were abandoning those states still under Blanton's rule as fast as they could . . . heading for those states that had aligned themselves with Ben Raines's form of government. Blanton could, and would for the remainder of his life, remember the words of Ben Raines spoken in this very office.

"I feel sorry for you, Mr. Blanton. We've handed you the dregs of society. We've left you with the whiners, complainers, the slackers and the dullards and the underachievers. That's one type we've left you. The other is the high-idealed and out-of-touch-with-reality person. They're the smart ones—to a degree. They have lots of book sense but no common sense. They're the ones who, for the most part, will form your staff and make up your House and Senate. They will write your speeches and pass the legislation and implement all the glorious and high-minded and totally unworkable and pie-in-the-sky social programs and foolish laws and regulations that will lead your government right back to the way it was when you first took office, more than a decade ago. The nation that I helped create is going to fly, Mr. President. We're going to soar. Just sit back and watch us. While you flounder."

Homer sighed and rubbed his temples with his fingers. He had a terrible headache. Thinking of Ben Raines always brought on a headache. He hated it when Ben Raines was right. Problem was, the son of a bitch was nearly *always* right.

Homer was well aware that a great many of his good people were leaving him. Not all were going to the SUSA, but those that weren't, and were going into the private sector, were leaving his administration rather than see it slowly sink into a morass of unworkable rules and regulations and total government control of citizens' lives.

And Ben Raines had predicted that, sooner or later, most of the fair-minded and reasonable people on Blanton's staff would leave him. Homer had scoffed at the time. He wasn't laughing any longer.

Blanton rose from his desk to look out the window. Those damn demonstrators were still out there. He picked up his binoculars and scanned the lines.

HOMES FOR THE HOMELESS.
JOBS FOR THE UNEMPLOYED.
EQUAL JUSTICE FOR ALL.

"Crap!" Homer said, and closed the drapes. "You want a job, move to the SUSA. Plenty of jobs down there. I'll even pay your way down there. One way. Problem is, Ben Raines wouldn't have any of you."

"I can't believe you said that," his wife chided him. She had been standing just inside the door to the new Oval Office.

"Why not? It's the truth." He pointed toward the window. "Those out there don't want jobs, they want positions. Most of them aren't willing to start at the bottom and work up, they want to start in the middle or at the goddamn top! And they're not qualified to shovel shit in a manure factory!"

His wife was shocked into silence. It would not last long. It never did. "Why you—" The First Lady found her voice. "You . . . damned . . . *Republican!*"

"Good God!" Homer hollered. "Can't you see by now that those people out there with their hands stuck out, waiting for the government to give them something, are nothing but whiners and complainers?"

"Oh, boo-hoo!" his wife sobbed, quickly changing tactics. "We've failed the people who need us most."

"Horseshit!" Homer said.

"It's true!" the First Lady shrieked—she'd been taking voice lessons from Rita Rivers and Harriet Hooter. "You've changed. You are a filthy Republican!"

"Oh . . . shut up!" Homer told his wife.

The president of the United States then had to crawl under the desk as the First Lady started hurling various breakable objects in his general direction . . . amid numerous vocal invectives.

Homer wondered if Ben Raines ever had to crawl under a desk.

Nine

Ben sure as hell was under a desk. About half a minute after he'd poured a fresh cup of coffee and rolled a cigarette, the creepies started a mortar attack that sent everyone jumping for cover.

What Ben did not know was that Bottger's commandos were now only a few miles from the DZ and were preparing to jump into the night . . . and the first drop zone was only a few miles from where Ben and his 1 Batt were bivouacked.

Mike Richards ducked and dodged and zigged and zagged and made it to Ben's CP without getting his head blown off by the incoming mail. He jumped into the room. "About fifty planes just showed up on radar, Ben!" he shouted to be heard over the crash of incoming. "They're coming from the east. It's got to be Bruno's bunch." He looked around the dimly lighted room. "Where the hell are you, Ben?"

Ben crawled out from under the heavy desk just as Mike was getting down on his hands and knees. "Here, Mike. What's this about jumpers?"

"It's got to be Bottger's people. They ought to be leaving the door right about now, Ben."

"Damn!" Ben got to his boots and waited for a lull in the explosions that boomed all around them. "Corrie!" he shouted.

"Right here!" she yelled.

"Can you verify unfriendlies coming in from the east?"

"Recon just reported the sky is filled with planes, boss. Wait a minute. All right. Hundreds of chutes, boss. West and south of us."

"Bug out!" Ben yelled. "Everybody head for Nimes. Make the bastards chase us. We aren't strong enough to hold here. Bump Therm and tell him what we're doing." Ben looked around for Mike, but his intelligence chief was gone. Ben figured that Mike would stay behind—his French was as good as any Frenchman— and see what he could learn. "Grab what you can carry and leave the rest," Ben said, picking up his Thompson. "Beth, rig the charges."

She grinned and gave him a thumb's up. Rebels were not known for their kind and loving ways toward the enemy. Every building they occupied was routinely booby-trapped for quick withdrawal. The charges were usually removed when they moved on, but in this case, they would remain active. The creeps and Bottger's men were in for a very unpleasant surprise.

The mortar rounds had ceased and quiet lay dangerously about them. Ben yelled, "Watch out. The bastards will be coming in now." The wind shifted, and he caught the familiar smell of creepies blowing in through the blown-out window. He turned and lifted the muzzle of his Thompson just as robed figures raced into in the yard, dimly visible in the moonlight. Ben held the trigger back and fought the rise of the powerful old weapon. The screaming charge of the half dozen robed shapes suddenly changed into a painful howling dance of death as the fat .45 slugs tore into flesh and shattered organs and bone.

"Let's go!" Ben said, waving his team toward the front door. Cooper was in the Hummer and ready to roll.

On the far south end of the town, a massive explosion rocked the night, foo-gas flames leaping high into the sky. Creepies or one of Bottger's commandos had touched off a booby-trapped building. The Rebels believed in using an ample amount of C-4 or Semtex . . . something to remember them by.

"Cassie—" Beth said, climbing into the Hummer.

"She's a big girl," Ben replied, placing one big hand on Beth's butt and shoving her into the seat. The discussion was closed before it could get started.

Lieutenant Bonelli's company had thrown up a defensive line around Ben's CP. As soon as Ben's Hummer had vanished into the smoky night, Bonelli ordered his people out, after laying out claymores. Another little surprise for the hostiles.

Beth struggled into body armor and pulled herself up, standing behind the roof-mounted 7.62 machine gun on the Hummer. She jacked a round into the slot and freed the weapon to swing. Jersey worked her arms up between the hole, and Beth fitted a throat collar around her. Beth was now protected from head to waist, only her eyes visible behind the clear impact-proof face shield. The body armor would stop anything up to a .50-round slug. Jersey then wormed her way to the rear of the Hummer and took up a cramped position, her M-16 ready.

While it irritated the hell out of the Rebels to be forced to give ground, when they had to do it, they did it swiftly and professionally. When in bivouac, the Rebels unpacked only that which was absolutely necessary for some degree of creature comfort, and no more. Consequently it did not take them long to pack up and bug out.

Cooper drove past Emil and his people, hastily throwing up defensive positions, and Ben told him to stop. "Emil!" Ben yelled. "Get the hell out of here."

"My position is rear guard, General," the little man said. "And that is where I shall be. Now get to safety. Be gone with you!"

Ben saluted Emil and received one in return. Cooper pulled away into the violent night.

"You can't short the crazy bastard for guts," Jersey spoke from the rear of the highly modified Hummer.

"For a fact," Ben replied.

"If they take Emil prisoner," Cooper said, "they'll regret it about fifteen minutes after the fact."

Ben smiled and said nothing. He clamped a tiny flashlight between his teeth and directed the sharp beam onto a map, studying it for a moment. "Corrie, bump our people and tell them to forget the airport at Nimes. It's too far out of town to fool with. We head directly into the city and take up positions. Where is the nearest squadron of 51's?"

"Toulouse."

"Tell them to be over our area at dawn with full payloads and be ready to raise hell. Right now, the paratroopers haven't a clue as to where we're bugging out. But they'll put it together soon enough. Bottger's people will commandeer vehicles and be after us. With any kind of luck, our people will catch them on the road at first light, and they can come in right on the deck and raise hell with them. Order our transports to start air-dropping us supplies and equipment at Nimes ASAP. Tell them to drop it right on the city. We'll find it. Field rations, water, medical supplies, and ammo for everything we've got. Did Chase get clear of the area?"

"Right, boss. He went back to Ike's sector."

"If Bottger's people follow us, they'll be making a very bad judgment call," Ben muttered. None of his team said anything; they were used to Ben talking to himself. But they all knew what he meant.

Bottger's commandos had jumped in with only light arms, with nothing heavy to back them up. Ben had set up his Rebels so that each battalion carried massive armor and artillery. The Rebels would be far outnumbered against the commandos, but they would be far superior in terms of withstanding any attack by the lightly armed paratroopers.

Travel was slow because of the abysmal road conditions, and it was hours before the long columns reached the outskirts of the city—the Rebels had split up, taking several different routes to reach the city. Cooper had worked his way to the head of the Rebel column, and Ben ordered him to pull over.

Standing outside the Hummer, stretching his legs, Ben glanced at his watch. Several hours to dawn.

"Mike and his people are positioned all along the roads to the city," Corrie told Ben. "They report that Bottger's jumpers are still several hours behind us but coming hard."

"Brave men behaving rather foolishly," Ben remarked. "All right. Let them have the first dozen or so blocks of the suburbs. Tell the tank commanders to get into hiding. Here. Mortar crews dig in. Here. Heavy machine guns stretched out along this line." Ben used a finger to lay out the positions on a map. "We keep falling back to this point. Suck them in. Order the pilots to lay back until they get word from me. See this relatively open area that stretches for blocks? That's where I want Bottger's people to reach. Then have the 51's come in and napalm the hell out of it. I want a wall of a fire followed by PUFFs. Got it?"

The last bit was unnecessary, for Corrie was already relaying the orders.

"You people rest," Ben said. "I'm going to check on things." As he was walking away, he glanced over his shoulder and found his whole team trailing along behind him. "I said get some rest!" he ordered.

"When you do," Jersey said.

"Oh, hell!" Ben muttered. "We'll all get some rest, then, damnit!" He glanced up at the sky. It had been starry, now it was overcast. "I think our luck is about to run out," he said.

When Ben woke up about a half hour before dawn, the weather had turned from crappy to shitty. Fog lay everywhere, thicker than two-day-old soup; nothing was going to fly that morning.

* * *

Just as soon as he laced up his boots, Ben immediately started doing some fast reshuffling. The fog was so thick that FO's were useless; nobody could eyeball anything so mortars and artillery were out. You could just barely see your hand in front of your face.

"The commandos have reached the outskirts of the city," Corrie said. "It's a large force, boss. Those planes our people thought they heard during the night?" She waited for Ben's nod. "More of Bottger's people. They landed to the north of us. Looks like they've got us boxed."

Ben winked. "Wouldn't be first time, now, would it?"

She smiled. "Not by a long shot, boss."

The commander of the paratroopers halted all advance at the outskirts of the city. He was very leery of the Rebels. He had spoken with people who had fought the Rebels at one time or another, and to a man, they had the utmost respect for the fighting ability of Raines's Rebels.

However the halt would not be for long. He had to commit his people. He knew the Rebels had plenty of armor and artillery, and he had nothing at all to match it. If he waited until the fog lifted, the Rebels would destroy his forces . . . and the colonel was professional enough to fully realize that.

He also knew what might happen to him should he fail and somehow manage to survive after the failure.

He turned to his radio operator. "Take the town," he ordered.

"Let them come," Ben said to Corrie. The fog was so unnaturally thick, he had ordered his people to fight with pistols and knives in order to prevent Rebel killing Rebel. He stood by an open window, a .45 autoloader in each hand.

On the north and south sides of the city, the thin ranks of Rebels silently stood or lay in position. Mike and his people had reported that Bottger's jumpers had not only landed lightly armed, they also wore no body armor, so any hit from a Rebel bullet would be a good one . . . for the Rebels.

Ben, as was his custom, had stationed himself right on the edge of the southern perimeter—on the first line of defense. He had pulled back all forward observers and recon and scouts. He wanted everyone on line for this hand-to-hand, eyeball-to-eyeball fight.

The men of the MEF were now so close, the Rebels on the front line could hear the occasional faint scrape of boots on brick or concrete.

"Hold your fire," Ben leaned close and whispered, and Corrie relayed the message to the Rebels on the south side. Ben had no way of knowing what was taking place on the other side of the city.

Then the Rebels sensed more than saw the first line of MEF troops suddenly stop. Ben guessed accurately that the first troops were no more than a hundred feet away . . . the point men closer than that. A cough or sneeze now would mean death for the offender and those close to the person.

The Rebels could hear the faint sounds of hoarse whispering.

Then . . . silence.

There was no breeze to stir the thick fog.

From the northern edge of the city, Ben could hear gunfire, light at first, then heavier as the Rebels and the MEF mixed it up.

Ben stared at the fog and blinked at the sight. A face had appeared in the window, the eyes under the lip of the helmet staring at Ben.

Ben lifted a .45 and pulled the trigger. The face blossomed into crimson and the fight was on.

Ten

Cooper used his entrenching tool to halt the advance of a MEF trooper trying to climb into a window. The sharpened shovel almost took the man's head off. Jersey stood in a window, a 9 mm in each hand and let the lead fly. Beth, knowing that any in front of her were enemies, was tossing grenades into the fog. Corrie knelt on one knee, a pistol in each hand, and let the lead sing its songs.

The men of the MEF went down like pins in a bowling alley.

"Shift!" Ben said, and Corrie relayed the prearranged directive.

The Rebels quickly shifted left and right, darting across sidewalks and alleyways and slippery streets.

Ben had guessed that the MEF would not have jumped in without rocket launchers and bloop-tubes. He was correct. But the mini-bombs exploded in empty buildings, thanks to Ben's orders to shift positions after the first contact with the enemy.

After the explosions, the MEF rushed the ruined and smoking buildings . . . and found nothing.

They ran out of the buildings, fearing booby traps, and stood in the fog, looking all around them. They could see nothing. They were fighting ghosts.

But well-armed and highly organized and trained ghosts. Ghosts who, a few seconds later, caught the MEF flat-footed in a killing cross fire.

"Back! Back!" the platoon leaders shouted the orders to what was left of their men.

But in the cotton-thick fog, no one was sure where back was. Turned around and confused, many of the MEF commandos ran right into Rebel positions and were slaughtered.

Then the sun suddenly began breaking through, highlighting pockets of MEF troops. The Rebels cut them down. Tanks roared into life and smashed through the walls of the buildings in which they had taken refuge. The Rebels stayed in their positions as the tanks, guns yammering and spitting lead, ran down the MEF troops and squashed them like bugs under a steel boot.

The back of the attack had been broken as the MEF troops ran for their lives. Those who ran to the south ran right into Mike Richards and his people, and Emil Hite and his group . . . waiting in ambush. The MEF men died in bloody heaps on the roads and in the ditches.

The fight for Nimes was over.

* * *

For Bruno Bottger it was a devastating defeat. One battalion of Rebels had destroyed almost all of three of his MEF battalions. Only a handful of men had managed to escape the slaughter in the fog at Nimes.

But unlike Hitler, the man he admired most in the world, Bruno did not go into a towering rage and screaming temper tantrum. Instead he sat quietly at his desk and tallied his losses and began revising his thinking as to how to stop Ben Raines and the Rebels.

He sat looking at a blank sheet of paper for a long time.

In Nimes the Rebels collected every piece of enemy equipment that might someday be used and cleaned, tagged, and stockpiled it. Old earthmoving equipment was found on the outskirts of the city, and the bodies were buried in a mass grave. Over twelve hundred bodies were buried in the scooped-out grave. The wounded were given medical treatment and held under guard at the airport, awaiting transport east for internment and questioning.

The commander of the three battalions of commandos had been captured and was now standing at rigid attention in front of Ben Raines.

The colonel had seen pictures of General Raines, but they had not prepared him for this face-to-face meeting. Ben's eyes burned with an unsettling intensity. There was an aura about the man that the colonel had never before witnessed surrounding any human being.

"Stand easy, Colonel," Ben said. "Sit down. Coffee?"

"Thank you, General," Colonel Housemann replied, taking a seat. "A cup of coffee would be most welcome."

Coffee and sandwiches were brought in, and Housemann ate and drank gratefully. He assumed this was to be his last meal, and he was, by God, going to linger over it and enjoy it. He looked over at Jersey. A lovely young lady, with some Indian blood in her. Unreadable eyes. Unquestionably loyal to General Raines. And dangerous.

It was especially galling to Housemann to be defeated by an army made up of all sorts of inferior beings. But defeated he had been, and defeated soundly.

"I am to be summarily executed, correct, General Raines?" Housemann asked.

"Not by us," Ben told him. "Are you wanted for any crimes in France?"

"Not to my knowledge, sir. I do not think I am wanted by the authorities anywhere."

"Then you are a prisoner of war and will be treated accordingly . . . with all due respect to your rank and position."

"I thank you again."

Ben did not question the officer about Bottger's strength or territory claimed, for he had a suspicion that he would get name, rank, and serial number from the man and that would be all. When Housemann had finished eating, Ben refilled both their coffee cups and sat back down behind his desk.

"Amazed that my people so easily took yours, Colonel?" Ben asked.

Housemann smiled, after a fashion. "To be frank, yes, I am."

"You are aware that the Rebels have never been defeated, Colonel?"

Housemann arched an eyebrow. "'No, General, I was not aware of that."

"We've lost a few battles, but never a campaign."

"That record might be broken when you cross over into Germany, General."

"I doubt it."

Housemann smiled. "If you are trying to anger me, General, you will not succeed."

Ben returned the smile. "It was worth a try. You can go visit your men, Colonel. We'll have hot showers up and ready to use in a few hours. And as you have no doubt noted, supply planes are landing at the airport now. POW camps are being made ready to receive you and your men. They are not being staffed with my people. They are being guarded by European Jews who escaped before Bottger's purge got into high gear—and some during the actual purge. As long as you do not attempt escape, you will not be mistreated. If you attempt to escape, you will be shot. And no Rebel will interfere. Is that understood?"

"Perfectly, General Raines."

After Housemann had been escorted out, Ben took a walk. Nimes was an ancient city, first settled in 121 B.C. Many remains of Roman occupation were in abundance in the form of old ruins, including a Roman amphitheater located in the center of the small city, a sight which Ben would not visit on this day because that part of town had not yet been cleared.

Rebel intelligence had been correct: There were no creeps in the city and had not been for some time. What people remained were mostly middle-aged and elderly. Rene Seaux had sent some of his FRF in and was arming the people. Any country that the Rebels had a hand in freeing—from whatever occupation force that was there against the will of the majority—would never against be the same. Although Blanton had almost blown a fuse and thrown a liberal temper tantrum, he had finally agreed: two of the stipulations Ben had insisted upon with the secretary-general of the United Nations before he would even consider taking the job were (1) the complete arming of the general population, and (2) his political teams could have a hand in setting up the government and framing the constitution. Any nation that objected to those terms would be not aided by the Rebels—so far, none had.

The prisoners were flown out to camps in western France, and the Rebels waited until the other battalions had pulled up more or less even on a north to south line with their position. But even then they could not push on because of the prisoners the other battalions were taking. Many of those punks who had boasted they would fight to the death were giving up. The winter had been a brutally savage one, and many of the gang members faced starvation and/or freezing to death in the bitter cold. There were only a few holdouts left, and they were waiting in Ben's sector.

Mike had showed up and dropped that news on Ben. "These people aren't going to surrender, Ben," the chief of intelligence told him. "We figure about eight to ten gangs left, total strength about three thousand— maybe less. But they've come together under one leader, they are heavily armed, and all have taken blood oaths to kill you or die trying."

"Who heads the group?"

"A punk named Tony Green. Known as Big Stomper."

"Duffy Williams and those aligned with him?"

"On the French/German border, waiting for us."

"And you can bet they've been beefed up with other expendables from the dregs of Bottger's followers."

"Right on the money, Ben."

Ben smiled at the man. "Drop it all on me, Mike. How strong a force are we facing at the border?"

"Ben, they keep shifting around. It's a ploy to prevent my people from getting any sort of accurate count. But I would guesstimate a force at least equal to our own. And this time they'll have armor and some artillery. Lots of mortars."

Ben mentally digested that news for a moment while Mike poured a fresh cup of coffee. When he had again seated himself, Ben said, "And the creeps are between us and the border." It was not a question.

"You got it. They have no place to go and nothing but death facing them in any direction. Nobody likes a creepie," he added.

After Mike had left, Ben sat at his desk for a time, studying maps. There really was no hard decision to make; the Rebels had to push on, regardless of the obstacles. Ben turned to look at the map behind him, the red pens denoting the last position of his battalions.

Two more days at the most, and the other battalions would be rid of the many prisoners they had taken.

Then the Rebels would have no choice but to push on.

Those members of the world's press that Ben had kicked out had appealed to the transitional government of France for permission to once more enter the country. But this was a much different government than that of the old. The members of this government owed their very existence to Ben Raines and the Rebels. This government chose to ask for Ben's permission.

Ben had always believed that wars could be won much easier if the boo-hooing, hanky-stomping, hand-wringing liberal press was kept out. It had always infuriated him to view or read reports from members of the press who visited enemy camps to interview members of the very army that the forces of democracy were currently fighting. As far as Ben was concerned, it was collaboration and treason and should be punishable by death.

With a great deal of misgiving, Ben finally agreed to let the press back into the country. With some very grim words of advice from him. "If I catch any of you in front of our advance, collaborating with the enemy, under the guise of getting a story, I'll have you shot on the spot. And don't doubt my words for an instant. You stay behind our lines at all times. You get caught in a cross fire, that's your problem. If a Rebel gives you instructions, you obey instantly—or you'll be on the

next boat back to whatever country you came from
. . . providing you're still alive."

"Is he serious?" Cassie was asked.

"Oh, yes," she told them. "Quite serious. Ben
Raines is very easy to get along with," she added with
a smile. "Just do what he tells you to do."

Those listening to Cassie's words tried hard not to
look in the direction of Dick Bogarde, who was standing with another group of reporters some few yards
away. Back in the good ol' days—when certain members of the press tried to dictate both foreign and domestic policy, through sometimes not-so-subtle innu-
endo and felt themselves above any restraints—had a
commanding general of any branch of the armed
forces dared to kick the shit out of one of their own,
that officer would have been crucified. The thorough
thrashing of Dick Bogarde at the fists of General
Raines had not even caused a small ripple.

Times were changing.

For the better, the majority believed.

The Rebels had landed at Normandy in the fall of
the year. The new year had passed, and February was
turning out to be the coldest on record, with snow, ice,
and bitterly cold weather. From Amsterdam to the
south of France, as the Rebels moved out to the east,
they reported finding pockets of punks and creeps frozen to death.

The majority of the press was learning, too. They
reported the findings without weeping, engaging in
verbal or printed snits, or twisting hankies concerning

the dead. Several made the mistake of bemoaning and lamenting upon the fates and deaths of the poor, misguided, misunderstood, politically deprived, society-mistreated, probably-abused-as-children, and surely good boys and girls who just took a slightly wrong turn and certainly didn't deserve such a horrible death. They quickly found themselves on ships back to their home country.

Two more press types made the mistake of slipping through Rebel lines (they really didn't slip through; the Rebels just made no attempt to stop them), and got themselves captured by a gang of punks.

When asked if he was going to send out a rescue party, Ben's reply was uncommonly blunt and physically impossible for those on the receiving end—no play on words intended.

The remains of the two were found the next day. The punks were so desperately short of food, they had eaten the choice cuts of the two.

"Remember," Ben said sarcastically to a group of reporters. "Always take the keys out of your car. Don't let a good boy go bad."

Cassie stood with a smile on her lips and shook her head at Ben's deliberate baiting of the press.

Eleven

At last the long line of Rebels that stretched all across France was ready to push eastward.

"The walled city," Ben said, as Cooper stepped on the gas, pulling away from Nimes.

"Beg pardon?" he asked.

"Avignon, Cooper," Jersey said. "The whole town's got a wall around it."

"That's cool," Cooper said. "But what's *behind* the wall?"

"Starving people, Coop," Ben told him. "No creepies and no punks."

"Well, where the hell are *they*, boss?" Jersey asked.

"Between Toulon and Monaco. It's warmer in the south. Don't worry, we'll get to mix it up with them. Then comes the more difficult part."

His team said nothing. They knew what he meant: Italy and Germany and Bottger's Minority Eradication Forces. Bottger's MEF had slammed down as far south as Rome, overwhelming the small Italian Resistance

Forces. Bottger was now a force that threatened the world.

And there was only one army in the world that had even a remote chance of stopping him: Ben Raines and the Rebels.

"We sure get all the shit jobs," Jersey summed up the feelings of all the team.

"We sure do," Ben said.

"Did it ever occur to you, boss," Ben said, "that just maybe Blanton and the UN secretary-general might be secretly hoping you'll get killed over here?"

"Jesus, Beth!" Cooper said. "Are you serious?"

"Yes, she is, Coop. And yes, I have entertained that thought, Beth," Ben replied. "Several times. But I finally dismissed the idea as false. Blanton is not a bad fellow. Not really. He's matured over the year that we've known him. He has, unfortunately, got some real shit-for-brains people around him. But I have a strong hunch that he'll slowly divest himself of them or push them far into the background where they can do no harm. He knows now that his nation cannot survive under a one hundred percent liberal rule. And he is far too intelligent to see his portion of America crumble and fail while all the other states aligned with us prosper and grow."

"You kind of like Blanton, don't you, boss?" Jersey asked.

"In a way, yes. I didn't at first. But I've grown to have some respect for the man. He desperately tries to do the right thing."

"Yes, but he tries to do it for everybody," Corrie said. "And that's not fair for those who will work at any job to get by and have to pay for those who won't work at anything."

That started a good discussion between the team members—one that Ben stayed out of as the miles rolled by. Corrie, Beth, Jersey, and Cooper were all too young to have many clear memories of the way it was before the Great War. They could remember family and friends and school, but were all too young to have any knowledge of economics or the day-to-day struggle of their parents to get by under the ever-increasing yoke of taxes laid on them by the democratic liberal government in Washington, D.C. What they knew of that they had learned from older Rebels—especially Ben. And he was an excellent teacher, being adamantly opposed to liberalism and socialism: two philosophies without a modicum of difference.

Avignon, the walled city, had suffered little physical damage from the punks and creeps. But here, as in so many larger towns, the citizens were mostly middle-aged and elderly. Their stories were the same: The young had been taken away to serve as slaves and whores for the gangs of thugs or traded to the creeps to be fattened and used as food.

It was at Avignon that Ben noticed, with some amusement, that his 1 Battalion had been gradually growing in strength by several full companies: armor, artillery, and ground troops. He knew perfectly well that his team was fully aware of the enlargement but had said nothing. He also knew who had ordered the buildup: Ike. He had taken several squads from each battalion and sent them in to beef up Ben's 1 Batt. Ben elected to say nothing about it. But it amused him.

Several Rebel battalions had reached the eastern-most French border, and Ben ordered them to halt and hold at the line until all of southern France was clear. Antwerp and Brussels had been cleared, and those battalions had moved to the German border. Ike and his 2 Batt had occupied Geneva and Dan and his 3 Batt had moved in to seize and clean up Lausanne. Other Rebel battalions, beefed up by French, Belgium, Dutch, Italian-Swiss, Luxembourg, and Free German Resistance fighters, were holding at Luxembourg, Metz, Nancy, Epinal, Besancon, Chambery, Grenoble, and Gap.

Ben had not seen Mike Richards in more than a week when the man strolled into his CP for that night and poured coffee and picked up a sandwich, then flopped down in a chair in front of Ben's makeshift desk.

"The gangs of punks under the command of Tony Green have been supplied, quite mysteriously, it seems, with heavy machine guns, rocket launchers, and mortars. They're waiting for you at Cannes and Nice."

"Bottger supplied them?"

"That's my guess. And they've been beefed up with the dregs of society. A fairly sizeable force, Ben. And they've also destroyed the runways."

"The runways can be repaired. But we need those ports." Ben frowned and drummed his fingertips on the desk. "So far, this has been a milk run. Marseille and Toulon are clean. But a suspicion keeps nagging at me that we're heading into a set up of some sort. It's just been too damn easy so far."

"I feel the same way but have no concrete evidence of it. What's your thinking on it?"

"The punks have made some sort of alliance with the creeps, and they're dug in deep, waiting for us to walk in before they spring the trap."

"I wouldn't argue with that philosophy, Ben. But if that's the case, they've done it smooth."

Ben nodded. "Very smoothly, Mike. And that makes me think the creeps did it. Those punks don't have enough sense to plan something that complex." He looked over at Corrie. "Get some of Buddy's special ops people to go in and give me a recon of Nice and Cannes and surrounding areas. We'll continue moving eastward a few miles each day so as not to tip off the creeps and punks that anything is wrong."

Mike stood up. "I'm going to grab a few hours of sleep. See you, Ben."

Ben smiled as he watched Mike leave. He might see the man in a few hours . . . or a few days or a few weeks. With Mike, you just never knew.

Ben leaned back in his chair. Buddy would have his people in place within hours. In a couple of days, Ben should have some idea of what the creeps and the punks had in mind for him. Ben had no way of knowing that Buddy was going in himself.

Buddy and his special ops people jumped into hostile country a couple of hours after receiving the request from his father. Buddy's team slipped through the night until they were within easy distance of the city, slept for a few hours, and were in position on the outskirts of Cannes just after dawn, while the other team was closing in on Nice.

Buddy's team studied the scene for several moments before what lay hidden in buildings became visible to them, and only then because one of the tanks farted to life and poked the muzzle of its main gun out a window.

"Shit!" Buddy said. "They've pulled in armor."

"You can bet the punks aren't manning those MBTs."

"Creeps. We've run into them utilizing high-tech equipment before. And since the movement started in Europe, years ago, this bunch is a lot more savvy than any we've encountered stateside."

The special ops teams watched and noted everything that moved before them in the two cities. Later that afternoon they pulled back and sent their findings by burst transmission.

Ben read the communiqués and told Corrie to get Georgi Striganov on the horn.

"Georgi, start moving your 5 Batt down from Digne. We'll hit Cannes and Nice from the north and the west. Those cities are not on the list of cities I was requested to save if at all possible."

Miles north and slightly east of Ben's position, the Russian chuckled. "So our pilots finally get into action, eh, Ben? They've been complaining to the high heavens."

"They can stop complaining. Now they can show me their stuff."

In the cities of Nice and Cannes, and at Bottger's headquarters deep in Germany, the mood was jovial and somewhat smug. The creeps and punks and men and women of the MEF were sure that the Rebels were about to get the surprise of their lives when they launched their assault against Cannes and Nice.

Somebody was about to get surprised, but it wasn't going to be the Rebels.

Georgi moved his 5 Batt over to Col St. Martin, and Ben moved his 1 Batt to the coastal town of Frejus. The highly modified P-51E's came roaring in at dawn, squadron after squadron, flying right on the deck at over five hundred miles an hour.

After dropping their payloads of HE and WP, the pilots kicked the rudders, did a chandelle, and came screaming back over the cities, machine guns and cannon yammering and booming. They made pass after pass, until they had exhausted their ammo. They left behind them burning and smoking cities, the streets littered with dead creeps and punks and assorted dregs of humanity. Before the stunned occupiers of the cities could recover from the initial attack, the smoky skies were once more filled with the second wave of P-51E's, roaring in from their base at Nimes. While the enemy was taking their second battering from the skies that morning, Ben and Georgi were rolling toward their objectives, MBTs spearheading the columns, traveling as fast as road conditions would permit.

Before the sounds of the P-51E's had faded into memory, two heavily supported battalions of Rebels launched their assaults against Nice and Cannes. For an hour long-range artillery softened the towns with rounds weighing up to 230 pounds. Buildings collapsed and buried crews and machinery before the tanks hidden in the old shells of brick and mortar and wood could lurch themselves free.

Before the last rounds had impacted, ground troops were storming the outskirts of the two cities. Ben and his 1 Batt hit the western edge of Cannes and began butchering their way toward the heart of the city.

"The law-and-order son of a bitch is not taking prisoners!" Tony Green screamed into the ear of his new ally, a robed and hooded creep.

"You were warned," the creep said, then turned and began fleeing for his life.

But there was no place to run except toward the sea. Ben had ordered Buddy's 8 Batt, the special ops battalion, to jump in between Nice and Monaco and also to fill the gap between Highways 85 and 202. Helicopter gunships and PUFFs were in the air, patrolling outside the cities, and they turned lawless living flesh into dead smoking and burned meat as the creeps, malcontents, and thugs tried to escape the burning cities.

Those who offered to surrender were taken prisoner, but few of them elected to give up. These were the hard core of the nation's criminals, facing the final certainty of a hangman's noose. They chose a bullet, and Ben and the Rebels were more than willing to accommodate their wishes.

Ben and team, fighting their way up Rue Felix Faure, toward the Casino des Fleurs, found themselves cut off from Bonelli's company and momentarily on their own.

"I swear you did this deliberately," Jersey panted,

flopping down beside Ben under the sill of a blown-out window.

"Not guilty this time, Little Bit," Ben said, ejecting an empty magazine and locking a full one into place. "What the hell is happening to Bonelli?"

"A pocket of creeps ambushed them," Corrie called. "They're pinned down tight. Just like us," she added.

"We got the bastard!" The shout came over a lull in the fighting. "Ben Raines is in that building right there. I seen the son of a bitch!"

"Bloop that group," Ben said.

Cooper and Jersey started lobbing 40-mm grenades toward the sound of the excited voice. Jersey put one right through the smashed remains of a window, and the explosion blew an arm out the opening. The severed arm lay on a pile of bricks, the fingers clenched into a fist.

"God*damn* you, Ben Raines!" a furious shout erupted from the building directly in front of Ben and team.

"Now he's going to tell us about his deprived childhood," Jersey said, sticking a piece of gum into her mouth.

Ben smiled. He didn't know much about Jersey's background, but he did know that she came from a grindingly poor family in the Southwest and never had a store-bought dress until she joined the Rebels as a teenager. But all that did not propel her into a life of crime. Jersey had even less use than Ben for those who blamed society for their problems.

Ben had once heard Jersey tell a minority gang member taken prisoner, "You think you had a hard time, asshole? I grew up on a goddamn reservation in the desert. My playmates were rattlesnakes, Gila monsters, and scorpions. I didn't know what running water and indoor plumbing were until I was ten years old. So fuck you and the horse you rode in on—*prick!*"

"Two rockets about to be fired," Corrie called from across the room. "Armbrust."

The bottom floor of the building housing the punks exploded in flames as the rockets impacted.

"Tell Bonelli thanks," Ben said.

"Not Bonelli, boss," Corrie replied. "Free German Resistance fighters."

"Then tell them *danke schoen.*" Ben stood up. "Let's take this damn city."

Mop-up is always the worst job. It means dealing with snipers and mines and booby traps and the fanatical hard-core enemy. But this time when the Rebels found a sniper hidden in a building, they called up tanks and poured on the artillery. A .30-06 is no match for a 105 mounted on the turret of a main battle tank. But two of the gang leaders got away: Tony Green and Tuba Salami. They took with them about 150 members. But nearly 4000 others lay buried in a mass grave between Cannes and Nice.

Cannes and Nice not only broke the back of the punks in France, it also astonished the hell out of Bruno Bottger and lit a fire under him. He had been sure the ambush would work. He was positive that the Rebels would drive right into it and that would have been the end.

Bruno Bottger had a lot to learn about Ben Raines.

Bottger gathered his generals and listened to their plans and theories about how to deal with Ben Raines and the Rebels. Bottger listened and then made up his own mind as to what strategy would be best.

"The Rebels are weary of the cold. So I believe Ben Raines will split his Rebels into two forces. One force will leave immediately, attempting to take the southern route through Italy, staying to the south until spring. Then they will cut north and attack Germany from the east, while the second force will push through from the west." Bottger stood up and walked to a huge wall map, picking up a pointer. "The push from the west will, in all likelihood, be on three points. They will jump off from Brussels, Luxembourg, and France. I am certain that Raines himself will be in command of the troops attacking Germany from the east. That attack will be two-pronged. They will attack from these two points: Salzburg, and drive toward Munich, and Passau, staying north of the Danube, and push toward Regensburg. I am convinced that this is the way Raines will think."

He was met with enthusiastic applause.

Bottger tossed the pointer to the table and glared at his people. "And then again," he said, his voice thick with sarcasm, "Ben Raines might do none of those things." He placed both hands on the polished table. "Listen to me, gentlemen. There is one thing about Raines that we must all acknowledge. He is unpredictable. No one, *no one*, can second guess the man. I can't, you can't. None of us will know what Ben is going to do until he puts his plans into action." Bottger sighed heavily and sat down. "That means we must be ready on all fronts. We must be ready to defend our homeland from the north, the south, the east, and the west."

"We can do that, General," one of his younger commanders said. "For we have something that Raines does not."

"Oh?" Bottger questioned, arching one eyebrow. "And what might that be?"

"God is on our side."

Bottger stared at the young officer for a moment, his eyes mirroring total disbelief at such an absurd statement. "Shit!" he said.

Twelve

For several weeks Ben let his troops relax. His engineers repaired the airport, and transport planes began flying into Nice and Cannes day and night. Ben ordered that each Rebel, and each member of the various resistance groups fighting with the Rebels, was to be given three days of R&R in the warm clime of the south of France. They relaxed on the beaches under the sun, swam in the warm waters of the Mediterranean, read, slept, ate three hot meals a day, and let the war be only a memory for a few days.

During that time, Ben met with his field commanders to map out strategy for the spring campaign: Vanderhoot of the Free Dutch, Rene Seaux of the FRF, Matthies of the German Resistance, Roche of Belgium, Plaisance of Luxembourg, de Saussure of the Swiss Resistance, Randazzo of the Italian Freedom fighters.

Mike Richards and some of his people had wandered back in after a two-week absence, and the chief of intelligence was sitting in on the meeting. Mike had reported massive troop movements inside Bottger's claimed territory, which included much of Switzerland, all of Germany, all of Northern Italy, and parts of what used to be known as Poland, Czechoslovakia, Hungary, Austria, and Yugoslavia. Mike was not sure just how far eastward Bottger claimed as his own.

"Too damn far," Ben had said with a grunt.

At the meeting Ben said, "Bottger has no idea where we're going to attack. He's shifting troops all over the damn place. And I am sure he is fully aware that by his doing so, he is weakening vital cross-points. But he has no choice in the matter." Ben pointed to General Roche of the Belgian Resistance, who had stirred restlessly in his chair.

"We must not forget that Bottger has thousands of civilian fighters aiding him, General. There are that many people in the countries he occupies who wish a return to the old ways . . . or at the very least, a change from the present. We're going to be outnumbered fifty to one."

Ben smiled. "The Rebels are always outnumbered, General Roche. I can't recall a campaign when we weren't. The trick to defeating our enemy is to be smarter, tougher, meaner, and twice as ruthless."

Roche smiled and said very dryly, "So I have noticed, General."

"So where do we launch our offensive, General Raines?" General Randazzo of the Italian Freedom fighters asked.

Ben shrugged. "I haven't the vaguest idea," he admitted.

* * *

Stateside, Cecil Jefferys, president of the SUSA, smiled at the latest domestic news. The economy of the SUSA and those western states who had aligned with the SUSA was booming; they were hard-pressed to fill the many jobs that were being created daily. A few companies had tried the Rebel philosophy—but had found it either too open or too harsh to suit them or too mystifying in its simplicity for them to comprehend—and had pulled out, heading back to Blanton's crumbling-around-the-edges-quasi-socialistic rule. But for every company that pulled out, ten stayed and ten more wanted in.

Blanton's Justice Department had, of course, informers within the SUSA, reporting to their superiors. Cecil was well aware of that and didn't particularly give a damn . . . as long as they did not try to stir up trouble. It was amusing to Cecil that the informers were scared to death every minute of the day and night that they might be found out.

Cecil looked at the men and women seated in his large office. They had come to the SUSA to look it over and try to understand what made it so attractive to other companies, and why so many people were flocking to it in droves, and some were frantically leaving.

"Mr. President," a lady from one of the newly emerging Fortune 500 companies said, "I don't understand your system of health care here. I spoke with a woman who was taking her family and moving out of the SUSA. She told me she had been refused medical care."

"I'm not familiar with the case, but I find it difficult

to believe that any resident of the SUSA was denied medical care."

"She had a cut finger."

Cecil blinked at that. "A cut finger?"

"Yes. She asked to see a doctor and was instead shown to some sort of para-medical person."

"That's common practice here. We have aid-stations all over the SUSA, staffed by EMTs and trained medics. They handled minor medical problems: stitching up cuts, tending to non-life-threatening wounds. That keeps emergency rooms clear for real emergencies."

"Some people might wish to see a physician instead."

"That's up to the medic at the aid-station. They won't tackle anything they're not qualified to handle. But many of them are so close to being doctors, I've seen doctors defer to them. Most of them have had years of treating combat wounds. There is very little they can't handle."

"So if someone had a burst appendix, they could operate?" a man asked.

"They could . . . and have. But unless they felt the patient would die before they could get to a hospital, they wouldn't. It's a judgment call for them."

"I'm not sure I would like to live in such a society, Mr. President," the man replied.

"It's strictly up to you, sir," Cecil said with a smile. "But before you make any decisions, why not visit those aid-stations and talk to our doctors about them?"

"Good idea. I shall."

"I don't understand the laws in this society, President Jefferys," another man spoke up. "People who have moved in here boast that this is basically a commonsense form of government. I'm baffled as to just what that means . . ." He shook his head.

Cecil started to speak, and the businessman held up a hand. "Please, sir. Allow me to elaborate."

"Go right ahead."

"I've subscribed to several of your newspapers for some months now, not trying to understand what is so special about this place but trying to *understand* it, period. I haven't seen a police officer since we arrived here several days ago. I see an occasional army Jeep or HumVee, with uniformed soldiers, but no police. Do you have police?"

"Yes. But not the kind you are accustomed to seeing. Mr., ah . . ." Cecil consulted a paper. "Mr., ah, MacKensie. We just don't need a massive showing of police in the SUSA. People who don't obey the law here don't last long. We either escort them to the nearest border and tell them not to come back, lock them up and throw away the key, or somebody shoots them. We've brought it all back to the basics here. My oldest and dearest friend, Ben Raines, used to put it this way: 'A smart person rakes his leaves, bags them, and takes them to the nearest landfill for disposal. A very stupid person, and the kind we don't tolerate here, rakes them, sets them on fire, and lets the smoke drift into his neighbor's window.' Cecil smiled. "Now, Mr. MacKensie, if you don't understand all the meaning behind those words—"

Again, MacKensie held up his hand. "Oh, I do, Mr. President. Are you telling me that should that occur, someone might pick up a gun and *shoot* the offending neighbor?"

"Oh, not the first time it happens," Cecil replied with a straight face. "We give everybody one mistake."

"What?" MacKensie blurted.

The woman seated to MacKensie's left smiled and then burst out laughing. MacKensie turned to her, irritation on his face. "Linda, I fail to see the humor in any of this."

"Robert," she said. "He's having fun with you. Can't you see that? I suspect the people who request to live in the SUSA are very conservative, law-abiding, and considerate. And they are fully aware of the unwritten laws in this nation. Isn't that correct, Mr. President?"

"Absolutely, Ms. Lambard."

"I'm still confused," MacKensie said.

Cecil said, "Mr. MacKensie, back before the Great War, I read of an account in New York City where a cop shot a thief and the thief sued and won something like three or four million dollars. Do you remember that incident, or one similar . . . of which there were many?"

"Yes, I do. So?"

"That has about as much chance of happening here as the possibility of my being able to flap my arms and soar with eagles. This is a law-and-order society. We teach it in schools. Public schools. There are no private schools in the SUSA. None, and there never will be any. There are no church-run elementary, middle, or high schools in the SUSA. None, and there never will be any. Every student receives the same type of education here. The finest in the world. We do have schools for exceptional children, on both ends of the spectrum. There is no such thing as social promotion. And there never will be. Our vo-tech schools are the finest in the world and so are our institutions of higher education. There are no crap courses. No easy courses. There are no sorority or frat houses, no basketball, football, or baseball teams. And as long as Ben Raines is alive, there never will be. Learning comes first. There is no such thing as a party school in the SUSA or in any of the states aligned with us. And there never will be. That is not to say the kids don't have fun, because they do. They have their beer busts and spring breaks and so forth. I even heard there was a panty raid at one not too long ago. When I mentioned it to Ben, he smiled and said, 'Things are getting back to normal, aren't they?'

"Teachers teach here, Mr. MacKensie. They demand respect from their students and they get it. They don't show up in blue jeans, and they aren't buddy-buddy with their students. They teach. There has been only one incident of a student assaulting a teacher in high school. The principal was walking by when it happened. He physically stomped the crap out of the kid, then put one foot on the kid's neck, held the kid down on the floor, took off his belt, and wore the kid's ass out with it. Then he dragged the student down the hall to the office, called the kid's parents, and told him to come get the kid and keep him until he could behave in a civilized manner. That young man is now a senior at Pal Elliot University and on the honor role. He plans to be a doctor. All he needed was a slight attitude adjustment. Are you beginning to understand how we work here, Mr. MacKensie?"

"Did the young man's parents sue?" MacKensie asked.

Cecil burst out laughing. "Are you kidding? You're not kidding. Hell no, they didn't sue. Even if they could find a lawyer to take the case—and in the SUSA that would have been extremely difficult, if not impossible—it would have been tossed out of court."

MacKensie was obviously shocked. Linda Lambard was amused at the recalling of the incident, as were the others seated in a half circle around Cecil's desk. With the exception of MacKensie, these were men and women who believed strongly in a law-and-order, capitalistic society—the only type of government that history proves actually worked.

"Your form of government is rather harsh, President Jefferys," MacKensie remarked.

"Works for us," Cecil replied.

"It is based on violence and total disregard for human rights," MacKensie countered.

"It's based on common sense, respect for the rights of others, and discipline," Cecil said with a smile.

MacKensie stood up. "I don't think I like your society, President Jefferys. My company will not be relocating here."

"Your option, sir."

When MacKensie had left, Cecil looked at the others. "And the rest of you?"

They were all relocating to the SUSA.

Cecil smiled. "Seven out of eight ain't too shabby," he said.

*   *   *

"Why is he waiting?" Bruno Bottger muttered the question as he stared at the wall map of Europe. Bruno did not expect a reply from any of the others in the room, and none was offered.

The harsh winter had broken, and a glorious spring had blossomed several weeks earlier than usual. The roads, for the most part, were clear and the valleys open. Bottger had repositioned his troops and all was ready. Still, Ben Raines did nothing.

Nothing was a word only in Bottger's mind, for Ben was doing plenty. Ships were arriving daily from the States with supplies for the next campaign. Fuel was being trucked to various jump-off points. Tankers were being made ready for the long pull into central Europe . . . and beyond. Special ops teams were training in preparation for the assault. Operations were being planned and carefully gone over and revised and honed to a razor's sharpness.

And Ben also had to separate, widely, Rene Seaux, commander of the Free French and General Matthies of the German Resistance. The two men did not get along at all. Especially after General Matthies said, "Goddamn French. You fuck with your faces and fight with your feet! You always have."

It took a half dozen men to break up the fist fight before the two inflicted serious injury upon each other. Ben then assigned Rene far to the north and General Matthies far to the south. General Matthies had a slightly higher opinion of the Italian Resistance . . . but only slightly.

Several times Ben put his people on high alert, knowing that Bottger had eyes watching him, as he had eyes watching Bottger. Each time he did that, Bottger was forced to throw his people on full alert, creating a lot of nervousness and unneeded tension among his people.

"The son of a bitch!" Bottger cursed Ben, after each alert proved to be false.

Bottger was learning, albeit slowly, about Ben Raines and his tactics.

Ben had moved his 1 Batt up and Dan's 3 Batt back to Geneva and shifted Ike and his 2 Batt down to the south of France. Everyone else remained in place. The Rebels knew it was time. They waited.

"We go in tomorrow morning," Ben told Corrie.

Thirteen

The assault was nothing fancy and nothing tricky. The campaign began with a straight-ahead push, and it caught Bottger by surprise, for he was not expecting anything so simple as that—not from Ben Raines.

This time Bottger did toss a bit of a temper tantrum. He stomped around his luxuriously appointed office and kicked wastebaskets and cussed and shouted at the walls. He had only the walls to curse, for everyone else had beat a hasty exit seconds after Bottger received the news of the assault.

Rage vented, Bottger shouted into the intercom, "Staff, in here! And don't disturb us for any reason! Any reason!"

The huge room slowly filled with staff members and field generals.

"Nothing from the north, south, or east?" Bottger demanded, hands on his hips, eyes burning as they glared at his people.

"No, sir," a ranking general said. "It was a straight-ahead assault. And it was very successful. Enemy troops are now inside Germany, Switzerland, and Italy."

But just barely. All along the battlefront, after the front-line troops of Bottger had recovered from their shock, they threw up defensive positions and held.

"The Free French came across the border and took Norden, Emden, and Leer," Bottger was informed.

Bruno blew his top again. "Are you telling me that a bunch of pussy-faced French Frogs overran my troops and routed them?" he screamed.

"Yes, sir."

"That's impossible!" Bruno shouted. "The French can't fight. Everybody knows the French can't fight. There must be some sort of mistake in decoding the communiqué."

The room fell silent as all could faintly detect a low roaring sound.

"What the hell is that?" Bruno asked, after listening for a few seconds.

"Probably a minor malfunction in the heating system, sir," a junior officer said.

It was about to get plenty hot, for a fact. But it had nothing to do with the old castle's up-to-date central heating system.

"Sounds like . . . planes," a colonel observed, involuntarily looking upward. "Prop planes. But the pitch is . . . well, stronger, somehow."

"Planes?" Bruno said. "Planes? Here? We are almost five hundred kilometers from the nearest border fighting. Don't be absurd!"

Before Bruno's words were through echoing around the marble-floored room, .50-caliber wing guns and cannon opened up from the lead planes of the three squadrons of P-51E's that had dared to cross nearly the whole of Germany, flying at treetop level, just to show Herr Field Marshal General Supreme Commander of the MEF Bruno Bottger that no matter where he might reside, he was not out of the reach of General Ben Raines and the Rebels.

Bruno hit the hard marble floor as slugs raked the room, whining off the marble and in general raising hell among the expensive vases and paintings around the room. One slug ruined the huge portrait of Adolph Hitler, stitching der führer from groin to nose. The heavy frame came loose from its mount and conked a general on the noggin, knocking him unconscious.

Bruno unceremoniously crawled under a desk just as a nearly spent slug slammed into his left buttock. It had enough force left to bring a wail of protest.

"Are you hurt, sir?" an aide yelled.

"Yes, goddamnit! I've been shot!"

"Where, sir?"

"In the ass, you idiot!"

Then there was no more time for words as the modified P-51E's banked and came around for a second pass, wing guns yammering and booming. The bombs they dropped on their first pass had exploded cars and trucks and set outbuildings on fire, and the smoke was thick and blinding to those on the ground. Bruno's people had surface-to-air missiles, but the planes were flying so low the missiles were useless against them.

One of the pilots was about a hundred feet off the ground and flying at over five hundred miles an hour. He grinned at an MEF officer as he roared past. The officer stood and gaped at the plane. A huge fist with a good ol' American middle finger was painted on the side of the plane. The officer stared in disbelief at the clearly visible rigid digit. By the time the officer recovered from his shock, the plane was out of sight, heading southwest to Switzerland.

Portions of the old castle has taken several direct bomb hits and were on fire. Limping badly, one hand holding the bruised left side of his ass, Bruno managed to clear the castle and give his men a chance to start pouring water on the flames.

"Get me a cushion!" Bruno bellowed.

Hilda Koller, Bruno's love at the moment, who was a 100 percent sadist and a closet dyke, came rushing out of her quarters of the castle, dressed in black leather and carrying her favorite whips and chains. She was cussing a blue streak.

"Mein Gott!" she hollered. "Vas is happening?"

Bruno gave her a very dirty look and tried not to grimace at the pain in his ass—literally and figuratively.

Dan had split off from Ben at Lausanne, taking Highway N1 toward Yverdon, Neuchatel, and Biel, while Ben stayed with E27 toward Bern. Ben ran into trouble at Bulle. A group of MEF regulars were racing toward the French border, and Ben's 1 Batt nearly collided with them. For fifteen minutes it was a battle of tanks. But in this war Bruno's tanks were no match for Ben's MBTs. The Rebels' main battle tanks were far superior in nearly every way: bigger and carrying heavier guns and armament. They blew Bruno's tanks off the road, and then it was infantry all the way as the two forces mixed it up.

Bruno's forces carried heavier-caliber rifles, mostly 7.62's. But they did not possess in any great numbers what the Rebels called Big Thumper: an automatic 40-mm grenade launcher that could spit out the mini-bombs at an incredible rate of fire.

After the MEF tanks were destroyed, Bruno's men slowly began giving up ground to the Rebels. But the commander decided to give ground too late. Ben had ordered two of his companies to flank the MEF, trapping them in a hellish cross fire. The commander of this contingent of the MEF was many things, but a fool was not one of them. He ordered his men to surrender.

It was particularly irritating to the commander when he saw what a mixed bag the Rebels were: Spanish, Negro, Indian, and just about every other race and creed one could name were included among their ranks.

"I don't know how you managed to whip these inferiors into any kind of effective fighting force, General," the MEF major said to Ben.

"I promised the Spanish people lots of tequila and tortillas, the blacks watermelons and chittlins, and the Indians lots of scalps," Ben said with a straight face.

Right on cue, Jersey whipped out a long-bladed knife and smiled at the major.

The major shut his mouth and did not open it again. But he could not understand why all the Rebels who were standing around General Raines were laughing at him as he was led away.

*   *   *

The Rebels rammed into Bottger's claimed territory and hung on with the tenacity of a bulldog. Bottger's men backed up, grudgingly giving the Rebels and the resistance fighters a few miles that first day, then began to dig in and hold as the first units of reinforcements reached them.

Ben had warned his people that this was not going to be an easy fight. He knew that Bottger's men were highly trained and just as motivated in their own way as the Rebels were in theirs.

The older Rebels could understand the motivation of the MEF, the younger Rebels could not. And Ben was very much aware that he had a few borderline men and women in his command who just might decide to adopt the views of the MEF and go over to them. The question of race had long been settled among 95 percent of the Rebels. But hates and blind prejudices could run deep, and among some, could never really be erased.

"There are good people and bad people among all races," Cooper said, the second evening of the eastern push. Ben's 1 Batt was bivouacked in a small town about fifteen miles from the city of Fribourg. "But no race of people is entirely bad. That's ridiculous."

Ben looked up from his maps. "You're all too young to remember the riots that started a few years before the Great War," he told his team. "It was a very touchy time in America. With certain members of the black community blaming all their troubles on the whites. And many whites blaming the crime upswing and dope dealing and drive-by shootings and personal assaults entirely on the blacks. Many whites just simply stopped watching the evening news on television because it seemed as though every evening some reporter was interviewing some black about some real or imagined problem. There was more racial discontent and hate bubbling just under the surface then than when I was a kid back in the sixties, when civil rights legislation was signed into law and real integration began."

Ben got up and poured another cup of coffee and picked up a sandwich from a tray brought over by the mess people. He sat down behind his camp desk and was thoughtful for a moment.

"I had been through a full-blown war in Southeast Asia and several brush wars in Africa and Central America before I settled down to build a more peaceful career. But those years before the Great War were the goddamndest years I had ever witnessed in terms of sheer absurdity and misunderstanding and miscarriages of justice . . . to name just a few things.

"It wasn't true, of course, but to many people, including myself, it appeared that every time a black was arrested for something, some damn group would jump up and scream racial discrimination. And I had never heard so many excuses for just plain lawlessness. A large percentage of whites just got sick of it—me included.

"You couldn't visit the nation's capital without fear of getting mugged or caught up in a drive-by shooting or some other act of mindless violence. Our nation's capital was a battle zone. That had to be one of the most disgusting and disgraceful pieces of news of the decade. I actually heard a damn network reporter say that he just didn't know what was causing the violence in Washington, D.C., and more importantly, who to blame for it. I laughed all the way to the bathroom so I could puke. You see, Washington, D.C., was a federal district. It was set up to be governed by Congress. Not to have a mayor or its own police force—all that was shoved down Americans' throats without their permission. But Congress was famous for things like that. The district should have been policed by the military. It should not have been allowed to turn into a welfare community.

"Now, with all the mindless acts of violence around the nation, many heretofore fair-minded whites began quietly turning against blacks . . . not just the lawless blacks but all blacks. And that was blatantly wrong. But the majority of blacks would not go public and say: 'Enough—we have a problem within our own community, and it's not the fault of the whites. Stop blaming the whites for the problems caused by blacks.' They wouldn't do it. So that caused more discontent and distrust and hate among many whites. Then the riots started. Whites sat in their living rooms and watched blacks and other minorities loot and burn down block after block of cities . . . and get away with it. Whites watched on TV as minorities violently and savagely and brutally attacked and beat innocent people . . . and received no more than a slap on the wrist for it. And then they listened to whining liberal excuses for what had happened. It was sickening and disgusting, and that spawned more hate among many whites.

"Not one mayor, not one governor had the guts to

order looters shot on sight. And then, to heap more fuel on the flames of racial discontent, who had to pay for the rebuilding of the cities those goddamn savages destroyed? The hard-working, overburdened, law-abiding American taxpayer.

"Oh, we *could* have stopped the drug traffic and the lawlessness and the terrible, mindless violence in America. But our elected leaders would not do it. They were too damn timid to take the harsh measures needed to do that . . ."

The large room was now crowded with Rebels; young Rebels and older Rebels. Rebels of all colors and creeds. Corrie had signaled a friend in communications, and the friend spread the word in about three seconds. For when Ben Raines started lecturing, his people listened.

"I lost my brother in a drive-by shooting," a black sergeant said, his voice filled with emotion. "The boy was walking home from school. He was nine years old. The goddamn system—I don't know exactly who was to blame—allowed a deal to be cut, and the shooters got a few years in prison and then walked free. If I ever find the judge who sentenced those punk niggers, I'll kill that son of a bitch!"

"That was part of the problem," Ben said. "Many judges and most liberals were opposed to any type of mandatory sentencing laws. Like the ones we have in the SUSA." Ben smiled. "And also part of the problem was the term you just used in describing the people who killed your brother."

The sergeant returned the smile. "A nigger is the lowest form of black person. Just like white trash is the lowest form of white person. I guess you have to be southern born and bred to understand that."

"So it's all right for a black to use that term, but not a white. Is that it, Sergeant?" Ben pressed.

"It sort of depends on who is doin' the callin' and who is on the receivin' end of it, General," the sergeant replied with a faint smile.

Cassie Phillips had joined the crowd early on, as had Frank Service and Nils Wilson, the only three reporters Ben would allow to travel with his command battalion. Cassie asked, "But where is the line drawn when it comes to name-calling?"

"That's where the rub comes in, Miss Phillips," the sergeant said. "Givin' the devil his due, back before the Great War, the liberals tried to do the right thing. But they went too far. Personal conduct and morality and consideration for your fellow bein' can be legislated only to a point. After that, common sense has to take over. Have you ever tried to talk common sense to a redneck?"

"Or to a nigger?" another Rebel said quietly.

"That's right," the sergeant was quick to agree. "Or to a nigger."

Nils Wilson closed his notepad. "I don't understand any of this," he admitted. "I have always found the word 'nigger' to be offensive."

"And I never like being called a honky mother-fucker," Ben spoke up. "But the way I interpreted the wording, one was protected by civil rights legislation and punishable by law, while the other wasn't. There is an old saying concerning the goose and the gander."

"Boss," Corrie called. "I hate to break in just when

this discussion is getting lively, but Bruno Bottger just sent word that he wants to talk to you—face to face."

"It's a trick!" Jim Peters, commander of 14 Batt said.

"I agree," Pat O'Shea of 10 Batt said.

Ben had gotten all his batt coms on a hookup to give them the news. "I don't know," Ben said, keying the mic. "He's agreed to meet anyplace I choose. That doesn't sound like a trick or trap to me. I'll get back with you all in a few minutes." He turned to Corrie. "Get me Bottger on the horn."

"General Bottger here, General Raines." Bruno's voice came out of the speaker.

"How about Paris?" Ben suggested.

"If you could guarantee my safety in that city, I would agree. Can you do that?"

Ben hesitated only a second. "No, General. I cannot guarantee your safety there."

"Then . . . where shall we meet?"

"I'm open to suggestion."

"I would be amenable to meeting in Geneva."

"I'm almost certain you would be safe there. I would pull back all resistance groups and have my 1 and 3 Batts secure the meeting place."

"I would insist that the secretary-general of the United Nations be present."

"I believe I can arrange that."

"Very good. And a top representative of the United States government."

"I can probably arrange that. In return, I would want the top officials of your government present."

"That shall be done. Then we are in agreement?"

"So far, yes. I'll be back with you in twenty-four hours, General."

"Thank you, General. Looking forward to it."

Much to Ben's surprise, Homer Blanton jumped at the chance to attend. What Ben didn't know was that Homer would have agreed to kiss the devil's ass for a chance to get away for a few days from VP Harriet Hooter, Rita Rivers, I. M. Holey, Dumkowski, and, hopefully, Homer's wife . . . he was running out of things in his office for her to throw at him.

"Please don't bring Harriet Hooter," Ben urged.

"God forbid!" Homer said.

"Or Rita Rivers."

"Don't even think that!"

"Perhaps I'll see you soon, then, Mr. President."

"I certainly hope so, General."

"Until then. And have a safe trip, Homer."

"Why . . . I think you really mean that, Ben."

"Oh, I do, Homer. If something were to happen to you, then Harriet Hooter would become president."

Homer Blanton hung up, cutting off his own laughter.

Book Three

"The time has come," the Walrus said,
"To talk of many things:
"Of shoes—and ships—and sealing wax—
"Of cabbages—and kings—
"And why the sea is boiling hot—
"And whether pigs have wings."
                              —Lewis Carroll

One

Secretary-General Son Moon arrived first, with a plane filled with aides and other UN officials. President Homer Blanton arrived the next day . . . with his wife in tow.

"Oh, wonderful," Jersey said, eyeballing the woman as she strode regally down the steps from the plane.

One of Blanton's aides came rushing up to Ben. "Where is the band?"

"What band?" Ben asked.

"The band to greet the president of the United States."

"They're not united anymore," Cooper said. "Or have you forgotten?"

From behind Ben, back in the ranks, someone started softly whistling "Dixie."

"Knock it off!" Ben said.

Jersey held out a harmonica. "Here. You want music. Toot on this."

The aide ignored her and said, "Why aren't your troops in dress uniform, General?"

"We don't have any," Ben told him. "The Rebels are not parade ground soldiers."

The harried aide rolled his eyes and went rushing about in a dither.

The Secret Service had been in Geneva for several days, securing and checking things out and arranging accommodations; they all wore worried expressions at the sight of so many guns.

They had really gone into a panic when Ben told them that more than likely there were still some creepies around the city.

Ben shook hands with Homer and spoke to his wife. She frosted him with a look. Ben laughed at her, and that really pissed off the First Lady. The two men rode to the hotel in separate vehicles: The president in his flown-over limo and Ben in his HumVee.

Homer and his staff and entourage took up one entire floor, the UN secretary-general and his people, another floor, and yet another floor had been reserved for Bruno Bottger and his people. Ben and his people bunked across the street in a warehouse, on the floor on inflatable mattresses. Many of the Rebels had been sleeping on the ground for so many years it was difficult for them to get to sleep in a closed room in a real bed.

A grand feast was planned for that night in the hotel's dining room. Ben thanked the aide and returned the invite with a polite no thanks. Ben's rule was hard and fast: He ate what his troops ate—always had, always would.

Bruno Bottger's plane arrived in the middle of the afternoon. Ben met his adversary at the airport, and the two men sized each other up. Bruno was younger than Ben, and Ben guessed him to be in excellent physical shape. Ben was a couple of inches taller, and wore his graying hair much shorter than Bruno's very blond hair.

"The famous General Ben Raines," Bruno said, shaking hands.

"The infamous General Bruno Bottger," Ben responded with a smile.

Bruno laughed. "Ah! But not as infamous as you have been led to believe, my dear General Raines. Not nearly so much. It will all come out in the meetings. I assure you of that."

"We'll see," Ben replied, wondering what in the hell Bruno had up the sleeve of his meticulously tailored gray uniform jacket. No death's head insignia here; no lightning flashes on the collars.

Bruno smiled at the puzzled look in Ben's eyes. "I have slaughtered no Jews, General. And there is much, much more. You'll see."

One of Blanton's aides came flapping up, his blow-dried and lacquered hair as stiff as a poker. "My dear General Bottger!" he blithered. "Come. Please. We are having a banquet this evening at the hotel." He glanced at Ben. "He refused to attend."

Bruno arched an eyebrow. "Oh?"

"I eat what my troops eat."

"Very admirable of you, General, I'm sure. Makes you just one of the boys, eh?"

Ben grunted.

After Bottger and his staff and the president's aide had left, Dan Gray said, "The bastard's got something up his sleeve, Ben."

"Yeah, Dan. But what?"

The first meeting was scheduled for nine o'clock in the morning. With typical Germanic precision, Bruno and his people were there on the dot. Blanton looked very presidential in his thousand-dollar handmade suit. Son Moon was wearing a suit of equal monetary value. Bruno was resplendent in a tailored uniform. Ben wore a set of freshly laundered and ironed old French Foreign Legion lizard BDUs and polished jump boots.

Son Moon gestured toward Bruno, and the leader of the MEF stood up. "I have been accused of operating concentration camps," he began. "Of systematically executing those of the Jewish persuasion. I categorically deny that charge, and furthermore I defy anyone to produce one person who has even a modicum of proof to substantiate those charges. I assure you all, your search will be futile because the charges are false. There are no concentration camps for Jews. None. There never have been any, and there are no plans for any to be built."

What he said was true. There was no hard proof that Bruno's MEF had imprisoned or tortured or killed any Jews. No pictures of the alleged atrocities.

"But we have ample proof that you forced Jews out of your claimed territory, General." The secretary-general was the first to speak.

"Guilty as charged," Bruno replied, sitting down. "I don't deny ordering that done. But it was done as peacefully, bloodlessly, and as orderly as was humanly possible. Yes, those that used force against us were killed or wounded. I admit that. And I also say this:

Those Jews were paid for their property—in gold. Anyone who says they were not compensated is a liar."

Ben remained silent, a faint smile on his lips. He thought he now knew what Bruno was doing, and if he was correct, it was a slick move. Ben would wait before speaking.

Bruno said, "Furthermore not all Jews were relocated. Oh, my, no. There are many of the Jewish persuasion still living and prospering in the territory we now control. Quite a goodly number, as a matter of fact. Most of those of Spanish ancestry were not relocated. Few Americans, English, or French who were living in Germany and the other countries who chose to align with us were relocated—"

"All white," Ben finally spoke.

Bruno smiled at Ben. "Correct, General Raines."

Son Moon and Blanton were both looking at Ben.

"The blacks, now," Ben continued. "They are quite a different matter, are they not?"

"They are proven to be genetically inferior beings," Bruno replied. "Not all. But many. At their very core is savagery. If you—any of you—try to deny that, you will be refuted by medical facts. The same applies to the group of people you Americans refer to as white trash . . ."

Ben let Bruno talk. He now knew exactly what Bruno was doing, and damned if he could figure out how he was going to defend against it.

". . . The species called white trash," Bruno said, "are genetically inferior beings. They possess the same moral deficiencies as Negroes. They breed like animals, without thought of how they will provide properly for their offspring. They are ignorant and happy to be ignorant, and in spite of all your efforts, the majority prefer to remain ignorant. Fuckin', fightin', fishin', and huntin' seem to be their preferred choices of recreation. Your own social programs in America, on which you have wasted billions and billions of dollars of taxpayer money, have produced nothing of substance. And you know it. It was a dismally disappointing three-decade-long social and fiscal failure. Oh, occasionally, one or two out of a hundred will crawl out of the mold and make something of themselves, but we have found it isn't cost-effective to allow that. The percentages are too low to be of any value."

Bruno poured a glass of water and thanked an aide who freshened his cup of coffee. He waited for reaction from Son Moon, Blanton, and Ben Raines.

Son Moon's expression was totally bland, his eyes unreadable. He said nothing.

Blanton wore a look of pure astonishment.

Ben Raines smiled and waited for Bruno Bottger to drop the other boot. A very heavy boot that Ben knew was coming—straight at him.

But Bruno was not yet ready to do that. He said, "We relocated Jews who aided Negroes and continually invented excuses for their behavior. We first spoke with them, urging them to stop it. Most refused. Those are the ones we relocated.

"We waited to see what the Negroes would do to help solve the crime problems created by their kind. Ninety-nine percent did nothing. *Nothing.* The same in America and you cannot deny that. You *can not* deny it. The only thing the Negroes did was blame the whites for their own problems. And the liberals in your government sat back and cooed and nodded their heads in agreement and created wishy-washy programs that cost millions of taxpayer dollars and in the end accomplished nothing. *Nothing!* And that is only the beginning."

Bruno took a sip of water and said, "You allowed the Negroes in America to teach myths to their young. Great centers of advanced learning in Africa. Bah! A lie. A lie that you all knew was a lie and allowed a myth to somehow become fact. Great centers of learning and fine universities in Timbuktu. A lie. Ben Raines has been to Timbuktu. He has read the accounts of Dutch explorers who were there centuries ago. What did those early *white* explorers find, General Raines?"

"Arabs holding black slaves used to carry mud in baskets to build homes."

"Any Negro centers of advanced learning, General Raines?"

"Not that early explorers could find, General Bottger. At least not to my knowledge."

"Oh! Well. Then who finally did discover the ruins of these great black institutions of higher learning? And all these marvelous cultures I keep hearing about?" He looked at President Blanton. "You answer that, Mr. President of the United States. You've had your nose up a nigger's ass for years. Surely you would know the answer to that."

Homer lost his cool. "I don't have to sit here and listen to this bigoted bullshit!" he thundered, slamming one big hand on the table top.

"Proof!" Bruno matched his shout. "Give me concrete proof of all these accomplishments the Negroes claim they had, and then were lost—quite mysteriously I must say—and I'll eat humble pie. People can lose their cultures, their past. I'll readily admit that. But something remains of it. Some shard of pottery. Some crumbling bit of stone with words on it . . . proving they knew how to read and write. But nothing like that exists, does it? Only lies and half-truths and myths."

No one in the room chose to reply to that. Certainly Ben didn't . . . and he was probably the most qualified of any there to offer a reply. He had worked in Africa while in the employ of the Company.

Bruno said, "I have seen with my own eyes remnants of a culture twenty thousand years old. Just to the west of us in France. Do you know of that, Ben Raines?"

"The Lascaux Cave. Yes, I know of it. I've seen it."

"Marvelous, isn't it?"

Son Moon spoke for the first time. "I fail to see what this line of conversation has to do with why we have gathered, General Bottger."

"Oh, it has everything to do with it, sir," Bruno said. "I'll get to it. Humor me."

Homer had his explosive temper back under control. Ben had never lost his. Son Moon's face was expressionless as he waved a hand, meaning unclear, but Bruno plunged ahead.

"My people have cold-bloodedly killed no Negroes. The outlaws aligned with us killed them as a test . . . a test that I did not sanction. Believe it or not—it's the truth. Negroes were killed—a few of them—when they resisted our efforts to remove them. I do not have now nor have I ever had concentration camps for *any*

group of people. I will allow the UN to send representatives to scour the countryside if you ask. They will
find no concentration camps. Now then, I do have
proof that citizens of the countries that my forces now
occupy—for want of a better word—asked me to send
troops in to restore law and order. I have those docu-
ments with me."

Bruno took a sip of water. "Gentlemen and ladies, I
control all of Germany, and we are a sovereign nation.
Austria, Poland, Czechoslovakia, Hungry, and the
northern half of Italy have asked to be aligned with us."
He cut his eyes to Ben. "Just as portions of Canada and
several of your western states asked to be aligned with
your SUSA, General Raines. Any attempts to invade
any country aligned with the New Federation of Germany will be considered an act of war and will be met
accordingly.

"Now . . . I will not tolerate Negroes in the New
Federation. None. I detest them. I think they are inferior beings, only a cut above savages, and I will not
have them residing in the Federation. And the UN has
no right to tell us who we might have in our country.
None."

"I cannot believe the good people of Germany
would allow this," Blanton said.

"The people will do what is best for our New Federation. Negroes have sullied everything they have
touched. Music, theater, sports, morals, values, the
family structure. You love them so much, President
Blanton, you take them. You're welcome to them. We
don't want them. There are damn few countries in the
world who do want them." He smiled. "And it was that

way for years before the Great War. Whether you will admit that or not."

Blanton glared at him but said nothing. Ben studied the blank notepad in front of him and was silent.

"What are you doing with those you so euphemistically call 'relocating'?" Son Moon asked.

"We're shipping them back to Africa just as fast as we can. They love that damn miserable country so much, they can live there. And by the by, South Africa is now and has been for some time under white rule. And it will remain so. If they ask for our help in seeing that their rule is maintained, we will give it."

"What happened to the blacks in that country?" Blanton asked, a depressed note to his tone.

"After a civil war that lasted for several years, the warring tribes were defeated and relocated."

"And you knew this was going on?" Son Moon asked.

"Of course."

"Then for years a lot of misinformation was sent out of Africa," Ben said. It was not a question.

Bruno's reply was a smile.

"Are you quite through?" Son Moon asked.

"Almost," Bruno said. "Once Ben Raines has pulled his troops off German soil and out of Italy, I will order my troops to leave Switzerland. They have not agreed to join our alliance, and I will certainly honor their sovereignty.

"You all have condemned me for my actions in dealing not just with minorities, but with certain types of people in general. You sent the greatest mercenary army in the world in to 'restore order,' as you so quaintly phrased it. I find that amusing. For you see, there isn't a modicum of difference between what I am doing and what Ben Raines has been doing for years."

I was right, Ben thought. *I had him pegged. Now here it comes.*

"Nonsense!" Son Moon snapped.

"That's ridiculous!" Blanton said.

"Is it?" Bruno questioned, a smile playing on his lips. "Oh, I don't think so. Do you, my dear General Raines?"

"Speak your piece, General Bottger," Ben told him.

"Oh, I shall. I shall. All the years Ben Raines has spent setting up his little nation within a nation, what has he been doing? Why, throwing out any and all who don't agree with the Rebel philosophy . . ."

That wasn't exactly true, but close. Ben said nothing.

". . . Search the SUSA until you collapse from sheer exhaustion," Bruno continued. "I'll wager you won't find a single white trash family in the SUSA. There are no niggers in the SUSA. Nobody who could work but won't on the dole. No shacks with a dozen junked cars littering the yards; no horde of half-naked kids with dirty diapers and runny noses. Ben Raines won't permit it. No grassless yards where those leaping savages spend their time playing basketball instead of working. He kept the cream and threw away the milk, so to speak. Back before the Great War, social services in my country almost bankrupted the nation feeding and housing and clothing and providing medical care to worthless people. Just like in America. Ah, but your precious Ben Raines, he got rid of those types of people. Just like I am doing. Yet I am condemned, and Ben Raines is allowed to continue his purging of citizens. Any of you care to deny that?" He met each eye in the room. Bruno chuckled. "No? I thought not. You, Mr. Secretary-General of the United Nations, you commissioned Ben Raines and his army of Rebels to destroy me for doing the same damn thing that Ben Raines has been doing for years! You, Mr. President of what is left of the United States, you went along with it because you knew if you sent your armies against General Raines, they would be defeated. And defeated quite soundly . . . and then Ben Raines would control *all* of North America."

Bruno cut his eyes to Ben. "You don't like the press, General Raines. But I love the press. Especially your American press. I intend to hold a press conference when this farcical meeting is concluded. Oh, my yes. Indeed I shall. I want the world to know what hypocrites you all are. I'm going to invite the press to come visit our New Federation. See our accomplishments. Film them, write of them. Pro and con. I will insist upon that. I don't expect glowing reports from them . . . just a few pros among the many cons will please me greatly."

He looked hard at Son Moon, then at Homer Blanton. "You hear me well, gentlemen. I have a standing army of a quarter of a million fighting men and women. With a reserve of over one hundred thousand. If you persist in sending Ben Raines and his Rebels against me, I will squash them like bugs." He smiled unpleasantly. "And then I will turn my armies against any who supported Ben Raines. But I will promise you this: I will never wage war against any country that does not first wage war against me. But I warn you all: Do not continue this fight against me. You cannot win. I will return to this meeting room tomorrow at nine o'clock in the morning. I shall expect your answer at that time. I pray it is the right one."

"We'll need a bit more time than that," Blanton said unexpectedly. Both Son Moon and Ben gave him sharp glances.

"Three days?" Bruno asked.

"A week would be better," Homer said, after cutting his eyes to Ben and receiving a slight nod. The man was catching on how to play the game.

"Very well. A week it is. I shall see you then. Not before. Now I will meet with the world press." Bruno and his aides stood up together and marched out of the room. The heavy door closed behind them.

"Jesus Christ!" one of Blanton's senior people said.

Every eye in the room turned to Ben Raines. No one could understand why he was smiling. Ben pushed back his chair and stood up. "I'll see you all in a few days. Here." He looked at Blanton. "Have your Secret Service people sweep this room for bugs." He walked out of the room.

Two

"He just might be able to field an army of 250,000," Mike Richards told Ben a couple of hours after the meeting had concluded. "And probably 100,000 to 150,000 of them would be crackerjack soldiers. The rest would be cannon fodder. He has practically no air force. What he has is some helicopter gunships and a few old prop transports. The group that destroyed Europe's jet fighters years ago did the world a service, I suppose. Although the reasoning behind that move still escapes me."

"They didn't just destroy the fighters over here," Ike said. "They systematically destroyed ninety-nine percent of the *world's* jet fighter and bomber fleets. PTV."

"Peace Through Violence," Dan said. "Interesting name. I wonder what ever became of that group? There must have been thousands of them."

"They vanished into history," Ben said. "What the hell has Bottger got up his other sleeve?" He glanced at Mike, but the man's eyes were clouded over. *His people are on to something,* Ben thought. *But he's not yet ready to spell it out.*

"The press types are hot to travel into Bottger's New Federation," Buddy said. "They're lining up in droves."

"Good," Ben said. "I hope they never come back."

Tina Raines laughed and leaned over and tickled her dad under his chin. Ben looked pained, and that brought roars of laughter from the roomful of Batt Coms, the majority of whom had flown in that morning while the meeting was in progress.

Georgi Striganov, the Russian Bear, grumbled at Mike, "What do you know, Mike? And you know something, I can sense it."

"Nothing concrete as yet," Mike replied. He stood up. "But I'll have something for you in seventy-two hours. I'll see you then." He left the room.

"Worse than the old KGB," Georgi muttered.

"Let's piece together what we do know but can't prove," Ben said. "We know that Bottger killed many of Europe's Jews—thousands of them—and then destroyed the death camps and planted flowers and grass and crops over the old sites. We know that to be fact. We just can't prove it."

"We know he killed thousands of minorities," Raul Gomez said. "Asians, Hispanics, blacks, others, and incinerated the bodies and scattered the ashes. Then dismantled the ovens."

"We know for a fact his hero is Adolph Hitler," Ike said.

"We know he despises blacks," Pat O'Shea said. "He's admitted that."

Ben held up a thin book with a tattered cover. "Bottger wrote this crap back in his youth. This is probably one of only a few volumes remaining. Years ago Bottger ordered all copies destroyed. In here he states that his lifelong dream is to find a way to rid the world of all blacks. I think this is the key."

"What do you mean, Father?" Buddy asked.

"I'm not sure. But one of the things Mike told me was that his people learned that scientists from around the world embraced Bottger's views some years back. Just before the Great War, they dropped out of sight. No trace of them was ever found, until now."

"Mike found them?" Nick asked.

"Some of them; probably all of them. They're working in a vast, underground complex in what used to be Poland. All these men and women share several things in common, the most important being the belief that all blacks are inferior beings and should be destroyed."

"I'll be damned! Have you told this to Blanton and Son Moon, Ben?" Ike asked.

"Not yet. But I will. I'm going to wait for Mike's next report. He's on to something."

Bottger and his staff did not leave their floor at the hotel. And no one saw Bruno for the next seventy-two hours. By that time Mike had returned.

The man was exhausted, but he would not rest until he reported his findings to Ben.

"Nothing solid, Ben. No proof at all. But Bottger's had his scientific minds working around the clock for months. About ten days ago the complex in Poland went back on a nine to five shift—with lots of happy faces. Lots of loud parties all over the small city; the complex is located just a few miles outside the town. Something big happened, but I can't find out for sure what it is. Ben, a Polish Jew died getting me the next bit. So bear that in mind."

"All right, Mike."

"Only a few of Bottger's scientists are German. Most are from other countries—the man who was shot getting to me was a scientist and a Jew, but he hid both facts and became a janitor in the complex. He died a few minutes after telling my man in Germany. He claims that Bottger's people have developed some sort of serum, vaccine, whatever it's called, that can be introduced into any sort of liquid: soda pop, water, coffee, tea, milk, beer—*anything*—and it does something to the female reproductive system. It renders them incapable of having children. And they're only days away from having the same sort of . . . *thing*, that will work on men. Destroys something in a male. Weakens the sperm, I think."

"Bottger's dream come true," Ben said in almost a whisper.

"Ben, a lot of people in this world would not be unhappy to see something like that come to be."

"I know. And some of the Rebels are included in that. We've got some discontent in the ranks right now. Only a few, so far; but it disturbs me."

"When do you tell Blanton and Son Moon?"

"Right now."

"Monstrous," Secretary-General Son Moon whispered. "The man must be stopped."

Blanton was speechless, his face pale with shock. He sat and stared at Ben for a full half minute before he was able to speak. "Bottger wants to control the world," Blanton finally said. "And with a weapon like this, he could."

One of Blanton's senior people asked, "Does this work on women of all nationalities?"

"I suppose so," Ben replied. "I don't see how they could make it work on one race and not the other. But then, I'm not a scientist. So I'm just guessing."

"With so few reports coming out of Africa, I wonder . . . ?" Blanton's voice trailed off into silence.

"I don't think so," Ben said, knowing full well what the president meant. "The serum or vaccine, or whatever it's called, has only just been perfected. If perfected is the right word to use."

"But they may have been experimenting with it over there for some time, and if that is true, only God knows what horrors may have come from it," Son Moon said.

"True."

"Bottger has to be confronted," Blanton said firmly. "We've got to act on this information. Mike Richards was a highly respected CIA operative before the Great War. People speak glowingly of him. I believe this report."

"Hold on," Ben warned. "Consider this. I'm here with two battalions. You have a dozen or so Secret Service people, and the secretary-general has his security people. But Bottger has ten or fifteen combat-ready battalions within easy striking distance of this city. And God alone knows how many more people he's been moving quietly into place—just in case something went wrong at the meetings. Like what we're discussing, for example."

"What are you suggesting?" Blanton asked.

"Getting you and the secretary-general clear of this place."

"He wouldn't dare harm us!" Son Moon said.

"Don't you believe that. He hates Homer. After he was elected president, Homer bent over backward in the direction of America's blacks. He angered a lot of people by doing that. And not just Americans. Something else you may not know is this: Bottger's mother was an American citizen. She was serving in the armed forces in Germany when she met her future husband. Bruno was very close to his mother; adored her. She never renounced her American citizenship. When Bottger was about twelve, she was assaulted and raped by a gang of blacks. Spent several days in a coma before she finally died from massive head injuries. Another reason why Bottger despises blacks."

"I didn't know that," Blanton said, a note of irritation in his voice.

"Your intelligence network is not nearly as proficient as mine," Ben said. "Congress puts too damn many restraints on yours."

Blanton gave Ben a dirty look, then managed a wan smile.

Son Moon quickly turned his head so Blanton would not see his own smile at Ben's blunt words. The secretary-general knew that during Blanton's rule before the Great War, Homer had allowed his liberal Congress to nearly wreck not only the military but also the country's intelligence-gathering network. Son Moon liked

Homer Blanton, but he did not have the respect for him that he held for Ben Raines . . . the two men thought very much alike.

"About a hundred or so press types have left for the New Federation of Germany," Ben said. "They were flown out early this morning for a guided tour."

"Any blacks in the group?" Blanton asked.

"Are you kidding?" Ben looked at him. "Just being this close to the border makes them very nervous. And I damn sure can't blame them."

Jersey opened the door to the conference room and stepped in, a worried look on her face. "Something weird is going on, boss. Bottger's troops have moved closer to the city and—"

Two grenades suddenly rolled into the room and went off in a blinding flash of sound. Ben had time to think: concussion grenades! They were followed by two canisters of hissing gas. Ben dropped into darkness wondering what in the hell had gone wrong.

Three

Ben slowly returned to consciousness. Groaning, he pulled himself up to a sitting position, his back to a wall, and looked around. Jersey was still out, as was Son Moon. Neither appeared to be hurt, just unconscious. Blanton's senior aides were sprawled on the floor.

Blanton was gone.

Ben had no idea how long he'd been out, but he thought for not very long.

Listening, waiting for full awareness to return, he could hear no gunshots. *It was a perfect plan,* Ben thought. He'd bet that nobody outside this floor knew that Blanton was missing. Bottger's people probably drugged the Secret Service agents' coffee, then tossed those . . . whatever the hell they were . . . in here and grabbed Homer.

How did they get the president clear of the building?

Old creepie tunnels probably.

"Son of a bitch!" Ben muttered. "This had to have been planned a long time ago."

Jersey groaned and sat up, a confused look on her face. "What the hell . . . !" she said.

"We've been had, kid," Ben told her, standing up. He was shaky and quickly sat down in a chair.

"I can't get my legs to work, boss," Jersey said with a groan.

"I know the feeling. Just rest there for a few moments; you'll be all right."

Ben managed to stagger to the hall door and open it. Rebels and Secret Service personnel were sprawled up and down the hall floor. Glancing at his watch, Ben saw that he'd been out about twenty or so minutes. "Goddamnit!" he cussed.

Ben made his way through the maze of unconscious bodies to the end of the hall. There he picked up a chair and threw it out the window overlooking the street. That got the attention of about a hundred people on the street and sidewalks below.

"Bottger's kidnapped President Blanton!" Ben yelled, leaning out the window. "Fan out to the edges of the city and seal it off tight." But he sensed it was a futile gesture. Bottger and Blanton were long gone. "And get some medical personnel up here, pronto!"

Ben was still very weak. He sat down in a chair near the smashed window in the hall of the old hotel and waited for his strength to return. Corrie and Beth and Cooper were slumped together in the hall, backs to a wall. He cut his eyes as Jersey came crawling out of the small conference room on her hands and knees, dragging her M-16 by the sling. She was cussing a blue streak, tracing Bottger's ancestry back to the caves and tree limbs and beyond.

"Settle down and lean against a wall, Jersey," Ben told her. "Your strength will slowly return."

Rebels and Secret Service personnel and UN security people were racing up the steps. They quickly filled the hall, followed by Rebel medics.

Ben pointed toward the conference room. "In there," he said. "Son Moon and all the senior aides are still unconscious." He looked at Dan Gray. "Bottger and his people had to have used old creepie tunnels to get clear. I'm sure the tunnel entrance is in the basement. Check it out."

Medics quickly checked Ben's heart and BP; normal. The effects of the gas were wearing off of everybody, and the hall was filled with groaning and moaning and cussing men and women. Corrie's radio crackled, and Jersey grabbed the mic and held one side of the headset close.

"Yeah. This is the Eagle's roost. Go on." She listened for a moment. "All right, sir. I'll tell him." She looked at Ben. "Dan's people found the tunnel in the basement, just like you figured. But it's wired to blow. Dan says it's gonna take several hours to clear all the booby traps . . . and that's just the ones they can see right now."

"Tell him to forget it. Those damn tunnels might run for a mile or more, and Bottger will have laid booby traps every hundred feet. It's not worth the time and people it would take."

"We'll take care of the tunnels," a Secret Service agent said. "We've got to find the president."

"Suit yourself," Ben told him. "All Rebels out of the hotel. Right now. Evac everybody before it blows."

The Rebels cleared the hotel in minutes, with many of those who'd been inside when the gas canisters went off carried out on stretchers.

"All Rebels clear, sir," Corrie reported.

"Son Moon and his people?"

"Clear."

"Eyes in the sky?"

"Everything we have that will fly is working in a widening circle on the edges of the city. Nothing yet."

"And there won't be anything," Ben said. "Bet your ass on that. Bottger and his people and President Blanton surfaced and were picked up ten minutes after they entered the tunnel. Everything was prearranged." Ben stood and cussed for a full minute. Didn't help much. "How about those troops of Bottger's that were reported moving closer to the city?"

"They're slowly backing up, eastward."

"Do you know what this means?" Ben asked Son Moon. The man was standing with his security people a few feet from Ben.

"I'm not sure what you mean, General," the secretary-general replied. "The kidnapping of the president of the United States is serious enough. What else could be worse?"

Ike was standing beside Ben. "I think I know," he said. "Jesus. Talk about things gettin' worse!"

Ben glanced at him. "Yeah. It means that Vice President Harriet Hooter is now going to assume the president's chair in the Oval Office."

A senior Secret Service agent paled. "God help us all!"

The ground beneath their feet shook as a mighty

explosion under the hotel belched out dust and smoke. Those Secret Service agents aboveground went running across the street.

Two more explosions ripped the earth under the hotel. The building shuddered and began coming apart. Cracks appeared on all sides as Rebels and others began quickly backing away from the structure. A huge groan escaped from the basement followed by yet another explosion, and the front and one side of the hotel caved in and collapsed into huge mounds of rubble. That was followed by the other half of the building collapsing. When the dust had settled, the old hotel was no more. Only some naked steel girders were left, twisted and stark against the amazingly bright blue of the sky.

"Give the bastard credit," Ben said, staring at the rubble. "Bottger planned it well. He sure outfoxed everybody." Ben grimaced. "Me included."

"I can't wait to hear how Vice President Harriet Hooter reacts to this news," Dan said.

"I beg your pardon?" General Bodinson, the chairman of the Joint Chiefs of Staff, said, after Hooter's short statement to him in the Oval Office.

"I said, 'Prepare our armed forces to invade the SUSA,' General!" she roared, rattling all the windows in the office. Hooter had a voice that would crack brass and a face that would stop a P-51E in a power dive.

After Bodison's hearing had recovered, he replied, "Yep. That's what I thought you said."

"Do it!" Rita Rivers yelled.

"Yeah!" Representative Dumkowski hollered.

"Right on!" Senators Benedict and Arnold chimed. They were both a bit behind times . . . in more ways than one.

"Destroy those damned filthy Republicans!" Immaculate Crapums shouted.

For a brief moment General Bodison felt he had been somehow transported deep into the twilight zone and plopped down in a nuthouse. "I thought we were discussing the nation of the Southern United States of America?"

"What's the difference?" Zipporah Washington said. "Rebels, Republicans, conservative malcontents, racists . . . they're all the same. Invade the SUSA and kill them all. Including those goddamn Uncle Toms down there." Zipporah had somehow managed to get herself elected to the House despite the fact that she was barely literate, and years before the Great War had served a two-year stretch in a county work farm for burglary.

"You're all nuts," General Bodison said.

"What . . . did . . . you . . . say?" VP Hooter shrieked.

"I said you're all nuts," the general repeated. "The Rebels have missiles trained at this very location. They have other missiles programmed to strike at every one of our bases. Four minutes after the order went out to invade the SUSA, Charleston would be a smoking ash heap. Forget it."

"I gave you an order!" Hooter hollered.

"Stick it where the sun don't shine," Bodison said, then got up from the chair and walked toward the door.

"I'll have your job!" Harriet bellered. "You chau-
vinistic pig son of a bitch!" Bodison flipped her the bird
and walked out of the office.

"Well . . . I never!" Harriet fumed. She probably
hadn't. She was rumored to have once propositioned a
famous porn star. He refused on the grounds that he
drew the line at bestiality.

The Secret Service and the FBI took over the case
of the missing president, a move which amused Ben.
"That'll last about seventy-two hours," he said to Ike.

"If that long," Ike replied.

Two days after the kidnapping, the Bureau and the
Secret Service came to see Ben at his CP in Geneva.

"You want to help us in this matter, General?" the
director of the Bureau asked. He had flown over immediately after hearing the news. He asked the question as
if the words hurt his mouth.

"Homer is still in Switzerland," Ben said. "Probably
not more than a hundred miles from here."

"How did you reach that conclusion?" the Secret
Service man asked.

Ben smiled. "Call it a hunch."

"I don't believe that," the Bureau man said. "I think
you know exactly where President Blanton is being
held."

Actually, a hunch was all it was. Ben shrugged his
shoulders. He wasn't about to confirm to anyone that
Mike Richards had people inside Bottger's New Federation. Deep inside. And not just a few people.

While Bottger's government and army and police

did set the decrees and enforce the harsh laws with an iron hand, the majority of the people did not agree with Bottger's policies. But for the most part, the people were helpless to act. For Bottger had taken a cue from America's liberal government and disarmed the people, thereby effectively rendering the citizens powerless to act except by the ballot. But when elections are few, and the few are rigged, the people are virtually helpless to change anything.

Nothing had been heard from the planeloads of press types that had taken up the invitation to visit the New Federation. Cassie Phillips and a few others had backed out at the last minute and stood on the tarmac and watched their colleagues leave. Ben had told her then she was making a wise decision.

"Do you think they're dead, Ben?" she asked him, a few days after President Blanton's kidnapping.

"No. But I do think they're being fed a load of horseshit and kept from the truth. Bottger doesn't have a free press. It's state controlled. Or Federation controlled. Same thing. I'll wager they know nothing about Blanton being snatched. They're probably being told that Blanton and Son Moon ordered me to declare war on the Federation and they're being detained deep inside Federation borders for their own safety . . . or something along those lines. And most of the bunch that went in with Bottger will jump at the chance to paint me as the bad guy."

Cassie shook her head at Ben's cynicism. "Those reporters are not stupid people, Ben."

Ben surprised her by saying, "You're right." Then

he smiled and added, "They're just out of touch with reality."

Homer Blanton had not been harmed. Indeed, he was being fed well and treated with the utmost respect and courtesy. But he was a prisoner. Problem was, now that Bruno Bottger had Homer, he didn't know what to do with him. On paper, the idea of kidnapping the American president had seemed a good idea. When the deed was done, Bottger realized what a stupid move it had been. It had accomplished nothing for his goals and served only to bring together Americans who, heretofore, had been widely separated by political and ideological views. Now Bottger not only had an American president prisoner, but two planeloads of reporters who were rapidly getting on everybody's nerves with their seemingly incessant questioning. Bruno didn't know what the hell to do with them, either.

One of Bottger's most senior people, a man who had been friends with Bruno since childhood, put it this way: "You fucked up, Bruno."

Bruno glared at the man. "Don't point out the obvious, Hans. Tell me how to get out of this mess."

"Free the man and let him go. He hasn't seen you. He has no idea you even had a part in this. He doesn't even know where he's being held."

"What about the press?"

Hans shrugged. "They can have an accident."

"*All* of them?"

"Certainly. We know of several of our pilots who are

secretly opposed to you. Have them pilot the transports and we'll shoot them down; blame it on Ben Raines and the Rebels."

Bruno was thoughtful for a moment. Then he smiled. "Excellent, Hans. Excellent. Yes, of course. It would work. But add this little touch to the play: We'll have a fake firefight among our people and 'rescue' President Blanton. We can say that malcontents from Ben Raines's Rebel army, working with Swiss and other resistance groups in Europe, kidnapped President Blanton and our own brave lads volunteered to risk their lives to rescue him and return him to safety. The shooting down of the transports carrying the reporters is good. They are such a meddlesome bunch. Yes. I like it. Everything can be blamed on Ben Raines and the Rebels. That will put Raines in a very unfavorable light in the eyes of that damn United Nations gook, Son Moon, and then Blanton just might order the American army in to kick the Rebels out of Europe."

"I'll start working on the plan immediately."

"Very good, Hans."

Mike Richards returned to Geneva and met briefly with Ben. After Mike left to grab a few hours sleep, Ben called for a meeting of those Rebel batt coms in the area.

"Blanton is being held in an old castle overlooking a lake right here." He pointed to a wall map. "In the town of Thun. I don't know exactly where the press is being housed, but Mike's people think they're just across the border in what used to be called Germany. My 1 Batt, Dan's 3 Batt, and West's 4 Batt are going after Blanton. Buddy and his special ops people are already in. They'll be laying out the DZ's here," he thumped the map, "just west of the town in these flats. Ike, you're in charge here."

"What do we tell the Bureau and the Secret Service?" Beth asked.

Ben said, "We'll brief the senior people only. I . . ." He looked at Georgi Striganov. The Russian was frowning. "What the hell is wrong with you, Georgi?"

"It smells like old fish, Ben. For days we don't have a clue. None of Mike's operatives can pick up anything. Then all of a sudden it just falls into our laps. I don't like it."

Ben sat down and was silent for a moment before replying. "You're right, Georgi. I should have picked up on that." He smiled. "Beth, after we brief the Bureau and the Secret Service, get Cassie Phillips, Frank Service, and Nils Wilson in here."

"The *press?*" she questioned, clearly startled at Ben's decision.

"The press," Ben said. "They're going to be fully briefed and allowed to go in with us. Maybe Bruno is trying to set us up for a hard fall. If so, the press will be right there with us."

Ike blinked in surprise. "Well, I'll be goddamned!" he said.

"We all might," Ben said, a grim note to his voice. "We're going in tomorrow, just before dawn."

Four

"Once you've been briefed," Ben told the three reporters, "you will not be allowed to leave this hangar.
There will be no communication with the outside. Period. If that is not acceptable, say so now."

"You're actually going to allow us to go with you on
a rescue operation?" Cassie asked.

"That's right."

"To get the president?" Nils asked.

"That's right."

"I wouldn't miss this for the world!" Frank said
excitedly, rubbing his hands together and grinning.
"This could well be the high point of my career."

"There might be more truth in that than you realize," Ben said with a smile.

Cassie narrowed her eyes at that remark. She knew
Ben well enough to know that he could pull rabbits out
of his bag of tricks when he set his mind to it. She felt
a tightness in her belly when Ben asked Corrie, "Everybody in place?"

"Right."

"Clamp the lid on."

"Yes, sir."

Ben turned to the reporters. "Any of you ever jumped before?"

"You mean like . . . out of an airplane?" Frank asked.

"Yes."

"Hell, no!" Nils said.

"All that is about to change."

"Oh, shit!" Cassie said.

"Nothing to it anymore," Ben told her. He motioned to a Rebel standing in the shadows inside the hangar. "Sergeant Mason here will give you some pointers. I suggest you pay attention. I'll see you all in the morning."

He walked quickly out of the hangar before they could ask him anything. But if looks could kill . . .

Ben and his 1 Batt were taking off from Geneva. West and his 4 Batt from Annecy. And Dan and his 3 Batt from Bellegarde. Enough planes had been found so that all three understrength battalions could go in together.

"What if this damn thing doesn't open?" Nils asked Cooper as they were walking to the planes in the pre-dawn darkness.

"Pull your reserve."

"What if that doesn't open?"

"How much do you weigh?"

"About 175. Why?"

" 'Cause if both your chutes fail, scoopin' you up

after you hit the ground is gonna be like pickin' up 175 pounds of Jell-O.''

"I'm sorry I asked," Nils muttered.

As soon as the jumpers had left the door, Buddy and his special ops people were going to storm the old castle—and it was old—built in 1191. At precisely 0600 hours, every fighter plane Ben had was to begin bombing and strafing Bottger's western lines; about two full divisions of troops, strategically placed on a north to south line, running roughly from Biel in Switzerland, down to the Italian border. In addition to the planes, Rebel long-range artillery had been quietly moved into place, and they would start shelling as soon as the bombing and strafing runs were through.

To avoid detection, the planes carrying Ben and Dan's battalions had to fly north and then cut east, and the planes carrying West's battalion had to fly far south and then cut east and north.

"How are we going to get out once we get the president?" Cassie shouted to Ben over the rush of wind and the roar of the engines.

He looked at her and hid his smile. "I haven't the vaguest idea."

"Oh . . . shit!" Cassie said.

Ben did know, of course. His intelligence people had learned that Bottger had no troops located between Bulle and Chamonix, and only a small contingent guarding the tunnel at Col du Grd St. Bernard. Ben planned on grabbing the president and beating a hasty exit southwest to Monthey, then down to Martigny, then through the tunnel to safety. He hoped. But Ben knew that war could change plans abruptly . . . often for the worst. He was fully prepared for the eventuality that the Rebels just might have to play this one by ear.

A crew member motioned to Ben and held up three fingers. Ben stood up and waddled back to the rear of the plane. The huge door opened ponderously and the plane filled with cold air. Then it was time to stand up and hook up and check equipment. Ben was not acting as jumpmaster this time—he was going to be the first one out. His team was right behind him on the left stick, Cassie among them. Lieutenant Bonelli was on the other side of the plane, leading his stick out. The green light popped on and Ben was out. The sky blossomed with chutes. Below, Ben could see flashes from the muzzles of guns. The attack was on. Then several miles to the north and west came a tremendous flash of fire and light. Ben had no idea what had happened, only that a plane had exploded in midair. But he knew it was not one of his. Then another flash of light fired the sky, almost in the same location as the first.

"What the hell?" Ben said aloud.

Then there was no more time for wondering about the strange explosions, for the ground was coming up fast. Ben hit, rolled, and came to his boots quickly. As he had during the previous jump, he had left his Thompson and now carried a .223 CAR.

"Buddy reports some strange doings at the castle," Corrie panted in his ear. "There was a firefight going on when he got there. Then when his people stormed the place, the people who were fighting each other both turned on him."

"Let's go find out what's going on," Ben said, ripping open an equipment pack. "This is looking more and more like a total screwup. Anybody hurt landing?"

"No, sir. Nothing serious. They're getting Nils Wilson out of a tree now. He's scared but not hurt."

"Lots of headlights coming up the road," Beth called.

"I hope they're being driven by Buddy's people and not Bottger's," Ben said grimly, looking at the line of vehicles heading their way.

It was Buddy and his special ops people driving the cars and trucks. Buddy hopped out of the lead truck and shook hands with his dad.

"The castle and town are ours, Father," he reported. "And President Blanton is safe. Bottger and his staff left earlier for Berlin, and the castle was only lightly manned. But some of Bottger's men were dressed in uniforms similar to ours, and both sides had blanks in their weapons. Taking the castle was a piece of cake."

Ben was stunned at the report. He could not make any sense out of Buddy's news. He shook his head and said, "Where's Blanton?"

"In the middle of the column. What were those flashes in the sky a few minutes ago?"

"I don't know. How many vehicles did you find?"

"Not nearly enough for three battalions, Father. I've sent people to check out those explosions. Do we occupy the town or head for the border?"

"Let's hold what we've got until full light and your people come back with some news about those flashes we saw. I've got to try and make some sense out of what happened here tonight."

"Good luck," Buddy said dryly.

"How many prisoners did you take?"

"Nearly all of them, Father. They didn't have anything to fight with except blanks."

Muttering under his breath, Ben walked over to greet President Blanton.

"I can truthfully say that I am very glad to see you, Ben," Homer said with a smile, shaking hands with Ben.

"Are you all right, Homer?"

"I'm fine. Can you tell me what is going on?"

"I have no idea. But I'll tell you what I'm going to do. Corrie, order all battalions to attack with everything they've got. Tell Ike to start his push through to Martigny and we'll link up with him there."

"Right, sir."

"Does this operation have a name, Ben?" President Blanton asked.

"Yeah," Ben replied. "Operation Fuck-Up!"

Bottger stepped off the plane outside Berlin and was handed a message by a frightened young soldier. The messenger backed up a few feet.

Bottger read the communiqué concerning the attack on the castle, wadded it up, hurled it to the tarmac, and started jumping up and down on the paper. "Goddamnit!" he shouted.

Another messenger came rushing up. "General! The Rebels have launched a full-scale attack all along our lines."

"Lines!" Bruno screamed. "I've got lines north, south, east, and west. *What* goddamn lines are under attack?"

The young messenger was so badly frightened at his supreme commander's fury, he began stuttering. Bottger grabbed him by the shoulders and started shaking him. "What lines?"

"I don't know, sir," he finally managed to say.

"Good God!" Bottger shouted, shoving the soldier away from him. "Find me somebody who knows what the hell is going on!" Bruno roared.

Troops of Bruno's MEF had expected an attack right after the abduction of the president. When none came, they began to relax. A lot of them would now be relaxed forever. Right on the heels of the fighter attack, artillery began pouring in rounds, then tanks roared in, followed by ground troops. Raines's Rebels, aided by resistance fighters, broke through at dozens of locations. The MEF were confronted, quite briefly at most points, by Rebels who were fighting with a fury that Bottger's troops had never before encountered.

Bottger's troops were spread out over hundreds of miles of lines, many of them far away in the east in what used to be called Poland.

The Rebels cut through Bottger's western lines like a heated knife through butter.

Ben and President Blanton were suddenly confronted by several dozen reporters who had survived the crash of the second plane in the early morning hours. The reporters were banged up and bruised, but none appeared seriously injured. The press, about half of whom were American, were startled to see the president among Ben's troops.

"What the hell are you doing here?" Blanton asked. "What happened to you people?"

"The Rebels shot down our planes!" one reporter shouted. "Our pilot managed to land in a field. These Rebels plan to kill you, Mr. President, and then take over the remainder of the United States."

"Don't be ridiculous!" Blanton snapped at them. "Ben and his people jumped in about an hour ago to rescue me."

"I don't even *want* the rest of the United States," Ben said. "It's filled with malcontents, ne'er-do-wells, liberals, and assholes like you people."

Ten minutes of shouting, cussing, and much armwaving ensued before the Rebels—aided by Cassie Phillips, Nils Wilson, and Frank Service—managed to get some semblance of order restored.

"Listen to me!" Ben shouted. "We're smack in the middle of about five divisions of Bottger's troops. Let's get out of here and then we can argue about what happened."

"Scouts report a regiment of MEF coming hard at us from the west," Corrie said. "Five miles away and closing."

"Get into ambush positions," Ben ordered. "We'll need their vehicles. So aim for the drivers and spare the vehicles. Get our cars and trucks off the road and hidden and get set. Move!"

Three battalions of Rebels sought cover in the small crossroads town only a few miles south of Thun, along the shores of the lake. The reporters—now that they had gotten over their anger at Ben and realized they had been had by Bruno—all marveled at the precision of the Rebels as they set up the ambush. It seemed to the reporters that one minute the streets were filled with Rebels, and the next minute they had vanished.

"How large a force is a regiment, General?" a reporter asked Ben.

"Oh, just a bit larger than three of our full battalions. We're under strength because we couldn't drop in tanks and artillery and engineers and all the other personnel that usually make up and go in with a Rebel battalion."

"Why are you suddenly being so nice to us?" the reporter with a cut on his forehead asked suspiciously.

Jersey looked at the man and shook her head in disgust. "Can't please the bastards," she muttered.

Ben chuckled. "Would you rather I be rude to you?"

"That's what we've come to expect from you, General," the reporter said honestly.

"Only because you people can't or won't understand that there are no rules to a war. That among other things."

"On the outskirts of town, boss," Corrie called.

"Get out of the way and don't interfere," Ben said to the reporter.

"Now you're back to normal," the man said, softening that with a grin.

"Yeah, welcome back, boss," Cooper said.

Ben grunted. "Nobody breathe. Here they come."

There were dozens and dozens of heavy trucks, and many other smaller vehicles. Many of the trucks were towing light artillery pieces.

Ben smiled when he saw those. "We might not have to run too far," he muttered.

"I see them," Jersey said, crouched by his side. "With them, we could make a stand."

"You got it, Little Bit."

"The lead truck is passing recon," Corrie whispered loudly enough for Ben to hear. "The convoy is so long we're going to have to let the first ten or so trucks clear the other side of town."

"Tell Buddy. Some of his people can take care of them."

"This is murder," a reporter whispered. "You can't call it anything else."

Ben cut his eyes. Beth had laid down her weapon and pulled a razor-sharp knife from a leather sheath sewn onto the outside of her jump boot.

"I don't care what else you killers call it, it's just plain cold-blooded murder!" the man said, standing up. "And I won't permit it. I've got to warn those soldiers. I've got to. Damn you all!"

The man jumped up to make a dash for the door and Beth tripped him, then cut his throat from one side to the other.

The reporter that had been talking with Ben puked all over his shoes.

Beth wiped the sharp blade clean on the man's jacket and sheathed the knife. Then she picked up her weapon and resumed her position by the shattered window.

"Back when I was working for the Company," Ben said, "I recall a saying we used a lot: 'Never bother the woodchopper when the woodchopper is busy chopping wood.'" He looked at the group of reporters in the building with him. "I'd keep that in mind if I were you."

The sounds of motors was getting louder.

Cooper bit off a piece of chocolate bar and passed the bar to Jersey, who bit off a chunk and handed it to Ben, who bit off a piece and handed it to Corrie, who took a bite and handed it to Beth, who finished the bar.

"Barbarians!" another reporter hissed at Ben. "None of you are fit to associate with decent human beings."

"Shut up, Paul," Nils told the man. "You don't know what you're talking about. Shut your mouth."

The reporter ignored the advice. "Charles Breedon was a good moral man."

"You want to join him?" Ben asked, as the first trucks began passing Ben's position.

Paul felt the coldness of a silenced pistol press against the back of his head. He had not seen or heard one of Buddy's special ops people slip up behind him.

"Shut your goddamn mouth," the special ops trooper whispered in Paul's ear. "And keep it shut."

"Buddy says it's now or never," Corrie called.

"Fire," Ben said.

Five

It was a slaughter—and a damn quick one. Rebels on rooftops rose up and raked the beds of heavy trucks with automatic weapons fire, while those at ground level on both sides of the street opened up. At the edge of town Buddy and his people were finishing up the front of the convoy. Rebels then swarmed over the vehicles, collecting arms and ammo and grenades and anything else they might be able to use.

"Hundreds of artillery rounds and cases of ammo for heavy machines guns and plenty of 80-mm mortar rounds," Corrie called to Ben.

"Good, good!" Ben said. He turned to President Blanton. "You up to a stand, Homer?"

"No retreat?"

"No."

Blanton did not hesitate. "Let's give them hell, Ben!" Then he grinned as hundreds of Rebels began cheering the president. Blanton was not accustomed to the military cheering him.

"What the hell's come over him?" Paul questioned.

None of the other reporters chose to reply to such a stupid question. Many of them were too busy having Rebels explain the use of the weapons to them.

Ben left West's 4 Batt at Thun and took his 1 Batt, Dan's 3 Batt, and Buddy's special ops batt and drove up to Bern. Homer Blanton went with him. Ben had put the president into body armor and surrounded him with Rebels, but Homer insisted upon being armed and not left out of any fight.

"The Secret Service is not going to be happy with me about this," Ben said.

"The Secret Service isn't here," Blanton replied. "Besides I'm having more fun than I've had in years."

Ben shook his head at the new Homer Blanton. "I've created a monster," he muttered. "Just be careful, Homer. Anything happens to you and I'll get the blame."

But Ben's warning was not necessary. Bruno Bottger's MEF people had pulled out of Bern. They had set up a line roughly fifty miles east of Bern, running north to south from the Federation border in the north, well into Italy to the south.

"Damn!" Blanton said, when the Secret Service swooped down on Bern and took away his M-16, his 9-mm pistol, and his knife.

"You're the president of the United States," they told him. "Not Rambo."

"I can't have any fun at all anymore," Homer bitched.

But pictures of him in full combat gear, smiling with

anticipation as he rode with the Rebels into what everybody assumed would be a full-blown firefight forever shattered his ultraliberal image.

And reporter Paul, who had watched Beth cut his friend's throat, was going to see to that.

After the rescue of Homer Blanton, even those reporters who hated Ben Raines were forced to write something positive about the man and his army . . . but Ben knew that would soon pass and many of the press would be right back taking verbal potshots at him and the SUSA.

"Shit!" Harriet Hooter said, upon hearing the news that Homer Blanton was still alive. She'd begun making plans to remodel the Oval Office. She thought the south wall would be a very nice place to mount the heads of Republicans.

Even the military leaders breathed a sigh of relief when they heard the news about Blanton being alive and rescued . . . especially the bit about being rescued by Ben Raines and the Rebels. As long as Blanton stayed in office, there would be no more talk coming from the White House about invading the SUSA.

But the military did know for a certainty that world war was imminent, and the United States, what was left of it, would be drawn into that war.

The chairman of the Joint Chiefs of Staff flew to Switzerland to meet with his commander in chief and Ben Raines.

General Bodinson and his aides and staff members sat in stunned silence in the conference room of the hurriedly remodeled and refurbished hotel in Geneva and listened to the full briefing from Ben Raines, Mike Richards, and finally, President Blanton.

"Monstrous," General Bodinson said, his voice no more than a whisper.

Ben sat on the edge of a table and looked at General Bodinson. "How many troops can you let us have?" he said, asking the question that the generals and the colonels in the room had been dreading to hear.

"A regiment," Bodinson said softly.

"Four full battalions?" Ben asked.

"Four short battalions," Bodinson replied.

About 2500 men under the United States Army's current system of 180 men to a company. Four companies to a battalion, four battalions to a regiment.

Ike's sigh was audible in the hushed room.

"Get them moving," Blanton ordered.

"It's going to be a mixed bag," Bodinson said. "Army and marines. We just don't have the men to spare since the goddamn liberals in Congress slashed us down to nearly nothing."

Homer suddenly got real busy studying his fingernails. He'd been warned by older heads not to cut the military so drastically. Something always came up where the military was needed. Now that "something" had reared its ugly head . . . and he didn't have the personnel to fight it.

"General Raines," a colonel said. "Back home we're having to act as policemen, firemen, guards, social workers; everything that we aren't trained to be."

"I know," Ben said. "It isn't your fault." He looked

at Homer. "And I won't lay all the blame on you, Homer."

"You might as well," the president said. "I signed the legislation allowing it to happen."

"Under pressure from dozens of liberals in your party and a lot of the newly emerging press types," Ben replied. "Now is not the time to drape yourself in sackcloth and ashes. We've all got to pull together."

"There is something else we'd better talk about right now," a Marine Corps colonel growled. "And you all know what it is. But I'll be the one to bring it up. What happens when a certain percentage of our fighting men say, and they will say it: 'Fuck the damn niggers!' "

Homer Blanton shook his head. He was still liberal enough to be unable to comprehend anyone saying something that cruel and unfeeling.

But not Ben. "I'm faced with that, too, Colonel," Ben replied. "I told them that this might start out with the blacks of the world, but Bruno will eventually use it to control every human being on the face of the earth. Most of them agreed with me. A few did not."

"I'd be interested in knowing what you did with those few?" another colonel asked.

"Nothing. They're good fighting men. And that's what war is all about."

The room was filled with silence for a moment. Son Moon broke that silence. "North Korea is the joker in this deck of playing cards. For years we thought they were finished. We were wrong. They don't have the army they once had, before the Great War, but what they do have is formidable still. And they still cling to communism. Even though they are definitely not the type of people Bottger cares to embrace, he just might in return for their support. We'd better think about that."

"If North Korea throws in with Bottger, we're finished," General Bodinson said. "We'd be facing a combined army of three quarters of a million. And North Korea still has nuclear capability, albeit limited."

"How about China?" a staff general asked. "Does anybody here know what's really happening there?"

"Torn apart by civil war," Mike Richards spoke up. "They've broken up into a dozen or more separate nations, with each nation fighting the other. For the time being, China is no threat to us."

"How the hell do you know all this?" Mike was asked by the DCI of the newly organized Central Intelligence Agency.

"My people are better than yours," Mike told him.

"The hell you say!"

Mike smiled in reply. Truth was, he'd gathered together many of the spooks that he'd worked with during the years before the Great War, and they had recruited others of like mind and capabilities. Ben's own version of the CIA was the best in the world. And it certainly should be, for many of the old hands who believed strongly that Congress should stay the hell out of CIA business and felt their continuous meddling would destroy the Company's effectiveness—which it had, back before the Great War—were now working for Mike.

The DCI glared at Mike, who was smiling sweetly at

him—about as sweetly as a mongoose smiles at a cobra.

"I say we strike a deal with this Bottger person," a man dressed in civilian clothes said.

"What kind of a deal?" Blanton asked, his eyes narrowed and real steel in his voice.

"You know what kind of deal, Mr. President."

"Say it!"

But the as yet unidentified man would only smile.

Blanton was steamed and made no attempt to hide it. "Goddamn you, Nichols. You're talking about the eventual extermination of an entire race of people."

"Who have been nothing but a thorn in the side of the white man for centuries . . ."

Ben now knew who Nichols was. He was a newly elected representative who had managed to get himself placed high on several important committees. Junior senators and representatives now held many of the top positions in the House and Senate, for most of the older hands were either dead, never returned after the Great War, or had retired. If Ben's memory served him correctly, Nichols was from Ohio. From a very conservative district.

"Now, you listen to me, Nichols," Blanton fumed.

"No, you listen to me, Mr. President," Nichols cut him off. "I serve the people who elected me. Truly serve them. And you know I was elected by ninety-one percent of the vote. I am their voice, and I will be heard. I'll be goddamned if I'll stand by and see what's left of the United States torn apart by your incessant kowtowing to every damn minority group that comes around whining and pissing and bitching about some problem they wouldn't even have if they would only, by God, conform to standards that are tried and true and helped to build America into the finest nation in all the world."

"Are you quite through, Representative Nichols?" Homer asked, his face pale with anger.

"No. I am not. Face facts, sir. We can't stop Bottger. We're not strong enough. Not after liberals like you destroyed our military capabilities. General Raines has admitted that even he doesn't know if his army can stop Bottger. Africa and Africans is simply not our problem."

"No, but Bottger damn sure is," Ben spoke up.

"Here and now, yes," Nichols said. "You think we should go into Africa, General?"

"Not until we deal with Bottger. And then only after certain conditions have been met with the leaders or warlords of each nation on that continent. When I take my people in to stabilize a nation, I will stabilize it."

General Bodinson and many of the other military men were smiling. They wished they could have the same authority as Ben Raines in dealing with thugs and punks and other human slime. It would make their job of trying to stabilize the United States—what was left of it—so much easier.

"Let's all take a break and cool off," Ben said. "I could use a cup of coffee and a smoke."

Blanton and Nichols left the room, the Secret Service doing their best to keep the two apart.

Outside, Ben turned to Mike Richards. "I think Bottger is bluffing, Mike. I don't think he has this serum. I think his people made some breakthrough; I think they're probably very close. But they haven't quite got it yet."

"We have no proof of that, Ben."

"We have no hard proof that he does have it, either. When will you have people in place in Africa?"

Mike looked uncomfortable for a few seconds, then he shrugged his shoulders. "I haven't found anyone who wants to volunteer to go, and I'm not going to order anyone, Ben. But I am working on it just as hard as I can. I may have found a few people. I'll know in a couple of days."

Ben sighed. "The hate runs that deep, Mike?"

"You know it does, Ben."

Ben shook his head. "I honestly did not know it was that bad."

Mike put a hand on Ben's shoulder. "Ben, ol' buddy, we go back a lot of years. We've never lied to each other, and I won't start now. I don't think you've ever really comprehended just how hated the black man is. Ben, I'm no fair barometer in this. You know how I feel: I like black people individually; I can't stand them as a race. I told you a few weeks back that Bottger has people all over America. Cells. They were planted a long time ago. Now they're emerging. Oh, not in the SUSA. Bottger isn't a stupid man. He'll save the SUSA for last. But he'll get around to us. Believe that—"

"Say what's on your mind, Mike," Ben interrupted him.

"All right, Ben. I'll lay it right out for you. The majority of the American people, both in and out of the SUSA, want Bottger stopped. But they want him stopped here. In Europe. The press doesn't know for a fact that Bottger has or is working on this serum. However, rumors are flying around like BB's. But a full fifty percent of the people don't give a damn what happens in Africa. They're tired of four decades of gimmie, gimmie, gimmie. They're tired of 'you owe me this, you owe me that, and you owe me everything.' They're tired of boogie-woogie jive shit. They're tired of a double standard in education. They're tired of excuses for savage behavior. They like the black man and the black woman individually, they just don't like niggers! And don't throw Cecil Jefferys up to me, Ben. Cecil is a good decent man. Cecil also knows that we can't have a double standard: one for black people and one for white people. Cecil knows there are classes of people, in black and white and red and brown and yellow. Cecil has talked to me about this. We both wanted to tell you but didn't know how. The hate's been building for years, Ben. Long before the Great War. Now it's boiling again. You know and I know that had the Great War not come along when it did, America was looking a race war right smack in the face. Now it's very nearly come to a head. Again. Next to the bottom line is this: The white race is not about to allow themselves to become a minority race. The bottom line is this: You'd better be goddamn sure you put the Rebels on the right side, Ben."

Mike turned and walked away without looking back. Ben stood for a moment, his team standing a respectful distance away. They had all heard Mike's comments. Ben looked at them. They met his eyes briefly, then averted their glances.

So there it was.

How the hell could he have missed it for so long?

Ben went off in search of Homer. General Bodinson intercepted him. "General Raines. I've talked it over with my staff. We all agree that Bottger has to be stopped. Here. I'll send you every man I can spare to stop Bottger here in Europe. But I'll be goddamned if I'll commit my people into Africa."

Ben nodded his thanks and walked on. He found the president sitting on a bench. By himself. Ben sat down and the two men were silent for a time.

"I feel so damned . . . *alone*," Homer said.

"That makes two of us," Ben replied.

"What are we going to do, Ben?"

But Ben had no reply to that.

Six

Doctor Lamar Chase found Ben sitting alone in his office. No further meetings were scheduled for that day. Each attendee was off by themselves, with their own thoughts.

Lamar poured a mug of coffee and sat down. For once he didn't have anything to say about the ashtray filled with cigarette butts on Ben's desk.

"What did you and Blanton agree on, Ben?" he finally asked.

"That it's lonely at the top."

"Are you able to see both sides of the picture clearly, Ben?"

"You know I can, Lamar. But neither side is very pretty from where I sit."

"And . . . ?"

"Do you want to go into Africa, Lamar?"

"Truthfully, no."

"Do you want to see an entire race of people destroyed?"

"I won't even dignify that with a reply, Raines."

"Have you spoken with Cecil back home?"

"About fifteen minutes ago."

"What did he say?"

"That you will do the right thing."

"Oh, that's just goddamn wonderful, Lamar!" Ben slammed a big hand down on his desk. "Thank you both for absolutely, positively nothing!"

"What the hell do you want me to say, Ben? That I have the answer? Well, I don't! I'm a doctor. An old one. But that doesn't make me Solomon. I do know from talking to our intelligence people that the majority of the German people despise Bruno Bottger. But they can't stop him because he disarmed them years back. Same with the people in all the countries that now make up his Federation. You've seen the latest figures on the size of Bottger's army?"

"Yes. He wasn't kidding when he said he had a 250,000 troops and 100,000 more in reserve."

"And . . . ?"

"I can't pull those battalions I left in reserve stateside over here, Lamar. And you know why?"

"You think the pot is about ready to boil over back home, Ben?"

"Yes. And so do you."

Mike walked in and sat down after filling a mug with coffee. "You want some more bad news from back home, Ben?"

"Oh, by all means, Mike. I mean, shit! Make my day."

"A group of people in the Midwest have surfaced. About fifty thousand of them. Well armed and ready to fight. They say the only way this race issue can be resolved is to round up all the blacks and put them on reservations . . . just like their ancestors did the Indians."

Ben threw his coffee mug across the room. It shattered against the wall.

Mike said, "You want to hear the rest of it?"

"Why not?"

"Blanton has just been informed that his government is on the verge of collapse. And the military is not going to intervene."

"Anything else?"

"The SUSA is solid. No trouble there. But thousands of blacks have gathered at our borders and are demanding they be allowed in."

"Demanding?"

"That's what I said."

"And I suppose that Cecil has handed that decision off to me, right?"

"The SUSA was your dream, Ben."

"And Cecil is president; the people elected him. I run the army."

"Bullshit!" Lamar said. "You are the SUSA, Ben. Always have been, always will be."

Beth walked in with a broom and swept up the pieces of broken mug. She dumped the shards into a wastebasket and poured Ben a fresh cup and placed it on the desk. "It's all right to praise one's past," the normally quiet Beth said. "We all should look back at our culture and our heritage and be proud, when it's deserving. You know I read a lot of history. And I've concluded that to a very large degree, conformity is now and always has been one of the keys to acceptance.

It's all right to be rebellious, I suppose. As long as it's confined to one's youth. But almost all of us grow out of it when we mature, look around us, and find that the majority is disapproving. We're either going to be one people, or we're going to be a nation divided. I don't like it when any group of people tries to jam an alien culture down my throat and demand that I accept it. Jersey is very proud of her Indian heritage. But she doesn't walk around wearing feathers and a loincloth. Jersey conformed and stepped right into the white culture with total acceptance. No one even blinked. She once summed up the American Indians' complaints with this statement: They lost the war; whitey won. And there were no prouder people on the face of the earth than the Apache. Jersey had enough sense to see that. Seems to me that other minorities could learn from her. That's my opinion." She walked out of the room.

"Well, now," Lamar said. "I couldn't have said it better."

"Nor I," Ben said. "But it doesn't solve the problem."

"Ben," Mike said, standing up just as Corrie entered the room. "This might be a problem that only has one inevitable solution."

"And that is . . . ?"

Mike shrugged his shoulders and walked out of the room.

"Boss," Corrie said. "Bruno Bottger has given the Rebels twenty-four hours to leave Europe. If we're not out by then, he'll drive us out."

"I never liked being ordered to leave a place," Ben said. "Put the Rebels on full alert for an offensive."

"And the situation back home, Ben?" Lamar asked.

"I deal with one problem at a time, Lamar. And right now the immediate problem's name is Bruno Bottger."